BLOOD SILVER

Published by:
Grand Mal Press
Forestdale, MA
www.grandmalpress.com

Thanks to Ellen Lawson for copyediting.
Special thanks to Araby and Berkeley for beta reading.

Library of Congress Cataloging-in-Publication Data
Grand Mal Press/Johnson, Ben

p. cm

Cover art by Grand Mal Press
www.grandmalpress.com

FIRST EDITION

For Hazel, my Little Crow.

BLOOD SILVER

by

Ben Johnson

Prologue

After coming from the land of the Vikings on the dragon boats, only a few years after the debacle in Ireland that had set him adrift across this Earth, the pale alchemist had met several people in tribes with hair shaved in strange patterns, much like the Roman helmets he remembered from his youth. The Vikings' established trade with these peoples meant that there were several of the Norsemen and women fluent in the thrilling new dialects, and he'd reveled in learning them.

When he said farewell to the Scandinavian traders and left with the native peoples, he hopped from tribe to clan down the coast and across the plains so full of the horned beasts in their thundering herds. He would live and learn languages, customs. He would hunt, and fight, and make love, and father a few children, and then he would move on, before whichever group he was with would notice that he remained the same age, never a new wrinkle appearing.

Back in Scandinavia, it had been brought to his attention by the young ovate from Erin that had left with him. Peik, the name he had been given by the norsemen, had noticed the same thing with the ovate. They had spent a decade with the Vikings, and the norsemen had started to grey and wrinkle, while Peik and the ovate looked exactly the same age as when they had arrived. Both of them knew where this was coming from, as the thing spoke to them in their dreams. Dreams both of the sleeping and of the awakened.

It was housed in a box of Sacred Oak, with gilt leaves of silver along the corners and hasp. When the box was opened, it sang and shone; the oaken and silver Spirit Snare of the Druids.

Made as a weapon for the ovate's people, it had worked marvelously, for a time. Soon after, though, the Christ-people who had invaded their land returned with an army. The ovate, the pale alchemist who had arrived with the Christian invaders, and the knife had fled to live with the Vikings.

The metal, fused with the blood of an aging and very powerful Druid, was called Blood Silver. It had been poured into a mold of an elliptical-bladed dagger, hollow on the inside. Oak branches, leaves, and acorns were depicted all along the blade and hand-guard, with gnarled roots as the handle.

As often before, Peik wondered what had happened to Eowen, the ovate; a too-trusting soul that Peik had drugged the night he'd escaped on a dragon boat, carrying the oaken snare along the freezing seas until they had reached Turtle Island. Probably killed by the Norse.

Once he made it to the "New World", no one found out about his eternal youth, as he never stayed in one place for too long. He hunted and harvested his way across the plains of Turtle Island until the Earth shot up into the sky on the horizon, and the red dust swirled in plumes and clouds. There, among the deep canyons and jagged stones, is where he met the Raven Man.

Peik had noticed the man twice, long before. Once while crossing the great river, forty years previous, and again a decade later in the forest to the north. Neither of those times had ended with a meeting, however, as the feelings Peik got from the man made him want to get farther away from him, not closer. On this third time, though, he had opted to meet the round, smiling man. Peik waved at him, and he waved back. The man smiled broader, then began to walk toward him. Peik's eyes were riveted as the large, dark-skinned man approached. With each step, the man seemed to blur and appear much closer than his size and gait would suggest, like he was skipping over large distances.

"Hello, traveler," the man croaked when he was near enough for conversation. His hair was matted with dirt the color of blood, and he wore what appeared to be the skin of an animal with a hole cut in the center, and nothing else. When Peik looked closer at the thing he saw its black incandescence resembled feathers. He gazed deeper, mesmerized, and the feathered poncho ruffled, a misshapen beak appearing. The beak wiggled, and he realized he was looking straight at the old man's penis.

"Hahaha," the man laughed, then, "Gluck." He made a noise like a stone dropping perfectly in the center of a pond.

Peik's head swam.

"It's the man who doesn't get older!" the man said in a dialect Peik could only barely make out. His crackly voice bounced off the strange columns of stone around them.

"I don't know what you're talking about," Peik said in the closest tongue he could, different only by mere degrees than the man's language.

"Oh, I think you do." His voice had altered, and in Peik's mind was reflected as exactly the dialect he had just used. "I really think that you do, man-from-across-the-waters." He cocked his head to the side, and his bloodshot eyes seemed to both move independently of one another, searching different places on Peik's face. It was alarming, confusing. Unnatural.

"I am simply a traveler, like you say."

"A traveler, yes." He nodded. "But not simple." His eyes came together on one of Peik's. It sent a ripple of nausea through his stomach. The larger man searched for a word. "Hm . . . complex," he said, satisfied. "Like you are many men at once, yes?" This time the dialect was thick, but the meaning clear. He looked closer at Peik, bending his head forward.

"A very white man with a shiny thing in a box," said the man. "What is that thing?"

In that instance, he seemed to have grown in size, almost doubled, his girth hovering over Peik, who pushed his bagged belongings behind him, as far from the man as possible, the snare in its box central among them.

"Get away from me," he said, clutching the strap of the bag so tightly his knuckles turned a flaming red on his pale skin. The contrast was startling.

Peik pulled a small knife from a sheath on his leg, strapped there in case of situations such as this. He held it tightly, blade down, ready. But a feeling overtook Peik; this was the first person he'd met in all his travels whose arcane knowledge matched or surpassed his own. Whatever he had, it was beyond the trappings of alchemy, or what Peik knew of shamanism.

"Another fun thing!" The big man was not intimidated, far from it. Rather, he made the sound with his tongue again, and Peik's muscles froze. The knife dropped from his hand, falling harmlessly to the ground. From inside the blanket-skin thing, the man reached out in a flash and grabbed it from the cloud of dust. Peik readied himself for the attack he knew was coming. But it never did.

When he looked from between his raised arms, the dirty man was holding the knife, handle first, towards Peik, offering it up to him.

"Heh, heh." The handle bobbled up and down from his chuckles. "That's not the one I'm talking about, stupid. Take this back, man-from-across-the-water, I want to show you some things. Things that will make you want to give me the shiny blade in the box of your own accord," he said, in the language of the Norsemen.

Slowly, Peik reached out, wrapped his fingers around the handle, and put it back on his leg. He wasn't going to be offered an opportunity like this again. This man, or whatever he was, had a control of things Peik had been chasing his entire existence. He looked up and saw him walking away, toward one of the large stone spires with holes in them all the way up to the top. Little cities in stone. The pale alchemist dusted himself off and followed the thick man toward the spires, and in the dust thought he could see huge black wings stretching off his back. Before he caught up, he looked after the man's figure. Beyond him, up in the cliffside crags, shone a golden light. It flickered, hidden in the sun's setting rays, then disappeared. Or had it been there at all?

1.

"Who wants to go for a walkie?" Buddy whispered.

The dogs' ears perked. Grifter jumped up on his hind legs, tail whipping back and forth, then backed down on all fours. Luna whined, staring at the boy.

"Shh. C'mon, girl," he said. "I need this. So do you. It's been three months, and I've waited. If they were coming they'd have done it by now. We'll just be gone a few minutes, honest." He reached down and tried to stroke her black-and-gold ears, cooing gently. The little dog dodged her head from side to side, avoiding his hand.

"You better come, or else I'll leave you here and you'll really be in trouble." With that, he walked out the door. Luna could see she was beaten, and followed Grifter as he bounded into the late-summer San Diego sun.

The smell of herbs and tropical plants on the patio wafted on the breeze. Buddy opened the rear fence into the long, thin canyon behind the house, slapped both dogs on the butt and took off down the trail that ran along the bottom. The warm wind whipped his face as the dogs yapped at his heels, unable to keep up. His body blurred into a streak as he phased into the lightning-quick rabbit spirit. He laughed. It had been so long.

Luna barked fiercely, angry at him for running ahead. Shadows grew long as the clouds turned pink.

Back in the house, Clementine had fallen into a late-afternoon nap, and when Buddy had slung the dogs' leashes over his shoulder and stepped to the back door, he knew it was the last chance he was going to get. Tomorrow she'd be back at work, and Helen would be watching him. Clementine's vigilance hadn't wavered in keeping Buddy hidden from the Stillwater's, but she had gotten comfortable with the idea he was safe, especially with Luna by his side. Helen, however, never got too comfortable, not anymore.

The Stillwater's hadn't located him. Buddy was starting to think they never would. The earth was still warm as he quenched the burning desire to run through the canyons. He had to be mindful, though, as his mom's naps were never very long. He'd been planning this for weeks.

The desert plants whizzed by, faster and faster, eventually morphing into a blur. Buddy couldn't help but let out a scream of delight as he tore down the dusty trail, beaming with joy. The dogs, thin and fast, were quite a way behind, but didn't dare let him out of their sight. Luna barked again. It had no effect on Buddy's speed. He was ripping.

• • •

Pearl Oca shooed away the singing mockingbird from the branch above her. The young girl, about to be thirteen, sat on the ground beneath a pepper tree, black hair pulled over her face, watching the spidery boy about her age sniff around the canyon trailhead that opened up off the bend in the road. When she heard another boy shouting from far up the canyon, she looked in his direction, but couldn't see anything except tall willow branches swaying from something moving beneath them. Moving very fast. A big red-tailed hawk soared away from its disturbed perch.

She turned her head back to the spider kid, but she'd lost him among the bushes. Not good. In the days she had been monitoring him, she'd found that he wasn't someone she wanted to be near. She could tell, though, if she kept watching him she'd see something pretty weird. It was obvious by the way he rooted around, always looking for something.

She'd never be a detective if she got scared off so easily.

Scanning the bushes, she finally located Spider, or whatever his name was, near the side of the trail where the thing shaking the trees was headed. He was crouched behind a laurel sumac bush, poised to leap. A twinge rippled up her spine, and without thinking she picked up a rock the size of her fist and heaved it toward the path. It sailed perfectly, and a cloud of dust exploded in the middle of the trail. She could see a skinny boy and two medium-sized dogs stop short, looking at the dust cloud. It was the boy she'd seen pouring trash and dog shit all over Eddie Calhoun's porch a couple months ago. The kid from the warehouses in the news. Pearl hadn't seen him since then. Her pulse quickened. This is who Spider's looking for.

The boy and dogs reversed course and tore back up the trail. Pearl again watched the willows bow in their wake. She had never seen something so fast. It was mesmerizing. Then the air popped, and he just disappeared. The dogs yelped, but kept running. Her mouth hung open.

When she finally shook her head free of wonderment, she tried again to locate the spider kid, jumping when she saw him looking back at her, still a way off, smiling a humorless grin like a hungry wolf.

Fear overcame her, locking her muscles, but the mockingbird returned and clicked a succession of notes into her ear, breaking her free of the frozen state.

The spidery boy stared as she got on her bicycle and raced toward home. She rounded a pepper tree and almost ran over an old man in brown coveralls.

"Sorry!" she yelled over her shoulder, churning her legs. The red-tailed hawk followed her with its eyes as she pedaled past its new perch in a Torrey Pine tree.

• • •

Buddy screeched to a halt when the rock hit. Beyond the dust cloud, he could see Oliver leering at him. Shit. He had no time to wonder who threw it as he reversed course and ripped back up the hill. Going full bore, dogs hot on his heels, he felt a sense of danger, something breathing down his neck. But surely Oliver couldn't go this fast.

From deep within, a frantic screech filled his ears, and his legs thrust forward even faster. A black hole the size of a trash can lid rotated in front of him, like an entrance suspended in midair. Buddy dove. When he popped through it, it was as if the air separated and left him drifting along iridescent filaments of the web, shooting along slick rainbow wires like data. Fat cables of light splayed off of braided tendrils, twisting wild like tornados against a background of silver and gold static. Pale, glowing clouds drifted above, casting shadows along the woven ground. There was no direction, only the silken caress of the web sliding him over a vast array. Time did not flow. He was and he was not. Orbits. Light. Distance. Revolution. Another hole. Green plants visible.

He popped out, barreling through the nut trees and into his back door, then tripping on the doorstep and tumbling into the kitchen. From far behind, he heard the yelping of the dogs. Seconds later, Luna's fur was on end as she ripped into the house, licking his face.

Buddy scratched her ears and locked the door, wondering what had just happened. How could he tell his mom about this? She already worried too much.

A distant voice, like wind, whispered.

He rides the web.

"Rupert?" came his mom's voice from her room. "What's going on?"

"Just reading books and lying around with the dogs."

She wasn't buying it. "What's that on your leg?" she asked, stifling a yawn while walking to the coffee machine.

Buddy brushed the smudge off. "Oh, some dirt from wrestling with Grifter."

"Uh-huh," said Clem. It was his last day. "Don't get too carried away." Truth be told, she wanted her boy to be able to run free, but it was too dangerous. After they had talked for a good while, she made some chicken and rice. They ate and talked about what to expect when she went back to work, then she put him to bed.

• • •

Deep in the night, Buddy shot up, eyes wide and skin sweaty. His dreams were dark, spattered with unknown attackers. Outside the window, leaves rustled. Something was creeping. He could feel it. Luna and Grifter were instantly alert beside him. When he met Luna's gaze, he could tell. They'd been followed. Shit.

She barked softly as Buddy nudged Grifter out of the way and slid from the bed. He opened the door and walked down the hall past his mom's room. The dogs followed, Luna growling.

From beside the back door, a small rattling started. The metallic ball attached to Luna's leash rose and bounced lightly off the coat rack it hung from.

He looked through the glass. A lit lamp dangled from the trellis, making a halo of light roughly six-feet-round that fell perfectly on a circular table. As he peered into the shadows beyond, a feeling in his gut told him something was there. He focused, concentrating on what lay beyond the light, when a hand clutching a small black cone swung up and shattered the bulb.

Grifter began barking furiously, and Luna ran to Clementine's door, leaping on her hind legs and scratching at it. The door burst open, and Clem, dressed in pajamas and gripping a pistol, came barreling out.

"What's happening?"

Buddy pointed. She saw the bushes sway on the far end of the backyard. Clem threw the door open, gun at the ready, but couldn't see anything. A sharp snap came from the front of the house. Grifter tore out the back door and raced around the side, snarling furiously. Luna stayed put, Buddy's pant leg in her clenched jaws for good measure.

"Don't move," said Clem, shutting the door and following Grifter before Buddy could protest. He followed her with his eyes to the front, craning his neck. Luna growled as something outside the back door clicked. When Buddy turned around, Oliver stood inside the house.

Luna exploded into a frenzy, lunging at Oliver. He slashed with the black cone, missing her by inches, then crouched low to the ground with the weapon pointed at her. She turned and attacked, diving through the air, but Oliver was ready, kicking her in the ribs. She flipped across the room and smashed into a bookcase, then fell to the ground, dazed.

"Luna!" Buddy shouted, facing Oliver. "Rrrrahh!" he screamed. From his mouth shot an opaque concentrated wave of energy, barreling straight and fast. It hit Oliver in the forehead like a battering ram, and he flew backwards, whipping out the open door and breaking through several tree limbs before crashing into the fence some thirty feet away. Instantly righting himself, he looked back, and saw Buddy inhale deeply, eyes like ice. Chomping his yellow teeth in frustration, Oliver vaulted over the fence and vanished into the canyon.

Buddy ran to Luna, who was standing up, looking more embarrassed than injured. "Are you okay?"

She licked his face as the front door opened, and Clem and Grifter ran back in.

Clem saw the open door and the wreckage leading to the fence. "Oh my god. What happened?" she asked.

"Oliver." Buddy's eyes were wide and wet.

"Oh shit." Clem felt betrayed by herself. Drawn outside like a rookie while they made a grab for her son. "Where is he now?"

"I got lucky. He ran off."

"How did you manage that?"

"He kicked Luna, and I screamed. When I did, something weird happened. Something new. It's like my scream hit him. Knocked him backwards."

"Through the trees like that?"

"Yeah, it was . . . gnarly."

"Wow." She didn't know what else to say. She was embarrassed.

"It's okay, Mom. I handled it. Who did you see?"

"Two people. Hard to tell anything about them in the dark. They were fast. I couldn't keep up, so I called Grifter and came back."

"Others will be coming. We should get more people too, Mom."

"I was thinking the same thing, Rupert."

Clementine shut off the light. Before herding Buddy and the dogs into the bedroom, she looked out the window one more time. In the dark recesses of the bushes and trees she saw a reflection. Unsure at first, she looked deeper, far into the folds of the bushes, breathing deep to steady herself. The glint remained. She moved her head to the left, and saw another matching glint, small, black, and round.

They blinked.

Clementine grabbed the gun and pointed her flashlight into the eyes looking back at her from the darkness. What the beam lit up was like staring at an out-of-focus picture. A smear in the dark, blinking its pitch-black eyes. Try as she might, she couldn't focus. Eyes shone on a blurred face. She felt sickened. Vertigo spiraled her mind.

She leveled her gun through the window. There was no way she was getting drawn outside again, but if she fired anything could get in. As she looked down the barrel, sights set between the two black orbs, waiting, the eyes and surrounding smear reverted to a dark mist. She stilled her shaking trigger finger, but the eyes had blended with the night and disappeared. Gone. Nothing reflected in the foliage.

"Did you see?" she asked Buddy.

"Yeah. Wow."

"What was that?"

"I have no idea."

"What did it look like?" she asked, unsure.

"Like somebody erased a drawing halfway."

"Okay. I just want to make sure we're seeing the same thing."

"Yeah, it was gross."

"Was that Abe?"

He looked at Luna. "No."

"Could Oliver do that?"

"I hope not. I don't think so."

She shook her head. "Damn. Let's get your people now."

"Yeah."

2.

Amy Munoz was aware that she was dreaming. The air held a thick mist as she walked into a darkened clearing with a large half-burnt tree in its center, still smoking from a recent blaze. Gnarled branches drew a path to the sky, and the smoke wafted around them in dizzying patterns. She drifted around the huge trunk, and beheld upon the smoldering bark a lone leafy branch. It was small and alive, about halfway up the massive live oak.

One leaf, then another, spun from the branch to the ground, already covered in leaves and ash. As she picked one up, its rough edges cut into the flesh of her palm. Blood rose quickly to the surface, pooled, then ran down her fingers, dripping next to an acorn loosed from its home.

Dust swirled in the hazy light, and a hairlike root stretched from the acorn, plunging into the small puddle of her blood. Immediately it began to grow, twisting until it mimicked the shape of the burnt oak next to it.

As the new oak grew, the old charred tree began to crumble and fall to the earth, sending billows of ashy dust into the air.

She placed her hand on its bark. To her astonishment she could feel a faint pulse through the girth of the trunk. A beating heart. As if guided, she plucked a leaf, and a lone drop of sap fell in slow motion until it landed with a soft thud in the ash.

The thud turned to an echoing plod, like footsteps. She became aware of an unseen presence around her, and searched in a circle, ending at the trunk of the oak. A knocking came from the tree, then around it stepped the grey suited and ponytailed man she had seen in photos, but never in person. A faint smoky presence trotted behind him.

"Hello there. I am Myron Fox," he said, extending his hand.

"I'm aware," she replied, surprising herself by shaking it. The older gentleman had a firm yet soft and reassuring grip, comforting her.

"You don't know me, but–"

"I know you work for Mr. Stillwater."

"I work mainly for myself," he replied, stone faced. "But I want to talk about my son, Gray."

Gray. Her lover. Murdered three months previous. "Your son?" she asked.

"That's right."

"Why weren't you at the funeral?"

"I was, of course. But under certain conditions it's best I stay behind the scenes."

"Conditions like your son's funeral? Why should I believe you're his father, anyway?"

"You know what's true," he said, "inside yourself."

His voice lulled her. She could feel it happening, powerless to stop it. A wave of calm washed over her, and she believed him, could actually see it. "But what's there to talk about? He's dead, and that's that."

Myron chuckled. "Well, that is what I'd hoped to talk to you about. Gray isn't actually, I mean, in the strictest sense, uh . . . how shall I say . . ."

"Spit it out, Mr. Fox."

"Okay, well, Gray's not actually dead, my dear, but in a very deep slumber. Trapped between worlds."

"What?" Hope and desperation collided in Amy's mind. Gray? Alive? How she hoped it could be true! But she'd seen Gray's heart get pierced with the Japanese suicide blade thrown by Frank Rawls. He died. That was that.

The only things she had heard about Mr. Fox were from Detective Clementine Figgins, with whom Amy worked, and Gray himself. One of the things both of them had to say about Myron Fox was that he is not to be trusted. A trickster. Somehow Gray forgot to mention he was his father.

"You're lying," she said, looking into his eyes. But her voice sounded so ridiculous, saying that. Of course he's not lying.

"You know I am not. Now know, also, that we can get him back." His dulcet tones relaxed her.

Her mind raced through sunlit pine forests with Gray at her side, the smell of needles baking on the warm red earth. "Your son is the only man, to me. Of course I want him back. Please don't be lying."

"I'm not. We want the same thing."

He was right. Hope was building to a crescendo within her. The dark depression that had overcome her since Gray's death, or apparent death, thinned. But she remained a scientist, and a decorated one. The best in the San Diego Police Department crime lab. Her pragmatism was hard to extinguish.

"But, if he was still alive, how come he wasn't breathing, and had no pulse?" she asked. "Kind of hard to mask that."

"Hard, yes. Not impossible. They were there, only they were moving so slowly that they didn't register to anyone or anything monitoring him, and was incorrectly identified as having neither. The nature of that particular weapon, or snare as we call them, is the slowing of life beyond any comprehensibility. A trait fused into it by its eastern makers. This tool is called a tantō, traditionally a suicide blade. Only this one is not strictly for suicide."

Myron tapped Amy softly with his finger between her eyebrows, and a rapid shadow play occurred in her dreaming mind. Robes, fire, silver and wood. A flash of gold. The faintest glimpse of an older weapon, hewn of ancient bone, used as a model for the maple snare being fitted with the metal. When the flickering play was complete, she recognized the blade that had pierced Gray, the one she had pulled from his body. She knew. In the vision she saw blood on the blade, her own hand wielding it, feathers in the wind. She shook the tendrils of disturbing imagery from her mind. "What do we do?"

"When you awake, contact Detective Figgins. Tell her what you have dreamed, what I have told you. Make sure that her son is there, and knows also."

"Wait, what? Rupert? Why him? She's only just had him back after ten years, and is understandably a little bit protective of him." Amy's suspicions rose, and for the briefest of moments she saw a house made of little bits of straw, blowing away in the wind. Gray, herself, Buddy and all.

A clicking from Myron's tongue shuffled that vision away.

"It is far too late to be protective of that child. And no plan that we concoct will be successful without him. He is . . . special. When you have convinced them to join you, meet me at the warehouses where Rupert was held."

"They won't want to go."

"I realize this. You must convince them."

"What if I can't?"

Myron lowered his head, peering. "Remove that option from your mind," he said, "You must do this, therefore it will be done, is the attitude. Use it. Be persuasive."

Acceptance and doubt danced inside her. Acceptance took the lead, pushed by Myron's words.

"What time?" she asked.

"It doesn't matter. I'll be there."

With that, Mr. Fox winked, then turned on the ball of his foot and walked back around the trunk of the oak. Just before he rounded from sight, his body lost its definition and turned into swirling smoke, and his translucent body walked next to a very large fox cloaked in the same haze. After a few steps they became one with the mist.

Amy remained, looking at the tree. Approaching it, she put her hand again to its bark, and felt its pulse. A lone tear broke down her cheek. She caught it on her finger, and brought it up in front of her eye. Slowly, she pulled it away from her face. The leaves, seen through the droplet, looked more like feathers. When the tear reached a certain distance, the tree turned upside-down in the visual filter of the liquid orb, and again they were leaves.

Another tear welled up, distorting her vision, which blurred until it became the ruby haze of the inside of her eyelids. She opened them, stared at the ceiling, and stretched. Something gleamed in the corner of her eye. Focusing, she saw the maple tantō, the blade that pierced Gray's chest, on her nightstand. She stared at it for a good while, then got out of bed o call Clementine.

3.

Clementine jerked when the phone rang next to her head. Amy. She stood up and answered, looking out the window into the still-dark sky. The horizon tinged purple to pink along the rocky desert mountain range to the east of San Diego, but it would be at least a half hour until the sun showed its face.

"Hey, Amy," She walked out of her room where the dogs and Buddy faked being asleep, leaving the door cracked. Luna and Grifter lay on either side of him as he lightly snored with one arm around each. They looked up as Buddy cracked his eyelids.

"Hi, Clem. how's it going?" Amy said.

"We had some visitors last night. None of them good. Oliver made it into the house." Clem walked to the kitchen, gun in hand, looking out the windows. There was nothing there now. She felt sure. But that's what they do, manipulate.

"Holy shit. What happened?"

Somebody lured me outside, then the little shit got in. Fortunately Rupert did something to him. I didn't see what, but it got rid of him."

"Ay cabrón."

"Yeah, there's more. But you called me. What's up?"

"I need to see you as soon as possible. I just learned something shocking."

"How did you learn anything at–" Clem looked at the clock on her stove, "–5 am?" As she asked, she already knew. "Another dream?"

"Mm-hmm. I'm gonna ask you to be open-minded about this whole thing, especially as it involves Myron Fox."

"I'm getting more open-minded by the second, unfortunately, but the head of security for Stillwater Enterprises? What's that all about?" Clem's radar was screaming. She got a bad feeling from Mr. Fox. He scared her.

"That's the thing," said Amy. "I'm not so sure of his loyalty to the Stillwater people. It may be a mole type situation with him. He told me some crazy things."

"In the dream," said Clem. Amy could almost hear her groggy friend's gears click.

Amy sighed. "Yes, in the dream. But these dreams, Clem, it's not like anything. Not like dreams at all. They're so vivid they make it seem like you're dreaming when you finally wake up from them, if that makes any sense."

"Like what?"

"He said Gray is his son."

"Wow. Interesting," She looked out the window again, relaxing a little in the new daylight. "Gray was that old guy's kid, eh? Well, they did show up together back at the design studios. What did he have to tell you about his departed son?"

"Well, for one thing, it appears that he isn't exactly departed."

The words hung heavy somewhere between the two phones. Amy was about to ask if Clem was still there when Clem said, "You're right. Hang up right now and get your ass over here. I'll make coffee."

Clementine did, thinking how easy it would be for Mr. Fox to shape Amy's opinions, using the memory of her lover, thought lost all this time. A fish in a barrel.

Fifteen minutes later, Amy pulled up in her little compact car, parking in front of Clementine's house as the sun's rays broke free of the mountains' shadows. As she walked through the gate into Clem's oasis, the flowering smells of late summer blossoms perked her nostrils. A hummingbird whizzed by between duties of pollinating the summer's last cactus blossoms along the porch rail. It made a sound, zif, then shot away. Amy watched it while Clem opened the door and handed her a cup of coffee.

"Hi there," said Clem.

"Hey, Clem," she replied, giving a quick hug. "How's it going?"

"We're all okay over here. So what's up?"

Amy sat down, letting out a long breath.

"Whenever you're ready, of course," said Clementine.

Amy pulled the black bag off her shoulder, then brought out the small Japanese sword from the towel it was wrapped in. Its blade shone bright silver and the handle was maple freckled with birdseye. A beautiful and terrible piece. Clem recognized it as the one that had claimed Gray's life.

"Okay, I'll get to it. Mr. Fox, anyway, in the dream, said that this knife is some sort of suicide blade related to the snare thing that Buddy had, that the Blackwing guy has now.

"So, this sword, called a tantō, slows down the life force until it doesn't register to machines or people, but it's there. The heart and the lungs still take in blood and air, only so slowly it seems to not be happening," she said. "Part of him is trapped in here." She motioned to the blade. "And he knows how to get him back out. He said he would meet us and we would know everything."

"Meet us where?" Clem asked, eyes fixed on the blade and its mesmerizing shine.

"Um . . . down at the warehouse complex," Amy said, batting her lashes.

"Jesus. Seriously?" Clem was wary, and rightfully so. Her son was held there for over ten years, and in the time since his return she had gone to revisit the scene quite a few times, mainly to get an idea what the next move of the group would be after the madman Frank had been done away with. Every time, she got terrible feelings spilling upon one another, like distortion in her mind. No other place, no crime scene had done that to her before. Now someone drew them back.

The timing was crazy. In the months since her reunion with Buddy, they hadn't been disturbed until last night. The very same night Amy has this dream. "Why?"

"He didn't say," answered Amy. "But that's not the bad part. He says bringing Buddy is crucial."

Clementine's eyes narrowed. Mr. Fox, from a dream, baiting her child back to the place of his imprisonment. "I'm supposed to take Rupert down to that place to meet someone we thought, until you dreamt otherwise, was an enemy? How sure are you that he isn't completely full of shit, bending you from inside the dreams?"

"I've still got instincts."

"They manipulate instincts." She didn't want to create a rift with Amy. On the contrary, they needed to be on the same page, but for that to happen Amy had to see the possibility.

The light clink of the metal dog tags behind them alerted them. Grifter walked from Buddy's side to the water bowl as Amy wrapped the sword in the towel.

"They'll be here soon," Buddy said.

"Hey, Rupert," said Amy, a little surprised. "Who will? And where's Luna?"

"She went to get my friends."

"The ones from the canyon?"

"Yeah, and some others."

"So that's our backup?" Amy looked at Clem, then Buddy.

"The only other cop we could tell is the one we're trying to get back from the dead, or whatever. So . . . yeah."

It had taken Clem a couple of weeks to get used to how silent and quick her son was. The world that he was a part of was nothing like the mostly straight ahead one of crime solving. It was almost like a parallel reality. His was a place of dark wonder, illusions and manipulations. His friends were kind, and protective, but all held some sort of indescribable power within them that mystified and terrified even the hardened police woman in herself.

"Rupe," she asked. "What do you know about him, about Mr. Fox?"

"Just that he chased us one time, him and a smoky fox thing. Abe and him have these animal deals, like, um, totem helpers or something, that's a part of themselves. So, Mr. Fox and his totem fox chased us, but Luna made a sound and the fox came apart, and we hit the road. Mr. Fox stayed with the smoky animal when we split," said the boy. "Stewart can't stand him."

"Stewart's another story." Clem shook her head. "But Mr. Fox didn't try to hurt you, right? I mean, even if he could?"

"No," he said. "Catch, though. Maybe he could have hurt me if he wanted to, I didn't want to stay around to find out."

"Of course not."

"Max told me to always assume that someone will do the worst thing possible if they catch you. Helps you run."

"Sage advice," offered Amy.

"Yeah," said Clementine. "Look, Rupert, this is your call. Can you go back there? And, should we?"

"If what you said could be true, we have to. Gray needs us. When we get Max and Helen, and Cora and Stewart, plus the five of us–" he motioned to the dogs, "–it would be hard for them to have a good ambush. Markuz went with my sister and the Bear Mother. That leaves Peik, Nuala, and Oliver who we know about. If we go soon, they probably haven't got many new people yet. But maybe some. All Frank's puppets are gone, I think. So we'd be dealing with rookies, hopefully."

"New people?"

He looked at his mom. "Frank wasn't the only one who ran tests."

Amy was impressed. "Well, that's some strategizing, Rupert, and not just for a twelve year old."

"Thanks. But Amy, call me Buddy."

"Baby, please," clucked Clementine.

"Sorry Mom. You can call me whatever you want, Amy."

"Alright, Buddy," said Amy, smiling. No matter what had befallen her, she had to count the whole thing a success so far, as they had gotten Buddy back. Now to keep him from the freak show of people after him.

Grifter barked at the front door. From the other side, Luna barked back. Clem pulled back the curtain and looked out at the dog standing with four people on the sunrise-lit sidewalk.

4.

Kim Song was a slim and cunning man known as The Korean. He knocked on the ornate hand-carved maple door and waited, assaying the live oak trees that stretched down into the canyon behind the house, then emptied into the golf course in Balboa Park. The sun was setting, blazing the San Diego sky with hues so bright they seemed unreal. He brushed his black hair out of his eyes and smiled. Life was good. The door opened, and the blonde woman bade him inside.

"Welcome, Mr. Song," she said.

The smile widened on Kim Song's face. Nuala was one to look at, even in her mid-forties.

"Thank you, Ms. McCafferty," he said. This was a business trip, after all. Who knew, maybe pleasure later? He'd heard about Frank's demise, of course, three months back. Maybe she was ready to move on.

"Please come in. You get a little sun? You're glowing," she said.

"A little."

She turned and walked to the table, feeling Kim's eyes on her.

He followed into the dining room, where one of Frank's old bodyguards, the older, pale guy, sat at a table with a brown-haired lady about Nuala's age. Thinner, more bookish. Guess they kept the pale guy on.

"You know Peik, of course," said Nuala.

Kim and Peik nodded to each other. "Of course."

"And this is Marie Stillwater."

Kim's eyes got wide. "Really? Well, these must be important."

"Our price was fixed, Kim."

"Naturally. It always is. Wasn't important enough for the man himself, though, huh? Still never met him. Couldn't be worse than Frank, though, may he rest in peace." He put a black leather bag onto the table and stepped back, his hands palm-up, a gesture of invitation. "I jest. Respect to your father, please."

"Oh, I don't know," said Peik, "they're just . . . different." He winked at Kim.

Marie stood and picked up the small tote bag, opening it. A faint glow lit her skin, and she brought out a small silver flute with five finger holes, etched to resemble tree bark. Oak, specifically. A muted glow cast off the instrument. She brought it to her lips and blew, and a high note filled the room. Glasses chimed, creating overlapping harmonies.

Sonic waves pulsed against one another, and a silver strand crept from the tip of the flute. Small leaves of light poked off of it. Marie trilled the holes, and the luminous branch snapped back inside it. She looked at Kim and raised her eyebrows. Behind them, a low hum sounded, somewhere beneath the floor.

Kim shrugged, smiling. "Well, it appears you don't need instruction."

The second item from the bag was a silver orb the size of a racquetball, carved to resemble a round acorn and glowing with the same intensity as the flute. Marie shook it in her palm. It chimed like a bell, light and fantastic. The air pressure in the room shifted dramatically, and their bodies swayed from the force coming off the orb. The hum grew louder.

"My father will be pleased," said Marie.

Kim looked proud. "I should think so. A most difficult find."

"Where did you locate them?"

"Information, like all my services, is costly." His smile was relaxed, confident.

Peik spoke up. "That won't be necessary. Why would we need to know that?"

"Yes, ah, of course," said Marie. "Naturally."

"Of course," said Kim Song, slowly. "Well, one piece of information included in the price is that these instruments bond to users, and not necessarily the first. They seem to choose. The only way to reverse this is if the recipient chooses against the instrument. Until they are bonded, anyone will have the same result. Once they bond, however, only the bonded one or ones will be able to play. Spirit magic, it is sometimes called."

"Very interesting." Peik brought a briefcase from beneath the table and slid it across the table toward Kim Song, who glanced in, closed it, and stood. "Well, then, thank you all very much, and please call if you are in need of anything else." His eyes flowed from Marie to Peik, then ended up on Nuala at the end of the sentence, as if 'anything else' was just for her.

Peik nodded, smiling. Marie dipped her head.

Nuala walked him to the door. "Have a good night Mr. Song."

"You know how to reach me," he said, looking her over.

She smiled, nodded, and closed the door, then turned back to the Stillwater's. "So what's the plan, then? I'm on pins and needles."

Peik looked at the instruments, then smiled at his daughter. "Good work, Marie."

Nuala butted in. "Are you kidding me? He's got to know who you are after that. He's paid to feel things out. Find untraceable objects. Once you corrected her, he knew." Her face was red.

"Somebody is really pissed off," said Peik. "So he knows who I am. Who cares? We have the instruments, and can proceed with the next step of the plan, so let's accentuate the positive, shall we?"

"Oh, shut up." Nuala slouched down in her chair.

"Yes, take a moment," he said, then turned to his daughter. "Marie, please get your philandering husband and bring him here. I think we can proceed."

"Yes, Dad." She walked down the hall. The sound of light chains clinked, then she emerged leading a man on a dog collar. Shackles bound his hands behind his back. His feet were similarly chained. In the living room, she kicked behind his knees and brought him to the ground. The man tried to speak around the ball gag forcing his jaw open.

"Shut up, David," said Marie. "You should have known this was what would happen when you were cheating on me." He tried to stand, but she put her foot on the chain and stomped down, slamming his face on the floor. She fastened the links through a hook next to his head, then stepped back.

Peik handed her the flute, shaking the chime gently. "Concentrate," he said.

She focused her intention and blew into the flute, a steady note, high and light. When Peik pulled open the door in the floor, silver tendrils grew like cilia, flowing from the steel machine humming beneath. They reached out for David, guided by the music's message. As they entered his nostrils, then his mouth and ears, his eyes twitched madly, pupils bleeding into the retina, blackening his eyeballs entirely. His jaw locked, biting down and grinding, splintering the ball with his teeth. Black pudding filled his eyes, and they bulged, protruding from his skull almost comically. He laughed, the mirth of a madman, then his eyes burst. Black spatter, like gooey plasma, shot from his sockets, burning into the wood floor. Wisps of smoke curled from the cavities. One last laugh made it past his lips before he fell down face first, clearly dead.

Nuala chuckled. "That went well."

"I'll admit we could use some adjustments." Peik stink-eyed her. "And now we'll need a new subject. Any ideas?"

• • •

The door creaked when Clementine opened it, and the mockingbird Klia swooped inside, clicking her tongue. Clem smiled and beckoned to Max, Helen, Cora, and Stewart, getting a feeling of security as they entered. Nothing would try to get Buddy with them around. She hugged them, bade them sit down.

After she had poured all the coffee into cups, she made a fresh pot and joined the group at the dining room table. The dogs made rounds and sniffed everyone while Klia pecked crumbs off of the kitchen counter. Though only three months had passed, everyone remarked on how Buddy had grown. And he had, curiously. Only just eleven, he looked more like a young adult.

"I guess I'm on time," said Helen. "But it's not just me."

"I guess so." Clem nodded. "It's good to see everyone, and welcome."

Amy looked at Cora and smiled. When Cora looked back, Amy felt a kinship, a sisterhood.

Cora's almond eyes settled on Clementine. "What happened here last night?"

Clementine explained, through occasional gasps from Helen.

Cora looked grave. "It was only a matter of time. The Stillwater's are ready to make a play, but now there are others as well. The ripples in the web call to them. Buddy casts them. The youngsters are seen as aberrations by some."

"Like who?"

"The blurred face is an attribute of a group called the Coyotes; agents of chaos. They will be trying to seize any scraps at this changing time. But there are many who feel threatened by your son. In terms of the weavers of the web, almost everyone does. The more power they stand to lose, the more they would be cautious of Buddy. Some of them may launch an offensive."

"You don't know who, though? Like, specifically?" Clem thought Cora had it pretty dialed in as far as the Web. She was a member of the Council, wasn't she?

"No, but the web speaks in different ways," said Cora. "Does anyone else have information?"

Helen cleared her throat. The smell of sage wafted over the table. "I have some things that I saw. You, in a dream, yes." She looked at Amy. "The smoky fox. His son with steel eyes fighting to return from the river of the dead. You, among the trees. So what did Mr. Fox say?"

It took Amy a second to respond. She felt almost frozen.

Clem walked over to her. "It's okay. We've got to start sometime."

Amy sighed, and told them the dream.

"Damn," Max said when she had finished. "I gotta say, how do we know the lurkers from last night aren't someone Myron's tangled up with? He's made moves before."

"Thank you," added Stewart. "He's the same guy who got my shoulder busted up, that gray-suit-wearing motherfucker with that smoke fox thing. Plus he tried to kill Klia, for chrissakes. It would fit nicely in his plan to have someone scare us the night he was working his angle with Amy."

"That's why we go in a big group," said Amy. "Who knows why he was chasing you, or what he meant to do with Klia? Or when he chased Buddy–"

"Hold up." Max stood up, waving his hands. "Chased Buddy? For what?"

"I don't know, he didn't catch me," answered the boy.

"My man," said Max, holding up his palm. The smack of skin rang in the air.

Stewart looked pensive. "There's one thing we're forgetting. When he chased me, after he hit Klia, the bear faced off against him and his fox thing, which means he can't be that popular with the Bear Mother. And those warehouses are one of the main entrances to her cave system."

"That's actually better," cut in Buddy. "My sister is with Ursula now. If the Fox guy starts anything, they could be there almost immediately."

"Yeah, except now they've got Markuz with them. Who knows about that guy?" said Stewart, rubbing his ribs. His entire body ached every day, all day, due to battling Markuz. He was nowhere near fully healed, and they were going to see the giant again. He wondered how different the circumstances would be this time.

Cora looked at Stewart. "Markuz can't be chosen by the Bear Mother and still be considered an adversary," she said.

"They're all adversaries, as far as I'm concerned." Stewart usually had a hard time listening to opposing viewpoints, but with Cora he softened. He looked back, nodded, and fell silent.

Amy chimed in, "We're just gonna have to go see. Now, what do you guys know about this?" She placed the bag on the table and pulled the tantō out. The small Japanese sword again glowed silver, lighting up the dining room though it was a bright late summer morning.

Stewart recoiled. "That's what Frank used to cut Nickel's head off. Fucking killing machine."

"It is," said Cora, picking up the blade, "if hacked or sliced." She swooshed it through the air, making everyone rear back. "How did you get this?"

"The dream," said Amy. "It was beside my bed when I woke up. I don't know how much time we have before someone sees it missing from evidence, but it can't be a lot. So let's not waste it."

Cora shrugged. "Okay. See the thin oval at the end? If stabbed, like so," she thrust it straight out, "It will trap the spirit, like its oaken counterpart. This blade is more complex than the alchemist's creation, though, and manipulates the vital signs of the body, rather than appearing alive and well, though dazed, as would happen with the oaken blade. The maple blade mimics death, the oaken an imitation of life."

Amy stared at the blade. "So, how do we get Gray from here," she held the knife up, "back into his body? Can just anyone do that?"

"Let me see." Cora, twisted it and looked down the hole as far as she could, clicking her tongue. When she was finished, she said, "We may actually need Mr. Fox a little more than I thought. I've never seen anything like this, and if he has a plan, and for some reason is on the level, he might be the only one among us who can reverse it."

"What? Why do you say that?" asked Amy.

"Well," answered Cora. "I'm not absolutely positive on this, but if the feeling I'm getting is correct, it will take someone who shares Gray's blood to undo the spell of the snare."

The room was silent, finally broken by a small whine from Luna, who walked over, hopped up onto her hind legs, and brought her forepaws down on Max's thigh. He scratched her ear and said, "Shit, let's do this. What time did he say to meet him down there?"

Amy answered, "He didn't. He just said he would be there."

Stewart grunted. "Sounds about right for one of those shitheels." Klia landed on top of his head and twittered. "Very funny," said Stewart.

Luna hopped down and trotted to the door as Max put on his jacket. Halfway to the door, he stopped and turned around.

"Let's go," he said, "there's work to do."

5.

The rolling chain link gate was open. Buddy looked into the warehouse parking lot from out on the street, lost in memories that came flooding back. Frank was dead, and the rest had moved on. Their presences no longer echoed here.

One by one they eased through the gate and into the center of the parking lot, forming a walking circle with Clem and Buddy in the middle. The din of traffic from the freeways behind them cast white static over everything. Stewart monitored the fences while Max and Helen walked ahead to try the doors.

Since all the action, the entire scene had been processed and re-processed by the police, every clue followed, to no avail. Other than the corpse of Frank, there was no trace of the others or their experiments. The authorities, under Clem's guidance, had extensively interviewed Marie Stillwater about the goings-on on her father's properties, but found nothing. When asked if they could speak to her father, they were repeatedly told he was "unavailable", a luxury reserved exclusively for the very wealthy.

Despite Clementine's protests, her Lieutenant officially dropped the pursuit of Mr. Stillwater, and decided that his daughter knew next to nothing. It was the responsibility of the leaseholder for the atrocities there, and not the Stillwater family, read the official police report. Conveniently, all the blame was put on Frank Rawls, who was dead.

Unofficially, the case was still being worked, by Clem and Amy. Knowing it would be solved in a less than legal manner, and being under pressure from her superiors, Clementine had eventually succumbed, letting the investigation stall. Everyone thought she was merely content with getting her son back. Besides, Frank got plugged by Amy after he'd killed Officer Gray Lowehaus. No Frank, no case. Though it was a sophisticated enterprise, her Lieutenant had forced her hand. Without Frank's leadership, most assumed anyone else in the organization would not have the drive to continue. Why this was assumed, Clementine had no idea.

Stewart walked to the smaller warehouse toward the rear. Its sides were corrugated metal, and it had a gaping hole in the steel door. In his mind, he could see Frank again, slicing through Nickel's neck without a second thought. Frank's eyes had been locked on Stewart.

With the remembrance came a chill, even standing in the sunlight. In contrast, the hole in the wall was a pitch black void which no light penetrated. Stewart peered in, his nerves on high alert as he braced himself for whatever lay inside.

When Myron Fox poked his head into the sunlight from the darkness, it looked to be hovering in midair. Before he could think, Stewart took a swing at the old man's face. The blow glanced off Myron's forehead, and Stewart's fist slammed into the metal door-jamb.

"Fucker," said Stewart, shaking his hand.

A dark shape burst from the blackness. Stewart recognized the smoke fox as it leapt, snapping its jaws on his forearm and scraping across his flesh, just shy of gaining purchase. Stewart howled. Blood filled the wounds as the fox sped back to Myron, spurred by his beckoning whistle. Stewart dipped his finger in the blood and put it in his mouth.

"Stop, Xorro," Myron said to the fox sternly. "No more." It halted at once.

A ruby sheen overtook Stewart's vision, and he prepared to lay waste to the old man and his stupid pet, walking toward them with a grin. "I am gonna fuck you and that thing the hell up." He giggled, cracking his neck from side to side. His eyes were manic rubies. "I've been waiting."

A sharp whistle sounded, and Klia dropped from a tree along the perimeter and flapped her wings, hovering in front of Stewart's face. While he was distracted, Luna trotted up and rubbed her nose on his leg. The rage drained. Cora wrapped her arms around him from behind, snuffing the remainder of his fire.

"I'm sorry about that, sincerely," said Myron. "He is quick to defend."

"Fuck off," said Stewart, applying pressure to his wounds with the tail of his T-shirt.

"Whoa, c'mon man," Amy said, standing between them. "Is he always like this?" she asked Cora.

"No. he's usually worse."

"Ha-fuckedy-ha," said Stewart. He gently pulled Cora's arms off himself. "Aren't we going to frisk this guy or something? What's the deal?"

"Babe. Relax, please. There are other things we have to worry about," said Cora. "Myron, what happens now?"

"If you'll follow me, I would be happy to show you. And, Stewart,

I do apologize for the attack. Xorro gets ahead of herself, sometimes, protecting me." He rubbed his head.

The blood had already stopped brimming. The flesh was repairing itself. Stewart began a witty retort, but Myron had entered the shadowy embrace of the doorway. The dogs went next, then one by one the humans followed, Klia swooping behind them. Before he walked through, Stewart glanced again at his arm, and saw the faint scabs vanishing from his skin.

It took several seconds before their eyes adjusted, and they could make out a morgue stretcher in the center of the warehouse. A canvas sheet was draped on top, spread over the tell-tale lumps of a human body.

"What the–?" said Clementine, "How in the hell did you get what I can only assume is Gray's body out of the morgue and down here? This is insane!" Her voice bounced off the steel walls.

Mr. Fox spoke in a soft, even tone while rounding the cart. "I am the next of kin. All this deception was necessary, as you will soon see."

"What've you been waiting so long for?" asked Clem. "It's been three months."

"There are times of year that have certain power, just like places or people, or animals, for that matter." He looked at the bird and dogs. "The cracks formed during the solstices and equinoxes are the optimal times for this sort of thing. And many other things besides."

Amy stepped forward. She and Gray had met three months ago, around the Summer Solstice. Tomorrow was the Autumnal Equinox. "What about his mother? Has she been notified?"

"Of course," said Myron, waving his hand dismissively. "She is from this world, and knows exactly what is going on. Now, can we continue?"

He was looking at Amy, knowing her love for his boy. She felt he was asking permission, respectfully. With a nod she gave it, dismissing her own questions, and Myron pulled the canvas blanket off.

Amy beheld the perfect body of Gray, and her desire for him to be back in her life multiplied tenfold. She brought the maple and silver tantō out of the bag. Its luminescence was a dull glow at first, but burned brighter and brighter until it was almost as intense as the sunshine outside. Silver and gold collided as the polish from the knife absorbed the distant sunlight, weaving among them, eddying metallic sheens mixed together. With a steady hand, she felt the hum of the web emanating from the blade. Without words it spoke to her, and she held it up, ready to use it herself.

Myron moved between Amy and Gray. "This needs kin blood, not a love spell."

With his tone, she felt her resolve soften. "Of course." She blinked hard, trying to clear her head, then handed it over to Myron. "I hope you know what you're doing."

"So do I, my girl." He held the blade as Cora had done, looking back down its length. "Gray, my boy, let's get you out of there."

Myron turned it so the tip faced straight down, pointed between the lowest ribs on the right side. Speaking ancient and jagged syllables that raked the air, he lowered it. The blade's luminescence gathered, concentrating into a beam that shone brightly on Gray's skin, as if aiming. Myron looked up and repeated the phrase, louder.

"Mojz Khujzuun."

As the words bounced from the walls, he thrust the knife down. The blade pierced Gray's skin, and his back arched. Eyes bulging, a bloodcurdling scream escaped his throat. Everyone covered their ears, even Myron. When Gray ran out of breath, he collapsed again. The look on his face after his grimace melted was that of a milky-eyed pawn. It reminded those who had seen them of the shuffling shell people. For whatever reason, this wasn't working.

"Stop! You're going to kill him again!" shouted Amy, amazed that Gray was still alive, albeit in a state of painful limbo. She jumped forward and put her hands over Myron's, pulling the dagger out. Gray lay still again, no visible breathing, no blood from the wound.

"I thought you said you could do this," Amy said, cradling Gray's head.

"It should have worked," answered Myron.

The rest of the group were wide-eyed. Clementine had her hand on Buddy's chest. Luna put her paws on the small of his back. He turned around.

Luna whined shrilly, looking at the boy.

Buddy asked, "Can I see that thing?" He removed Clem's arm and stepped forward. Before she could protest, Luna whined again. Clem reluctantly let her hand go limp.

The blade in Myron's hands began to buzz and hum. The vibration turned to shaking, the hum intensified. The small sword magnetized toward Buddy. Burnt ozone and metal charged the air.

Ribbons of light exploded off it, blinding them. The sound was deafening now, filling the room with a massive rumble. The ribbons whipped around Buddy's arm and pulled harder. After a moment the blade finally shook free of Myron and flew handle first to Buddy, guided into his open hand by the blazing filaments.

When he curled his fingers around the wooden grip, the hum silenced immediately. Clementine, as shocked as everyone else, looked at her son in amazement. His hair stood on end, slowly rippling like grass in a breeze. She could feel the energy coming off him in waves.

"Who, may I ask, is this boy's father?" Myron asked, an intrigued look on his face.

She took a second to respond, without taking her eyes off Buddy. "His name is Miguel. A ceramics teacher. Last I heard he was in a coma, somewhere in the mountains."

"Miguel who?" Myron's eyes grew hungry. "Miguel Dos Santos?"

A chill shot up Clem's spine. "Yes, that's his name. Why?"

"Miguel Dos Santos is the half brother of Zelia Lowehaus, who is Gray's mother," he said. "One big happy family. Well, young man, meet your first cousin." Myron stepped back and fanned his hand toward Gray. "The blade seems to think you'll do a better job than I."

"What? No," said Clem, doubting the whole affair. "He can't do that." Her head swam as she slid between Buddy and Gray.

Amy bit her tongue, not wanting to interfere with Clem's parenting, but realizing Buddy was the key to restoring her trapped lover. She merely played the outcome she wanted over and over in her brain, and was unsure if it were due to her influence or not when Buddy stepped forward.

"I can do it, Mom," he said, sounding sure. "I'll be fine. Gray needs me."

His eyes crackled with energy, and Clem could see the spirit and resolve of her boy beneath the dazzle. She shook her head as she stepped out of the way, and Buddy walked over to the stretcher.

"First I must teach you the words," said Myron.

"No," said Buddy, "they're not necessary."

Myron shrugged and backed off, the curling smile returning to his lips.

"Gray," said Buddy. "Get off your ass and give us some help here."

Without hesitation he jammed the knife between Gray's ribs. Gray's scream ripped the air and he opened his eyes wide. The smoky film dissipated to about half the intensity. There was a consciousness beneath that hadn't been there the first time. This was Gray, mostly.

Covered in sweat, Gray bent his head over the side of the chrome stretcher and vomited out long yellowed strands of goo. The stuff reeked.

The tantō stuck out from his side awkwardly, like a pen-knife in a baked ham.

Amy pulled a handkerchief from her pocket and wiped away the mess from around his mouth. He wrapped his arm around her waist and pulled her close. She slid the sword out of his side, and his eyes bugged out, then his breath evened and he looked peaceful. She handed it to Buddy and placed a towel over the wound, holding it tight and fighting back tears.

"Hello again," she said, sniffling. "Drink this."

She held a large metal water bottle in front of him. Gray accepted it and gulped down the entire thing, then pulled Amy closer. She leaned down and kissed him on the lips, and forgot for a moment the pain and misery she had lived inside for the past three months. He was alive. Gray. Her man.

"Hello . . . Amy," he said, with difficulty. He was panting and covered in sweat as he rubbed his eyes, still slightly glazed with milkiness. As he sat up and looked at the others, they appeared as if through a veil.

Which world am I in, he wondered.

Amy tried not to be concerned with his eyes. He seemed normal other than that. It would probably go away after a while. "Baby, I'm so glad to see you!" She held his head against her, arms wrapped tightly.

"You . . . too, Amy." He squeezed her waist reassuringly. "Thanks . . . for getting . . . me out of there." It was hard to form words.

"That wasn't me, Gray. It had to be someone who shares some of your blood to get you out," she said.

"Well . . . thanks, Dad." He looked at his father, who shook his head.

"Guess again," answered Myron.

Gray followed his father's gaze to the young boy with the knife, flanked by the dogs. Filaments shot off him, cascading from his body. Gray wondered if anyone else could see it.

"Meet your first cousin, Gray. Rupert Figgins. Or Buddy? What do you like, young man?" asked Myron.

"It doesn't matter," said Buddy. He didn't even have a name a few months ago, and now had several. "Whatever you like, Gray. Nice to meet you." He held out his hand, getting the hang of common courtesy in the three months since he'd been reunited with his mother.

Gray looked with wonder at the child. The hand was like a bonfire blazing."You . . . too, Buddy. Clem's kid, eh?"

Gray took Buddy's hand. A crackling current rippled up their arms.

"Whoa," Gray said, pulling his hand away.

Buddy was shocked. "What was that?"

They stared at one another, arm hairs on end.

Myron looked concerned. "Everything alright?"

"Yeah, we're good," said Buddy. He still didn't know if he should share information with Myron, despite the circumstance. Especially here in the warehouses. "Hey, you guys? Now that we've got him back, can we get out of here?"

Clem wrapped up the knife, handing it to Amy, who slid it into the bag hanging off her shoulder.

Max, Helen, and Stewart fanned out once they exited the doorway into the sunlight, always watching. Klia flew high into the bright sky, her shadow darting around on the ground. Another shadow swept over the asphalt, and Max looked up at a raven, high in the sky. Helen saw it too, and monitored the bird until it tucked into a barrel roll and jetted away, cawing, on the eastward wind. Higher still circled two large hawks, hidden in front of the autumn sun.

6.

Julio had worked all summer. Odd jobs. He hated it. After finally renting the grinder and paint sprayer, he'd just gotten the last bit of spray paint off of his metallic blue race car parked on the front lawn. His hands hurt from using the grinder all week. The car was his pride and joy, costing at least three times per month what his rent was. Maybe he'd paint it a different color this time, get a new start. Plus, it would be easier to track down the little fucker that did the damage in a car that looked different.

"Nice car."

Julio turned around. Some lady in yoga pants and a tank top stood on the sidewalk facing him. Brunette, like forty years old. Mami was pretty fine, though, in that sexy librarian way.

"Yeah, thanks." He looked her up and down. "How you doin'?"

She walked forward slowly, setting sun at her back. "I'm doing great. I didn't think you'd ever get all that paint off."

He didn't recall seeing her before, and he was pretty sure he'd remember. But she'd been watching him. He had no problem with that. "It took a while, true that."

"You look like you could use a drink." She pulled a handbag on a strap around from her back, unzipped it, and pulled out a bottle with no label. "Thirsty?" She popped it open without waiting for a reply.

"Damn, it's like you can read my mind," said Julio, taking the bottle and swigging half of it. He brought it down, offered it back to her. Shit was good. Crazy good.

"That's okay. I'm good, honey." She swung her hair around when she said it, and the sweet smell combined with her locks glowing in the sun did something to him. It was like he'd always known her, always trusted her enough to tell his deepest secrets to. Even the ones he wouldn't tell his friends or family. He wanted to tell her now.

"I know where the boy is that did that to your car," she said.

"What the fuck?" He looked shocked, but intrigued. "Why don't you come inside and tell me about it, lady?"

She smiled. "I thought you'd never ask."

Marie Stillwater followed Julio into his house, reaching into her handbag. "Thank you, Julio," she said, walking inside as he held the door for her.

"Yeah," said Julio, "you got it." Did she say my name?

• • •

The fading light hit Gray's long-unused eyes, knocking him backward. In the whitewash, he could barely make out the buildings around him. He squinted across the blacktop to the place where he had been trapped, or killed, still unsure which it was. He felt his body here, in the daylight, being helped along by Amy and his father. The energy Buddy had given him was draining. Crashing.

He could also feel himself in that moment when his chest was pierced by the tantō while he held his gun on Frank Rawls. As he looked across the asphalt, he saw himself impaled by the Japanese sword. Yet another part of his spirit, a third shard, was still in the knife. They all were true, floating in existence together, yet separate. In the space of an instant, he saw his fractured planes of spirit spread across the landscape, overlaid like translucent maps. He walked between them. Between the worlds.

"You alright?" a familiar voice asked.

His father looked into his face with concern.

"Yeah . . . I think," somebody answered.

Myron, alarmed, looked at Cora and said, "We need to get to my house, and now."

She saw it too. "Let's move, you guys."

Amy was near hysterics. "What's happening?"

Myron answered. "The echoes of his spirit being trapped still resound here. While these are necessary to call him back from where he was, they are dangerous afterwards. We must leave, and be somewhere we won't be disturbed. No one will come after him at my house. His spirit is drifting back between the worlds. If we don't hurry, he'll be trapped." He picked Gray up and hastened to the cars.

Once he had eased Gray into the back seat, Amy slid next to them, with Buddy and the dogs riding shotgun. Clem fired it up and flipped a u-turn, flooring it.

Cora followed in her huge clunker with Max, Helen, and Stewart. Klia sat on top of the chrome woman that served as a hood ornament, the rising wind ruffling her feathers until she hopped off and let the wind carry her over the roof of the speeding car. Near the trunk, she fanned her wings out and shot up into the red sky, bright with the setting sun. Flying in a great loop, she came around in front of the hood, then tucked in one wing and shot into the open window, landing on Stewart's finger.

"That's one hell of a bird," said Max.

"Yeah, she is," returned Stewart. "Thanks."

Klia made a tone that mimicked Stewarts voice. Zzsshht.

Cora hit the gas, trying to keep up with Clementine's car as they twisted deeper into the canyon neighborhoods. Little roads with more dead ends than through streets whizzed by while Cora and Stewart craned to see the blue coupe disappear constantly around the next corner.

"Turn here," said Myron, leaning forward and touching Clem's shoulder. "After the tree."

With his hand on her, she could see in her mind's eye the route to take, like a glowing filament overlaid against the trees and shrubs. She hit the brakes and pulled beneath the low branches of a gnarled pepper tree. Its flowing limbs were covered with leaves and peppercorns, obscuring a one-lane dirt road that wound into the confluence of dusty red canyons.

Tall grass grew between the tire tracks, with smaller weeds in the ruts. The road rose and dipped, turning between several trees before coming to a stop in front of what appeared to be a rusty old bus. The vehicle, chipped green paint falling off, was from the thirties, maybe older, and its nose stuck out from the burly braided roots of a live oak tree and a Torrey Pine. The two trunks grew away from each other with branches that formed an antlered array against the darkening sky, like a massive elk head in the desert canyon. The branches and roots wrapped around the rear of the bus, looking as if the trees had swallowed it.

Clem parked. They got out, lit by the headlights on Cora's beater, which scraped the earth as it came over the last bump and sent a billowing plume of dust into the air. The big car backfired as she stopped the engine. Klia chirped and flew into the trees when Stewart opened his door.

"Come! Bring Gray. Time is precious," said Myron as he disappeared into the cavernous bus.

Putting his arms over their shoulders, Max and Stewart carried Gray up to the door. Gray's feet slid along the ground, not even trying to step. Amy was right behind them as they turned sideways and pulled him inside.

One by one, the others followed. Inside, the driver's seat was still in place, with the steering wheel, clutch, and pedals. That was it as far as what came stock, the rest was custom. Bookshelves stocked with books, skulls from small game, and myriad curiosities lined the walls. Sofas and cushioned chairs were spread about with tables and lanterns beside them. Myron was striking matches and lighting lanterns and candles, their flickering glow making shadows dance along the walls.

Near the back was a long table with seven wooden chairs. Max and Stewart pushed away the few books and plates that sat on it and hoisted Gray on top. His eyes opened and he coughed ectoplasmic strands over the edge. The yellow spit spilled like ribbons. Amy stroked his hair. He looked ashen.

Myron sifted through bottles on a shelf in the corner, mumbling names and setting small glass vials and larger jars to the side, emptying occasional ingredients into a stone bowl.

"How are you, baby?" Amy asked Gray. She tried to mask her emotions as she watched the cloudiness thicken in his eyes. Just a thin line at first, the haze rose along the underside of the iris, brimming along the ridge of the lid and lashes. She was losing him again.

"Nouht goo," said Gray.

His voice was hollow, too deep.

His tongue lolled around in his mouth, beyond control, then his eyes.

"Oh baby, hold on." She looked at Myron and yelled, "Whatever the fuck is happening, let's get on with it!"

Cora looked at Mr. Fox, who seemed to be dawdling around, then she bolted out of the front door of the bus. Outside, the sun was down, and the moon hadn't risen. She ran into the clearing, having to slow down so she didn't trip over the uneven ground. The Fox's terrain. It had gotten dark so quickly. She opened the door to her car, grabbed a canvas shoulder bag and sprinted back.

"Any day now!" Clementine glared at Myron as Cora ran back inside.

"Look out!" she shouted, running for Gray. "Hold him down. Amy, get the sword."

"God, don't stab him again." Amy had tears breaking down her cheeks."I can't take it."

"You won't have to. Please get it." Cora's voice was short, but calm. She put a leaf in her mouth, chewed, and spit it into her palm, then poured one drop each from three bottles onto the chewed leaf and rolled it, pulling it apart into two even chunks and laying them down on Gray's exposed chest.

Myron observed, stoic, grinding the mortar and pestle.

Cora motioned to Buddy, who brought a candle from one of the smaller tables. She chewed up another ball of herbs and held it over the flame of the candle. It began to sputter and crackle, birthing a tiny ember that sank down into the center. She held it aloft, and smoke drifted from it as she offered it in six directions; east, south, west, north, earthward, skyward.

The smoke wafted in jagged swirls as she sang a clear, sad note, and plunged the burning ball down into Gray's open mouth.

Amy was aghast. "What the fuck? What are you doing? My god."

Cora spread the remaining herbs on Gray's skin. "Please. Be calm. Help me."

With a choking sigh, Amy placed the sword beside Gray and held his arms down.

His body jerked, and he moaned, but his voice wasn't the deep and weird sound she was expecting. It was his own. Amy saw the terrible milk recede from his eyes.

A black mist wafted from his nostrils, then poured out in a steady stream. The smoke from the smoldering herbs on his chest rose in a grey plume, which swayed lightly in the still air of the bus before drawing into his misty breath.

They swirled together, drawing the ill effects from his body. Then the toxic mixture began to gravitate toward the humming silver of the tantō. When the blade had sucked in all the smoky mist, it shone with a darkly silver light.

"Get that thing back in the bag," said Cora. "Right now."

Amy did, then returned her attention to Gray, who was choking, his skin turning from pale to a light blue. "Help him, please."

"Of course," Cora said. "Step back."

With both palms, she pushed down on Gray's solar plexus. The ball of herbs in his throat shot into the air, trailing smoke like an asteroid burning through the atmosphere. At its apex Cora reached out and snatched it, then rubbed it between her fingers until it snowed down in a mixture of ash and leaf on his body, sinking into his skin. After the mix had vanished, his eyes closed. Color had returned to his skin, and his chest rose and fell evenly with sleeping breath.

"He may stay asleep for a while," Cora said.

"What was all that?" asked Amy.

"I had to troubleshoot. That knife is very different than any I've seen before, more complex. Part of its essence stayed inside Gray, corrupting him. With the herbs, I absorbed that essence, and neutralized it. Then the blade re-incorporated what remained."

"Damn," said Amy. "What the hell were you doing, Myron?"

"Oh, I knew Cora could handle it." Myron was pouring water into a glass. He mixed it with a spoon when he was done, walking back toward his son on the table. "I was making something for now, when he has been healed, but will need something to keep him that way," he said. "Drink this, my boy." He offered the cup to Gray.

"No way," said Amy, stepping between them. "Not after you were just humming and hanging out while your son is dying."

"I, and he, were doing no such things. You forget how well I know Cora, Ms. Munoz. She is more a healer than I am. Now please," he said. "He needs this."

He pushed past Amy and poured the water down Gray's throat. Though sleeping, Gray gulped greedily.

"Easy, my boy," he said, pulling the glass back. "A little goes a long way."

7.

Detective Jim Garrett was at the point of no return. Up until now he had been a pretty dirty cop, as far as San Diego Police went, which was considerable. Never, however, had he been this far gone.

Taking the occasional wad of money from criminals to ignore a certain corner, or infraction, had been commonplace in his work, even after being paired with Detective Clementine Figgins, a woman that the term "straight-laced" didn't even begin to describe. She was so vanilla that he hadn't even tried to turn her as he had done so many rookies in the past. Instead he skirted around the ambitious detective, keeping up as much of his double schedule as possible. She was no rookie, anyhow, having risen to detective rank in no time and working for years with Hector Alcazar, who had gone so deep undercover he still hadn't come up for air. Jim didn't miss Hector, another idealist that was bad for business.

This new assignment, though, was beyond those secretive dealings. It was sent from someone who expected results, and whose penalty for failure was substantial. Fatal, even. Bigger paydays have bigger risks, he told himself. Jimbo wanted bigger paydays. He had a pretty good instinct for who was going to bend, usually. However, he'd been surprised at who had given him this assignment.

Fortunately, Clementine neither trusted nor enjoyed working with him. In the three months since the Stillwater case, when her son came back, he hadn't worked with her at all. Soon she'd return full-time, however, and that would change, though possibly not as much as the change happening now.

The sky was clear, turning from morning to afternoon. The San Diego heat radiated off the asphalt. Jim, dressed in plainclothes, sat in a subcompact car, parked in a diagonally-painted spot in the shade of a jacaranda tree. He wiped his brow, then checked the rearview mirror to make sure he hadn't moved his fake beard.

He'd bought the car for $750 off the street three days previous, as per his instructions. The car's former owner had just been putting the sign in its window when Jim caught him. No phone call. No record. The man was delighted to get cash without doing anything, and had handed Jim the sign as a kind of joke, feeling strange when the big man neither laughed nor smiled and threw it directly into the trash can of the gas station they were next to. Jim took the keys and title and drove off without so much as a deal-clinching handshake or thank you.

Now, from the car, Jim watched the door to the back of the county jail swing open, its frame filled by an obese man waddling out of lock-up. He watched the bloated mass of Crazy Garth exit the door, the one reserved for released criminals or drunk tank temporary residents, away from Broadway and any respectable person entering the Justice Building from the front. An old man in brown coveralls swerved off the sidewalk to avoid him, looking back and shaking his head as he passed.

The huge man swayed, trying to find his balance. Jim hoped Garth made it all the way to where he was parked. He was a good block and a half from the station, as close as he dared. He scratched an itch beneath the beard, watching Garth through the trees. The man usually camped somewhere in the canyons on the other side of the 5, up on Golden Hill. He'd had some sort of fight with Clementine's son up there before he got locked up these latest couple times.

Jim was parked on the most direct route from the station to the canyon, right next to the liquor store Garth would find irresistible. He wouldn't need to enter, though, as Jim already had a pint of the cheapest stuff next to him, and another beneath his seat.

In agonizing slow motion, Garth stumbled and swerved, sitting down to catch his breath twice before the final stretch to the liquor store. Once he had some booze inside him he'd walk straight. He'd be able to breathe. Until then he was at the mercy of the ever-present throbbing in his brain. As he neared the store, he reached his hands into his pockets. Realizing he had no money caused painful gears in his head to clank and turn, searching in vain for a plan to procure vodka. Stealing it wouldn't work, he'd be back in lockup before he could take a swig.

A voice came from behind him. He tried to ignore it, but turned his head as an automatic response. His reptilian brain recognized the red and white label with just the right touch of baby blue that advertised his favorite vodka–Skipper's–in the cheap plastic bottles that would split down the seam if you sat on them.

Like a donkey to a carrot on a string he rose, hand grasping, and walked to the small car that had the bottle sticking out of the window. When he got near, the door swung open. The bottle sat on the seat, drawing him in. He picked it up and sat heavily. The car's springs groaned as he shut the door. "Hey, thanks."

"I got a lot more where that came from," said Jim, breathing through his mouth to minimize the stench of piss and vomit as the giant drunk eased back and cracked the top off the bottle, then poured the entire contents down his throat. "Wanna take a ride?"

Without waiting for an answer, he started the car and backed out, then drove away from the police station. Jim brought another bottle from beneath his seat as he watched the big slob lick at the last drops of the first, blissfully unaware of the small amount of white silt clinging to the bottle.

"Yeah," answered Garth, wiping his mouth with the back of his hand. "But who're you?"

"I'm your friend, Garth," said Jim, adjusting his beard that had begun to drift off to the side of his face. "I work for Skipper's Vodka. We're giving you a lifetime achievement award and ten cases of our product."

"Just . . . like they . . . said. I knew . . . my luck would . . . turn around . . . someday." The stuff was working.

"Hm? Oh, it has." Jim smiled.

Satisfied, Garth opened the second bottle, took one gulp. He watched the houses go by, and then Golden Hill Park, where he had stayed for so long. "Thass where I live," he said, pointing at the tree-filled canyon and grassy expanse with a one-way road around it. His finger poked the window, then slid slowly down.

"I know, Garth, but that's not where the vodka is," answered Jim. "Why don't you tell me what you know about the other people who live out there? Like Max and Helen, and the kid and the dog?"

"They're all a bunch of fucking bitches," he answered, taking another swig off the bottle as they continued east.

"Yeah, they are," agreed Jim. "But what do they do out there?"

Garth's face screwed itself up, confused. "They're homeless, What the fug do you thig they do out there? I don't fuggin' know. What the fug a vodka guy wanna know about those peeble?" He grew more animated, waving his fat hands around. He looked out the window, but didn't know where they were headed.

"Market research. We don't give out awards to just any garden-variety Joe. You're special, Garth. We need this information to continue with your prizes. Now, didn't you notice, when you tried to get the kid, that he could do . . . weird things?" Jim asked the questions he'd been told, racing to beat the drugs and booze that were overtaking Garth.

"Okayokayokay," he said. "He def'nit'ly shunta made me fall off the cliff. He's real fast. Plus that fuggin' dog. We almost there, man?" He drained the second bottle and threw it out the window,. It bounced against the curb and ricocheted, coming to rest in the middle of the street. "Thad fuggin' dog."

"Yep." Jim followed the bottle with his eyes in the rearview, then pulled down to a little cul-de-sac with a house on either side, one black, one white. A grove of live oak trees started just before the houses and flowed down into the canyon beyond. The lattice of shadows from their branches and the strong midday sun mesmerized Jim for a moment when he got out of the car. He shook his head, steeling his resolve before opening Garth's door, pulling on the fat man's collar to get him up.

"Dafuggoffme," said Garth, hitting Jim's hand. The force and speed of the strike surprised Jim, who thought Garth would be pretty docile with the barbiturates in his system. Damn, he's big.

Garth, a little wobbly, stood up and said, "So where'sa hooch, man?"

"Over there, behind the black house," said Jim, pointing.

The darker of the two wood houses lay on the southern side of the small dirt circle at the end of the road. It was matched in everything but color by the lighter one to the north, the side of the street that the sun fell on for most of the year. Magnetized by the call of booze, the large man rumbled and shook as he jogged behind the black house, almost skipping.

Rather than an endless supply of vodka, he stopped and stared at a six foot cube of missing earth. Confused, he turned around from the giant hole in the ground and was blasted by Jim's baton straight to his face. The blow burst open the old wounds that the little dog had given him. They'd taken so long to heal. An explosion of acrid blood sprayed into the air between the two men. Stinky droplets hovered as Garth wobbled on the lip of the grave.

Before he had drank the vodka, the blast and the drugs would have knocked him out cold. Now, however, with just enough liquid courage inside of him, he felt impervious to the pain. Alive. Awake. The familiar rush of booze ignited him, canceling out any effects of the drugs Jim had spiked it with. The promise of vodka was an even greater force, though it looked even to Garth's pickled brain that that could have been a ruse. Once planted, the seed was dying hard.

Teetering, Garth shot his hands out and grabbed Jim's forearm near the wrist, knocking the fake beard into his eyes in the process. Jim pushed him, but Garth held fast as he fell backward, carrying Jim with him into the gaping hole.

Jim steered the bigger man's body beneath him, and Garth came down on the back of his head and shoulders, smashing to the hard earth and wrenching Jim's forearm until his elbow and shoulder felt like they were going to disengage.

Jim's head hit on Garth's shoulder and he breathed in the stench, feeling like he might choke. Garth squeezed. Jim's radius and ulna were going to splinter apart if he didn't do something. He dropped the baton and grabbed on to Garth's pinky finger, jerking it backwards. Garth howled in pain as he jammed his free fist into Jim's kidney.

Jim felt his ribs crack, and he coughed up a spray of blood into Garth's face. The world spun in the vertigo of pain, but he managed to focus enough to lurch forward and attempt a head-butt. He came down hard, aiming for the bridge of Garth's nose, but Garth turned his head. Instead Jim hit his eyebrow ridge on Garth's cheekbone. A white flash of pain lit up his eyes, burning into them. He was really in trouble now.

The synapse finally fired in Garth's brain; this guy with the fake beard was trying to kill him. When the realization hit, Garth whipped into a frenzy, twisting Jim's arm until Jim felt fissures forming along the bone.

In desperation, Jim pulled Garth's finger hard toward his mouth, stabilizing it just enough to get it there. When Garth saw what was happening, his sausage-like finger was already being bitten into.

The stench of pickled blood overtook Jim's senses, but in order to be the one who walked out of this grave, he spurred himself on, grinding and gnashing the skin and muscle apart, never relenting for a second. Garth let go of Jim's forearm and paused, unsure.

Jim took advantage, gnashing his teeth through, splintering the bone apart along the cracks. Blood shot from the stump into his mouth as he spit the severed finger into Garth's face and followed up with another head butt. This one connected perfectly on the bridge of the fat man's nose, and when the cartilage crushed Jim smashed down again. Over and over he blasted Garth's nose. With each successive blow there was less movement, until finally he lay still, wheezing.

Jim pushed himself off the big man and stood up, covered in the stinking spray of Garth's blood. It combined with his own, running down his face and neck. He located his baton in the dirt. As he stepped over the big man's arm to get it, Garth grabbed his pant leg and jerked him back, then nailed a perfect strike to Jim's balls from beneath. Jim fell forward. Before stars overtook his vision completely, he made sure he dropped on top of the baton. With it securely in his hand, he turned around to see Garth righting himself.

If he touches me, thought Jim, I'm fucked. His forehead, kidney, balls, wrist, and almost everything else were afire with sharp pains now. Ignoring everything, he prepared for the finishing strike.

Jim faked forward and to the left, and Garth bit. When the fat man lurched where he thought Jim would be, Jim cut to his right, planted his foot on the wall, and got behind him. Running along the wall, he planted again and pushed, turning in the air and landing on Garth's back, then slipped his baton beneath the folds of flesh to the Adam's Apple. His bad wrist wasn't going to hold up. Holding the baton with his good hand, Jim placed the other end in the crook of his elbow and heaved backward as hard as he could.

Garth's nearly four-hundred-pound frame smashed into the wall, with Jim between him and it. Jim felt his teeth loosen, but he couldn't relent with the choking. It was truly him or Garth now, or everybody dies.

With Jim still hanging off his back, Garth slammed into the wall once more. Jim swallowed a mouthful of puke. Then a wobble, a sway, and Garth finally fell face first onto the grave's floor. Jim held the baton there for five minutes that felt like an hour while Garth bucked, flailed, and rolled, at one point nearly crushing Jim's leg. Finally, there was no breathing. He'd done it. Garth was dead.

Jim lay on Garth's back, trying to catch his breath. The problem was that with every gasp he inhaled the stench of Garth's skin and blood, increasing his desire to vomit. After a valiant effort not to, that's what he did, choking out his stomach's contents next to the bloated corpse.

When he was finished, he tugged and pulled his baton out from the folds of Garth's neck and threw it out of the hole, then tried to climb out himself. The dusty lip gave way at the top, making him fall backward. His landing was surprisingly soft, and he found himself sitting on Garth's ass.

A bubble popped from Garth's throat, and Jim scrambled upright frantically before realizing it was not a sign of life, but gas being forced from the body. The stench was unbearable, and Jim dry heaved once, then swallowed the saliva in his mouth. It was bitter, like old milk.

Cursing under his breath, he pulled Garth by the armpits, grunting and heaving until his body sat propped up in the corner, fat back resting on the junction of two walls. Jim set his foot on Garth's shoulder and hopped up so his hands were on the lip of the grave, then stepped on his skull and crawled out of the hole. He sat there, catching his breath, covered in their commingled blood and the brown earth. A muddy, bloody mess.

After he could breathe, albeit with some difficulty, he got to filling in the hole. He meant for Garth to be lying at the bottom, but with the other changes to the plan Jim thought maybe the corpse being buried while sitting upright was pretty insignificant. The sheer amount of dirt was quite a chore to replace, considering his injuries. His kidney, balls, and hand were killing him. Nevertheless, he grunted and strained through the ordeal.

When he was finished, there was still a pretty massive pile, since the dirt had been aerated. Not to mention there was four hundred pounds of dead man inside. Jim made a mound with most of it, then used a fallen branch to sweep the rest into the live oak, sagebrush, and willow that grew behind the black house.

As he left, carrying his shovel and baton with him, he didn't notice the large raven eyeing him from high up near the crown of a craggy live oak tree, nor would he have thought anything of it if he had. The bird clicked a sound among the trees as it watched Jim pull off, driving up the street and away.

As his car rolled on to the paved street at the top of the hill, the raven spread its wings and dropped down to the freshly replaced earth over the grave, making the sound again. Glunk. Like a great stone dropping into the center of a still pond.

Jim drove south, underneath the freeway, took a couple lefts and pulled into a gas station on Market street. He knew this place's cameras weren't hooked up to anything, having cased it many times. There weren't even cables coming off the old things.

He locked the bathroom door and washed the blood off of his face and hands. His mouth tasted like he drank a glass of chalk dust, and drinking the water didn't help. In the mirror, a battered and swollen man looked back, blood still trickling from the goose egg on his forehead and the gash over his eyebrow. He held paper towels over them until the blood stopped.

When he pissed, the stream was pink. The drunk had injured his kidney enough to release blood in his urine. Hopefully no one would know how sloppy this affair had been, or he could be in just as much trouble as if he were still fighting in the grave with Garth.

Getting back into the car, he put on his fake beard, and drove southeast, zigging and zagging at each block. a couple miles later, he cut up a small street lined with houses strung together with years of random materials, stuck between vacant storefronts and warehouses off Commercial Avenue. He pulled to the curb, looking around before opening a rolling gate. Inside were several cars in various states of rebuild. He drove the car into the chop shop and locked the gate behind him.

The magnetic license plates popped off in his hand. He put them in a brown paper bag with the latex gloves and fake beard and stuffed them into a small brick stove in the corner. He used a saw to cut up the shovel and baton and threw them in as well. After they had burned up, he sifted through the ashes to make sure nothing was left but the charred shovel head, which he threw in the corner. Satisfied, he walked to the back and opened a small door. Outside there were two high fences made of corrugated metal siding. They formed a hallway that looked like a dead end, but at the end revealed a zig, then zag, and a gate held shut with a combination lock. He popped the lock and walked through a pathway behind the buildings, a hidden no-man's-land of dirt and weeds. At the other end, he entered the back door of a small garage. Opening a trapdoor beneath a rug, he descended a flight of stairs and opened a door to a tunnel, then walked underneath the neighborhood until a ladder brought him up inside the safehouse.

• • •

The large raven hopped around the disturbed earth in a circle. A throaty caw escaped its beak, and it spread its wings wide. Dancing smoke curled around feathers, gaining a solidity as they turned to the hands and body of a stout man. When the smoke had cleared, he sat on his haunches, thick hands spread over the mound, fingers splayed and palms downward. Raggedy trails of his poncho and other scraps of clothing hung from his wide body. Again his tongue made a clocking sound as he reached his hand under the poncho, bringing forth a conical blade made of silver and oak.

The snare, made across the sea to the east a thousand years ago. A deep chuckle came from inside as he held the blade up into the last rays of sunlight that filtered through the oaken boughs above him.

Silver and gold light shot from the setting sun's reflection off the blade, and the beams fanned slowly downward, coming to rest perfectly on the square of turned earth. A hum, high and light, rang out. The earth inside the grave was glowing, like an illuminated cloud. The hum grew louder.

Abraham Blackwing sang a low note beneath the snare's high pitch. He clocked his tongue again, stopping both. Silence dropped like a curtain. The world paused. Even the bugs on the breeze were frozen in time.

When he stabbed the oaken spirit snare into the earth covering Garth's grave, the world moved again. Heavy soil was buoyed by light, and it rose. Abraham blew upon it, spreading it back among the trees and bushes to the rear of his house. It thinned and dissipated until through a dusty haze he could see the head and shoulders of the drunkard Garth, sitting propped against the wall, staring through dead eyes into the darkening sky. Abraham made another sound, sharper, higher. The dust moved as one, swaying in a circle and gaining speed until it whipped around like a tornado, sucking the dirt out of the hole and coating the surrounding foliage, wrapping around Abe without touching him.

As it cleared, Garth was uncovered like a sped-up archeological dig. Abe walked around the pit until he was crouching just above the crown of Garth's head. He hacked, bringing up something from his throat, then spit dark saliva down onto the dead man's scalp, right where three sections of skull had fused a soft spot long ago. He rubbed it in, saying a word forgotten in this world, and stabbed the knife's point through the scalp and into the brain. Abe's hand jittered on the handle.

Garth's eyes rolled, and a roar escaped his lungs. Abe looked at the knife and laughed.

The monster stood, massive belly shaking back and forth, and spit black blood from its mouth, which sizzled as it hit the dirt. It grunted, then punched the wall. A huge chunk of dirt fell from the lip onto the floor. Massive hands, pale and bloody, raked more earth down, making a slope.

Abe laughed again. When the monster looked at him with its dead eyes, black pools covered with a sheen of milk, it roared louder. Abe roared back, eyes bugged, mimicking.

The beast stopped and cocked its head, not breaking eye contact, then it crouched down and leapt out of the hole at him.

Its strength was impressive, Abe could see, as the creature fanned its arms above his head, sailing by. The monster was even more powerful than it had realized, but soon it would understand.

Abe whipped around, trying to monitor the thing's progress, but it had already righted itself and charged. It caught him with a shoulder to his ribs, squeezing hard as they flew down into the grave.

Just before impact, Abe clocked his tongue, and his body reverted to smoke. The monster fell through the haze and came down face-first in the far corner.

It stood up with a crooked neck and scanned for its target. The smoky cloud drifted, shimmering on the lip of the hole as it gathered into Abe. He walked backward into the live oak trees and away from his house, again making the comical roar.

It sprang after, chasing him into the woods as Abe turned to a smoky cloud which formed itself into the shape of a huge raven, flying low between the trees. Shadowed wings whispered past the trunks, drifting off in smoky eddies. The monster chased the bird until it got distracted by the silver knife sitting by the roots of an old fig. Growling low, it picked up the snare, looking it over. The blade glowed like a phantom.

The great raven flew in a circle among the trees, then came back to the monster and landed on the ground. Smoke swirled and rose, then dissipated to reveal Abraham. The stout man stood in front of the monster smiling, beckoning.

"To me."

The beast breathed in, prepared to roar, but Abe clocked his tongue, and its breath hitched.

"To me," he repeated, looking at his hand, then back to Garth.

The beast made a low, long growl, then turned the blade, handle pointed toward Abraham.

"Thank you, Garth." The old man wrapped his fingers around it, and the blade disappeared into the folds of his cloak. He pointed between the monster's brows, poking sharply. "Now go get the others." He nodded into the trees.

The beast's head bobbed as if a wave had rolled over it. On heavy feet it ran into the live oak grove, low to the ground, sniffing and searching.

8.

Pearl watched from behind a hibiscus bush as Eddie Calhoun sat next to the liquor store, looking for a mark to score him beer. His eyes bugged out at the blonde woman in her forties. She was old enough to be his mom, dressed in a modest business suit with a skirt.

Eddie couldn't put his finger on it, but something about her was amazing. Not, however, the type to score beer from the local liquor store for a nineteen year old kid. Well, almost twenty. As a joke, he decided to give it a shot anyway.

"Hey lady, do me a favor?"

She surprised him by stopping, and again by smiling. "What's that?" Her eyes got him lost, took him off his game.

"Uh, that is . . . ah."

"Spit it out. I don't have all week."

Wow. This lady knew how to take charge. "You feel like scoring me some beer?"

Her smile grew. "I got something already. Let's go drink it together."

That really wasn't the response Eddie was expecting, but he damn sure was going to take her up on it. This lady was full of surprises. "Really? Right on!" said the boxer's kid.

"Yes, right on," she answered.

Pearl stayed low to the ground, hiding as the lady led him to her car, then followed carefully as they drove to the park.

• • •

In the side canyon of Golden Hill Park, the beer's fizz tickled Eddie's throat, warming as it went down. They sat on a sprawling live oak with branches that filtered the sunlight through its high canopy. The visual effect upon the canyon floor dazzled him.

"What do you call this stuff?"

"It's a little something I brewed up. Do you like it?" Her words echoed, a honeyed reverberation. "It's called TLC."

"Yeah. I mean, it's amazing."

"I know." She looked into his eyes, deeply. "Hey Eddie, do me a favor? You owe me one."

"Heh, yeah. You're right. What do you want?" He didn't remember saying his name.

"Take off your shirt."

"Damn. Yes ma'am." He crossed his arms and tried to pull it over his head, but it got caught in his armpits and he almost fell off the branch. "Wait. I got this."

"Take your time, baby." Her voice lulled, a cooing thing.

After a struggle, he got the shirt off. "Now what . . . baby?" His eyes were droopy, but expectant.

She brushed her fingers on his arm, up to the shoulder. In its trail, a burning desire flooded him. He reached out to touch her as well, but she stopped his hand. "We can do all of those things, but there's something you've got to do for me first."

"Anything." He meant it.

The woman pulled out a black, conical knife. "I need to put this right here." She brushed her fingertips on the bottom of his ribcage.

The warming sensation reached a climactic wave, and Eddie heard his own voice, as if from afar, say, "Anything you want."

From behind a prickly pear cactus patch, Pearl suppressed her desire to scream as she watched the blonde lady slip the knife between Eddie's ribs.

• • •

Later, Rick Oca and Eddie cracked their bottles on the roots of a fig tree in the center of the park. "Careful what you say. Little Crow might be listening," said Eddie.

Eddie had given Pearl the nickname after he'd been thwarted trying to rip off the neighborhood liquor store. He'd never proven that she was the one that blew the whistle on his beer pilfering, done in the store's one blind spot from the cameras stationed throughout, but he just knew. She was always around.

He hadn't checked that day, feeling comfortable, but for some reason one of the cameras had been moved, and he'd been caught on tape. The next time he had gone back to the store he had been given two options; pay back what they had calculated was missing and be able to come back afterward, or go to jail and be banned from the store, in which case he would still be held liable for the expenses. There was no choice. He couldn't run. Everybody in the neighborhood knew where he lived due to the regional fame of "Rockin'" Royce Calhoun, his father, an Olympic boxer from years past.

He didn't put it together at first, but each time he saw Pearl in the vicinity of something, the situation went south. Now, in the park, drinking quarts of malt liquor with Rick, he brought up the subject.

"Your sister's a spy or something. Like a narc."

"Dude," said Rick, shaking his head. "She's not a narc. She's a twelve-year-old girl that thinks she's Sherlock Holmes."

"Well, whatever. Every time she hangs around, well . . . "

"Like I said, twelve. You gotta watch what you say around kids, dude. Plus she's insanely smart, and actively tries to listen."

"Like a little crow," said Eddie. He looked up into the trees, into the eyes of a black bird amidst the branches. It warbled, and his stomach felt queasy. "Little Crow. That's your sister's Indian name."

"Are you for real? Pearl is her Indian name. We're fucking part Ipai."

"What is that?"

"An Indian name."

"I thought you were Mexican."

"That too. Let's just move on. Pearl will ruin your plans, so be careful what you say. It's not that hard to avoid her if you're aware."

"Little Crow," said Eddie, tasting the words. "It wouldn't surprise me if she was the one who put all that shit on my porch."

"I doubt it."

"Yeah, but you don't know."

Rick shrugged. It would be just like Pearl to do something like that, actually, but he kept it to himself.

"Besides," said Eddie, "little crows have a thing for garbage."

"Easy with that little crow shit, dude, seriously. What did you want to talk to me about? Not my sister, hopefully."

"Not at all, okay. Anyway . . . " Eddie's voice drifted off. Rick followed his gaze to a small black-and-gold dog across the grass in front of them. A forty-pound baja mutt with a black bandana around its neck. It whined, staring at Eddie.

The sound of retching made Rick turn his head. Eddie was puking his malt liquor into the sprawling roots. When Rick looked back, the dog disappeared behind a copse of miniature palms.

Pearl, hiding amidst the palms, was shocked. The little dog did something to Eddie, that neanderthal. She'd seen the little dog before, with the cop's kid from the news. Just yesterday.

She'd been spying on Eddie's house one day when she saw Rupert Figgins the first time. Three months ago, before all the news stories. He was about her own age, taller and stringy. Everyone was taller than Pearl, it seemed. He covered the porch with garbage and dog shit and rang the doorbell with a stick, then hid across the street and watched. She'd told her brother Raul all about it, except for the part where the boy moved like a blur after he rang the bell, so fast her eyes couldn't follow. This dog was with him then, too.

Then came the news, and after that she'd been trying to find him until yesterday when he was being tracked by that spidery kid who was missing a finger. This time he moved even faster, so fast he wasn't there. She couldn't tell anyone about that. She wouldn't even tell her grandfather, if he were around to listen.

Now, with Eddie throwing up his beer, the little dog walked past her hiding place where she had been reading lips. It looked right at her without breaking stride, gave a muffled bark, and took off like a shot across the one-way road into the pine trees.

Keeping the palms between herself and Eddie, Pearl picked up her bike and followed. She got as far as the pine break before she lost sight of the dog over the cusp of the canyon. When she saw it again it was up the other side, almost to the golf course. She pedaled as fast as she could, careful she wasn't re-entering her brother and Eddie's line of sight.

A mockingbird squawked to her from a bouncing branch. She looked as she passed by, and couldn't tear her eyes from it. Her front tire hit a root in the path and she ended up crashing off the trail and rolling into the weeds.

"Dang, bird," she said. "Why'd you do that?"

The bird screeched and took off on the trail of the dog, landed on another bush and looked back. Pearl dusted herself off and picked her bike up. It flew away down the wooded hill, and when she reached the branch it had been on, she searched for it, but the bird was gone.

If she was going to find that boy, this was her best chance. A twelve-year-old girl couldn't find out where a big-time detective lived using a computer. The kid hadn't even started school yet. Until he did, this was it. She bombed the hill, letting her instincts guide her, like her grandfather used to tell her. Across 26th street she pushed her bike up the hill to the golf course parking lot, then looked all around for the dog, birds flying into the air, leaves rustling, anything. But it was still. She passed Irene's restaurant and rode down forgotten stairs into the canyon next to the driving range, where she heard a deep warbling. A big black bird dropped from the electrical wires stretched over the canyon and spiraled down to the path. It looked at Pearl with its head cocked to the side and made a sound that froze the marrow in her bones. It was familiar.

As she stood motionless, the bird hopped around her, sizing her up. It clocked its tongue, and a familiar, earthy scent wafted up her nostrils. Her muscles relaxed, felt wonderful even. A stream of thoughts without words danced like ribbons in her mind. She looked into its eyes and spied the dreams of birds, then the thing turned to a swirling column of smoke.

Little Crow. That is me.

"Hello, Grandfather," she said.

"Hi, Pearl," said Abraham Blackwing. "Are you prepared?"

"Yes."

9.

"Fellows, will you follow me downstairs?" Myron pulled back a curtain in the corner, revealing a black, wrought-iron spiral staircase curling into darkness. He walked down without waiting for a response. Stewart and Max looked back. Cora and Helen nodded, and the men followed Myron. Klia watched from the table near Gray, and clicked her tongue.

At the bottom, the temperature dropped by several degrees. Sound became muffled, falling out of the air. Mr. Fox pulled a wooden scrolling door down, closing them in the room below the bus.

"Hold on. What are we doing down here, man?" asked Stewart, his hand on Myron's forearm.

"I'm sorry, there's a few things we need to speak about in private," said Myron, lighting a small lantern.

"Bullshit," said Stewart. "What could you have to talk about without the women present?"

"It's not the women part as much as the cop part that worries me, as we need something stolen from somewhere."

"We?" asked Stewart, incredulously. "The fuck you mean we? I'm barely 'we' with this guy, which puts you definitely not in that circle."

"Thanks, I guess," said Max.

Myron said, "When you hear what I have to say you may sing a different tune. The thing we need to steal will save us from imminent peril, perhaps death. There is a monster that's been made, and it's hunting."

"Who and what are you talking about?" asked Stewart.

"The man you call Garth," Myron answered.

He told them a tale of the raven and the monster. When he'd finished, Stewart said, "God, that fucking Abe dude pisses me off. So infuriating."

"That's his job, Stewart. Of all the tricksters, he is king." Myron had an amused glint in his eye.

To Stewart, the look reeked of condescension. "Yeah, dude. I get that. Let's just get on with it." Rage, like bile, bubbled in the back of his throat. This fox guy didn't like him. He wasn't too gaga about Myron either.

"Listen up, and try to relax." Myron put his hand on Stewart's shoulder.

"What, motherfucker?" Stewart slapped his hand off, then balled his fists up. "Tell me to relax again, dude, I fucking dare your ass." His nostrils were flared, eyes wide, leaning toward Myron.

Max got between them. "Stewart, Can you not try to fight everybody all the time, please? Damn, dude."

After a tense few seconds, Stewart put his hands to his sides. It took longer for him to stop shaking. Once the rage rose from within him, it was difficult to bottle it back up. Cora had been teaching him. It was easier with Klia around.

"What we need," Myron said, "are the twin blades of stone. One green, one gray. Only if the monster is stabbed by both at once will the twisted spell be silenced." The words hung heavy.

"Where are those?" asked Max, shuddering as he thought of Garth as a mindless corpse.

"Cora had one, but lost it at the assault on the warehouses," said Myron. "I've traced it to Marie Stillwater's house. The other is in police evidence. Both locations have their own sets of problems, of course."

Stewart eyed him. "Didn't you get the one up there from evidence?"

"Yes. But I work with the police, and it was used on my son. I have no such connection to the stone blades."

"Well," said Stewart, "we're gonna have to go get 'em, then. Where to first?"

Max looked corner-eye at Stewart. "No offense, man, but you're kind of lacking in the stuff that makes a good thief. Like silence, levelheadedness, the propensity to disappear rather than brawl, things like that."

"Well, what else can we do?"

"Can one person do it?" Max asked Myron.

"Yes, with one of the mockingbirds," he said. "But unfortunately the boy, Buddy, seems to have a natural feel for the blades in general. Not everyone can handle them. Even I had trouble with the tantō," he said. "If you went, and couldn't handle the blade for some reason, we wouldn't get a second chance."

Max shook his head. "I can't take the kid. Clem won't let me, even if I wanted to."

"But the monster is searching now. Our options are limited. He's a very talented child."

"No kid. No way." Stewart's eyes narrowed. "This is bullshit. I'm fucking going with, and that's that. I can handle a goddamn knife, and I happen to have a mockingbird friend."

"Fuck," said Max. Hopefully Stewart wouldn't get them both killed. "It's you and me, then."

Myron stood firm. "I wish you'd reconsider."

"Get used to disappointment," said Stewart, pushing past Myron and opening the scrolling door. "Because I'm going." He walked up the stairs. Max shrugged and followed, leaving Myron to blow out the candles.

Upstairs, Helen and Cora had Gray sitting on their crossed arms while they walked off the bus. He was asleep, with his arms over their shoulders.

"Where are we going?" asked Max.

"To my house," answered Clem. "So he can be looked after properly."

Myron came last off the bus, singing a tune under his breath.

• • •

As she pulled from under the pepper tree's hanging limbs, Clementine's radio squawked to life. The dispatcher said there was an anonymous tip concerning a buried body behind a house among the canyons. Not recognizing the street name, Clem asked Amy to look it up, and found it was within a mile of her home.

"Okay, dispatch, show 274 responding," Clem said, to Amy's surprise.

"10-4, 274."

Amy's arms were around Gray, who was asleep sitting up in the middle of the back seat. "God damnit," she said. "Why?"

"It's too close to my house. Could be connected."

"I get to go to the crime scene? Nice!" A beaming smile spread on Buddy's face.

"Not a chance," said Clem. After few blocks of shooting down Buddy's bright ideas on how to tag along, she pulled up in front of their house, then approached Helen as she got out of Cora's car. "Helen, can you please look after Gray and Buddy? Amy and I have to check out a crime scene near here, just got called in."

"Of course, baby. Whatever you need."

Buddy kicked a rock as he walked through the gate.

"Thanks," said Clem, following him with her eyes.

Amy was trying to pull Gray out of the car. Helen tapped her lightly on the shoulder, moving her to the side, then reached in and effortlessly lifted Gray's sleeping body from the back seat. As she carried him into the house, he nestled into her arms, comforted by her intoxicating scents.

Clem cranked the wheel and flipped a U-turn, then sped down the street toward the crime scene.

Cora watched the car's taillights vanish around the corner. "Where are they going, Myron?"

"Abe's house, I think, though I don't know why."

Stewart interrupted. "Myron said Abe made Garth into some monster who's collecting all the old knives for him."

Myron scowled. "You're no fun."

"What are you talking about? That's a banishment offense." Cora was steaming. "Who has the Maple Snare?"

"Fuck." Stewart had a sickening knot tightening his stomach. "The Japanese thing? Amy's got it. Does anyone have her number?"

They looked at Buddy, who shook his head.

• • •

Where the map said to turn, there was nothing. Clem had Amy look on her phone, throwing the map-book down on the seat between them.

Something caught Amy's eye. "Stop," she said.

Clem obliged, and was curious when Amy got out and picked up an empty pint bottle from the middle of the street.

Amy put it in a bag and got back in. "Long shot, but this is the same kind of bottle as the ones littering Garth's camp when we were there," she said. "Coincidences are becoming more and more rare."

"I'll say," said Clem, swallowing the knot in her throat.

Half a block later, a thin driveway peeled off to the right. Clem turned the wheel hard between two clusters of trees. Peering through hanging branches, they could see two houses, one on either side of the end of the street. She got a familiar feeling as she looked at the small statues barely visible in the approaching night. The light-colored one to the north had eerily happy figurines of people in animal suits. The dark one to the south had misshapen figures of bundled wire and string. Neither had an address.

"This has to be the place," said Amy, taking the safety off her service revolver before putting it back in her holster. She rounded the car and pulled Clem's reserve crime tech kit from the popped trunk, eyes tracing tire tracks on the gravel.

"Yep. I've got one of those gut instincts everyone's so fond of," answered Clem.

"Yeah, me too. These tracks are fresh, but I can't get a read off gravel. Later I can look up farther where there's dirt, alright? Let's do this."

They walked to the lighter house first, fanning beams from their flashlights along the ground. As they circled it, weaving between the thick bushes toward the back, they saw no disturbed earth that would signify a recent grave. Clem shined her light through a window covered in dust, making the beam glow pink inside. Nothing moved in the cluttered house. A plush chair sat by the fireplace in the large living room. Bookshelves were stuffed with books, statues, figurines, glass jars. So many things she had a hard time focusing. They moved around to the front and crossed the dirt road to the darker home.

Amy felt a chill when they neared the front porch and looked around, shining her light into the bushes. She was unable to shake the feeling of eyes following them.

As they rounded the side, Clem shone her light in a window. Black drapes were drawn tight. Nothing was visible except dark fabric. She took a deep breath and followed Amy around the back.

The huge hole wasn't what they expected to find. This looked like a freshly dug grave, except the six-foot cube of missing earth had one side raked down until it formed a hill. At the bottom Amy saw clumps of wet soil, not the sort of thing that occurs six feet down in the bone-dry summertime in San Diego. She rounded the hole and turned backward to ease herself down as Clem surveyed the ground surrounding the pit. Broom marks. The dirt had been swept clean of footprints.

After dousing it with luminol, her swab shone pink in the light. "I got blood, Clem." Amy held it in the beam. "And a dirty puddle that looks like puke."

Clementine noticed a grey cylindrical object the size of a rolled taco behind Amy. She was about to call it to her attention when they heard a loud pounding, like something very heavy banging on steel.

"What the hell?" said Clem.

"Go check it out," said Amy. She moved quickly, bagging up the swabs and latching her kit. "I'll get this packed up."

Clementine ran around to the front of the house, shining her light on the car. The beam lit up the backside of an obese person slamming their hands down repeatedly on the roof.

"Stop! Police!"

The man's head whipped around. He gave a guttural snarl before rushing at her with alarming speed.

"Stop! I will shoot you!" She fired her pistol into the dirt, but he didn't even break stride. "Last chance!" She fired again as he drew near, three times. Chunks of bloodless flesh, grey in the light, exploded off his torso. Her legs took over and she ran, chancing a look over her shoulder. She recognized Garth, the pervert from the park, moving quick.

He was right behind her as she rounded the building to see Amy trying desperately to claw out of the large grave. Clem turned, squeezing the trigger. His hand knocked her aim down before she could apply enough pressure. In the muzzle's flash she saw a tortured, dead look in his eyes. She'd interviewed him a few months ago. He had been a drunk, but assuredly alive and human. What had happened?

The bullet shot through his leg, provoking no reaction as the huge beast collided with Clem and grabbed on to her. They fell to the bottom of the grave with Garth on top, crushing her. As they hit, her breath whooshed out, and she couldn't draw a new one. It all felt broken. Stars flashed in her vision, then blackness.

Amy screamed as they flew over her. She leveled her pistol, but with Garth atop Clem, she couldn't fire. Easing behind him, she aimed at his temple.

The monster instantly snapped its neck sideways, its thick cranium hitting the barrel. Amy squeezed the trigger, and the bullet shot into the side of its neck, lodging in its shoulder. She tried to shake off the concussed numbness and maintain her grip.

Black blood oozed like thick pudding from the monster's gaping wound. It rose, towering over Clem and shifting its focus to Amy. A hopeless fear, the likes of which she had never encountered, covered Amy like syrup. There was nothing she could do.

One moment. Frozen. Inside this eternity she fought and scratched, ridding herself of the saturating terror. Somehow she was able to get her gun up. Her fingers relaxed, just a bit, and she leveled the pistol at Garth's eye and fired. The monster felt this one. It entered just beneath its eyeball and exploded out the back of its head. Blackened skull and brains sprayed onto the surrounding plants.

A howl of pain ripped through the canyon. The beast's hand shot to its face as it thrashed around blindly and fell to the ground.

To Amy's relief, Clem was awake and rolling out of the creature's range. Amy backed up into the corner, with Clementine opposite her. The monster stood between them, so that there was no chance to fire on it without risking grave injury to one another. She reached into her pocket and fumbled around. To her relief she had one quarter. Taking a step to her right, she threw it, hitting the monster's cheek on the ruined side of its face.

The monster lunged in the direction the quarter had come from, and Amy cut the other way. She ran toward Clem, put her boot into hands forming a stirrup, and was thrown up onto the lip of the grave. Instantly she turned and gave Clem her hand, hoisting her out.

They turned back, pistols raised, but the monster was already launching itself through the air toward them. A dozen bullets tore through its arm, raised to protect its one good eye. Chunks of flesh spattered off as it propelled its body clear of the grave, shrugging off the effects of the large caliber bullets like so many flies.

Amy jumped one way, Clementine the other, and Garth fell headlong, tumbling between them. The beast righted itself, and looked at the guns, then down at its mangled body. A clunky gear clanked in its mind, and it turned around and ran into the trees.

They fired after it, in disbelief at how little harm they were inflicting. The horrible groaning voice faded into the darkness as they grabbed Amy's kit bag, picked up all their spent shell casings, and ran back to the car.

Clem looked into the back seat, where the monster had been trying to break in. In the crack of the upholstery, tucked down with the hilt protruding out of its wrap, she saw the tantō. The ancient sword emitted a silver glow that lit up the inside of the car.

Amy held Clem's radio handset in her palm, staring mutely at it. "What do I say?" she asked, stymied.

• • •

Marie's house was empty as Oliver stood outside the front door. In his hand he clutched a sparrow. He brought it in front of his face, chomping his teeth. The bird chirped frantically, trying hard to flap its wings, but the boy's grip was iron. He squeezed the bird as it made its next sound, holding it in front of the keypad, and the terrified chirp tripped whatever sonic code was needed to open the door. A hydraulic whoosh pushed it ajar, and he smiled.

He looked at the bird, bringing it closer to his mouth. He had no more need for it. The bird had other ideas than becoming a snack to Oliver, however, and in a last act of defiance pecked its small beak on his knuckle, making his grip slacken ever so slightly. The bird broke free. He swooshed his hand after it, catching it between the tips of his fingers. It pecked and chirped bravely as Oliver brought it close to his mouth, clacking his teeth together in a chilling rhythm. As its head entered his mouth, the bird gave a final cry. Oliver's insides knotted up in a sickening way, but he forged wis will and bit through the bird's neck. An electric charge trickled down his esophagus as the bird's blood coated it. Oliver sucked the rest out and growled, a little blood only made him want more. Dropping the dead sparrow on the ground, he fought off the urge. There wasn't any more blood, anyhow, not anymore.

Tiptoeing over the creaky hardwood floor, he reached down and pulled open the trapdoor. A smile parted his bloodstained lips. Yellow teeth glinted in the light of a half moon shining through the large bay window. Like a shadow, he raced down the hall to the bedroom. Gears and magnets slid, and he came back clutching the flute and chime.

Putting the flute to his lips, he looked down at the metal machine and blew. A pale light shone from beneath the floorboards, accompanied by a deep hum. Silver tendrils wound their way through the air, drawing to his touch like moths to a candle. They wrapped themselves around him, and he could feel the changes growing inside of him.

His eyes felt so full.

10.

The night breeze blew east, through the branches where Raul Oca waited. He was good at it, making no sound, no movement from his perch high up in the pine tree. A lightweight black canvas tarp was pulled around him, covering all but his eyes. He'd been taught well by his grandfather in the ways of stealth.

Pearl, his little sister, had relayed a message from their grandfather concerning musical instruments hidden somewhere in the house he was casing. When Grandfather asked, they obliged; Pearl, Raul, and their brother Rick who hung out with some unsavory types, even by the Oca family standard, but was generally trustworthy considering family business.

There was some weird shit going on in this one. He watched the scene with the thin kid and the bird, not really believing what he was seeing. Then there was the following light show. After the house had lit up like lightning was striking inside, the spidery kid had run out of the house and disappeared into the trees, hands over his eyes.

Now the house was dark, the canyon quiet. Pine and oak branches swayed in the light eastern wind, carrying the smell of the harbor. His limbs quivered as he waited for the right moment. This era, one that had people so paranoid they no longer used lock and key, had also made them overconfident in the security of computerization. All you had to do was witness a keypad being punched and you were golden. After waiting weeks, he'd finally seen the brown-haired woman enter her combination without blocking his view. He'd waited hours after she left, only to see the spider kid use the bird. Not even his grandfather had shown him something like that.

The sun had gone over the western hill while he sat in the tree. He could see the joggers running along the golf course to the west. Fortunately no one looked up.

Waiting. Such is the life of a thief. The sound of hushed voices slithered to his ears, but it was just the neighbors. The man and woman, tipsy from the looks of it, staggered up some steps and into a craftsman house across the street. Then the area was quiet, save for the low rumble of the nearby freeways.

It was time.

He shoved the tarp to the bottom of his bag as he ran to the front door, punching the numbers into the keypad. The door clicked, and a hydraulic pump kicked in, opening it slowly. The house was dark and quiet as he stood in the doorway.

Headlights shone from around the side of the house, surprising him. He pulled back on the door, but the pump was strong. It slowed, but kept opening. He quit pulling and pushed. It opened all the way and the pump clicked off. Then he pulled it shut, quickly scampering into the bushes before the car came into view. Its headlights turned off before they hit his spot in the shrubs.

Cars were so quiet now, much more so than when his grandfather had originally taught him the thieving way. The sleek black sedan parked. Two women–one blonde and one brunette–stepped out.

"Are you sure you're up for this, Marie?" asked the blonde. "I could volunteer, you know."

They walked to the front door. Marie punched the numbers into the keypad. "Up for it?" she asked. "Oh, yeah."

"Not everything's a gift. You saw what happened to David."

"There's others, and when one works, I'm next, Nuala. Nice try."

"Good luck."

Marie chuckled, unamused. "Thanks."

The door shut, cutting off their conversation. Raul retreated into the bushes, then scampered up an oak on the canyon's ridge. He watched their animated discussion through the large bay windows while they walked from room to room.

Behind him, tires crunched on gravel. Raul hugged tightly against the cracked bark of the live oak and watched a pale man exit the sedan. He opened the rear door and pointed toward the house, mumbling something Raul couldn't make out. Someone he recognized stepped out of the car, a friend of his brother's, some wannabe banger named Julio. Dude was neighborhood-famous for his car. A car that got tagged up pretty good a few months back. Pearl said it was that cop's kid.

Julio walked stiffly, like a cartoon sleepwalker. The pale man followed, opening the door and guiding him inside. Raul could see the women straighten up.

After a short conversation, the pale man looked at a silver object on the table, the one Oliver had left. He twisted it, and it became two; one long and thin tube, the other a ball the size of a child's fist. The objects Pearl had described.

Marie stood in front of them, facing Raul through the window. With the house lights on, and the canyon dark, there was little chance she could see him. Still, her eyes rested precisely where he was sitting. It creeped him out.

She turned around as the pale man blew into the silver tube. Nuala rocked the ball back and forth, rolling it around her palm. Julio stood between them, straight and unmoving. A hum issued from within the house, shaking the earth around it. Raul's tree vibrated, and prickly leaves spiraled to the ground.

He peered into the house in wonder as vapors rose from the floorboards. They were blue and metallic, and looked alive, probing slowly around Julio's body. When at last they came into contact with his skin, they seemed to gain purpose, snaking around his arms and legs, then over his torso. They slithered up his head, leaving only holes for his mouth and nose, writhing like glowing worms.

The pale man held his hand up, stopping the music. Nuala placed the chime in his palm. From where the tendrils grew, he pulled up a trapdoor. A bright blue glow illuminated their faces, and Julio in his bindings. The pale man reached down inside it, and the hum and glow intensified. The tendrils rose, lifting Julio's body.

Raul's mouth hung agape as Julio hovered in the center of the room, quaking. It was so bright now, he was getting scared they would see him through the window. He hugged all but a corner of his eye behind the trunk.

Julio stayed aloft as the tendrils removed themselves, then reattached in different areas of his body. After long minutes crawled by, the steely wires began to slink back into the floor. The lights dimmed, the hum quieted, and he was lowered to his feet. His pants and shirt had holes all over, the size of cigarette burns. His eyes were black voids.

"Show us," said Peik, stepping back. "Fulict Lazhou."

Julio turned his head to the side, opening his mouth. The sound that came out was like the hollow and cavernous cry of a whale. Smoke cascaded to the ground and surrounded his body, climbing all the way up to his eyes, then enveloped him completely. The column of smoke stood still, then drifted across the room and swam up the chimney. Julio was gone. Where his body had been was now an empty spot on the floor. The pale man looked on with delight as the wisps of smoke vanished.

Raul was close to panic watching his brother's friend turn into a black cloud. He got a hold of himself, breathing deep, and was about to jump down before he looked to the house one last time and froze as the black smoke drifted from the chimney toward him. It gathered into a ball, floating in front of Raul's tree, and shaped itself into Julio. Through pitch black eyes he stared at Raul, who waved his hand to shoo him away. Julio pointed, his mouth opening. Raul just knew some horrible sound was about to come out of it.

At that moment, the pale man trilled into the flute. Julio reverted to smoke and was sucked back through the chimney as if magnetized.

Raul looked inside as Julio gained solidity. Peik beamed, but the women seemed skeptical. Julio lumbered to the window and looked out toward Raul, raising his hand and scratching the glass.

Stop fucking doing that, thought Raul, ignoring the gooseflesh on his arms. He'd never seen anything like this, or been this scared, but his grandfather had taught him how to remain calm. He breathed deeply and relaxed his mind.

The pale man said something to Marie. She nodded, and stood next to Julio. The pale man played the flute, and Nuala the chime. The hum began again, and the floor sent forth more tendrils. These, though, were thick, fewer in number.

Eight braids of midnight blue, glowing from within, attached themselves to Marie. The first, also the thickest, came to rest on the base of her skull. The second guided itself to the other end of her spine, at the tailbone, then her hands and feet. The last two were much thinner, tensile braids, glowing dark blue. They snaked up and attached themselves to her eyes.

The pale man and Nuala changed pitch, starting a slow, eerie song with four notes, rhythmic and repetitive. Marie's body rose off the ground and shook. Her hair stood straight out, an electric blue dandelion, and her body pulsated with the blue light, illuminating her from within. Strobing lights dashed along her veins, nerves. Her breaths were quick and shallow, and her head rolled from side to side. The lights gained speed, zipping along her insides until they blended into the color of her skin, now a pale blue porcelain, then lowered her to the ground, disengaging themselves.

When she opened her eyes, they were electric blue. She blinked, swooned, and fell sideways. Before she hit the ground, the pale man caught her, moving so quickly Raul couldn't follow. He was a couple yards away, then he was scooping her up. No in-between. He motioned to Nuala, who picked up Marie's legs while the pale man got her shoulders, setting her down on the couch. Her breasts rose and fell with the rhythms of sleep. Julio, eyes black, watched from his spot across the room.

The pale man crouched over the hole in the floor, snuffing out the light. Raul saw flashes from the silver objects as the man put them back together, then walked down the hall and shut the door.

The blonde was looking out the window, next to Julio, typing something into her phone. She had barely slid it back into her pocket when the pale man opened the door and came back down the hall. He said something to her, and she spoke to Julio, who walked toward the door. They were leaving.

It was sketchy, but Raul couldn't wait to get into this house. Something pulled his will beyond his rational self. He'd robbed places when people were home before. The only person staying behind was asleep, and he was filled with an undeniable confidence. One his grandfather would have warned him about.

He tied his bandana around his face and watched them lead Julio to the car. The gravel crunched beneath the tires, fading into the distance, then Raul dropped from the tree, dashed to the keypad, hit 3712, and slipped in.

Once inside, his thudding heart felt like it may burst from his chest. Could she hear it? Marie lay on the couch, still sleeping. Wanting her to stay that way, he walked heel-to-toe down the hallway, feet near the walls rather than the well-worn and probably creaky center. Following the route of the spider kid, he crept into the bedroom at the end and looked around. Bizarre-looking statues on shelves with books and jars, jewelry on top of a vanity and a chest of drawers. Nothing so far.

After looking behind paintings and in the closet, he found what he was looking for. The corner of a rug was curled up, and on the floor was a piece of the hardwood that looked odd; the slats around it had wider gaps than the rest. Scooting the rug aside, he stuck his fingernails into a crack and pulled it up to reveal a safe sunken into the floor. He smiled. Safes were the first thing his abuelito had shown him.

He pulled tools from his daypack and had it open in seconds. Up close, the things didn't look very valuable at all. The stem of the flute resembled an oak branch, and the round chime was magnetized to it. Could silver be magnetic? He wasn't sure, but if he hadn't seen what they could do, he'd have never thought to steal them. Not his usual score.

Next to where they'd been in the safe were several black conical objects with etched markings on them. Beside them was a polished stone knife.

When he placed the silver items in his bag, the orb gave a solitary chime that seemed to come from everywhere at once. Raul balled the bag up, silencing it. After listening for a click, he snatched up the stone blade and gripped it tight.

His mind drew a picture of a cold cave with a glint of far off light. It sent a vibration through his body that filled him with desire. Pearl didn't mention a knife, but she did warn him about taking extra things. The temptation was too great, though. Surely his grandfather would be proud of him. He put it in the bag with the instruments, tearing his grip from it.

The black cones stayed. Looked more noisy than useful.

He closed the safe, put the floorboards and rug back, and crept back up the hall toward the front door, peeking around the corner at the now-empty couch. Shit.

He stepped forward, hand held protectively in front of his face. An iron fire poker whizzed by, glancing off his forearm and into the wall, cutting into the plaster and sticking fast. At its other end, Marie grunted in frustration.

In one leap, Raul bridged the distance to the front door. When his thumb came down on the latch, the hydraulic system made a deafening click. He looked back at Marie. She wore a curtain of rage on her face as she tried to free the poker from the wall. Her blue eyes glowed electric fire. She looked inhuman.

The door opened with agonizing slowness. Abandoning the poker, Marie hurried toward him. Her hands and eyes glowed bright, energy crackling off her like lightning. Raul stuck his fingers in the crack of the door and pulled as hard as he could on it. Slow ass door. He got his elbow in, forced it wide enough to squeeze through, and took off into the canyon just as the door was hit with a bright blue bolt of energy which nearly blasted it off its hinges.

Once out in the night, Raul ran like never before. He heard Marie come outside as he made it to the thicket of trees behind the house. Weaving through, he looked back and saw her sniffing the air. Her face was a sickening grimace. Small blue tendrils of light peeled off her glowing hands, snaking into the air.

She smelled him. Bright blue ribbons flowed from her eyes as well, stretching and twisting into the dark grove, splayed out in front of her like antennae. Searching for him.

Raul was rapt, but when the tendrils turned towards him, he tore his eyes and ran up a bushy path between two small, older ranch houses. Marie, gliding along on the tendrils, followed his tracks in the dirt. Just before he turned a corner around an old apartment building, he looked back again. She was scratching at bushes, fuming. She cursed, hot blue spittle flying off her lips, and turned back toward her house.

He cut between the buildings, ending up on a quiet street. Accelerating at every corner for six or seven blocks, he finally slowed to a walk in an alley. Catching his breath, he took his bandana off his face and turned his reversible jacket from black to green. As he unzipped the bag, the stolen things cast a glow. He reached in, grabbed his hat, and put it on, closing it as quickly as possible.

His mind was spinning with the thrill of the chase and filaments of light as he looked to see if he was still being followed. Seeing no one, he got on his way, sticking to the shadows. A few miles later he came to his squat. Like a shadow he descended the steps off of the street level, moved the sculpted cardboard-box-and-trash gateway, and entered the place where he lived and played music with his bandmates in secret. Unknown to anyone, underneath an old building downtown.

11.

Alec and May were gone. Raul was happy about that. He needed a little time to figure out what the hell he was thinking, robbing that house with someone inside. He had rules, and that wasn't one of them. But he had the silver ball and whistle, plus the stone knife.

When he took out the instruments, they gleamed in the dim ballroom,. As he pushed the orb to the side it made the faint chime again, brightening. He looked in wonder, picking up the flute. It was a short, straight whistle with four holes on top and one on the bottom, six inches long that tapered at the mouth, etched to resemble an oak branch complete with a solitary leaf and two acorns. The air became charged with a static that filled his vision, dancing and mingling with the light off the silver. He placed the mouthpiece to his lips and blew into it.

From the end came brilliant ribbons of silver light, reaching up into the large high-ceilinged room. Raul maintained a steady breath. His abuelito had taught him breath control, used to great effect in both music and thievery. He watched enraptured as the streaming filaments wrapped around themselves, forming a glowing tree trunk. Weaving limbs grew from each node into leaves and flowers.

When he finished the note and drew the flute from his lips, a massive oak tree filled the ballroom, its exposed and ghostly root system binding the tables and chairs stacked against the far wall, pushing into the musical equipment set up near the corner. The trunk was twenty feet wide with branches as thick as his body, glowing bright as day.

The canopy mesmerized him, leaves and branches swaying on a breeze that he couldn't feel. In his daze, he let his focus drift off into the web of lights. He jumped back when he saw a blurry face looking back at him. A girl, or woman, it was hard to tell. Just as quickly as it had appeared, she vanished.

Movement along the glowing bark shifted Raul's vision, and in it he saw May, his roommate, descending the steps to the ballroom with a grocery bag in her hand. A portal, happening now.

Instinctively, he put the whistle back to his lips and blew a short trill. The tree began to unravel, sucking back into the flute.

Just as the final branch disappeared, a scrape sounded from outside. The door made a pop, then its wheels rolled along the ground a few feet before May came around and shut it tight.

"What's up, Raul?" she said. "When did you get home?" She pulled the rope that brought the trash heap up against the outside of the door. That was one of May's contributions; a bunch of trash and whatnot glued and taped together so it looked like an impassible wall of garbage, but had a handle and rolled on small wheels effortlessly when pulled. No one from the building wanted to clean a homeless encampment, and no one checked it out too closely. The two boys were as impressed with her creation as they were with her musical ability, which was undeniable.

The basement was where May and Raul lived. There was electricity, but no water. To bathe they went to Alec's house, shared with a few deadbeat roommates, but to use the toilet took more ingenuity. Raul, however, had been boning up on the blueprints to the building, thanks to Alec's job in the city records office. Alec had found it, and Raul got them inside, then siphoned electricity. Soon he'd have the water situation figured out.

Raul nonchalantly put the flute and orb into his bag. From the ball came a faint chime.

May cocked her head, looking for the sound, finally settling her eyes on the cymbals surrounding the drum set. "What the hell was that?" she asked. She pinched one to silence it, but the sound didn't alter. She pinched the rest with the same effect.

"What?" asked Raul.

"That, like, ringing, dude. Or chiming. You don't hear that?"

"I don't hear anything." Raul shook his head.

"Huh." May looked to see if an amp was left on.

"Probably outside of my register." He put his hand on top of the bag.

"Yeah? Anyway I can't hear it anymore. Weird. Want some rolled tacos?" She held a white paper bag out towards him.

"Big time," he said, opening the styrofoam package, dipping the taquito in salsa and biting it in half. "Fankf," he said around the food in his mouth.

"De nada," she answered, and followed suit. As they ate, May noticed the tiniest sliver of light from Raul's backpack. Just a thread really, but it piqued her interest. Her face got the same intrigued expression, only more intense. "What's that light from, dude?"

Raul was starting to really like May. It's important to like the people you play with, especially at the inception of a band, when you need to be together a lot to come up with enough songs for a set. But Raul was actually attracted to May, and he felt the attraction was mutual.

However, he wasn't ready to confess to the whole thieving life, just as he wasn't ready to throw everything his grandfather had ever taught him out the window. Perhaps just some tidbits would satisfy her. He pulled out the ball.

"Just this trippy metal ball I found in some bushes." It rocked back and forth in his palm, chiming louder this time. May looked up from the orb.

"You hear that, don't you?"

"Yeah, now that you mention it. Is that what you heard?"

"Fuck this," said May, her eyebrows creased. "Raul, the reason I left my home, years ago, is because my father is a liar. Everything that came out of his mouth was a lie, even when it didn't need to be. He looked a lot like you look right now. So tell me, if you want me to be a part of your life at all, what in the fuck you are lying about?" Her eyes bored into his.

"Shit. Okay, but it's weird."

"I don't care. Show me."

"Lo siento, Abuelito," he said. When he put the flute to his lips and blew, the tree of lights streamed from it, dancing and writhing. This time, many faces were discernible in the bark. Men. Women. Children. Swirling. Changing. May's eyes brimmed, awestruck.

She stood up beneath the limbs, reaching up to caress them, and a tear broke down her cheek. As if obeying a distant voice, she picked up the metallic orb and shook it lightly in her hand, and the leaves changed their shape. Little eyes blinked as they separated from their branches, folded into wings, and flew around the tree's trunk in an ever-widening circle. Avian heads poked from the bodies of light, and birds filled the air, alighting and perching on every surface, including the transfixed couple, who marveled at the flock. May brought her hand, holding three weightless finches, close to her face, studying them.

A great squawk arose, and they jumped as the birds took wing, circling high against the ceiling, whooshing around the tree's huge trunk. When the sound had reached a nearly deafening crescendo, they formed a stream and barreled into the orb in May's hand. Its chime dulled, then was gone completely. Raul repeated the trill as he had done before, and the tree shot back into the flute. A sheen of sweat covered them, and their bodies hummed with a silver tone until the flute and chime no longer glowed.

"What did we just witness?" asked May.

"I have no idea."

"Where did you really get these things, dude?"

"You're not gonna like it."

"Come here," she said, a hungry look on her face. She put her hands behind Raul's ears and drew his face close. With puckered lips, she kissed his cheek, more than friendly, then the other, the corner of her mouth touching his. After that she looked into his eyes and kissed him on the mouth in a way that no one ever had before. It was the kind of kiss that made him hope no one ever would.

"Now that we got that first one out of the way," she said, "I'll like whatever it is you tell me, as long as it's the truth."

Raul had always liked May, but Alec had made it known he would be bummed out if anyone in the band were dating each other. Now Raul saw her in a new light; stronger, more confident, sexy. Screw Alec's ideals.

"Okay," he said, "but let's have one more of those first."

Raul leaned over, cradled her head in his hands, and kissed her. When they were done, they leaned back on the cushiony love-seat and he told her of his time at Marie Stillwater's house.

When the story was finished, May was intrigued. "Who are these people, and how'd you find out about them?"

Raul paused for a moment. A cardinal rule for the entire twenty-five years of his life, and especially since age ten, when his grandfather began to teach him, had revolved around one theme: tell no one what you have done. Not friends, not family or lovers. If you get caught, do not tell your fellow inmates. Very simply do not breathe a word to anyone. Ever.

That wasn't an option with May, he needed her. The flute and chime were out of this world. That Marie lady would be coming for them, with her friends, and who knew what they could do? Plus he didn't know where his grandfather was. He never did.

"Well, you asked for it," he said, shrugging. "I'm kind of a, um, cat burglar. A thief. That's what I do for work, sort of. I found out about the house through my Grandfather, he needed me to get these things." He motioned to the whistle and orb. "So I grabbed 'em."

May's interest was piqued. "And here I am working at a damn coffee shop at the golf course. Wow. Is that what you've always done?"

"Since I was like ten, yeah. Grandfather taught me. He's kind of a legend in the thief game, although no one really knows his identity. They only know him as El Pàjaro, because he leaves so few clues people swear he can fly."

"Jesus . . . He can't really fly though, right?"

Raul looked at her sideways. "Of course not, May."

"Of course not. How stupid. It's just, that tree and those birds made out of light . . ." Her voice drifted off.

"Yeah, I know, I've never seen anything like that either. This is the first time he's asked me to get something so . . . magical."

"Wow." She looked at them. "Well, before we give them to him, how can we use these things to our advantage?"

There it was. "I don't remember telling you 'we' were a team."

"That's because I'm telling you, baby. This band is okay, but it takes more than music to make money, chiefly luck, and these things look like some pretty good luck to me. Plus after seeing that stuff and hearing your story, there's no way I'm going back to the cafe, dude. I'm sick of that place. So how can we use these?"

Raul marveled at how quickly May had bent his will to her own, and realized her talents were greater than he expected, but she didn't really get the concept of thieving yet. Too eager. "Well, I guess the first lesson is about stealth, and these things are about as stealthy as a herd of buffalo, so I couldn't tell you how to use these to our advantage, 'baby'. This is a serious business, not a game," he said.

"No, no, no." She waved her finger. "No macho bullshit. I don't care if you learned from your macho grampa or not. Don't talk down to me. Fucking man code crap.

"First of all, you haven't tried more than two things with the flute. Only you did the same things twice, like you said, because you're a dude, and lack imagination. Plus, if you used the lights to create a diversion that someone couldn't tear their eyes off, then it would be easy to steal from wherever they weren't looking."

Raul blinked several times. May was thinking in ways he himself never would, and she wanted this life.

"I'm sorry. I shouldn't condescend to you. Everything's been a secret for so long. I've never showed anyone what I know." He reached forward and grabbed her hand, "but it'll feel good to teach you, I think."

"I think so, too, if you mind your p's and q's." She mussed his hair playfully. "Where do we start?"

Leaving the instruments in the bag, Raul instead concentrated on what he knew of the thieving game. For the remainder of the day, before Alec got back from his job, Raul started on teaching May how to pop open locks. He had a canvas bag filled with knobs and deadbolts, and tools for picking. His fingers would guide hers with the tools, and told her which one best suited which lock. After hours of this her fingers began to cramp, and Raul rubbed her hands with oil.

A sly look crossed her face, and she led him to her futon in the corner, taking off his shirt then her own. He looked up at her curvaceous body as she lay him down on his back, kissing and undressing him. Raul got dizzy looking into her eyes. The good kind of dizzy.

When they were finished, they lay in each other's arms, dreaming big, until they heard the familiar clop of Alec's shoes descending to the hidden entrance. They got dressed, kissing one last time before Alec pushed the big door open and slipped inside. He shut it and pulled the rope.

"What's up, guys?" he asked, squinting in the room.

Raul was tuning a drum, and turned around when Alec spoke. "Not much."

"You weren't playing those, were you?" asked Alec.

"We all know not to play till seven, dude," said May.

Alec liked most things about May; she was relatively nice, smart, and a great musician. One thing he didn't really like was how much she said 'dude', even by southern California standards. Oh, well. Small potatoes, really.

"Good. Well, what is going on? You guys just hanging out?" he asked.

The mumbling began to tell a story. When Raul finished what he was tinkering with and faced Alec, his unzipped pants added a chapter. Alec shrugged and walked over to his amplifier. It had only been a matter of time before they hooked up, despite his protests.

The thing he had come for, his jacket he had left here after practice last night, was draped over his amp. He put it on.

"Well, see you chatterboxes in a couple hours for practice. I'm gonna go shower and eat something at home." He reached into the inside jacket pocket, pulled out a pipe and some weed, took a hit, and offered it to them. Curiously, they turned it down. That never happened. He shook his head and made for the door. "Later," he said, blowing smoke up toward the high ceiling. It swirled slowly.

"Alright. See ya, dude," said May.

Raul, who had noticed a breeze, was zipping his pants up. "Bye Alec."

As he pushed the door shut from the outside, Alec thought of the many shifts occurring in his world ever since he had met the lady cop. Three months ago, Clementine Figgins had come into his work and looked at blueprints to some crazy buildings, but not this one. He'd hidden it.

Thing was, after she had gone, he'd found her buildings had the same owner as his. He'd looked into it. Not only had the properties not paid taxes for over half a century, most of them had been scrubbed clean on their records. Water, electricity, and other utilities were all functional, but on paper, or more accurately these days on computer, the properties didn't exist. Under Stillwater Enterprises there were roughly seventy properties on the books, including the warehouse stuff he'd read about. The one where Detective Clementine Figgins busted some sort of slave operation or something. The articles he had read were a little cloudy about what had actually been happening there. But her son was involved. That was the newsiest part.

Off the books, Alec had found about two hundred more secret Stillwater properties. On old blueprints he had located several blocks in the city that had 'holes'; properties that had no deed or record, but he could see where they were. They weren't online. In order to locate them, you had to have access to the blueprints, and only three people even knew where they were. The other two wouldn't have a reason to look.

He walked up the stairs two at a time to the street level, so lost in thought he almost ran into the fit and fortyish blonde woman walking toward him. Excusing himself, he met her gaze and felt a shudder run over his body, quickening his pulse. He followed her with his eyes. He couldn't help it.

Trailing her perfect legs up to the skirt which hung just above the knee, his eyes drifted over her shapely butt and up her back to her silken blonde hair. His libido screamed, and the beginnings of an erection tightened his pants.

Shaking his head, Alec broke from the thought of trying to pick up on the cougar and detached his gaze from her ass. When he swung around, he was surprised to see a pale man, very nearly chalk-white, wearing a blue track suit and looking at him with interest, a toothpick in his teeth. The man smiled at Alec, whose member instantly shrank to its most flaccid state. He lowered his head and hurried past the man down the street.

12.

Inside the ballroom, May's nervous laugh had gained momentum. Now she was heaving on the ground, tears streaming down her face. Like after a fart in church, Raul got caught up in her mirth. He laughed, letting his guard down. The giggling sounds were so loud, he wasn't sure whether or not he had heard a soft rapping on the door. Shushing May wasn't easy, but when he did they both distinctly heard it; three soft taps, then a pause, followed by three more.

Just in case one of them forgot their key, the trio had a sort of secret knock. This wasn't it. No one knew about this place, and really shouldn't be knocking at all unless Alec had been careless while leaving, which he never was. They froze in their positions.

"What do we do?" May whispered in Raul's ear, almost silently.

"Just wait. They'll leave."

The pause after the last round of knocks stretched into a minute, and they finally dared to breathe. Raul grabbed the bag carrying the knife, flute, and orb, pulling it around his shoulder, then crept to the light switch and turned it off. The knocking came again, louder this time.

There was no way he was opening that door for anyone, Raul thought. If someone made it in here, they were going to have to do it without his help. As if in response, the lock clicked, then the door creaked and opened just a bit. Raul darted back to May's side.

"Anyone in here?" came a woman's voice, raspy. The door slid open as the words echoed. Light shot in, making a long shadow that stretched across the floor. Raul and May ducked behind the loveseat, keeping in the dark.

"Hello?" came the voice, closer.

Raul slipped the bag off, then pushed it beneath the loveseat. May's nails dug into his forearms. She chanced a peek, and found her gaze being met by an unfamiliar woman standing over them. Blonde and slim, older, attractive.

May shook Raul, the jig was up. He recognized her from the house he'd robbed. Then the pale man stepped through the door.

"I believe you have some things that belong to us," said the woman.

"I don't think so," answered May. "We don't have too much around here."

The man breathed an exasperated sigh. "Shut up," he said, "and give me the items you stole."

He grabbed the loveseat and pulled it away, exposing the bag. Raul grabbed the knife and flute from inside, but they snagged on the strap and he lost his grip. The ball fell out of the open bag at the same time, and they clattered to the floor, all bouncing in different directions. Pings echoed around the room.

Nuala dove for the flute, but May got there first and flicked it back to Raul. When Nuala landed in front of her, May punched, but she moved her head and May's fist hit the floor.

"Ow! shit," she said, shaking her wrist.

Nuala took advantage, punching May in the neck. May stumbled backwards, wheezing. This lady knew how to brawl, and she was fast.

Raul put the flute to his lips and blew, hard. At once, thick filaments of light burst from it, streaming for the pale man. They flew into his mouth and nose, around his neck and limbs, then lifted him into the air.

To Raul and May's dismay, a low rumble came from the man's throat, and the filaments spasmed out of control, falling off his skin, so white it nearly glowed. He dropped to the ground, landing on his feet.

Behind them, Nuala hummed a similar pitch, creating a harmonious wave which washed over the ballroom and forced the filaments of light back into the flute.

With the lady distracted, May grabbed the orb, shaking it maniacally, to no effect. Whatever they were doing to the flute was also working on the orb. Realizing their new toys weren't going to help them, May rushed Nuala.

Having left home at a very young age, May spent a lot of her life being raised by the street, and she knew how to fight. Through countless adventures she'd learned when to defend, to walk away, and when to strike. This situation fit snugly in the third category. Before the blonde woman could respond, May took two big steps and delivered a devastating kick to her solar plexus, making her gasp for air, and stopping the hum.

"I can fight, too," said May, shaking the orb. Raul followed her lead.

"Nuala, get up!" shouted the pale man.

With Nuala's voice silenced, The combined tones from the flute and chime overcame him. Tendrils again wrapped his limbs. He looked shocked. Still playing, May and Raul retreated to the far corner of the room while he struggled to regain control.

On the wall nearest them was a grate that covered a vent. Ductwork ran from it into the bowels of the old building. May worked on the old grate with one hand while Raul blew into the flute.

Nuala coughed, then resumed the humming harmony just as May got it open. The grate hit her hand and the silver ball fell to the floor. A feeling of hopelessness overtook the two musicians. The older couple advanced upon them with confidence.

Raul pushed May farther into the duct, shielding her with his body. With him between her and the strange couple, the mind-bending tones were dampened, the dismal feelings receded. She tried to pull Raul after her, but he wouldn't budge.

She scrambled up the tube. When she had gone several yards, it bent upwards into blackness. She wedged her body inside and began climbing up, her feet on one wall and her back against the other, pushing with her hands near the small of her back. The progress was going slowly, and she began sweating, which didn't help things. Raul screamed, then the voices got louder. The dread returned, but she pushed on.

A steady tapping echoed from behind. Footsteps. Someone was running up the tube after her, stopping at the point where it bent up. Faint light came from a grate ten feet above, about half the distance she'd already come. Chancing a look down, she saw someone looking up at her. A skinny boy. He hissed, and May caught a glint of light reflecting off yellowed teeth and dark, unnatural eyes.

She focused her energy on reaching the grate, but was moving too slowly as the boy began to climb up behind her. He had one hand and one foot on each side, something May felt she wouldn't have the strength for, and was moving twice as fast as she could. He was almost upon her by the time she reached the grate. She kicked it with all the force she could muster. On the third hit it began to give way.

Just as it clattered into the room on the other side, a thin hand wrapped around her ankle and pulled. She lunged forward and wrapped her hand on the lip of the hole, now hanging on with the spidery boy dangling from her leg.

She shook to get him off, making the metal housing cut into her palm, and repeatedly stomped his face with her heel, smashing his nose and yellow teeth. Every kick made her hand sing with pain.

The kid's grip was firm, and he started jerking down. The edge cut deeper into her palm, She held on as long as possible before the pain became unbearable. It was let go or lose her fingers. As the blood ran down her arm, she opted to fight. Fuck this kid.

She let go, and they plummeted down the slick tube, echoing with the terrible song from the ballroom. With the boy below her, she shifted her body, and soon was kneeling with one foot on his collar bone. She landed a solid punch to his throat. He coughed, and tried to bite her ankle. His teeth clacked together, giving a sickening beat to the paralyzing music.

He grabbed her shirt, pulling as they slammed to the bottom of the tube. Her foot slipped up to his neck, ramming his head into the floor, and she jammed the butt of her cut hand into the bridge of his nose. A ringing pain shot up her arm.

Breaking free, she ran down the tunnel, straight for the blonde, who stood at the opening humming that goddamn sound. Shock and nausea from the fall hadn't taken full effect yet, and May shot from the dark tube, elbowing Nuala squarely on her cheek.

Reacting instantly, Nuala snagged May's hair and yanked. May's momentum swept her into the air, six feet up. Time stood still for a fraction of a second before Nuala brought her down hard, smacking the rear of May's skull against the floor tiles.

"How do you like that?" said Nuala.

May's head sang with pain and her vision began to blur as she watched Nuala pick up the bag. From the corner of her eye she saw Raul, hands tied. The pale man loomed over him. Raul didn't struggle. May thought they must have done something to him, like drugs or whatever the hell these people did.

The blonde lady held the flute and blew. No sound. No lights. She handed it to the pale man. Same result.

"Grab everything," said the man, looking deadly serious, "and everyone."

May tried to keep awake, aware, but everything was so hopeless. A bright light had entered her life, then just as quickly it was snuffed out. More lies. The story of her life. She felt her hands being bound, and saw the spidery boy emerge from the ductwork.

"Good job, Oliver," said Nuala.

The kid growled, no look of pride or thanks. He walked up to May, staring with dead eyes into her soul. She shuddered in fear. He smiled, then lunged forward, teeth snapping close to her neck. His progress was stopped short.

The reason he hadn't bitten her, she realized, was that the pale man had intercepted the attack and was holding a handful of the boy's hair in his hand.

"That," said the man, "will be enough of that. We need them alive."

May, barely conscious, expected the boy to listen to the older man, seeming all the world like the leader of this group. She was surprised, though, when the boy turned to face him, twisting his head with his hair still clenched, and wrapped his thin fingers around the man's neck, He squeezed and shook the man's head.

The man pulled the boy backward by the hair, prying him off almost effortlessly. His arms were longer than the kid's, and when the boy's fingers slid off, the man made another tone, throaty. Dark blue threads of web, speckled white, poured from the man's mouth. A great spilling glut of luminous tentacles wrapped themselves around the boy's arms, legs, torso, and neck, and shot him up in the air. His head was as high as the crystal chandeliers hanging from the ceiling of the great hall, a good twenty-five feet up, before the pale man ceased the song, and the tendrils whipped the boy down to the floor. He hit with an earth-shaking crunch, a sound like hundreds of bones compacting. The tentacles slid back into the pale man's mouth.

"Frank's fucking pet becomes more of a nuisance every day," he said, tying the boy's hands after the tendrils had retracted. "Unpredictable little mongrel."

The boy groaned, and the blonde woman sighed in relief that he was alive. "He did help capture her, though. He's just got a little temper, Peik."

"My ass, Nuala," answered Peik, exaggerating her name. "He should have died with Frank. Now he wants to kill me. Look at him. If you don't control him I'll use this on him." He pointed to the knife.

"Well, then it would be useless," she said. "Besides, if it weren't for your daughter's screw-up, we wouldn't even be here."

"She will do her penance," he countered, never looking away from Oliver.

Nuala could see something terrible was about to happen. "Oliver, let it go." She stepped between them.

The last thing May saw before she passed out was Oliver attempting to smile at Nuala. She thought the boy must not have had much practice with the whole smiling thing. It didn't come naturally to him.

"I miss Markuz," Peik said. "This trip made Frank's kidnappings seem tidy by comparison."

"Oh, boo-fucking-hoo," said Nuala.

May was jerked awake moments later, and the couple followed her, Raul, and the spidery boy through the door to the street. Raul was looking better, more aware, to May's relief. They glanced at each other, and a world of meaning and communication branched out between them.

"You guys try anything beyond looking at each other and you'll be dead, guaranteed." said Nuala, pushing them up the stairs and across the dark and deserted street where their car was waiting.

May knew that getting in the car was a point that, once crossed, would yield no return for them, but another thought accompanied it.

If they wanted us dead, they'd have killed us already.

With that, she eased back in the seat and breathed deeply, trying to set her mind right to see what this strange future would hold.

• • •

Peik pulled from the curb and drove east, creeping down the street as Nuala held the flute up to the light. It sparkled, illuminating the interior of the car. Oliver struggled against his restraints in the backseat between Raul and May.

Raul gazed at the thing, and the blonde woman, mesmerized. From the corner of her eye, Nuala watched, and his pulse quickened.

"Whatever the fuck you're doing, bitch?" said May. "Cut it the fuck out," Oliver chomped his nasty teeth at her, protective of Nuala. "You too, dude. You sick fucking thing,"

He hissed, lunging with his neck.

Nuala put the flute down and turned to May, waving the grey stone knife through the air.

"Oh, I'm sorry," said Nuala. "Did he already lose interest in you, sweetie? So sad." She touched the tip of the blade upon May's cheek.

May could feel a rivulet of blood trickle down to her dimple, cut by a blade so sharp there was no feeling, no pain accompanying the slice. The wound tingled, like a vibration. She'd be dead before she even knew it with this thing. A shiver passed over her while the car motored through a tunnel beneath the 5, almost to the western slope of Golden Hill.

"Put that thing away," said Peik as the car ascended the steep grade. "You want someone to see you? C'mon."

Her eyes drifted over to Peik without losing their potency. She smiled, not friendly, and pulled the knife away from May's bleeding cheek.

May breathed a sigh of relief, then the night exploded.

Smash!

Halfway up the hill, the high creak of twisting metal ripped the air as a thunderous force rammed into the side of car, low and hard. It spun completely around, rising off the street. When it dropped, the mutilated face of a monster roared at them from outside the passenger window. The thing was massive. Maybe four hundred pounds. Its gray face was destroyed, and a good chunk was missing from above its left eye. The eye itself was crushed, and black pus oozed from the socket. Huge curls of fat dripped off its neck.

Everyone but Peik screamed. Clashing waves of sound filled the car. The monster was confused. It put its hands over its ears, raised one thick leg, and kicked out Nuala's window. A tattered and filthy boot hung in front of her face until Peik floored the gas pedal and shot up the hill with the monster hanging on to the door by the crook of its knee. The back of its head bounced off the pavement every few yards.

Nuala tried to force the leg up and out of the window. The beast grabbed the spinning tire next to its head, and the car shot to the right at the crest and smashed into a small coupe parked at the corner, trapping the beast's head and hands between them. It flexed its muscles and pushed back, scooting both cars along the concrete.

Peik opened his door, but before he could undo his seatbelt the monster threw the car straight up into the air. When it fell, it smashed its grille into the concrete, then rolled onto its roof in the middle of the intersection, spinning.

The beast stopped it, then grabbed Nuala, trying to drag her out the window while she still had her seatbelt on. Peik unfastened his and fell to the ceiling, then ran around and gurgled a sound that grew a filament from his mouth. It sped toward the creature.

Splitting in two, it wrapped around the monster's thick wrists and jerked it back towards Peik. The creature fruitlessly tried to shake them off. When it stopped that and yanked back, the force ripped them apart.

Peik grunted, seizing up with pain. No one had severed his filaments before. He felt it deep within his intestines, like boiling bile.

Wide awake with their captors preoccupied, Raul and May maneuvered enough to push the releases on their belts, and dropped onto the ceiling. Raul easily looped his wrists under his feet and brought his hands in front of him. He located the bag with the flute and ball, tucked under Nuala's ass, and pulled hard on the handle. The stone knife popped out, almost stabbing him. He grabbed it, turned it inward and cut his restraints, then, avoiding Oliver, did May's. She had to crawl underneath Oliver, as the monster was blocking her door. Oliver tried to kick her, but she caught his foot and twisted. When he jerked his foot back she slid under and joined Raul.

Once out on the street, there was a brief moment of silence. When Raul turned around, the giant monster was above him. Knife in hand, Raul slashed, and the sharp blade cut a deep groove in the monster's arm. It howled, batting its hand upward into Raul's fist. He couldn't maintain his grip, and the blade flew over the car, then hit a curb and rebounded toward the crest of the hill.

Empty handed, Raul faced the monster. This was it. His fear turned to wonder when the beast chased the knife instead of him.

He started to run after it until May pulled him the opposite direction. "Let's go!"

Abandoning the knife, they ran down a small side street, looking back before vanishing into the bushes between an apartment building and a small house and fleeing into the canyon along the city mechanic's yard.

Peik, in brutal pain, focused. The knife slid along the intersection, about to carry over the lip of the steep hill overlooking downtown. He ran, diving just in time to trap it beneath the tips of his fingers on the cusp of the hill. He heard the thundering footsteps and roar of the creature closing quickly, and turned when the sound became unbearable, stabbing with the blade.

The creature's roar turned to a scream as the blade sunk into its wrist and stuck fast. It wrenched its arm backwards and pulled it from Peik's grasp. Unnaturally quick, it snatched the blade out of its arm, taking some skin and muscle with it, and looked down with a corpse's eyes.

Peik thought his long life may be at an end before the monster exploded down the hill, holding the knife high like a trophy. At the bottom, it crashed through the fence near the entrance to the city maintenance yard. Its voice echoed as it disappeared down a gully that flowed into a huge tunnel beneath the city, carrying storm water from the long creek bed to the harbor.

"Shit," said Peik, facing Nuala and Oliver, free of their seat belts and standing outside of the car. "Nice of you to help out."

"Screw that," said Nuala. "What the hell was that thing?"

"That's what we're going to find out."

Nuala shook her head, still in shock.

Oliver had done the trick he'd seen Raul do with his wrists under the feet, and was gnawing the zip-tie off of his wrists, staring at Peik.

Peik's gaze was ice. "You better control your little monster as well.

You don't want anything happening to him."

Nuala turned to Oliver and whispered, "Oliver, this is very serious. You need to apologize to Peik, and he needs to believe you, okay? Do it now."

He stepped around her. "I'm sorry, Mr. Stillwater. I forgot my place, and got too excited with all the activity. It won't happen again. I'll behave. We'll move as a team," he said. His voice cracked from disuse.

Peik broke into a slight smile. "It's alright, Oliver. I was young once, very long ago." He made a mental note to never let his guard down, remembering his own coldness at such a young age. "Now let's get out of here."

• • •

A couple had come from their house, looking out upon the scene: three people gathered around an upside-down car in the middle of the street.

Peik, Oliver, and Nuala convened on the side of the car farthest from the couple. Hidden from their view, tendrils of dark light came from Peik's hands, and rocked the car until it creaked and rolled, bouncing onto its tires. To the couple, it looked like a man, a woman, and a kid, none of them physical marvels, had actually pushed the car back upright themselves. They were wide-eyed as the battered sedan started and drove up the hill to the east.

Nuala looked on the front seat, then underneath it. After she'd also scanned the rear she asked, "Where's the bag with the flute and bell?"

"I'm sure you're not asking me," returned Peik. He was swooning. Too much energy lost from the ripped tendrils. "Now we have no blade, flute, or chime? I'm sure those little assholes have them. And the monster took our knife." His pale knuckles turned bright red as he strangled the steering wheel.

13.

Time was of the essence. Stewart and Max didn't know how much they would have, but both knew it was in short supply. They'd gone over the plan several times: get in the house, locate the safe, Klia would pop the lock, then they'd grab the blade and vanish.

Cutting through the canyons on small game trails near the golf course, they made it to Marie's adobe ranch style home; a one story house that sprawled out along a peninsula of red earth, surrounded by tall trees, mostly live oak and pines. The house looked empty. As did the neighbors on either side.

Max's brow wrinkled, and he nodded to Klia, who landed on the branch in front of them. She pecked on the bark, chirped, and they set off toward the front door.

"Something is weird," said Stewart, sniffing the air.

"I feel it too," Max replied. "But we're here. Let's do it."

Stewart held Klia, perched on his finger, in front of the keypad. She made a click-whistle combination, and the lock popped. A hydraulic pump kicked in, and the door slowly opened.

The air was thick inside, heavy. Smelled vaguely to Stewart like panic sweat. There was a light chiming, almost imperceptible, on the air, and clicks sounded from beneath the floor, like old heat pipes cooling. Stewart scrunched his nose, trying to smell out what was bothering him. Max grabbed him by the collar and pulled him down the hallway as Klia jumped on his shoulder.

In the bedroom, Max saw something in the corner. A rug had been moved. Along some of the slats there was a thicker groove than on the other parts of the floor. He put his fingernails into it and pried it open to reveal a safe.

Klia dropped from the corner of the bed and chirped into the safe. Stewart jumped as gears clicked, and the safe door jostled. Inside were canvas bags, rolled up and bound, beside a stack of black metal cones. Jagged etchings adorned their sides.

The stone knife wasn't there.

"What the fuck?" Max looked around the room for any other place it could be, although Mr. Fox had detailed the safe exactly. He stood up and began opening drawers.

"This is fucked. C'mon, man, we gotta go." Stewart eyed the cones.

"Should we take these?"

"No." Max shut the safe. "We don't know what's going on with those things."

Klia clicked sharply, warning, and both men froze. The next sound was the latch of the front door popping and the pump kicking in. Max pulled the rug over the floor above the safe and joined Stewart in the space behind the open bedroom door, looking through the crack above the hinge. Here came Marie Stillwater, storming down the hallway, eyes a blue blaze.

They squished behind the door. Marie walked past them and kicked the rug aside, then threw open the slatted floor piece. As she turned the safe's dial, Max and Stewart rounded the door, shuffling sideways so they could keep her in their sights.

She pricked her ears as the floor creaked, locking eyes on Stewart as he was swinging the door shut. He jumped backwards, slamming it as Marie screamed.

The power from her voice buckled the door, knocking Stewart backwards, but it held. Waves of sonic energy slammed it again, forming splinters. Klia flew past Max to the front door, clicking and chirping. It opened, and in agonizing slow motion the hydraulic system engaged. Max squeezed partway through, hearing the bedroom door atomize down the hall. Marie stepped out, her skin glowing pale blue.

Klia flew over Max's head and into the canyon. Marie screamed as Max popped out, and the force of her voice knocked Stewart into the open door crosswise. He ricocheted, tumbling into the living room. When he came to rest, a brass hook was in front of his face, sunk in the floor. Marie drew a deep breath. He rolled over and pulled it, and a door in the floor opened up. He covered his body with it as she screamed again. The hinges buckled under the force, but the thing held. When he looked, she was standing over him, hands glowing blue.

He swung his leg around and kicked out her knee before she could react. As she went down, a thick blue filament shot from her hand and bashed Stewart in the temple. Half his vision became static as blood pooled behind his tongue. He swallowed, looking down at a weird metal machine beneath the floor. Its cylinders and cones ran in knotlike patterns, connected to a fat tube in the center. The visual static became rubies as he stood.

Marie's thick blue tendrils shot from her hands. They smashed into Stewart's face, but under the influence of the red rage they bounced off harmlessly. Stewart was as surprised as she. He smiled.

Marie stepped backward, eyes wide. Stewart ran at her, ramming his shoulder into her ribs and running through the open door. Once he was outside, Klia chirped and flew down to him, landing on his shoulder and rubbing cheeks, then followed the path Max had taken. Stewart sprinted behind, rage draining. A bush erupted in blue fire as he passed it.

They could hear Marie's screams as they sped down a hill and into the cover of the canyon, running until their lungs ached.

• • •

"Dispatch, this is Unit 137. We've got an 11-99. CSI Amy Munoz and I have been attacked. Assailant at large. White male, six-one, 400, brown, brown. Headed southwest off thirty-second, through Switzer Canyon toward the golf course. May be injured." She shot a glance at Amy, who nodded. "Send a chopper."

"10-4. Big boy," said the dispatcher. "Do you need medical assistance?"

"Negative. But get a few ATV's to my location."

"On their way."

They waited, searching the perimeter with their flashlights until they heard the blades of the chopper, then saw the beam from its searchlight sweeping across the golf course. They watched it circle for seven agonizing minutes until a pickup pulling a trailer with two black-and-white police issue ATV's parked across the road. A concerned-looking uniformed officer jogged up to the sedan.

"Que Paso, Amy?" he said. "Are you okay?"

A smile curled upon Amy's lips, despite the situation. "It's weird stuff, but I'm fine, Juan. Clem, this is my primo, Juan Carrillo." Amy hugged her cousin tightly. He squeezed back.

"Mucho gusto," said Clem, shaking the young officer's hand.

"Tu tambien, Clementine. I've heard a lot about you. This is my partner, Tommy Whiteoak. Genuine Kumeyaay tracker badass," he said, motioning to the officer unchaining the four-wheelers. The well-muscled man looked over and waved, continuing his work. Clementine had heard about Tommy Whiteoak, as well. The Indian tracker looked as legendary as his stories; chiseled and cut with a thick braided ponytail down to his belt.

"So a big ass white guy ran that way?" said Juan, pointing to the wide swath of broken twigs and branches cutting down the hill.

"That's the deal," answered Amy.

Juan cracked his knuckles. "Alright. Let's get tracking."

Clem and Amy grabbed their gear from the car and walked with him to the ATV's. Amy put her kit bag which held the tantō over her shoulder, latching it tight to her body as she hopped behind her cousin. The chopper hovered to the southeast, blades whipping the treetops.

Clem jumped on behind Tommy, clasping her hands around his stomach as they set off down the hill into Switzer Canyon. His braid smelled of earth and cedar.

It was no trouble following the path of the monster. The four-hundred-pound beast left a considerable trail of chaos. It had run the length of the canyon, going over 30th Street and down the other side, then through the dry creek bed of Switzer until it got to the golf course. They lost the trail for a few moments, driving along the concrete walkways until they found a hole through the surrounding brush. Following, they crossed the entire course, driving through another giant hole in the chain-link fence at the south side.

Tommy gave a low whistle. "That ain't easy to do," he said, stopping for a moment at the maimed fence. "Hold on."

Clem wrapped her arms around him as he gunned the accelerator and bounced through an oak grove and up the steep dirt hill, weaving between the trees. Feeling the ripple of Tommy's muscles reminded her she hadn't been with a man in a long time, but she focused on her job and let the feeling pass.

On top of the hill, they cut through the grassy flat of Golden Hill Park with Amy and Juan behind them, and rounded the old stone fountain. Beneath a Torrey Pine he turned right, then left at the terminus of the park. Tommy noticed that along the monster's path, the leaves on the trees had begun to brown.

The chopper's beam hovered two blocks away. When they caught up to it, they looked around at the drops of blood and shards of broken glass which littered the plateau of B Street before it plunged down the steep hill to downtown. Evidence of car wreckage, but there was only one dented car, a white subcompact parked at the corner with hardly enough destruction to match the debris. Plus, the blue paint on its fender, and in a large scraped circle in the center of the intersection, didn't match any of the cars parked there.

The beam of light drew down the hill to another chain-link fence, and another gaping hole ripped into it. The ATVs followed the light, driving through the fence and down into a gigantic drainage ditch. The gulch turned into a ten-foot-round tube and disappeared into total darkness beneath the city. Very large and very fresh footprints were sunken into the gritty soil at the mouth of the tunnel.

"Chopper. You can go back to base. Thanks," said Tommy into his radio. His voice echoed in the blackness before them.

"10-4," said the pilot.

The deafening blades receded into the distance, leaving the idling of the four-wheelers as the only sound before both men cut the engines.

"Whoa," said Clem. "What's with turning them off?"

"Listening," said Tommy.

"You gotta let the man work," said Juan. "He's the man." One raised finger from Tommy silenced Juan, who shrugged and raised his eyebrows as if to say, "see?" then turned back to the tunnel. Tommy crouched and listened.

Clem didn't hear it. Neither did Juan.

Glink.

The small sound came bouncing up the tunnel, a plopping stone.

"This," said Tommy, pointing into the void, "is a trap."

"So what do we do?" asked Clem.

"Spring it."

He fired up the ATV, and Clem hopped on. The lights illuminated the round tube as they drove deeper beneath the city. As they progressed, the light seemed to have less effect, as if the blackness was eating it. Every so often they would pass smaller tubes from the side, far too narrow to have let the giant monster escape up one, though Clem saw she could fit into one easily. The tubes dripped stained water onto piles of wet trash. Many of the piles had been kicked through.

When the tube turned, Tommy had to slow down for the curve, leaning into it. The wheels slid on the wet concrete floor, and they found themselves slipping sideways. The headlight swished along the wall as he turned the handlebars to correct the skid, but their momentum was too much. He whipped them back around before they tipped over. The ATV spun wildly as Tommy coasted through it, not wanting to exacerbate the problem by braking.

Heavy pounding echoed from beyond the curve, enough to vibrate the tires off the floor, nearly capsizing them. After a few hairy seconds Tommy brought it under control. When at last they stopped, the rhythmic pounding was deafening. Tommy reversed and corrected. Juan and Amy rounded the corner and their headlights lit up Crazy Garth.

The obese monster burst around the curve straight into the headlights, too quick for something so large. It opened its mouth as it ran down the tunnel, a roar shaking the air. Sonic waves battered the cops. Another sound, short and deep, came underneath the roar, from behind the beast. Amy, Clementine, and Juan felt a physical terror which froze their muscles solid. All control was gone.

But not Tommy. He drew his .45 revolver from his hip and blasted the monster in mid stride. A large chunk of gray flesh exploded off its hip, but didn't slow it. The thing was ten yards away when Tommy reached down into his boot and pulled out a small pearl handled .22, pointed it at the monster's heart, and pulled the trigger. The Saturday night special flashed and sent the bullet screaming into Garth's chest.

The monster's scream resounded. Frozen muscles thawed. The creature that had been hit with .45 caliber slugs and not made a grunt was now screaming in pain from what should have felt like a pinprick. The thing held its massive hands over its heart, wailing.

Tommy whistled to Juan, making a twirling motion with his hand, and put the little gun in his teeth. Juan turned and revved the engine, gunning it back toward the entrance with Tommy's ATV right behind.

The beast's howls ceased seconds after they sped off, replaced by footfalls that rattled the tunnel. It had recovered quickly. The call of the Blood Silver sang out in the creature's mind, and with jumping steps it gained on them, its fat head narrowly missing the curved ceiling.

Its hand swooshed behind Clem's head, standing her neck hairs on end. One more step and it would hit her. Did Tommy know? Without aiming, she shot her own gun over her shoulder blindly. If she looked, he'd grab her, she knew in her gut. The ensuing pulpy thud told her she'd hit it, and she turned. Its progress had barely been slowed, though a chunk was missing from its shoulder. She thought the only way to kill Garth now would be to whittle him away into nothing, or use Tommy's .22.

A flash of panic sparked in her mind; this was the jailed, almost incoherent man she had interviewed about her son. He didn't look like the same guy, but something occurred to her. She hoped Rupert was safe, and this wasn't an elaborate diversion in this world of tricks and illusion.

The creature gained. Clementine turned and faced it, pistol leveled. Instead of torso shots, which seemed to have little effect, she fired at its legs and feet.

A select few can hit a considerably small moving target while turned around on the back of a speeding vehicle. Clem was not among them. The errant bullets sparked just to the sides of the creature's feet, throwing light on the space behind it.

Another presence flew through the darkness.

Horror saturated Clementine when she looked into the abyss of a giant raven's eyes, a shadow flying in the monster's wake. It opened its beak to reveal a jagged row of human teeth along its ridge. Drool seeped out and flew in ribbons down its chest, bouncing off feathers and splatting on the floor.

She felt Tommy's stomach muscles ripple. He'd seen it too, in the mirror. She holstered her firearm and wrapped her hands around Tommy.

Tommy cut the throttle and braked hard on the wet concrete, turning the handlebars all the way to the side. As they spun around, he pulled the .22 from his teeth and fired. The bullet whizzed past the beast, between its ear and upraised arm, and into the gaping mouth of the bird in the darkness.

The air was filled with the raven's shrieking. When they had spun a complete 360 Tommy twisted the throttle, angling up the wall. When the wheels hit the dry sides of the tube, the four-wheeler buckled, bumping up on two wheels. Clem held tight as Tommy leaned hard and got it back down the wall safely. They sped after Juan and Amy, the tunnel ringing with the raven's cries.

The thudding of the monster's steps slowed, then stopped. Clem couldn't make anything out down the dark tube. The red taillights were swallowed by the blackness. At last they made the final turn and found themselves at the mouth of the tunnel.

"What was that?" asked Clem once they'd made it back to B Street.

"That was a monster," said Tommy.

"What about the bird?"

"A different monster. Worse than the big guy."

"Is that what we're putting in our report?"

"In the police report? No," he said. "But when we go meet with your friends at your house, we can really talk about what's going on."

Amy creased her brow. "How do you know about that? We didn't mention it." She glanced at her cousin.

Juan was three shades whiter and covered in sweat. He tried to smile, but it was crooked and sad. "Like I said, Tommy's the man," he said, feeling sick.

• • •

The monster followed the bird into the tube, watching as it unraveled into a column of smoke, barely visible in the blackness. When it cleared, a burly man stood there, poncho hanging off him. He doubled over and retched into his hand, and out dropped the slug of the small bullet. Casting it aside, a great cough loosened his lungs, and he spat out the metal that had coated it. Small drops sprayed out, then rolled along the lines of his hand, collecting themselves into a solitary mass. As they cooled in the frigid air, a small ball remained. From his ragged poncho, he pulled the stone knife, then poked the silver ball, making it roll along his lifeline.

"Good job," he said to the beast as he tried to stand. His legs buckled beneath him, and he almost fell before the monster picked him up and cradled him in its arms. Man and beast proceeded deep into the tunnel beneath the city.

After about a mile, Abe clicked his tongue. The monster stopped and put him down. Abe stood steady. When he pointed to a steel handle bolted into a concrete square on the wall, the monster put its hand through it and heaved. Nothing happened. Abe took the Spirit Snare from the folds of his poncho, striking its handle on all four corners of the square, then made a boosh sound from the pit of his lungs. A stream of vapor drifted from his mouth into the monster's nostrils. Abe clicked again, and the monster put both hands through the handle and pulled harder.

Crick.

Concrete ground upon itself, one click at first, then a steady stream. Low grinding filled the tunnel until the cube slipped out of the wall and fell heavily to the floor. Echoes bounced up the tunnel.

"Haha," Abe chuckled. "Stand watch now."

He pulled his poncho around his shoulders and over his head. It fell to the ground, and black smoke drifted into the hole in the wall. The monster watched the tunnel with vacant eyes.

14.

At Clementine's house, Amy ran in to check on Gray before she headed to the lab to deliver the blood evidence. He was pale, sweaty, his breath shallow. Seeing his eyes closed, she gave Myron a questioning glance. Myron shook his head.

"These things can be complicated," he said.

Amy had no response. She walked over to Gray and bent over to kiss his slick forehead, then dabbed it with a handkerchief from her pocket. After that she straightened herself up.

"I'll be right back," she said, hugging her cousin, then walked out the door. She wanted to cry.

• • •

Inside the crime lab, the new guy, Rory, looked up from his work. "Hello, Amy," he said, pushing his glasses up onto his nose.

"Hi, Rory." She walked around him, to her work station, and pulled out two vials.

"Need to run some DNA?"

"Yep."

It sounded final. He noticed her clothes were covered in dirt. A question formed in his mind, but before it escaped his lips he shut it away. Her answer, and tone, were so direct that he decided to observe from his place across the room, to speak when and if he were spoken to. She put her evidence in a vial and put it in the new machine, started it. The vial shook and the machine hummed. Lights flashed on its face. She put the vodka bottle next to everything on the table.

Amy was consumed with thoughts of Gray, the blades, and the monster that was formerly a guy in jail. A guy connected to the disappearance of Clementine's son. Besides all that, she needed to run tests on the blood. Tests whose results would take hours. She needed help from someone trustworthy.

In the time since the showdown at the warehouses, she'd noticed that Rory was compassionate. When she had wandered around in a daze over Gray's demise, he'd picked up her slack in the lab, making sure the jobs were done until she could get her shit together, rarely taking credit.

"C'mere, dude," she said, waving Rory over.

"Okay."

"We got called to a scene. Somebody gave a tip about a fresh grave. When Detective Figgins and I got there, the grave was empty, and there was blood at the bottom. This is that blood."

"Different samples?"

"Two pools. Might be one, two, or more" she said. "That's what we're gonna find out."

Though it was the latest tech, the new machines still took time, two hours at least. With multiple samples, that was time Amy could ill afford to spend in the lab. She wasn't going to cover for anyone. Whoever's blood came up in the search deserved what they got. Someone had been buried there, dead or alive. Someone should pay for it.

She had to trust Rory eventually.

"Hey, are you going to be here a while?" she asked

"All night."

"Well, I have urgent family business, and I have to leave. Is there any way you could babysit my evidence until I get back?"

"Just the two samples?"

"Yes. The bottle probably has prints and DNA, plus what looks like drugs at the bottom, but we found it away from the crime scene, so if you get to that and you're not busy, it might be something. Do it last, though."

"I really am gonna be here all night," he said, flatly.

"Please?" She smiled, used her sing-songiest voice.

The turn in her demeanor towards him was dramatic, but he had been working on helping her cope, in his own way. Finally, maybe, it was paying off. He was trying to make his time in this lab as productive as possible before he got the call from a bigger, or at least more organized metropolis.

"Sure," he said. Or she was just using him? Oh well, we'll see.

"Thanks so much." She patted him on the shoulder as she exited the lab, then walked faster toward the main door. When she was out front, she ran to her car and peeled out of the parking lot towards Clementine's house.

• • •

As Amy walked through the front door, Max and Stewart were confessing their robbery of Marie Stillwater's house. Clem was pissed.

"Unbelievable! For what? It had better be damn important. I'd hate to think you endangered your lives and came up empty-handed." She was a cop, and didn't need the merry band of yahoos breaking every law and then coming back to hang out at her house.

"Uh, prepare to be disappointed," said Stewart.

"Grr." Clem turned and faced Helen, "did you know about this?"

"No, Clem, honey. They very wisely did not tell me about it. The last thing I want in the world is for you to not want us around Sugar. I'm as mad as you, I promise that," Helen said, boring her eyes into Max, who didn't look back.

Myron sat near Gray, looking crestfallen. "No! Where is the grey blade? I was sure it was at Marie's house."

"In case you missed it, the trip didn't go so hot," said Max.

"I should say not. What happened?"

"A couple things; if it was there, then someone beat us to the punch. The knife wasn't in the safe. Don't think it was anywhere else in the house, either. Something's weird with that place. The energy is haywire."

"Yeah," said Stewart. "It's haywire because there's some sort of crazy machine between the floorboards. All tubes and spikes."

"I've heard about the machine." Myron met his gaze. "It must have been used to change her."

"Change her? She wasn't like that before?" Clem asked.

"Not at all," said Myron. "She's the public face of Stillwater Enterprises. They're taking drastic measures if they've transformed her."

"What are you talking about?"

"Basically the same thing as the monster, Garth. Only he was done through older, more complicated methods. There are many ways to alter individuals. I've heard rumblings about a very powerful transformer made one hundred years ago, but never finished."

"Well, until now," said Stewart.

"It would seem," said Myron. "They must be stopped. This is not good."

"How do we do that?" asked Amy.

"The knife that Stewart and Max were trying to get is one of a set of two. They were made to dispel monsters. The machine is new technology for a very old and complicated rite, called upon to create these beings of the half-death. The old way is time-consuming and cumbersome, but very effective. Those knives will be necessary for anyone who has been transformed, whether by machine or webcraft, to be neutralized."

Stewart screwed up his face. "So in human talk we would need to stab Marie with both knives to kill her, just like Garth."

"That is correct," said Myron. "As far as we know."

"Where's the other knife?" asked Amy.

"It was in police evidence. If it's gone, Stillwater would surely transport it to one of his more secure holdings."

"It won't be secure if that thing finds them," said Clem.

"I better get down there," said Amy. "Plus I've got Rory in the lab by himself waiting on my DNA results."

"Wait, Rory, the new guy?" Clem was wide-eyed.

"The circle widens itself, I guess. I couldn't stay, and I'm choosing to trust him."

"Alright," said Clem. She was skeptical, but it was Amy's call.

"How many Stillwater properties are there?" Amy asked.

"I know of seventy," answered Clem. She thought of Alec, the quiet clerk who had been hiding something when they had first met. She'd have to pay him another visit, to see if there were other holdings not on the books. Maybe that was his secret.

Myron said, "There are far more than that."

"I was just starting to wonder. Mr. Fox, does the acronym HOME mean anything to you?"

"Yes. Of course. A group of architects from one hundred years ago, responsible for some very memorable buildings here in town. Most, as you probably know, owned by Stillwater."

"Memorable for what, exactly?" Clem asked.

"Intricacy, chiefly. The men were at the top of their craft."

"Mm hmm. Why?"

Myron leveled his gaze. "Sound bending. For control of the webs. It is most likely they who drew up the plans for this machine."

Clementine and Amy had been brought more or less up to speed on the networks of webbing that connect all things, and though they couldn't talk to any police about it, there were things they had come to accept as real that they never would have believed before.

Amy's cousin Juan Carrillo did not have that luxury. "Alright. I've had about enough of this big secret everyone but me and this guy know about," He jerked his thumb toward Tommy, who looked at him with soft eyes.

"Sorry, Juan, but it's my world as well," said Tommy, widely considered to be the best tracker in the history of San Diego law enforcement. "This guy's a true legend." He nodded to Myron.

"Have we met?" asked Myron, extending his hand. Mr. Fox was not opposed to a decent ego-stroke.

"We have now. Tommy Whiteoak. Nice to meet you."

"Jesus," said Juan. "Man, I hate to interrupt this make-out session, but does that mean that I'm the only person here who doesn't know what's going on?" In desperation he looked to Amy.

She nodded. She hated to see her cousin so vexed, but this world was rough. You entered it when you were least ready, she thought, like this life is trying to see how much you want it. "Sorry, Juan, but you'll be okay. Look at me."

Her phone vibrated. After looking at it she grew concerned and said, "But I have to go." she pointed at her kit bag, then hugged her cousin, said good-bye to Gray, still asleep on the couch, and walked out.

Stewart put on his jacket. "Lemme know what you guys come up with," he said. "I gotta go to work."

15.

It didn't disturb Alec that his bandmates had hooked up, though he'd initially said otherwise. He saw the way they looked at each other. It had only been a matter of time.

May worked at Irene's Cafe by the golf course, and Raul said he was sort of a handyman for a bunch of different properties, but Alec never saw him with a toolbox, just his backpack that was never far away, and a smaller canvas bag, hardly bigger than a wallet. Handyman made sense, though, after seeing what he did to get electricity in the ballroom.

Alec scampered up the stairs into the small craftsman cottage he shared with his roommates, who were playing video games with glassy eyes as he mumbled a salutation on his way to his room. They mumbled back. Such was his relationship with them. At least they paid the rent and bills on time, though he had a sneaking suspicion that if their well-to-do parents knew how they spent their time, they might not be too willing to support them. But what did he know? He'd given up the living room to them long ago. His own room was by far the biggest, with its own bathroom and deck, so he rarely dealt with them anyhow.

He took a shower, changed his clothes, made and ate a sandwich, then said good-bye to the roommates, still in the same positions on the couch. The cool evening air invigorated him as he stepped down the stairs and into his car. He rolled down all the windows as he drove to the ballroom.

When he got out in front of the old building, dizziness hit him. He breathed deep until it passed. A strange tingling remained as he opened the heavy door and saw the disarray the room was in.

The first thought to cross his mind was a lover's quarrel, hot on the heels of Raul and May's first hook-up, but the destruction was beyond that. There was a center to the chaos, with the love-seat upturned in it. He followed a path of blood drops to an old metal grate torn from the wall. Beyond it, the tube into the building's innards was black, and he turned the flashlight on his phone on, shining it up the ductwork tunnel. There were more drops, and scuff marks in dust leading to a shiny black puddle beneath the area where it curved upward. He stepped closer until he could see it was a puddle of blood, then scrambled back into the ballroom, avoiding the droplets.

His pulse was racing, unsure if some attacker was still in here. His eyes darted around the room, and he picked up a mic stand to use as a weapon.

He kicked the grate back into the wall, then locked the door. His fingers shook as he called Raul. When the connection rang, he heard the snare drum buzz. Walking over, he saw Raul's phone vibrating on top of the drum. His voicemail came on, and Alec hung up, eyeing May's phone on the floor beneath the drum stool. Shit. This was looking worse.

Anyone he asked for help would immediately realize that this situation was illegal, and if they were on the official level they would shut his place down, whether they located his friends or not. Well worth the risk if they turned up okay, but maybe that shouldn't be his first move.

However, if he were to tell any of his peers, namely other musicians and the people who worked in the bars he played in, they couldn't help him at all. No resources.

From within these two threads of thought came two different ideas.

The only cop he'd ever met that didn't send him into a panic was the lady detective he'd met at his job, who treated him like an expert in his field. What was her name? He remembered the word association game he'd used; two fruits. Oranges and figs. Tangelo Figgers? No. Clementine Figgins. Detective Clementine Figgins. That was it.

From the music world, he remembered a man who, when Alec had first met him, made him feel as if anything were possible. Every time he saw the guy, the same emotion would wash over him. He didn't come around very often, though. Alec had mainly seen him at Auntie Frieda's Rock Club, Alec's favorite place to play in town. The guy was related to Auntie Frieda, the owner, and sometimes did odd jobs for her as well. He was her cousin, Maximilian, whom everyone called Max. Alec used to watch Max play guitar in various bands. Guitars melted like butter in his hands. The dude was some serious shit. He hadn't played around in a while, though.

The cops should be the last resort. He'd try Max first.

He walked out, careful not to disturb anything further.

Please let them be okay.

The heavy door rolled, shutting fast with the sculpted trash in front of it. Keeping his senses on high alert, he ascended the staircase, looking around as he came up to the sidewalk level. Seeing nothing out of the ordinary, he slipped into his car and drove toward Auntie Frieda's.

• • •

The club had just opened, and it was almost an hour until the first band played. Alec shook hands with the doorman, a huge smiling guy with the easygoing confidence of someone who could take care of themselves, no matter the situation.

"Alec, my man," said Winton. "What is the haps?"

"What's up, Winton?" Alec shook Winton's big, dark hand. "Who's playing tonight?"

Winton checked behind himself, then said, "One of those new 'it's cool to not know how to play an instrument or sing' bands, dude. Soundcheck was murder."

"Lots of those right now," said Alec. "What's the cover?"

"You're okay. They already got the guarantee. Sold a bunch of advance tickets. Apparently it's popular, man." Winton paused and smiled as a spindly kid with his hair in his face stepped by, then pointed his thumb at the kid's back. "His band," he mouthed silently.

Alec chuckled and held out his wrist, which Winton stamped. "Hey, is Frieda here tonight?" Alec asked.

"Nah, man. Not tonight. She understandably does not like this stuff, but you won't hear her say that. Why you wanna see her? You know she doesn't book shows at night, you gotta email her now."

"It's not that. Actually I'm looking for Maximilian for something," he said.

"Max?" said Winton, wrinkling his face. "I'm lost, bro. Do you even know that dude? 'Cause he's a trip."

"Yeah, I know him a little, and it's some trippy shit I have to talk to him about," he said.

"Well, that's his area of expertise, 'trippy shit', but he's not here, and neither is she. Stewart's tending bar, though, and he's been hanging out with Max lately, I think. What a team, right? Probably know where to find him. Better than me, anyway." He shook his head and chuckled.

"Right on, Winton. Thanks."

"No problem, bud. Good luck," he said, stepping out of the way to let the smaller man through, like a human gate.

There were only about twenty people in the club, early-comers ready for drinks or to just post up near the stage. Alec looked over their heads to Stewart, who was finishing an order, and smiled at Alec when he walked up.

"What's up, man?" said Stewart, then leaned down close to Alec and in a low voice asked, "You're not here to see this crap, are you?" without moving his lips.

Alec chuckled nervously. “No, man. I actually need to ask you a question.”

“Oh, yeah?” said Stewart, intrigued. “What about?”

“Well, uh, do you know how to find Auntie’s cousin, Max?”

It was hard to tell in the diminished lighting of the bar, but Alec could have sworn he saw Stewart’s face grow pale at the question.

“Why you looking for Max?”

“Well . . . can you step away for a few?”

Stewart hated to leave the bar, chiefly because it cost him tip money, but he flagged down his barback and led Alec into Frieda’s office.

“So what’s the deal?” Stewart asked as he turned the deadbolt on the door. “Why Max?”

Alec had a difficult enough time coming to terms with telling Max what had happened, and wasn’t eager to tell Stewart, a notorious hot-head. Who knew how he would react? But time was of the essence.

“It’s some fucked up stuff. Please don’t tell anybody.”

“That ain’t me,” said Stewart.

“Right. Okay. I work in the city records department, and I found this old sealed-up basement ballroom that no one’s used in a long time, and we jacked some electricity. Anyway, Me, Raul, and May have been practicing there. It’s kind of how I got them to join the band. So, they live there, pretty much, except the water’s not on so they have to go outside to go to the bathroom–”

“Stay on point, Al.” It wasn’t a suggestion. Stewart was a bitter old dude who spoke directly. Everybody knew that. “I don’t have all night.”

“Right. So I got off work and swung by, and they were there. Then I went home to shower. When I came back the place was a wreck, and they were gone. There was blood, and their phones were still there.”

Stewart got the same feeling he had not so long ago when his house had been torn apart while he listened from the balcony next door. The thing that had done the thrashing then had been his now-dead friend Nickel, his spirit trapped apart from his puppet body.

“Who knows about your place?” he asked.

“Just the three of us. I’ve never told anyone, anyway, and I don’t think they would. It would fuck up their living situation.”

“Not everyone is taught not to shit where they eat,” said Stewart. “These other two, they a couple?”

“As of recently, I think. Does that matter?”

“I have no idea,” said Stewart. “What do they do?”

“You mean for work? She works at a cafe, and he’s like a handyman or something?"

"Are you asking me?" Stewart glared, making Alec lose his train of thought.

"I, uh, I don't . . . that is, I'm not sure what he does."

"You ever see any tools?"

"No, but he always has a backpack, and inside he has another cloth case with a zipper, it's always closed, though," said Alec. "He's pretty secretive about that thing. I've only seen it a couple times, and by accident."

"How big is the cloth case?" asked Stewart. "This big?" He spread his index fingers and thumbs out in an 'L-7' shape.

Alec was amazed at the guess. "Yeah . . ." he said.

"Your friend is a thief. That's his kit." His eyes got a twinkle Alec had never seen before. "That's who got our knife. Shit. I gotta get back to work. You stay here until I get off, then we go to your ballroom. Okay? Do. Not. Leave." He poked Alec's chest with each word.

Alec thought to ask about the knife, but it could wait.

"Yessir," he answered, then asked, "You mean I have to stay in the office?" His head was swirling with Stewart's information. He didn't know which end was up.

Stewart actually smiled. "No, dude, but stick around."

Alec chuckled, "Ah, alright."

Winton and Stewart were right; the band was god-awful, and popular. Alec whiled away his time near the back of the club where there was a pool table and a pinball machine, trying to wrap his brain around Raul being a cat burglar.

He played pool against a girl with silver and brown hair which hung down her back. She was much better than he was, and slaughtered him. At least she wasn't the sort to try and offer 'tips', and even said 'good shot' on his only one he made. He shook her hand when the game was done, and a guy with hair like hers put two quarters in the table.

Hearing the rumble of the balls leaving the gate, he walked aimlessly over to the pinball machine. May loved pinball. His thoughts wandered to May and Raul, and the fact that he was sitting around playing games while they were missing. This was getting stupid. He decided he was going to go back himself, and start looking for a trail, a clue. Stewart could just meet him there, or wherever else he ended up.

He walked up to the front to tell Stewart he was leaving, but saw he was busy with multiple people jockeying for their place in line. A fruitless quest, as Stewart always knew who was next. Out of the corner of his eye, Stewart saw Alec behind three people, looking sheepish.

"Alec! Do not go off by yourself," said Stewart, pointing at him from over the others' heads. "Stay right there."

"Yeah, Alec," said the girl from the pool table as she swirled her straw in her drink.

Stewart opened a beer and put it in front of him, leaving no room for conversation. As he grabbed it, a man whose turn it was next clicked his tongue in exasperation.

"You wanna cry, or get something to drink?" Stewart asked, staring.

Sipping the beer, Alec braved the caterwauling singer's voice and made small talk with the girl. She was cool, if a little younger than the cougar age women he preferred.

"That your boyfriend?" He pointed to tongue-click guy.

"Haha. No."

He asked for her number.

"Fuck that," she said. "Just friend me and we'll set something up. Phone number is down the line, stud." He did, and she wandered off. He tried to think about his missing bandmates, but drifted back to the girl with the wild hair at the bar, kind of against his wishes. Where did she go? He looked up her profile on the social media site he'd friended her on. The profile pic was a wild dog or something. None of the pictures were her. It wasn't just the hair, either. The skin tone, age, height, everything but the sex was different. Why would anyone say they were someone they weren't? He looked around, but she was gone.

The final song finished, and there were only a few errant claps from the sold-out crowd jammed around the stage. The people didn't move, and the band came back for an encore, as if everything was expected, scripted.

A few minutes later they finished the one-song encore, and the people started filing out. Alec hung by the bar as Stewart finished the closing duties with Winton and the rest of the crew, then said good-bye to his co-workers.

They got into Stewart's beater with Alec riding shotgun. As they pulled from the curb, Alec saw a bird following them. When they parked at the ballroom, a similar looking bird landed in the jacaranda tree at the top of his stairs, staring at him. A mockingbird, he thought.

The first thing Stewart noticed when they pulled open the door was the smell of iron permeating the air. "Where's the blood?"

Alec pointed to the grate on the wall. "There's drops that lead over there," he said, looking around the room nervously.

"What are you looking for, dude? Are you trying to set me up? Who's in here?" Stewart got in Alec's face.

Alec thought he'd lose control of his bladder. "Nothing, no, no," he said. "I'm just scared, I swear."

Stewart grunted, satisfied, and walked between the blood droplets toward the iron grate. Alec watched him work, careful not to disturb the process.

He pulled the grate off with a popping scrape, and crouched on his haunches, leaning his head into the vent and sniffing into the darkness.

"Hm," he said, crawling deeper. He pulled his long-sleeved T-shirt down over his hands and walked on the sides of his feet. When he came to the L-joint, a puddle of blood caught his eye. Something was shimmering inside it. He dug a lighter from his pocket and brought it close to the puddle. Silver ribbons swam, worms slithering to the bottom where they reflected through the blood.

Stewart extracted himself from the ductwork, careful to step in his own tracks. When he emerged, he shook his head. Alec peeked over the stack of amps.

"So, you don't know anything about what went on in here?" Stewart asked.

"No, man. When I came after work I thought they had just hooked up, y'know? They were just chillin' here waiting for me to come back for practice, as far as I know."

"Alright," said Stewart. "Whose bag is this?" He pointed to a duffel bag near the bass equipment, then started rustling through it before Alec could answer, pulling out a small canvas zip bag.

"Is this his kit?" asked Stewart, holding the bag up for Alec to see.

"No, the one I've seen is green, and I've never gone through his bag."

"What, you don't want me to look for them, now?" Stewart bubbled, threatening to boil over.

"That's not what I meant, just stating a fact, Stewart. Please, dude."

"Okay," said Stewart, relaxing a little. "This is his back-up kit. Like I thought. Lock-picks, cutters, tension wrenches, and well, looks like some magnets. Maybe for safes." He held a tubular magnet in front of his eye. "So, I'm thinking your friend, who is thief enough to have two separate lock-picking tool kits, may have stolen something from the wrong person or people, and I think I know who. Has there been anyone you didn't recognize that gave you a weird feeling? Like for no reason you felt scared, or confused?"

"What about horny?"

"What are you, twenty-three? That's a little more common, dude. I'm thinking beyond sporting wood from seeing a hot chick."

"No, I'm serious." said Alec, "When I left to run home, this blonde cougar lady walked by me. When she smiled at me I got like ragingly horny, then when I ran into the pale guy it went away."

"A blonde cougar lady and a pale dude, huh?" asked Stewart, sticking the thieving tools in his back pocket and walking for the door, "Funny, that's exactly who I was thinking about. This is a pretty bad situation, holmes."

"Where are we going?" asked Alec, falling in step.

"We're gonna go find Max. And a couple other people. You passed my test."

They pushed the trash sculpture back and walked up the stairs. The mockingbird sang from the jacaranda. Alec was familiar with the birds, and the sounds they made, but he'd never seen one land on someone's shoulder like this one did right now.

Stewart didn't even break stride as Klia nuzzled her head into his cheek. As he scratched her neck, she turned to Alec and made a razzing sound, then jumped off Stewart, flapped her wings a couple times and landed in another jacaranda, where she commenced her night songs.

"What the fuck is up with that?" asked Alec.

"That's my bird, kind of. More like my partner, really," said Stewart. "Her name is Klia."

Hearing her name, she blasted three high tweets, then flew from her perch to a signpost just beside Stewart's car. She dropped down, hovering beside the door, and tweeted some quick chirps that made the lock pop up.

"Showoff," said Stewart, holding the keys. Klia clicked her tongue.

Alec was slack-jawed and bug-eyed.

The bird hopped on the dashboard when Stewart opened the door.

Alec got in. Stewart scared him more now than ever, and he was petrified of him before. He tried not to move or talk very much on the drive to wherever it was they were going. The bird, with its steel-grey penetrating eyes, stared at him. Alec had a feeling his emotional ride was only beginning.

16.

At Clementine's house, Alec almost shit himself as he looked down three gun barrels.

"It's okay," said Clementine, lowering her gun and motioning for Juan and Tommy to do the same. "Get in here."

As Stewart stepped around her, she caught her first real look at the young man behind him. A feeling overcame her as she looked at the clerk from the hall of records who had helped her three months ago. She wasn't sure whether or not she should be surprised, and she wondered if there was a word for that.

"Nice to see you again, Alec," she said.

"Uh, you too, Officer Figgins," Alec said, bewildered.

Once Stewart had filled them in, Alec asked for a glass of water.

"Of course," Clementine said, wondering what to make of his story. How did the clerk get himself wrapped up in this world? She handed him the water and turned to Stewart.

"How sure are you that it's the Stillwater's? What made you think that?" she asked him.

"Alec saw them before they went in, as he was leaving," said Stewart. "Plus, I smelled their blood. Since the fight at the warehouse my sense of smell is insane. So, when we checked out the blood, I saw little silver ribbons in it."

At that, Mr. Fox stood up and stepped forward. "The silver, it was inside the blood?"

"Yeah," said Stewart. "And it kind of, like, hid from me, or the light."

"Hm," said Myron. "Curious."

After a long pause, Stewart asked, "Are you going to enlighten us about what is so curious? Or should we guess?"

"One may be as good as the other," said Myron. "But I think the artifacts, made from a very unique metal to begin with, are starting a mutation."

"Dumb it down a little," said Stewart.

"Blood Silver," said Mr. Fox. "Listen now."

Stewart grabbed a cup of coffee.

Myron cleared his throat. "These blades, or snares, some are weapons, others are tools, as individual as their makers. There are also different instruments, some ancient, and some newer. Age matters, but not as much as the process by which they are made. That is the power, the magic, of these things, and how they are used to amplify the effects of the web. The Blood Silver is the amplifier."

He looked around the group. Some nodded with understanding. The less fortunate were lost, but they'd have to sink or swim. There wasn't time for personal instruction.

"To make these," he continued, "or their ilk, takes an addition of spirit into the molten metal, and when it is cooled, the trappings of that spirit remain within the knife. These trappings are held in the drops of life-force that is added; human blood, and usually that of someone well-versed in the knowledge of the Web. When one of these pierces the flesh, minute particles of the silver enter and overtake the will of the blood. This is bad enough, but now the silver seems to move on its own accord. A new development. Even I don't know exactly what that means."

Cora nodded. "The Council is deeply concerned with the sudden rise of snare tech."

"The Council is concerned with a great many things, and rightfully so," said Myron. He looked around, making sure the message was delivered. "In short, these knives hold, and can also be made to control, blood. So, how many in this room have been stabbed, even slightly, by one of these things?"

"Me." said Buddy, stating what almost everyone already knew.

Helen held up her hand as well. "I did also, and Max."

Max nodded and slipped his hand around her waist.

"Anyone else?" asked Myron, "I'm feeling the frequency of another."

Cora nodded, letting her eyes slip out of focus, seeing the ethereal strands of web permeating everything before her. In her will she separated the frequency from the others, following its path to the man whose spirit she had helped turn into a berserker while trying to unite him with his rightful Raven's gift. Her lover. Stewart Zanderson.

"Stewart," she said. "You weren't stabbed by anything, were you?"

A gleam caught the corner of her eye, hanging on the rear wall of the house beside the dog door. Ping. The frequency. Thin webs, almost invisible, drew eye her to the leather strap. Funny that you can often see things in the distance but not that which is in front of your face, she thought.

Stewart watched her. "No, lots of other stuff, but never stabbed."

"Buddy hit you with this, didn't he?" She pulled the leash with the silver ball attached from the hook on the wall.

"Oh, yeah," said Stewart, rubbing his dented shinbone; since Buddy had attacked him with the leash, he had a steady throb there, one of many injuries accumulated since discovering the webbed world. "Big time."

"Where'd you get this, Buddy?" Cora asked. Buddy looked at the ground.

"It's okay, Sugar," said Helen. "I gave it to him."

"But you didn't make it, did you? I mean, you and Max don't know how to make these, right?"

"You mean the metal ball? No. Jeb did. He was supposed to teach us before he got killed," said Helen. "He said he had unlocked the final secrets of the alchemist, Mr. Stillwater."

"Wait a second," said Clementine. "Mr. Stillwater the what?"

"Alchemist. He made the ancient blade that drew Stewart back. He also taught Jeb most of his secrets. But Jeb took that knowledge and ran with it, coming close to finishing the machine in Marie's house."

"Stillwater made the ancient blade? How old is he?" Clem asked.

Helen looked to Myron. "At least one thousand years," he said.

"You've got to be kidding me."

"Sorry, no."

"How old are you? And Abe?"

"Older than that."

Clem looked at Cora.

Cora smiled, her almond eyes soft and kind. "Let's catch you guys up real quick." She explained about the long-standing and tenuous relationship between Peik Stillwater and Abraham Blackwing, and the relation of both men to the Council of Webs, whose leader, Golden John, the Eagle, viewed them as enemies.

She explained how Markuz had left Stillwater during the battle at the warehouses, joining Ursula, the bear mother, in the vast winding cave and tunnel system beneath the city. Clementine could see this hidden world expanding in her mind, like webs stretching out and covering everything, including herself, and especially her son. Buddy was a lynchpin. The more she knew, the closer she wanted to stay to him. This case was falling into the webbed world. Only knowledge would help her solve it.

"So, Abe made Garth into this undead thing?" asked Clem. "Using one of these snare deals?"

"That's what it looks like."

"But why the Council? Isn't Abe on the Council?"

"He's more what you would call 'on probation,'" Cora said. "He, like Ursula and some others, no longer see eye to eye with Golden John's Council on several issues pertinent to this changing time. I work for the Council. I was assigned Abe, and he tricked me, like everyone else. I should have seen it coming, no matter how it seemed."

Clementine stared. Cora was like a web-cop? "Well, what are you, then? I mean, you worked with him, or for him, forever. I just don't get it."

"My role is called a Second. In your terms, the closest thing is a probation or parole officer," she said. "Abraham was treading a very thin strand as far as the Council was concerned, and they assigned me to make sure he didn't do anything completely off the rails. Which of course he did anyway."

"Don't beat yourself up too much," said Clem. "He seems pretty good at getting into trouble. I admit I'm still wrapping my brain around my son's talents, let alone some bat-shit bird wizard," said Clem.

Cora smiled.

"Okay. Who are the most likely suspects in killing Garth?" Clem asked.

Cora pointed at Myron. "Him, for one."

"I did no such thing," said Mr. Fox. "If I were to frame Abraham Blackwing for murder, you can rest assured I would have done a much better job than this barbarism. Besides, what would I have to gain from doing so?"

"Who benefits, then?" asked Clem.

"I would look to the Council." Myron sat down heavily.

Cora narrowed her eyes at Myron. "While I would look toward the tricksters like you and the Coyotes. Spreading chaos to feast on scraps. Elaborate ceremonies."

Myron rolled his eyes, an indignant half-frown on his face. "Stuff and legends. There are no Coyotes left."

Cora was silent as she sized him up.

"Who?" asked Clementine. "What now?"

"Sworn enemies of the Council." Cora said. "Coyotes are the servants of chaos. They are notoriously difficult to track. At any one time, each one only knows about five others."

"How many are there?" asked Clem.

"Dozens? Hundreds? The reason for doing it is so no one knows that or any other information. Obscurity. It is said that even when you stare right at a coyote, the only detail you remember are the eyes. The rest is always a blur."

"That's who was here before you all came over," Clem said. Who was who anymore?

"I'm pretty sure, but of course the more adept of the Webspinners could mimic that look." Cora's face was grave. "Whoever it is is one step ahead of us."

"Crap. Who isn't one step ahead?" Clem waved her hands in the air, frustrated. "Let's back it up. We have two problems. First, the Still-water group grabbed your friends for some reason," She said to Alec. "We've got to find them."

"Uh, yeah." Alec was trying to see how many of these people bought this story. It appeared like they all did, even the cops.

Clem wanted to have pity on Alec, and explain things, but there was no time. Hopefully Buddy or Cora could inform him later. "Second, someone tried to frame Abraham, so he in turn made this monster," she continued. "How do we deal with this?"

Cora answered. "Abe wants the blades, and has the monster to collect them, though even I don't know why. As Myron said, to kill these monsters, we need the blades. Find them, find the story, even if it comes from within the Council."

"I thought you worked for them?" Clem asked. "Wouldn't you know?"

"I am a part of them, but I follow no one blindly. There is great power in the Council, and power corrupts. If Golden John is the one doing this, I can't in good conscience stay aligned with him."

"What if it were useful?" asked Myron. "Staying aligned, that is."

Cora stared at him in silence. All eyes watched the tension mount until Juan broke it.

"Hey, hey! Alright. Where do we start?" he asked, getting between Cora and Myron. Once their staring contest was interrupted, they both relaxed.

Tommy spoke. "The monster follows the knives, and may already have one or more. Much easier to follow a four-hundred pound puppet than a little knife. Begin at the scene of the crime, I say."

"Sounds good," said Max. "So back at Abe's houses?"

"Exactly," said Tommy. "And Detective Figgins should gather evidence at the ballroom."

"What about the Coyotes?"

"Coyotes live on the fringes of society and the edge of night, so we look in the small cracks of the world. I know these cracks."

"Okay" Clem nodded, impressed but wary. Tommy knew when to speak, and what to say. Maybe too much.

Juan had stars in his eyes. "I keep telling you guys, Tommy is the man."

17.

"Man, what happened to you?" Lalo said. His brother Julio looked like a junkie, shuffling past his unpainted car and up the steps to their house with bags under his eyes.

"Shit, dude. I was working on the car and some old hottie came inside with me. She gave me something to drink and . . . fuck. That's all I really remember except being down the street."

"What time was it?"

"Man, I didn't look. I was working, then looking at her."

"Ay cabrón," said Lalo. "Where was the sun in the sky?"

"Setting."

"Well, it's dark now, and I was here all day. You're missing a day, bro. Who did you say she was?"

"Fuuck. What the FUCK?! I have no idea." He held his head in his hands.

"That's ok, hermano. We'll find out."

• • •

The baker walked away from his oven, leaving the bread. He pushed the glass door open and wandered into the night.

His assistant, Q, called out to him as he left, but got no response. He followed the baker to the door, opening it and calling his name out again, louder, but his voice fell on unwilling ears. With a sigh, he watched the baker go, wondering what had come over his friend, but not able to follow him, lest the precious bread burn in the ovens. Then where would they be?

The people smoking cigarettes in front of the bar watched the baker. He had a glazed look. The bar's doorman, a regular at the bakery, waved and called out to him, and was a little concerned when the man who seemed so friendly at his own place of business was so cold outside of it. Then the thickset doorman noticed the baker's milky eyes, and thought he must have a secret drug problem, as he looked blasted, yet walked straight.

"You alright, bro?" he asked as the baker walked through the group, not slacking his pace or turning his head at all.

"Guess he's not, huh?" said some chunky guy with glasses, a beard, and a baseball cap that looked like he bought it that afternoon.

"Guess not." The doorman watched the baker round the corner into the alley.

He turned right at 24th Street for half a block, then left at B. The bright lights of downtown twinkled as he walked down the steep hill and under the freeway, shambling past the knot of onramps, through the community college toward the heart of the city, but he didn't notice them.

As he neared the old stone building, a blue sedan pulled past him in the opposite direction. Magnetically his head swiveled, following the car, and his body fell in line, turning away from the place he had come so far for.

Behind him, another body shuffled in the same direction, a glassy-eyed woman with bushy hair. The baker didn't give any indication he noticed her as she walked behind him. As they walked, others with the same look fell into step, a slow, shuffling line.

• • •

The young couple sat on their porch, drinking beer, sharing a joint, and discussing whether or not an old man, a fortyish woman, and a teenaged boy could push a car from its hood back onto its wheels. As the woman, athletic and thick, exhaled a smoke ring, her face grew puzzled. The scraggly man followed her gaze to a group of six people walking by, shuffling their feet and looking dazed. They turned left, up the U-shaped streets that touched the canyons of Golden Hill Park.

"What the fuck? Look at that. C'mon, Chase," she said, tugging on the man's sleeve.

"What? No way," he said, taking another drag off the joint. "I'm not following some weirdos into the canyon at night, Viv."

"Suit yourself." She drained her beer and set the bottle down. "I'll tell you how it goes."

"Very funny." He didn't really want to, but if she was going, then he was too. He knew that much. He hit the joint once more, then put it in the ashtray on the porch while finishing his beer. His hand hovered with the bottle before he stuck it in his back pocket, having no other weapon in case they needed anything.

Vivian was halfway down the block already, and Chase had to jog to catch up to her. As he rounded the corner, the last shuffler disappeared between a one-story house and a three-story apartment building. A trail from there led into the canyons, that much he knew.

He put his arm on hers. "Viv, grab a rock or something," he said..

"Why?"

"Shit, I don't know. What if they're zombies or something?" he whispered. "They fucking look like zombies."

"Zombies? C'mon dude." She should have a weapon though. Who knew what these randoms were doing out here? She picked up a shard of paving stone from someone's yard, about eight inches long. "This'll have to do," she said with a shrug, then slipped between the buildings.

The trail dropped down into a grove of tall eucalyptus trees and a few pines. They could see the shufflers ascending the other side of the small canyon. The couple stayed still at the top and watched the group cut to the right behind some houses, then ran after them, coming out on a small street which ran alongside the park, separated by a fence. When they emerged from the bushes, they couldn't see the shufflers anymore. They searched yards and driveways, and finally Chase spotted them disappearing into the trees.

Vivian ran, waving for him to follow, but he was almost over it. Now he was thinking the group was just a bunch of people on drugs or something. His thoughts drifted back to the porch and joint and beer the longer he was separated from them. He watched her disappear in the direction of the shufflers, but he was barely even jogging anymore, not much faster than the plodding group. Vivian was in much better shape than he was. He stopped, hands on his knees, breathing heavily.

Giving up on him, she accelerated her pace and crossed 26th street where it cut through the park. She saw the people enter a small side canyon between the street and golf course. Beneath a tall Torrey Pine, the group was gathered around two people, a young man and woman, standing back-to-back with a canvas shoulder bag between them.

"Hey," she said.

The woman looked from the milky-eyed people to Vivian. Next to her, the man was hyper-aware. "I know you," said May.

"You're May, right? From Bludgeons? Who are these people?"

"I don't know, dude. Freaks. You're in that band with Stewart from Auntie's, right?" May looked around. No one she recognized. Three men, three women, not too much to make them look like they belonged together, either. "How 'bout, you, babe?" she asked Raul.

He shook his head. "This guy owns the bakery. Hey!" he said to the baker, snapping his fingers. No reaction. He whistled at the wild-haired woman and clapped his hands, which had much the same result, then he got a thoughtful look on his face. May scowled as he brought out the flute and chime.

"What are those?" asked Vivian, taking in their glow with hungry eyes. "Wow."

"Nothing," said May. "Just a whistle and bell thing." She held the silver orb in her palm and turned her back to Vivian as she shook it.

A wave passed through the entranced people, like wind pushing tall grass. Recalling May's barb, Raul tried something different as he blew into the whistle, instinctively trilling notes that made the group stir. The glaze drained from their eyes.

• • •

The baker came out of his spell in a small canyon. He was surrounded by a group of people. He didn't recognize three of them, but he did know the five men and women with whom he had been held against his will in the warehouses near Juniper Street Canyon for several months. He shook the cobwebs from his brain, remembering his bread in the oven, and without a word to the others turned and set out for his bakery. He almost ran into the young bearded man as he left the thicket, then righted himself and walked away.

Chase pushed through the bushes, panting. "What happened?"

"Nothing," Vivian answered, looking at him with a touch of scorn. She was getting a little sick of his whatever attitude. A girl needed some excitement. "Just some people taking a walk."

Chase didn't appreciate being brushed off. "Taking a walk to meet these guys in the canyon? Yeah, right."

The others were rubbing their eyes. A short woman, almost as wide as she was tall, said, "Who are you?"

A tall man with a scar on his cheek looked at her. "Have we met?"

The woman looked back, and a twinge of recognition did stir, but she didn't know from where. Possibly from the time of her captivity. When she had emerged from the truck following their release, she had warned herself that if she ever thought she was near someone from the warehouse, even by accident, she would do whatever necessary to avoid that person.

She read the news reports concerning the case surrounding the warehouse after she'd made it home. They hadn't caught anyone that had kept them prisoner. One man was dead, but in a cloudy way she remembered there being a large group helping him. Certainly one person would not be able to subvert the wills of so many.

Fighting back a wave of nausea, she realized these were the people that had been her fellow prisoners, or her captors. She burst from the small canyon into the street, her high-pitched wail fading in the distance.

Without words, three more backed away into the brush. The last of the group, the man with the large camera around his neck, extended his hand to Vivian and said, "Hello, it is very nice to meet you."

Vivian, stared. "Well, if we're meeting, what's your name?" She made no move to accept the handshake.

"Oh, how very rude of me," he said. "My name is Emiliano Flynn."

• • •

Peik drove east, strangling the steering wheel. Not knowing what would happen if these kids started the machine at Marie's, they were instead headed to Nuala's house to figure out their situation. Things were slipping away, but he would right them, and soon. His scowl was repellant, and neither Nuala nor Oliver saw fit to speak.

As he turned up Golf Course Drive, a curious look came over his face and he swung the car around, rolling down the windows and slowing. He stuck his head out and drove past two people walking out of the canyon, separately. Peik recognized one of Frank's people. A baker. He drifted past the man and shut off the motor, gliding onto the gravel. The tires crunched as it rolled to a stop. He got out and listened.

"What are you—"

"Quiet," he whispered. His nose twitched, and he beckoned. Stepping slowly, he pointed to the base of a lone pine in the side canyon between the gym and 26th street. She followed him down the south side of the canyon as Oliver vanished into the bushes to the north.

• • •

Emiliano Flynn's eyes lit up at the sound of the car's engine dying, then the crunch of gravel beneath feet. "It is not safe here," he said to the young people surrounding him. "Come with me."

He walked down the canyon to the street, but after only a few steps turned around. No one had followed. He shook his head, parted the branches blocking the trail and vanished.

Bushes up the hill shook noisily. People emerged.

From one side stepped the pale man with a grimace on his face, followed by the blonde woman. From the other crawled the spider boy with the jagged teeth. He smiled at May, who nearly wet herself from fear, then pulled on Raul, trying to run. However, both Raul's feet were firmly planted on the ground.

The spider boy clacked two rocks together while a clear note spilled from the blonde woman's throat, and Raul, as well as Chase, stood entranced. Vivian, who still held the paving stone, threw it hard. Nuala tried to catch it, but it hit off of her hand and bounced into her ribcage, stopping her voice.

Raul and Chase snapped out of it. Peik, in a flash, was upon May, grabbing her wrists while Oliver ran at Raul.

Nuala held her ribs, glaring at Vivian, then attacked. With movements so quick Vivian could barely focus, Nuala hit her with an open palm over her ear. Vivan's head was filled with a pop, then a loud ring. Nuala grabbed her hands, twisting them the wrong way, and immobilized her in no time.

Chase, the odd man out, had wide eyes brimming with fear as he turned and ran away.

"You fucking pussy!" Vivian called after him.

Peik held May's wrists while retrieving a zip-tie from his back pocket. As he tried to loop it over both hands, she kicked him and screamed. Peik slapped her in the face, cutting off her voice, but not before a light came on in a nearby house. He got the zip-tie on her wrists, then brought out a cloth from his blue track suit and put it over May's face. The gaseous vapors overtook her, and she passed out on her feet.

When they had secured all three sleeping prisoners in the car, Nuala and Peik got in front. Oliver stood outside.

"You know what to do," said Peik. "Do this right and everything's going to be okay with us, boy."

Without a word, Oliver sniffed the air and bounded off after Chase, thinking how much he hated being called "boy".

• • •

Chase slammed the door after he got in the house, then fell down, wracked by sobs. His chest heaved, out of control. He hadn't run that far in years, and despite going out with Vivian, who was far more fit than he, hadn't planned on doing it again. Why did he leave her? Fuck. Panic had kicked in and the rest was history. He lay on his back, trying to control his breathing enough to call the police. Hopefully she'd be back soon and–Crrr-r-r–the floorboards on the front porch creaked.

He still had the bottle in his pocket, and pulled it out, then thought he'd find something much more useful in the kitchen. He put the bottle down and walked on his tiptoes onto the linoleum tiles. When he rounded the corner, he was shocked to see the spidery youth from the canyon sitting on top of his old stove with a large butcher knife in his hand. Chase reached for something to defend himself with.

When Chase diverted his eyes, Oliver leapt into the air, knife held high, and brought its steel blade sweeping down into the side of Chase's neck. A stream of blood exploded into mist as it hit against the hilt. Chase shook and struggled, but Oliver's grip was iron.

Oliver pulled the knife out and closed his mouth over the fountain of blood, gulping hungrily. Peik and Nuala hated when he drank the blood, but Frank had given him a taste for it, and he loved it still. Peik and Nuala weren't here, anyway. Just him and this loser.

Chase grew faint, watching as the boy drank the life force out of his body. Survival instinct kicked in, and he thrashed with an energy never felt before, but it was nothing but the flurry of a gnat's wings to Oliver,. After a few long minutes, Chase fell to the ground, unmoving. Dead.

Oliver, stomach full of blood, crawled off. He'd never drunk so much before. His body swooned, nauseous, and he vomited all over the kitchen floor. Bile and blood dripped from his chin as he crawled out the window into the night.

18.

Julio rose from his bed, something beckoned to him in his sleep. His eyes were open and full of milky liquid as he walked noiselessly out of the house and into the black convertible driven by the fine librarian mami, who zipped him away.

• • •

Every heartbeat made May's head throb with pain. She peeled her eyes open, just a crack at first, and saw the silhouetted shapes of Peik, Nuala, and Oliver, blurry through her eyelashes, in a dim room. They spoke softly, beneath her register, and stood in a tight circle off to her left.

She tried to memorize details of the room in case she lived long enough to describe it later. Old books sat displayed in a glass case. They seemed valuable.

There had to be a way for someone to track the titles, if she ever got out of here. She followed the kidnappers' movements until they turned away from her, then opened her eyes all the way, peering at the dimly illuminated books in the case, but something was wrong. The books, with dyed leather bindings, had titles in a different language than any she had ever seen. Jagged marks embossed the spines, obviously a language used by someone, but who?

As she looked at the bookcase, she saw what appeared to be a reflection of a face. At first it was difficult to tell if it came from inside the case, or if she were imagining it, but soon realized it was very real, and was two faces, not one. Her body jerked when she focused on the amused grins of the dark-haired man and woman reflected from behind the chair she was strapped in. The woman's blue eyes glowed unnaturally. The man's were black coals with a hazy sheen over them. They had a hungry look.

"Good morning," said the woman.

May didn't answer, but the others turned around when they heard her. Peik's eyes caught May's..

"Someone is awake." His voice sliced the still air as he approached.

"Yes," said the woman with the electric blue eyes, rounding the chair and ogling May. "Someone with such smooth skin. How does she do it?"

The woman, of average height, raised her hand and brushed it along May's cheek. From behind her head, May felt someone else stroking her hair. She glanced into the reflection in the display case and saw the man, both hands running through her red locks. His touch did something to her that the woman's did not. It gave her a feeling of comfort, and, curiously, a yearning. She adjusted her hips.

They looked intrigued, the way a carnivore attends to a new and exotic type of meat. May began to shiver, her freckled skin growing goose pimples, though the room was not cold by any means.

"Raul! Get the fuck up!" May yelled, struggling against the new emotions. Raul groaned. In the display case's reflection May noticed someone. Focusing, she saw the girl that had come across their scene in the canyon. Vivian was tied to a wooden chair, behind her and to the left. May hoped the new girl had a better plan than she did.

"Feisty," said the black-eyed man, pulling May's hair tightly in his fist. He brought his face close to hers. "Like to play games, mami?" His breath was sweet.

The woman laughed when May screamed.

"Oh, yes. Wake up the others," she said. "I love new friends." A solitary fingernail pushed up against the bottom of May's cheekbone, stretching her skin against the sharp tip.

May could feel the nail about to break through, and started to panic.

The two pulled May's psyche in different directions, and a twisted yin and yang of fear and desire dizzied her. Intoxicating. The pale man observed them, interested but not enough to intervene. Oliver was hiding behind the blonde lady, who watched stoically. A ripple passed through May's muscles as she realized Oliver was fearful of the man and woman. The little boy assassin wanted nothing to do with the man and woman. She could see why. This was nauseating.

"That's enough. We actually need them for some answers before you do whatever it is that you do," said Nuala. She corralled Oliver behind her.

The brunette, still poking the skin of May's cheek, looked from the corner of her eye at Nuala.

"What do you say, Dad?" she asked. It was easy to see that the blonde woman wasn't someone she'd be taking orders from.

Peik chuckled, not answering, and leaned down to peer at the boy. "Not so brave now, Oliver?" He raised his hand, signaling them to stop. As one, they separated themselves from May's chair and drifted back among the shadows to wait for direction.

Peik approached May, the indentation of the fingernail still deep red in her cheek. "Who are you people? Who told you about us? And who is that?" he asked, fanning his hand. Following with her eyes, May saw Vivian propped in a chair with her head lolled forward, chin on her chest, and hands tied behind her. Her eyes moved ever so slightly behind her closed lids.

"I don't know what you're talking about, or who that is. She just showed up out of nowhere."

"How clever of her," said Peik, who had drawn his face so close to May's that she had trouble focusing on his eye. She felt a pang of nausea deep in her innards. "Marie, Julio, wake the thief."

Slipping from the shadows, they picked up the wooden chair that Raul was bound in and glided with it back over to Peik, setting it down next to May's recliner.

Marie bent down, drawing in her breath inches from Raul's face. Vapors, thin as mist, snaked from Raul's mouth. Marie inhaled them, licking her lips. He groaned in his sleep, then opened his eyes, jerking when he saw Marie so close. As he did, he felt a tug on his guts, like he was attached to her in some way. Marie laughed, then exhaled. Raul's lungs filled, then expanded painfully. Just before they began to rip, the pressure decreased.

"Remember me? Haha. Guess you picked the wrong house, thief." She chuckled, stepping back and away. "He's awake."

Peik lifted up the bag that housed the flute and chime, set the chime on a table next to them, then held the flute in front of Raul's face. "How did you know about these?" the pale man demanded. "Or my daughter's house?"

"Dumb luck," Raul answered. "I've been hitting houses around there for years."

"You can't expect me to believe that," Peik said, then reached out and pinched Raul's eyelid, twisting it hard and pulling.

"Ow! The fuck, man?"

"Let's try again. Who told you about Marie Stillwater's house?"

"Nobody, man. It was just next on my list. I swear," he said, eyelid throbbing and growing purple.

Peik, shaking his head, brought the whistle up to his lips, "We shall see." he said, and blew into it.

Nothing happened.

He shook it, and blew into it again, then shook the ball in his hand while blowing trills, to no avail.

"Son of a bitch!" he yelled out. "Come here," he said to Marie and

Julio, waving his hand. They stood around Raul and Peik told them to blow into it. Each tried. Still nothing.

"Little bastards bonded with these, like Kim Song said," he said. "I wasn't convinced at their little ballroom, but I see now." Peik shot Raul a murderous glare."Renounce your bond."

"Why don't we just kill them?" Nuala said.

"Because if that doesn't work, these instruments are less than useless, and we need that machine. They must give up control of the instruments willfully." He spoke as if addressing a child. "Now, renounce your bond, thief."

Nuala was not amused.

Raul chuckled nervously. "Why would I do that? You'll kill us."

"Oh, no." Peik shifted course, his voice velvet. "If you do, We will show you things you can't have possibly imagined. We've been waiting for you, Raul. We want you to join us."

Raul's eyes lost their focus.

May felt this world of wonder she'd just discovered was about to leave her behind. "Hey Raul!" she shouted. "Stay with me!"

To her surprise, his body swooned, a wave coursing through him. It seemed their bonds to each other, heightened through these instruments, could override the group's influence.

Peik was irate. He glared at May. "If you don't renounce control, we'll kill that other girl. You have ten secon–" He turned, gesturing with a beet red hand to the wooden chair, which now had ropes hanging limply from its armrests.

"What other girl?" said Raul. "Who?" He craned his neck around and saw the empty chair.

"Oh, haha. No more bartering chip," added May.

Raul and May's ears felt as if they would explode with the roar of fury from Peik's lungs. Marie and Julio shot to the open window, then turned around and took off toward the door, gliding out of the darkened room and away like sentient shadows.

19.

Vivian had experience with ropes. Part of the reason she had hooked up with someone as dangerously close to burnout status as Chase was because her first boyfriend, a guy long before Chase or Stewart, was so intense.

Things were okay with Frank Rawls at first, but then the sex got weirder, and what he would talk about was worse. She finally called it off with him after he had made her put on doll makeup and pigtails, then left her tied up to a bed for sixteen hours, with no food or water. Somehow, she had chewed through her gag and shouted at the window when she heard her neighbor walk by. Frank hadn't returned until three days later. He never spent a second in jail, for reasons she could never find out. She took solace knowing she would never be with the jackass ever again, and the years slid by until she hardly remembered him, though she did stay familiar with knots and knives.

After Frank, she had learned a great deal about rope. How to tie and untie just about anything, and how to slip out of it. She also stretched her hands and feet every day, increasing their flexibility to the point where she could almost use her feet to mimic hands. For a thick and muscular woman that was no easy task, but she had vowed never to get herself into a situation where she was helpless again. That knowledge, and learning to fight, gave her back the confidence Frank had tried to rob her of. For the first time, she wondered about what could have happened to Frank. He'd get along great with these assholes.

She'd gotten so adept at it that her muscle memory kicked in when they'd tied her up, flexing her wrists. When she had awakened from her drugged stupor, her taut muscles relaxed, creating enough slack for her to worm herself free. Their attention had been centered around May and Raul from the band Bludgeons.

Smelling rope and old leather, all those memories of bound imprisonment, where every minute was a lifetime, came flooding back to her. She kicked, stopping as quick as she had begun, and her movement was passed off as a dream tremor by the spidery kid, the only one who saw.

From the corner she played possum, watching her surroundings through slitted eyes. Breathing deep and slow, she ferreted out of the straps binding her. The scene in the room was freaky, but she ignored it, concentrating.

A window was open. To Vivian that meant that either this group was so arrogant they believed themselves infallible, or there was no escape. One thing repeated in her mind; if she stayed, she was as good as dead. Crossfire does not favor the ignorant.

Straining, she flexed her skin as it slipped beneath the rope, pore by pore. At last she popped her hand out, and the bindings fell like limp noodles across her lap. She slowly pushed them down her legs. As they slid to the ground, she rose and slipped out the window, not looking back.

It was pitch black outside. She hung from the window sill, feeling around for something to stand on, until she realized there was a small iron balcony, wide enough for a potted plant. Sliding down, she looked over the edge into blackness. The balcony, more of a decoration, strained under her, unstable. She evened out her weight and took one long breath, slowing her pounding heart.

The rear of the house hung over a wide canyon. Long stilts supported the two-story building in the back, while the top story opened out to street level at the other end. It was one of several in a row of its kind; boxy houses considered modern when they were built into the sides of the canyons decades ago. Its rear end hovered thirty feet in the air. From the small balcony there was no staircase, no escape.

Her thoughts raced. She searched for a solution. A jump into blackness was still better odds than what was going on in that room.

Both her hands were on the rail, and she brought one foot to meet them, staring down to gauge the depth of her fall, impossible in the dark. Over the groaning of the bolts, she heard a rapid stream of clicks from her right. She jerked in shock, teetering over the void, then righted herself. Peering toward the click, a glint of light reflected off the ruby sheen of a hummingbird's throat. Now that her eyes had a moment to adjust, she could make out a eucalyptus tree's trunk and hanging leaves.

She looked where she had been about to jump off, and could now see a pile of jagged stones below. The hummingbird flew to her face from its perch, and clicked three clicks while hovering in midair, then shot back to the tree.

Hearing the bird, Vivian was filled with confidence. She had seldom felt anything this strong, this sure. Embracing it, she launched herself through the air and into the branches of the massive tree.

As her feet hit, they slipped on the smooth bark, but she turned, favoring all her limbs equally, and stayed braced in the crotch of the merging branches. She stood, relieved, but it was still a long way down.

The bird hovered down below her foot, clicked, and landed on the fleshy ridge left from a branch being lopped off years ago. Shaking, she reached her foot down, at last coming in contact with it. Another click, another ridge. This continued until she was about fifteen feet off the ground. Fearing time may be running out, she jumped off, landing on an incline and rolling, unhurt.

Righting herself, she stood behind the tree trunk and looked back up to the balcony. No movement, yet.

"Zif," said the hummingbird, then zipped down the canyon. Vivian felt she had no choice but to follow, not knowing in which direction she was running. The bird sped ahead into the bushes while she ran as fast as she could, trying to keep her eye on the glint from its feathers. She needed to put as much distance as possible between herself and the weird house before they noticed she was gone.

Finally able to see the trail she was following, she flinched at a click, then a whir which slashed the air next to her head, and poised herself to attack before she saw the hummingbird flying next to her, matching her speed. She brought her mind out of attack mode, but still didn't know what to make of the little bird out here at night, or why it was helping her.

Hummingbirds aren't even nocturnal, she thought as it sped deeper into the branches ahead. Vivian redoubled her pace to catch up to it. The path zigged then zagged up a hill, and she chanced a look back in the direction of the house. A pit opened up in her stomach when she saw two human shadows, slipping in and out of the bushes and trees behind her, barely discernible in the darkness. Suppressing a scream, Vivian fled after the hummingbird as fast as she could go.

Through thick and spiky shrubs she sprinted, clawing with her hands through the densest parts. There wasn't even a path anymore. The hummingbird was her only hope as she followed it into smaller and smaller holes in the brush. A flash of memory came to her of some sort of insect or fish that did this to its predators, leading them into confounding mazes and leaving them trapped to starve to death. She hoped this wasn't one of those situations.

Before long, she could hear the thrashing hands of her pursuers, but didn't dare turn around. That's how mistakes happen.

Twigs cracked and leaves rustled. They were gaining on her. She could hear their breath now, mixed with the swish of unseen cars driving by on a road above them.

There was no way she could reach the road before they caught her, she knew, crawling as quickly as possible through the thick brush. Something grabbed at her shoe, snagging. She instinctively kicked, pushing off someone and launching through the far side of the plants, coming to a stop against two stone stairs that opened into a black cave-mouth. Chiseled steps disappeared into the depths. Finally chancing a look behind, she saw the woman's eyes glowing blue.

Without hesitation, Vivian fled down the black tunnel. Cool air blew from below as she stumbled on the uneven footing.

The hummingbird whizzed by and vanished into the darkness. She heard their voices checking each other before falling silent. For an instant she thought they'd turned back, or stopped, but the clacking of a dislodged rock bouncing down the staircase told her that they were not far behind.

"Where are you going, lady?" Julio sounded amused, like he was in his element. The chase. His voice bounced by her, echoing off the stone walls. She picked up two rocks and threw them at the voice. The first clattered off stone, but the second hit something hollow.

Clonk!

She followed the clicks of the bird blindly, hands splayed in front of her. Her feet slipped on a wet patch, but she evened her balance and pushed against the wall, then kept running. Up ahead, a faint glow pulled her forward as it seemed to pulsate, giving her hope as she came flying out of the tunnel and into a massive arching cave.

Streams of green light ran along the walls like rivers impervious to gravity, casting an eerie glow over the three people and massive bear that stood in the center of the huge cave.

The bear roared, making Vivian skid to a halt.

"Help me!" she cried.

Time seemed to stand still as the huge man looked to the old woman, as did the teenaged girl. The old woman, grim and resolute, snapped her fingers, and the bear exploded from behind them, barreling toward Vivian.

With a scream, Vivian threw herself to the side. Like a runaway train, the giant bear flew past her and ran straight at Julio and Marie as they entered the cave. With feline precision Marie cut to the left and Julio to the right. The bear missed both, its inertia carrying it past, scuttling its feet and sliding sideways, then slamming into the wall. Its rumbling voice filled the cave as it righted itself amidst a cloud of dust. Julio and Marie regrouped and ran low to the ground from different directions at Vivian.

Marie's skin shone blue, electric. She held her hand high and shot a tendril of light from her palm. It scorched the air as it flew toward Vivian, hitting the ground next to her. Dust flew into the air from the huge divot left by the blast.

Vivian surprised Marie by counter-attacking before she could respond.

It worked. Vivian dodged Marie's flailing arms and grabbed her by the neck and armpit. She swiveled her hips into a spin, lifting Marie off the ground and twisting her through the air before slamming her into the stone wall from three feet away.

Marie tried to stand, but her eyes floated on a sea of pain, and she collapsed with a groan, blue eyes fading.

Vivian turned around to find Julio with his fist cocked above her. His body seemed to hang, then the bear snagged him out of the air with its teeth.

Its powerful jaws clamped down on Julio's torso, piercing vital organs. Julio reacted instantly, punching the bear in the eye several times, his hands a blur. The bear shook its head, ripping flesh, then released him, sending him bouncing along the ground. He righted himself, then cut beneath the animal and back toward Marie limping, with blood seeping heavily from his wounds.

Vivian kept the bear between herself and them, backing farther and farther away from the melee and the women who stood and watched. All eyes were on the bear as Vivian slinked off toward the wall. She didn't know these other people, and wasn't going to trust them either.

Julio picked up Marie, whose skin was now glowing blue. Before the massive bear could strike again, Julio let out a growl of his own, higher and more urgent in its pitch than the voice of the bear. Black smoke, like living shadow, poured from his mouth and wrapped around them, rendering them invisible. When the smoke cleared, there was no sign of either one.

The old woman, eyes like granite, called to Vivian from across the cave. "Come here, girl." Her gnarled finger beckoned.

Vivian faced the woman, then ran. Her strong legs made two good strides before a strange sound froze her muscles and she fell to the ground. Using all of her energy, she was able to roll her body over and look back through the dust.

The teenaged girl, tall and a little awkward, as if she hadn't yet grown into her body, held her hands in front of her, palms raised to the sky. She blew a humming tone through her teeth with a whistling sound beneath it, all the while staring at Vivian.

Vivian's life had been hard, and the streets had raised her just as much as any parent, but looking into the eyes of the girl made her remember when life was easy, a time before her body grew curves and attracted so much of the wrong kind of attention from all the men in her life. Rather than calm her down, the thread continued, pulling her into the darker memories of her own teenaged years, culminating with the freak who loved the ropes so much. More rope. More knots.

Reaching deep within herself, Vivian strained against the memories, pushing them from her mind, retreating into the survival mode which at one point had been her bread and butter. She stood, leaving the memories, and the girl smiled at her.

"Welcome," she said.

"Hi, and thanks," said Vivian, then walked backwards slowly. "But no thanks." And she ran away.

The old woman watched, her arm on Markuz's chest as Vivian fled into a tunnel. He stood still, muscles flexed, ready to chase her down if the need arose, but the old woman held her hand until Vivian's echoing footsteps had faded.

A clicking filled in the cave, and the ruby-throated hummingbird hovered in front of the old woman. "Yes, Zif." She nodded, and the bird shot up the tunnel.

"I'm sorry, Ursula," said the girl.

"There's nothing to be sorry about," said the old woman, running her fingers through the girl's hair. "All is as it should be."

• • •

The blackness was total. Vivian had to slow down after the path turned to stairs. The staircase forked in front of her. She sat between the two, listening, smelling, and trying to see. From behind her came a whirring sound, echoing along the tube until a wind raced by. She screamed, and her voice bounced along the walls. After the reverberations subsided, she heard the click of the hummingbird's tongue, and saw a faint ruby sheen off the bird's neck, though there was no light for it to reflect.

"Oh yeah?" she said to the bird. "Why should I trust you?"

The bird clicked its tongue.

Vivian turned to the other tube. Something moved. She fought the urge to run and stared deeper into the blackness. Eyes peered back at her, glowing yellow and as big as saucers. In the blackness, a woman's figure was revealed. But for the eyes, she appeared out of focus. A blur. Vivian couldn't tell if it was a trick of the darkness or what, but the effect was nauseating. The woman tilted her head to the side, long hair swaying. Inquisitive eyes wandered over Vivian. "Hello," she said.

The woman raised her hand toward Vivian's face. Just as the woman touched her, a wavelike shiver passed over her body.

"Where are you going?" said the woman.

"I don't know." She had to get out of here.

The little bird flew away, wings beating a trail for Vivian to follow. She struggled, finally tearing herself from the rapture of the woman's touch. As she broke free, the woman grabbed a fistful of her hair and jerked hard.

Reacting instantaneously, Vivian kicked backwards, hitting squarely on the woman's kneecap. She heard the woman curse as she sprinted after the bird, running blind, feeling along the stone walls. Hazy light bled down as she neared the surface.

The tube bent, and air blew from above, carrying wafts of sagebrush with it. Vivian inhaled the desert air as she sped out of the cave's mouth, looking up at the clouds, glowing pink with the reflected lights of the city. The moon, one-quarter full, hung in the sky, shooting silver rays through a perfectly centered break in the clouds. Vivian could see more vividly from its light than she usually did in the daytime.

In the middle of the moonbeam sat the big-eyed woman. A dark-skinned man with a deep scar above one eye stood next to her, long hair falling around his shoulders. The woman wore a dress of thick black fabric, a smile on her pursed lips.

"Hello, Vivian."

"Who are you?"

"We've met." The woman winked.

"No, we hav–" she stopped. A flame of memory sparkled. "What the fuck?"

"We're just trying to help you."

"I doubt that," said Vivian. "People say that, but they don't mean it."

"Well," said the woman, snapping her fingers, "We're not exactly people."

The man next to her raised his hand, opening it and blowing fine dust at Vivian. Before she could turn her head, it shot up her nose. It burned, and her vision grew blurry with tears.

"So you can find us," came the woman's voice, "and we can find you." When Vivian had wiped the mess from her eyes, they were gone. The hummingbird clicked from its hiding place in a bush behind her and sped into the bushes.

"Thanks a lot, bird," she mumbled, following it into the scrub willow growing along a drainage ditch at the base of a hill. Flashes of meeting the owl woman at Auntie Frieda's, then something more. She couldn't pinpoint the rest.

Above the willows were eucalyptus trees. Their tall lanky stalks shot up and blocked the three-story, cheaply-stuccoed apartment building at the crest of the incline.

On the other side of the ditch was a smaller hill, and above that a freeway. She climbed up the shorter hill to suss it out, and found she was at the crossing of the 15 and the 94 freeways, to the southeast of her house.

As she stepped from the willow, she looked south. No headlights. She tore across to the other side and down an incline, farther beneath the freeway to a long cement drainage gully. She looked up the inclines. The juncture where these met the roads were prime locations for urban party spots and homeless encampments.

"Hey, baby," a man's voice floated down. A thick shadow of someone dressed in rags sat atop the hill. The hummingbird zoomed down and clicked in her ear.

She stared at the shadow. "Hey, shithead. You say one more thing, I'll come up there and beat you with a fucking rock, okay?" She was over dealing with people's crap.

He eyed her, and she picked up her pace, turning and walking through a rip in the chain-link fence. The hummingbird, flying up toward the man, made a series of clicks and whistles, then zipped after her. The man chuckled.

Through the fence, she saw the warehouses where they'd found that police lady's kid, the one from the news. Yesterday she might have wanted to check it out, get a little excitement with old boring Chase. Now, thinking about it, she got a feeling in her gut, and took off running toward her house. She'd figure it out with Chase, smoke a joint, have a beer, maybe get laid, and they'd get a plan going. Together.

Her lungs burned, but she pushed on, thinking she might not have given Chase enough of a shot. There were worse things than boring. Hell, after tonight, she'd embrace boring.

She wasn't concerned when the door to her house was open, they passed out like that a lot. However, when she saw the wreckage inside, alarms began to go off. And when she saw Chase's body, so pale it seemed blue, with blood spattered all around it, she realized there was no going back. They already knew where she was. Whoever they were.

There was no plan B. She shivered, chills sweeping over her body. Consumed by sadness, she slipped down into a heap on the floor, next to Chase, holding his cold hand and crying until she couldn't breathe.

The eastern sky grew rosy with dawn, and Vivian realized she'd have to call the police. Staring at her phone, she tried to think of what she would say.

20.

"Alright. You in, Juan?" Tommy Whiteoak asked, ready to walk out Clem's door.

Juan's usual response to situations was to keep it light, joke around a little. However, it was becoming difficult to maintain his chippy exterior now that the subject matter was so removed from reality. His eyes drifted from Tommy, his partner he hardly knew.

Cora could see his dismay. "It doesn't stop because you want it to," she said. "It doesn't stop at all, if my experience means anything, but it makes sense after a while, kind of."

"Yeah, I never believed in magic, or whatever this shit is," said Juan. "But, well, I don't know . . . " He looked at Tommy, but the brawny tracker had turned around, and Juan watched Tommy's braid swing back and forth.

"This may be beside the point," said Cora. "But it's not magic, it's science. Only a different branch than we're taught when we're young, if that helps."

"I'm not sure it does, but thanks," Juan replied. "Anyway, fuck it. Yeah, I'm ready. But what do we do if we find the crow dude first?" It was as if a light had gone on inside of him.

"Raven," said Cora. "Don't confuse the two, it's not a good idea."

"Claro, lo siento," he said. "What do we do if we find the raven dude first?"

"Plug your ears," said Cora. "He's very influential."

Clem nodded and took the lead. "Okay. Three groups. Cora's on the trail of the monster and Abe. Tommy and Juan are on the Coyotes. I'll pick up Amy from the lab and try to find the Stillwater's."

"Who's gonna stay with him?" Buddy asked, pointing at Gray.

"I will," said Myron. "He's my boy."

"You, responsible for the safety of my child?" asked Clem, incredulously. "I don't think so."

"I can go," said Buddy. "I can help."

"No." she said, simply and sternly, eyes wide.

"I'll stay," said Helen. "Watch over Sugar while Myron looks after Gray."

Helen. Rupert would be dead or worse ten times over if it weren't for her. Of everyone from this case, Helen was the one who garnered

Clem's trust, and would know what to do if anything went south at the house.

"Thank you," said Clementine. She couldn't stop herself from hugging the large lady. Helen had that effect. Clementine breathed in Helen's scent of dust and desert sage, calming her nerves.

Luna stood next to Buddy and barked. Grifter flanked him on the other side. There would have to be an immense amount of power to get the dogs away from the boy. Myron twiddled his thumbs and looked at Luna.

"Mr. Fox," said Clem. "if I hear from my child, or anyone else, of any deception on your part, I will hunt you to the ends of the Earth."

"Of course." Mr. Fox smiled. "I wouldn't have it any other way."

Walking out of the house, Tommy Whiteoak put his hand on Clem's shoulder. When she turned around, he offered her his pearl-handled .22.

"I have a feeling you're going to need this more than I am."

She shoved it in her boot.

After they had gone, Myron stood in the kitchen, humming a tune as Gray slept on the couch. Myron's soft voice had the effect of a lullaby on Buddy and the dogs. Without thinking it out of the ordinary, Buddy walked slowly to a large comfortable chair and sat down, drowsing to the music, heavy eyelids falling shut. Grifter and Luna stretched at his feet and laid down on their sides, twitching immediately in pre-dream cycles.

Once he was snoring, Helen grabbed Myron's arm. "If this doesn't work, I'm going to kill you," she said.

"My dear," Myron responded, "if this doesn't work, you'll have to stand in line."

• • •

Jim Garrett had a thin layer of dust upon him as climbed up the ladder and pushed underneath the door in the floor, opening it. The house was dark, as the sun hadn't risen.

The burrowed tunnel stretched a mile and a half beneath the neighborhoods along the harbor, big enough for several people to walk shoulder to shoulder, with long strands of lights running down its entirety. Solar fuel cells atop the house powered the tunnel so no ridiculous charges appeared on the electric bill to alert the authorities, one of many precautions.

Brushing the dust off, he shut the closet door that was the tunnel's exit, went into the kitchen, poured himself a glass of discolored water, and sat on a lumpy couch in the living room.

His body ached, and his mind was weary, neither being assuaged on the long tunnel walk. Fatigue overtook him, but he looked out the window to the street. Seeing no car, and no way for him to leave without being seen, he sat back down. His sitting became lying, which in turn made him fall fast asleep.

The room was no longer dark when he awoke to the sound of the door closing. Jim popped his eyes open. His contact for the job, Myron Fox, wore a grey suit. That and his ponytail were crisp and impeccable. His stare gave Jim the chills.

Jim sat up, rubbing his arms.

"Detective James Garrett." His name from Myron's mouth sounded like a mockery. As if there was something the detective should be detecting, but he couldn't put his finger on it. "You look like shit."

Jim felt the knob on his forehead, still a little gummy with undried blood. "Uh, yeah. Did that job for you."

"So it seems. Let's get going."

"Wait a goddamn minute. What about getting paid?"

Myron didn't pause. The screen door slammed, sending a billow of dust into the living room.

"Son of a bitch," Jim said, tying his shoes.

The car was a small brown coupe with a blue spoiler on the back. It looked ridiculous. Myron sat in the driver's seat, engine idling.

"Very nice work," said Myron when Jim had sat down. "Quite tidy, considering."

"Well, I am a professional," said Jim.

"Certainly, and you should be compensated as such." He handed a black canvas tote bag to the detective. Jim looked inside at the stack of bills and zipped it back up, tucking it between his legs as Myron pulled onto the street, zigging and zagging at each block. Jim's phone vibrated in his pocket.

"Garrett," he answered, then listened intently for a few moments, looking into the rearview mirror at the curious eyes of Myron. "10-4. Thanks, hon," he finally said, and turned around.

"That was my girl on the switches," he said. "One of the houses on the hill you wanted me to monitor just called to report a murder."

"Where?"

"B Street hillside, the one near the mechanic's yard."

"What's the manner of the death?" asked Myron. "Anything interesting?"

"Exsanguination, she said. Pique your interest?"

"It does indeed." He put his foot to the floor, and the car that looked like a clunker joke rocketed back to Golden Hill in minutes, surprising Jim.

He thought he'd have to explain that he needed to appear in his own car at the crime scene, and not be dropped off there by a civilian, or at least give directions to his house. However, he was surprised, and not pleasantly, to find Myron make all the proper turns precisely and deposit him outside his house, right next to his sedan.

Jim didn't say good-bye. He ran into his house to stash the bag of bills and change out of his clothes, flecked with blood and dust, so he could hit the crime scene clean and without arousing suspicion. While he was in the house, his phone rang. He watched the coupe pull away and around the corner.

The Lieutenant was calling.

"Garrett."

"Hey Jim. Just wanted to let you in on the fact that Mr. Stillwater and all of his operations are no longer under the protection of Special Investigations."

Jim's sun-blanched skin turned white. "And the people in his employ?" he asked, hands shaking just a little.

"Everything's off. They are offered no protection from SDPD. None."

"Got it." He looked back out the window, but Myron Fox was gone.

"Where are you now?" asked the Loo.

"Responding to a possible homicide in Golden Hill. West side. You can see the house from the station."

"Let Homicide handle it. I need you for something back here." He paused. "Wait . . . what's the address?"

"1284 20th."

"Belay my order. Go immediately. Then call me when you know the details," he said, offering no explanation for the 180 degree turn.

"Roger that," said Jim, hanging up. He felt dizzy, and devoted several seconds to not vomiting, then headed to the murder scene.

• • •

Back at the house, Myron walked in. Helen breathed a little deeper. Mr.

Fox snapped his fingers, waking Buddy and the dogs. They acted like nothing had happened.

"Who wants lunch?" asked Helen.

Everyone did.

21.

"Back in five minutes," said the sign on the evidence desk. Amy had waited fifteen. She didn't have a key to the locked gateway, and couldn't keep waiting. Cursing, she walked back to the lab.

Rory jumped when she came through the door. His hair was matted with sweat and his face was pale. "Shit. You scared me."

"Sorry. Are you okay?"

"Not really. I got the results. Jim Garrett is a match to one of the signatures from the evidence you gave me. From the empty grave."

"Fuck. Seriously? Who else?"

"I'm still working on it. Garth from lockup is one. We knew that, but there's an unknown. Possibly two."

Amy's stomach knotted. "Shit."

"I really don't like this, Amy."

"Me neither. But I need you now."

"At least tell me what the hell is going on." He was starting to sound desperate.

"Okay," she sighed. "It's complicated, though, so listen carefully." Her phone vibrated in her pocket. "Hold on, please." She answered it. "Hi, Clem . . . Right now . . . ? Okay."

She hung up. "The explanation's gonna have to wait, Rory. I have to go somewhere with Clem. But I promise I'll tell you next chance I get."

He was reluctant. "Alright," he said, shrugging as Amy walked out of the lab. He got back to work. After a few minutes the doors opened again.

Looking up, he said," What can I do for you, Lieutenant?"

• • •

"Did you get to evidence?" asked Clem, driving Amy and Alec to the ballroom.

"Damn gate was closed and no one was there. Left a sign," said Amy. "Rory had some news, though."

"Do tell."

"Well, the blood pools from Abe's place yielded a few signatures. One was Garth, one or more are unknown, and the final blood spiller is our very own Detective James Garrett."

"You are freaking kidding me! He's that far gone? We've got to report him."

"To whom? Who can we unequivocally trust?"

"Well, the Loo, for one."

"You're one hundred percent sure of that?"

"Well . . . no. Of course not."

"Exactly," said Amy. "What about Tommy and Juan?"

"Reporting something to them wouldn't help. Christ, I outrank them."

"You're right. Anyway, what would we be reporting? Just because he bled there doesn't mean he killed Garth."

"We need some evidence." The air lay heavy for a few seconds. Clem tried to lighten it up. "So, what are the chances of, you know, me and Tommy . . ." She flashed back to holding the tracker's muscular abs as they raced down the subterranean tunnel.

"Seriously?" Amy asked, confused.

"Hey, I'm just asking. I'm starved for a little male companionship now that I solved the case of my life."

"Clem, baby. Of course you deserve some lovin'," Amy said. "You're a great mom, and Buddy's safe. That's not what I'm talking about."

"Well, what is the big deal then? He's certainly hot."

"Oh, big time." That was undeniable.

"Hey Alec," Amy asked. "You gay?"

"I'm not. You can't tell?" he asked, leaning forward on the back seat.

"Actually, I can. I knew you weren't. How 'bout you Clem? You think Alec was gay?"

"I have to admit I didn't think about it one way or the other."

"Hey, Alec, you think my cousin was gay?"

"Pretty much, yeah."

"How about that Tommy dude?"

"Had a feeling."

"Yeah. Good job," She faced Clem. "You know how my cousin is constantly saying that Tommy is the man? That's because Tommy is his man. Tommy and Juan are partners partners. Like a couple," Amy chuckled. "How do you work in San Diego for, like, ever, being a kick ass detective, and not have any gay-dar?"

Clem saw it. How Juan spoke so highly of Tommy, like he was

transfixed. She didn't blame him. She'd also been blinded by the dark, mysterious tracker. "I guess I just couldn't see past his sculpted body."

Alec joined their chuckling, relieved to find Clem had no current love interest. Though almost twenty years her junior, he found her magnetic. He made a mental note to work out more, maybe grow his hair, as he directed them to the ballroom.

He was leading the police to his great secret. Funny how things change in the blink of an eye, he thought, as he pulled the trash sculpture from in front of the door, unlocked it and pushed it open.

Alec stepped around an amp and turned on the lights. The women gasped at the enormity of the ballroom, its furnishings and decoration in very good condition due to being locked away from any harmful elements for decades. Lights from the crystal chandeliers illuminated gold and scarlet sculpted curtains of plaster curling from the crown moulding to the floor. Tables had been moved and stacked on one wall to the side to make room for the circular set-up of musical instruments and amplifiers where the band practiced. When they had finished admiring the room, Alec pointed to the trail of blood leading to a grate over an air duct in the wall. "Here's where it happened."

"Thanks," said Amy. It was pretty obvious where the struggle went down, but she kept her comments to herself. "What color are your bandmates' hair?"

"Hers is red. His is dark brown."

She squinted her eyes, knelt down, and with some tweezers plucked a long blonde hair from the rug. It glimmered as she bagged it and put it into the kit. She saw something else, and grabbed a thicker, shorter, hair. Its silver sheen reflected the light, giving it the appearance of motion. Weird. She bagged it as well.

Though the room was plenty bright from the chandeliers, Amy used her flashlight, fanning it back and forth as she walked toward the covered opening. From roughly ten feet away, she pointed it straight at the grate, and was surprised to see a teenaged boy looking back from inside the twisted wrought-iron work. His eyes were dark, almost black. Poor kid, she thought.

"Hey there, what's going on?" she asked him. "You lost?"

As she walked toward the wall, she blocked Clem and Alec's line of sight to the grate.

"Who are you talking to?" said Clem.

Amy put her hands on the grate.

"Amy!"

The kid smiled and nodded as Amy tried to get the corner out. Kid's not used to smiling with those nasty teeth, she thought. He pushed the same spot on the grate from the other side. The wrought iron creaked against itself, slowly sliding from its housing. The ends of the boy's three fingers peeked from around the edge, then quickly pulled back as Clem kicked the grate closed with a bang.

Amy snapped out of her trance as she watched the boy disappear up the tube, his body lit in the weblike patterns from the flashlight through the wrought metal.

"What the fuck?" she said, shaking her head back and forth in an effort to clear the cobwebs. "How did he do that?"

Clem pushed her gently out of the way without answering, grabbed the grate and tugged on it. It squeaked as it dislodged, then clattered to the floor while she pulled out her pistol and flashlight. Shining the beam up the tube, it lit his ankle vanishing into the duct-work at the end. She followed. When she reached the junction, her shoe splashed into a puddle at the bottom. Cursing, she pointed the beam up at his ascending body.

"Stop! Police!" she yelled, watching him punch through a grate thirty feet above her head and disappear into a hole in the side. He'd made good time up the chute. Faint light bled from the hole, then the metal grate came tumbling down, banging against the sides as it fell.

She leapt out of the way, and it clattered into the puddle. Kicking it aside, she looked back up. No movement, not even a flicker of a shadow from the uncovered hole. The boy was gone.

She walked out of the tube shaking her head. "Lost him."

"I don't know what came over me," said Amy. "In a way I knew who he was, but it just never occurred to me he wasn't a lost kid who needed help."

"That's how they do it, these people. That's Oliver." Clementine said, rubbing her scarred bicep. Something caught her eye. On her pant leg. "There's blood on me."

"On it." Amy pulled out a swab and vial. "Hold still,"

Clementine complied, and Amy crouched down and rubbed the swab along the rubber sole.

"Stop moving," she said.

"I'm not."

"Sorry," said Amy, "I was talking to the blood."

"What?" Clem looked down. The drops of blood were rolling up her shoe. She gasped, prying one shoe off while Amy attempted to corral a droplet with the swab. As her foot popped out, Clem bumped Amy's hand, and the squirming drop of blood transferred to her pant leg, shimmying upward at once.

Alec watched, mouth agape, as the fit older officer stripped off her pants and left them in a pile over her shoes, followed by her shirt

Amy pulled a large, clear plastic bag from her kit and threw the lot of Clementine's clothes into it, then shoved the shoes on top before sealing the zipper lock. The drops of blood remaining on the floor gathered together, rolling in a line toward the ductwork. Amy put down the bag and chased it.

"Is there any on me?" Clem, in bra and panties, turned in a circle in front of Alec, who dutifully inspected her body for any cause of alarm.

"No. You're clear," he said, after an inordinate amount of time.

"Okay. Shit. Does your bandmate have any clothes here?"

"Yeah, and we have band shirts," answered Alec, trying his hardest not to ogle. He turned around with maximal effort and opened a drawer on May's bureau, by the guitar cabinet.

"Just get me some shorts and a t-shirt, and like some flip flops or something," said Clem. She'd noticed the lingering looks, and while Alec wasn't remotely her type, she was flattered. She did keep herself in good shape, after all. It wasn't a crime if a young man enjoyed the sight of her. He was cute, if only half her age.

Alec came back with what she asked for, although befitting a rocker more than a detective. She was just glad to have something without moving blood on it, and she put on the cutoff camouflage cargo shorts and new black shirt that said BLUDGEONS! in white and red with two crossed clubs dripping blood down a human skull.

"How do I look?" Clem asked.

Sweaty and breathless, Amy was walking back, inspecting the blood she'd corralled in her vial. It sloshed against the sides, hitting the top. She smiled at Clementine. "Pretty badass."

Clem was glad they were a team. "That's fucking right. Now, what do we have here?"

"Wow. I don't know. I have to go back to the lab. Are we sure that kid's gone?"

"Well, he went up the tube, then out of it about thirty feet up, into an opening. He could be anywhere." She turned to Alec. "Is this whole thing the insurance company, even the bottom floors?"

"No, just the top few, the couple on the bottom are independent lawyers and a title company, plus a couple miscellaneous ones that turn over pretty quickly."

"You keep tabs, Alec?"

"I feel like it's my responsibility."

"I like that word," said Clem, winking.

Alec's heart skipped.

Amy cleared her throat. "I should get going. This is the key," she said, holding the bag up.

As they stepped out and up to the dawn-lit street, they looked for Oliver on the sidewalks, in the windows of the building, in cars, everywhere, but didn't see him.

Clem started the car, and her mother's intuition went crazy. "Something's wrong at the house," she said.

22.

The cars came to a stop a little up the street at Tommy's signal. He didn't want anybody stepping in any tire tracks or footprints, and guided them to the rear of the house where they stood around the hole in the ground, far enough away that they didn't disturb the tracks in the dust.

"That's a big-ass grave," said Stewart. Klia clicked from her perch in a tree.

Max looked at him sideways. "You haven't seen this guy yet, huh?"

"No. Everyone says he's pretty big, but this big?" Stewart looked at the raking finger marks along the rim where chunks were pulled into the grave, forming a hill. Deep gouges were stomped into it.

"Massive. And nasty," said Tommy. He sniffed the air, nose wrinkling with the acrid scent, then crouched low, shining his light along the top of the rippled earth. "When you go, follow this path," he said to Max, pointing to the tracks through the oak trees. "This other one will be a long circle before the big guy returned and lost some of his mass. After that's when Clem called us, and we chased it down to the tunnel by the mechanic's yard, so when you exhaust the pathways you can pick it up there. Be careful, though. The tunnel's dark and wet."

"Thanks," said Max.

Tommy turned, stepped around the disturbed earth of a struggle, then shone his light into a bush and squinted. "Juan, can you come here please? We should get a sample of this."

Juan, kit in tow, almost leapt over to help. With his tweezers, he pulled the gray fleshy hunks from the bushes and put them into vials.

Stewart busied himself sifting his fingers through the earth at the bottom of the hole. His hand brushed upon a fleshy tube-shaped item. For a reason he couldn't explain, he curled the thing into his palm, hidden away.

"Okay," said Tommy. "I got what I need from here. We're going back to the street. Separate the tire tracks. We'll get a hold of you guys when we know what's going on." He and Juan waved and walked back toward the cars.

"Let's get to work," said Cora.

Max didn't answer. His jaw was hanging open in disbelief at what he saw Stewart doing.

"Stewart! Stop! No!" shouted Cora, waving her hands as she

watched him put what appeared to be a gray thumb into his mouth.

Klia, from her perch high in a live oak, flew at Stewart shrieking and squawking.

Like he knew to breathe air, Stewart knew this would lead them to the monster, and to Abe. He put the finger into his mouth, and the putrid taste of death flooded his senses, rushing with an irresistible force. A black onslaught of slime overtook his mind, and he felt his muscles twitch and spasm, control waning. Black void. Pounding deep rhythms reverberating.

Battling to keep his mind from losing itself, he burst from the hole, raking dirt behind him as he propelled himself up and out like a wolfen creature. He grunted, looking at Cora with a crazed animal's eyes, then disappeared into the trees. He could hear the sap pulse through their branches.

Klia shrieked and followed him, flying fast.

Cora and Max tailed him, too. Up ahead, they could only just make out Stewart's body flashing brief glimpses between the trees. They soon topped out their speed, but it was no match for Stewart and whatever was propelling him. Very soon they had to resort to following his tracks through the canyons at night.

Max's vision, like Cora's, was excellent, but the darkened conditions, as well as Stewart's wide gait, made the going slow. They had lost him for now. Cora let her mind drift on the web, and she was able to see, or rather feel with her eyes, a faint trail in Stewart's lingering wake.

"Here we go," she said, and stepped onto a pathway Max hadn't seen.

Max looked back, then followed Cora, jogging slightly to catch up.

The voice of a bird. Wings shoving the air. His bird. Klia. The sound of dew forming. Surface tension. Droplet sucking into droplet, popping together. Clouds filling with water. Crashing like waves in the sky. Each leaf dropping from its stalk and whispering on its way to the ground. Distant tires hum on asphalt. A chorus of Crickets. Sprinklers. The call of an owl luring the sleeping squirrel.

Stewart heard the rhythms of the world. The patterns of everyday life. Human. Animal. Machine. The all-embracing song. He listened, charging through the canyons, his eyes a viscous haze.

23.

"Nine-one-one," said the woman's voice, "what's your emergency?"

"It's my boyfriend. He's dead." Vivian said.

"What's your address, ma'am?"

Vivian told her, reciting the numbers as if in a dream.

"Okay, what happened?"

"I came home and the house was a mess. He has a huge hole in his neck and he's blue."

"Ma'am," said the dispatcher, "are you alone?"

"Yes." Vivian wiped the tears from her cheeks with the back of her sleeve. Then it hit her. "Shit. You think there's someone in my house?"

"I didn't say that," the woman said, staying calm. "But is there a secure room with a lock that you can go into until I can get an officer there?"

Before the woman could finish her sentence, Vivian had locked the bathroom door and checked behind the shower curtain, then just for good measure checked beneath the sink, though no one could really fit there. She wished she could tell the woman on the phone that the people she was hiding from could turn themselves to smoke and disappear, so locking herself away might not work, but she thought better of it.

"Okay," said Vivian, "I'm secure, for now."

"Good. A car is on its way."

"Thank you."

"You're welcome. I'll stay on the phone with you until they arrive. Are you injured?"

"No." She checked to make sure. Hurt, yeah. Not injured.

The main police station was less than a mile from her house, and one minute later a knock came from the front room.

"Hello? Police," a male voice said.

Vivian thanked the dispatcher and cracked the bathroom door until she saw two uniformed officers on the porch. She crossed the room and unlocked the front door.

"Hi, thank goodness you're here. Please come in."

The two police–a shorter but buff Hispanic man and a pudgy white officer with a mustache–cleared the house before settling on Chase. The round man gestured with his eyes for the muscled one to talk to Vivian while he checked the body and called the detective and crime techs.

"Hello, I'm Officer Gustavo Gonsalves," said the officer once he had gotten Vivian out of the house and into the front yard, away from the sight of her slain boyfriend. "What's your name?"

"Vivian," she said. "Vivian Cartwright." A black van pulled across the street, and a man and woman in coveralls with tool kits walked into her house.

"Okay, Vivian. What can you tell me about what went on here tonight?" said Gustavo, waving his hand to break her staring at the crime techs.

What can I tell you? she thought, Almost nothing.

"Okay. I came home from being out, pretty much all night, and found the house torn apart and Chase lying there dead." A tear broke on her cheek. She wiped it away, streaking mud.

"Where were you all night that you got this dirty?" asked the young officer, looking her up and down. Her clothes were covered in dirt.

"Well, it's kind of a complicated and long story."

Gustavo looked at her with a serious expression. "I like stories."

As Vivian tried to decide where to start, the lights of another patrol car, this one unmarked, fanned across them as it pulled around the corner.

A plainclothes officer–fortyish, tall, and fit–stepped out of the sedan and nodded to Gustavo, then Vivian. A gory knob adorned his forehead. He extended his hand to the girl, smiling as warmly as he was able. "Hello," he said.

"Jesus, what happened to you?" asked Vivian.

"Hazards of the job," said Jim.

"Wait up, Jim," said Gustavo. "You ain't homicide."

"Take it up with the Loo," Jim said. "Wanna call him? Didn't think so."

Gustavo clicked his tongue, then motioned to Vivian. "Vivian Cartwright," he said, "girlfriend and roommate of the victim."

"Detective Jim Garrett," said Jim, grabbing Vivian's hand, "I'm sorry for your loss."

"Mm. Thanks," responded Vivian, flatly. The ambulance arrived seconds later, and two EMTs, a male and a female, jumped out. They had no trouble identifying Vivian as the caller and rushed to assess her.

Jim had no choice but to look on as the paramedics checked her out. After sizing up Vivian for a few minutes he walked into the home, greeting those already inside.

When the paramedics were satisfied, Officer Gonsalves asked again.

Vivian managed to belay him, telling him that the story was so intricate she wanted to tell them both at the same time. Gustavo said that she'd have to tell it several times at a minimum. This was, after all, the murder investigation of her lover, wasn't it? Still she refused, and, after groaning about it, Gustavo fell silent. Finally, Jim emerged from the cottage.

It was time to tell them something. She hoped it was good enough as she watched the mortuary team roll Chase's body out of their house.

Her tale began with the people who shuffled by in the night, setting the whole thing in motion. After that Chase had gotten separated from her when she had been chased by the people, but it was so dark she couldn't recall anything about them. She'd been a little buzzed, and when she escaped the crowd she'd gotten lost among the winding canyons around the golf course. When she came home, Chase was dead and she called the police.

They pressed her for any details of the crowd. How many were there? Height? Race? Sex? Anything?

"Sorry," said Vivian. "It all happened so fast. I really can't remember."

Officer Gonsalves closed his book. "Do you have someone you can stay with?" he asked.

"Yeah. I need to get out of here. Can I go now?"

"Go where?" asked Gustavo.

Vivian screwed up her face. "None of your business, officer."

"Okay, whatever," he said. "I'm just trying to help. Jim?"

Detective Garrett eyed her with suspicion. "No. I'm done too. You need a ride?"

"No, it's just up the hill. I'll walk."

"I don't think that's advisab–," Jim didn't bother finishing his sentence, as Vivian had already left. He watched her round a building, out of sight.

She walked quick. The bar she was going to was just at the top of the hill.

"Bye, Gus." Jim pulled his car out in the opposite direction and looped around the long block. As he approached Vivian, walking towards him on the sidewalk, he turned his lights off and slowed to a crawl, rolling down the window. When he stopped, Vivian stared down the barrel of Jim's service revolver.

"Hey, smartass," he said, "get in the fucking car."

Vivian looked up and down the silent street. Her hand hovered over the door handle before she jumped sideways and dove behind a parked car.

As Jim popped the cruiser in reverse, lights appeared behind him. Vivian watched from underneath the car as he put it in drive. The cruiser's tires very slowly pulled down the block. When he turned right, she heard his motor rev hard. He was coming around again. She got up and fled across the street, jumping through the bushes between two apartment buildings. She listened to his motor roar around the corner as she ran toward the back. The shared yards were thick with plants and trees, then opened up into a pathway between the stuccoed buildings. She thought she saw a person behind a bush, but when she blinked she saw it had only been the bush's shadow.

She kept going, toward the alley, walking between two old garages surrounded by trees. The walk seemed longer than the block it was on. It didn't make sense. Her hands trembled, and she tried to still them. Through an opening in the trees, a staircase led down to a swimming pool reflecting the half moon. A warm wind carried the scent of desert herbs.

"Hey, Vivian," said the Lieutenant. "How's life as a CI?"

She jumped, scared. "Damn, man." She was shaking. "What are you doing here?"

"Standard contact protocol," he said.

"Jesus. Well, yeah, it's a little more than I bargained for."

"Sorry about that."

"Nobody said Chase was gonna die. That wasn't part of the deal."

"I know," he said. "That wasn't us."

"Fuck. Who was it?"

"We're working on it."

Vivian didn't feel reassured, and that feeling multiplied when she saw a figure in the shadows descending a staircase.

• • •

After Vivian gave him the slip, Jim drove to the crime lab with the evidence. He dropped it off to Rory, saying he needed a rush job for the Loo. He paused, looking at an empty bottle of Skipper's vodka standing between vials on a metal tray. He thought of trying to grab it, but Rory wouldn't stop looking at his knot on his forehead, so he left the lab, firing up the computer in his office.

Vivian Cartwright. Chase Edwin Drake. Who were they? Why did the Loo care so much? After coming up empty, he returned to the lab.

"Got any results?"

Rory jumped when he heard Jim's voice behind him.

"Oh, hello, Detective Garrett," he said, wiping sweat from his brow. "Yes. The blood pool matched the contributor of the hair sample taken from the Golden Hill residence. Chase Edwin Drake. Thirty-one years old." He showed Jim the matching signatures on the screen.

"Now, the vomit is a mix of turkey, potatoes, Mr. Drake's blood, and bile and saliva contributed by someone unknown. No match."

"So, nothing," said Jim. "Crap. If you figure anything out, you call me immediately, you got that?" The vodka bottle wasn't there anymore. His stomach tightened.

"Okay. You got it." Rory sat down. As Jim walked out of the lab, he opened another folder on his computer. The one that showed Jim Garrett had a blood event with crazy Garth, the drunk from lockup. He bled. Garth bled. What happened then? Now, Jim shows up to investigate Chase's death. Jim wasn't even Homicide. And now the bottle with the drugs and the other substance the gas chromatograph/mass spectrometer was having trouble with.

Rory opened Amy's folder from Craig James' house, where Detective Figgins got attacked months ago, and checked the signature of the attacker. As he thought, they had a match to the Golden Hill murder.

The fucker's all over the place.

In his mind's eye, he could see tendrils begin to connect with each other, the cases being drawn together like a spider's web. He thought about transferring back to Chula Vista's smaller but less dysfunctional crime lab.

• • •

Back in his office, Jim got an idea. Running Vivian and Chase's names through the search engine at the same time, The Skeez came up. There were two incarnations of the band. Stewart Zanderson, at one time a suspect in the abduction of Clementine's son, was in the first and not the second. Couldn't be a coincidence.

Following up with the other band members, Jim found out that a year ago, months before Clementine was reunited with her son, Stewart and the rest of the band had had a disagreement, which led to Stewart's ouster. He'd also gleaned that Vivian had been Stewart's girlfriend before going out with Chase.

He ran a check on Stewart Zanderson. DNA on file. Drunk in public a while back.

Jim licked his lips. Stewart Zanderson. Revenge murderer? As he was about to go find Stewart, his phone rang. "Garrett."

His Lieutenant spoke from the line. "Jim. I need you to check out a couple things from evidence."

"Sure thing. Now, though? I just got a lead on that homicide in Golden Hill."

"The band guy?"

"Yeah, is there another?"

"You tell me. Anyway, first I need all the evidence from case #274b brought to my office, then you can get back to that."

"The warehouse case."

"Yeah, there's a weapon. A knife made out of stone."

"I remember," said Jim. "No evidence it was used for anything, though, as I recall."

"We got some new intel. We need the blade."

"From who?"

The Lieutenant paused. "A confidential informant, Garrett."

"Of course, sorry."

"Yeah. And one more thing. May be related, maybe not. Cold case. Same C.I. told us of a murder from '98. Man found bludgeoned in alley. Common-law wife at the time was cleared for lack of evidence, but was a really good suspect. Need the whole box from 137-7."

The case rang a bell. "That common-law wife wouldn't be named Helen, would she?"

"How'd you know?"

"Just a hunch. I'll hit evidence." As he hung up, he could see connections forming. He hoped his own ties to this case weren't nearly as visible.

Jim punched the code that unlocked the steel gate to the evidence room. After two lefts and a right, beneath the yellow and dying lightbulb, he pulled box #274b from the top shelf. It felt light. He pulled off the lid and saw why. The stone knife was missing. The manifest said it should still be here. The lieutenant wouldn't be happy, but then again he rarely was since returning from his vacation to Rosarita. Seemed pretty uptight. He'd gotten a deep golden tan, though. You'd think he'd be pretty relaxed.

He hurried down the hall to box 137-7.

24.

"Who was that girl?" Peik pointed in May's face. "Enough lies. You were speaking to her."

"I really don't know," May answered. Vivian had come out of nowhere, and now had disappeared back into it. "Her name is Vivian, but I barely know her."

He leaned down, quivering with energy, and stared into May's blue eyes. "Yes, you do."

She closed them, trembling. Peik, with a firm hand, reached out and pried one open with his thumb and middle finger. She tried to look straight up into her eyebrows. With his index finger, he touched the corner of her eyeball, squishing and rotating it down until she had no choice but to meet his gaze.

His skin moved, rippling. The effect increased until his face appeared to bubble, then boil with a visual dissonance, rendering his features a blur. The boiling gave way to the birth of hair-like tendrils snaking their way out of his pores. The effect was nauseating.

When they had grown an inch, they shimmered and waved in unison, smoothly migrating to the center of his brow, where an electric blue filament grew. Each hairlike thread that was absorbed thickened the stalk. Soon his face was clear, but for the one filament, poised like a cobra.

The snake-like thread shot down and struck May between the eyebrows. She was paralyzed as it wormed its way into her most private thoughts. Memories blended together, obscuring events from her past. Her own ideas were cast aside as it violated her mind with its groping. Time had no meaning, only the nausea which controlled her.

After an eternity, she could feel them retreat. She gasped, trying to breathe, to remember how. Her thoughts had never been so murky.

"She wasn't lying, they aren't aligned," said Peik as the tendrils absorbed back into his skin. He took one step backward, then swooned as if caught in a wave. He steadied himself, then sat down in a chair. His breathing was rapid and beads of sweat covered his skin. He wiped his forehead. He'd pushed himself too far. Twice in one day. This didn't used to happen at all.

May's vision blurred, the entire room swayed, and against her wishes she slipped beneath the blanket of sleep. The action had taken its toll on her as well.

Nuala watched May drift to sleep while Oliver scampered over to the kitchen and returned in front of Peik holding a glass of water.

"Hm." Peik took the glass and drank, emptying the cup. "It makes no difference," he said. "Marie will have her back here soon, and then she will cease to be a problem."

"I'm glad you're so confident," said Nuala.

His breath was coming back. "Marie is a damn sight better than the ridiculous innocents that you and Frank spent all those worthless hours trying to corrupt. That, my dear, was his downfall. Always with the experiments, those Rawls boys. Too much 'why', not enough 'how'."

Nuala sighed. "The experiments were Jeb, and my, ideas. And good ones. Frank's downfall is that he wanted to have little girl slaves, but I always thought for a criminal enterprise, you need criminals, not babies."

"Ha, I guess we'll see how it works with your young, suggestible street hoodlums before I buy completely in. But enough of that," he said, rising from the chair and shakily walking to the window. He felt better, but still needed some time after the strain the probe put upon him. He breathed deep, looking out into the dark canyon.

Raul saw Peik's knees wobble, and turned his eyes to May. She was breathing regularly, her skin returning to its normal rosiness. Her eyes were closed, hopefully only sleeping. Whatever the pale man had done to her scared him. Though she hadn't yet been hurt, this was his fault, and he vowed to get her out of here or die trying. Satisfied of her health and safety for the time being, he cased the room. Nuala and Oliver had their eyes glued on Peik as he watched the canyon. Behind his back they gave each other a look. It was one that Raul had no trouble deciphering.

He opened his mouth to speak, but at the sound of his lips parting Oliver dashed from Nuala's side and stopped in front of him, smiling through his yellow teeth and shaking his head.

Peik saw the reflection in the window and turned to see Oliver about to bite into Raul. Instantly Peik vanished, then appeared in front of Oliver and pushed him backwards.

"Vile creature. I should end you before you ruin everything." Peik swooned, more pronounced this time. He felt sick.

"Oliver!" cried Nuala. "What are you doing?"

Raul seized the moment. "She's lying, she knows. They were going to try something. On you."

Peik turned to Raul, head at a tilt. "Do tell."

Just as Raul began, thick black smoke spilled from beneath the door to the hallway, swirling in a tight column before molding into the shapes of Marie and Julio. Julio, breathing heavily, was covered in blood, and cradling Marie in his arms. Her body hung limp, arms and legs splayed on the ground.

"We lost them in the caves," he said. "Marie's unconscious."

Peik hobbled toward them, eyes glued to his daughter. A blur raced by him. Before he could react, he saw it was Oliver, rushing on all fours like a dog, complete with trails of saliva running from the corner of his mouth. In a snap he was on Julio.

Julio turned to brace himself, but Oliver was already wrapped around him, jamming his sharpened fingernails deep into Julio's neck, then twisting and ripping out a chunk of flesh. Blood pooled up in the wound instantly.

Julio pulled Oliver's hand off, ducking down and throwing the boy. Oliver sailed over Marie and slammed upside-down into the wall. As he slid down to the floor, Julio counterattacked, getting his hands around Oliver's neck. It was hard to keep a grip with all the blood. Julio opened his mouth wide, and a hollow sound came from the pit of his stomach, creeping and low. Smoke drifted, binding Oliver.

As the black cloud enveloped him, Oliver spat into Julio's open mouth, sizzling when it hit. The smoke recoiled as Julio choked. Water brimmed in his eyes and he held his throat. Free now, Oliver craned his neck and bit down.

Guarding Marie's body, Julio lurched backward, avoiding the snapping teeth. Oliver leaped over him and bit into Marie's shoulder. Oliver's face went rapt. Julio slammed into him with his shoulder, knocking him off Marie and onto the ground.

"Enough!" Peik's voice, full of authority, crashed around the room in waves. Julio halted, obeying. He wobbled, covered in his own blood.

Not listening, Oliver used Julio's complacency to his own benefit and rose from beneath him, crouching into a ball and exploding with such speed that he was already curled around Julio's head and sinking his teeth into his ear before Julio could respond.

"Oliver! Stop this instant!" screamed Nuala. It seemed Oliver, one of Frank's final experiments, had finally risen to the point where he wanted to run the show, just like Frank had. Only Frank was dead now. If Oliver continued, he might be as well.

Dark blue tendrils began to snake from Peik's palms. He saved these for the most dire circumstances.

"I can get him to stop. Give me a chance," Nuala said, voice breaking.

"Too late." The tendrils shot out, flying like arrows at the thin boy.

Oliver, his teeth like a vice, swatted Julio's flailing hands away and pushed against his head. Blood came down in a curtain as his ear began to rip off. Too much blood, Julio thought.

Peik's tendrils made contact with Oliver's skin. Oliver's muscles tensed, and he released the ear with his teeth, but still had an iron grip with his fingernails cutting into Julio's scalp.

Desperate now, Julio landed two blows to Oliver's kidneys. No effect. Oliver turned his head, gurgling blood from his mouth, and gripped one of Peik's tendrils, pulling it toward his mangled teeth and biting down into it. His eyes rolled back into his head as the tendril split apart and its electric juices oozed down the spidery boy's esophagus.

Peik wailed in shock. The little mutant had caused him actual pain. It had been a while since he'd felt this much. His tendrils waved in the eddying currents of the room.

Julio landed a solid punch to Oliver's face. His expression didn't even change. He jerked his head forward in a blur and sank his teeth deep into Julio's neck wound.

The blood was charged with a powerful taste, like the atmosphere itself was bottled up in it. Oliver drank greedily, knowing he may get sick from the glut of blood, but not caring. The only thing that mattered anymore was the delicious and invigorating life-force filling him. It tasted so different from the burnout guy.

Julio's body wavered, smoking, but Oliver hummed low as he drank, and the smoke turned back to flesh, now grey and wrinkled. Ashen.

Peik was weak, watching Oliver feast on the blood. By the time Julio realized what was going on, his lifeless body had fallen to the ground. Oliver let the bloody corpse slip from his grasp, then crawled over to the woman lying beside him.

"No!" Peik let loose with a blast of tendrils with all his remaining strength, something he was remiss to do as it could leave him so vulnerable. This was no time to quibble, however. The filaments zipped to Oliver's body and wrapped around his limbs, neck, face, everywhere. They picked the boy up and slammed him against the wall. Bones audibly broke. The window smashed, falling on the rocks in the canyon.

Through the blanketing tendrils emerged a thin hand, then another, and a foot. Oliver twisted and fought until at last he fell out and hit the ground running. Peik's final blast of filaments whizzed by him as he made it to the window and leaped out into the darkness.

Peik and Nuala ran to the window, looking out into the blackened canyon. Nothing stirred, not even a leaf rustled in his wake. Somehow, he'd vanished without a trace.

Peik was furious. "What," he asked, "was that?"

"I truly don't know," Nuala said. "He's been hard to control since we left the warehouses, but this is ridiculous." She looked at Julio's body. Next to him, Marie groaned, stirring.

From beyond the grave Frank Rawls still fought. One of his final experiments had just murdered one of Peik's new minions.

"It most certainly is." He turned from the window. "You," he said to Raul. "What did you see?"

Raul's eyes darted between them. "Nothing. was lying."

Peik was contemplating. His brow quivered. "Clever, are we?" He knelt down and felt Julio's neck for a pulse. He found none, as he suspected. Most of his blood was on the floor or in the belly of Oliver.

Marie opened her eyes, and saw Peik kneeling down over her. "What's going on?" she asked, "Did Julio get her?" Her last memory was of Vivian in the tunnels. Part of her was still there.

"No, child," said Peik, cradling her head.

"I'm sorry," she said.

"No, Marie, I'm sorry."

That was unexpected. Why should he be sorry? "What do you mean?" Concern was etched on her face. "Where is Julio?"

The bond of the maker machine had united Marie and Julio since their transformations. A string of consciousness connected them. With this news something hollow, like a dark echo, brewed in her center. She propped herself up on her elbow and looked at his body, splayed on the ground with a dark trail puddling from his neck. His skin was blue and bloodless.

Her thoughts ran in dizzying circles. "How?" she asked, standing up.

"Oliver."

"And where is he now?" She rubbed her hands together, trying to bring feeling to her numb fingers.

"He got away, unfortunately," Peik saw her eyes glow brighter than before. "We'll deal with him later."

"I'll deal with him. He's mine," said Marie.

"Well, okay," said Peik. He hoped her hubris didn't lead her to her demise, but she seemed determined. "Not yet, though. There are other things to attend to." He motioned to the instruments.

Marie walked around Raul, bound in the chair. He looked up to her face and she smiled at him. Though he was frozen in shock, he found his mind on a slow breeze, lofting him skyward. A suit of cottony clouds snuggled his skin.

Her features softened, she was the only person there. The only one that mattered. She made him forget May was in the room. Made him forget everyone was in the room, or that there was even a room.

Marie picked up the silver flute from the tray behind her and held it in front of his face. "You want to join me, don't you, Raul?" she whispered, slowly and softly. A dulcet monotone.

Raul had never wanted something so much in his entire life. She drifted upon silver clouds, face lit by dawning sun. Her glow was peace, happiness.

"Yes," he answered, through a filter of dreams. Marie's eyes glimmered hot blue as she opened his mind, probing.

"All you have to do is renounce the bond that you made with this silly whistle. It's a matter of what you want; to come with me and drift on clouds, ruler of your domain, or a whistle."

"I want to go. I want to rule."

"Good. So say it. Say 'I renounce my bond with the flute.'"

"Yes," said Raul, dreamily. "I renou–"

"Raul!"

May's voice slapped him back. Raul opened wide his half-lidded eyes and saw her screaming. He looked at Marie and recoiled. Her honeyed expression changed to fury. She slapped May in the face, hard.

Raul snapped out of his stupor, launching himself backwards when he saw May assaulted. As he fell, the chair hit Marie. She lost her grip on the flute, which skittered beneath a table. When Raul hit the floor, a leg broke off the wooden chair and the slack in the ropes gave enough room for him to wriggle out within seconds.

Peik, ignoring his weakness, leaped toward Raul.

Raul rolled to the side, ropes hanging like limp spaghetti, and Peik missed. Raul scrambled for the flute. Peik was inches behind him, and Nuala was closing from the side as Raul brought it to his lips.

Slowly. A thought came.

He blew a long, steady note, and the world ground to a halt.

Peik and Nuala were stuck in midair above him, moving so glacially they appeared frozen in time. Marie stood like a marionette with the strings turned to stone.

Raul, continuously blowing, twisted and turned his body, writhing until the remainder of the ropes had almost fallen off.

"What the fuck?" May's voice spoke at normal speed.

He looked at her, but couldn't answer. He had to keep going with the note. Only one knot remained, slung around his shoulder. As he switched hands the note ceased. In the fraction of a second where it paused, Peik and Nuala fell toward him. He blew again, and they slowed, inches above.

Intention. The word tickled his mind. His grandfather used it all the time.

Understanding, he breathed in a circle through his mouth and nose so the note stayed true. Untying the ropes from May's chair with one hand as any accomplished thief could, he freed her in no time. She grabbed the bag and silver chime, then they ran out the door. The flute's slow, steady note lasted until they were down the street, where, finally short of breath, Raul had to stop blowing. They found themselves on a curving street with one side disappearing into a steep canyon. As they left the road, spiky branches jabbed at them along a thin path.

The stars twinkled around a crescent moon as they slowed, feeling their way through the dark bushes. Raul pushed a branch out of the way and led May down to a dry creek bed. As her eyes adjusted, May could see a pathway to the left, about eye-level. She scrambled up the ridge, holding on to roots to balance until she had both feet on the trail. Raul followed, barely able to see through the thick bushes.

From behind them, a whirring neared. May gasped as a small, dark shape glinted a speck of ruby light. She shielded her eyes as it shot up into the air, then descended in a flash of red and landed on her pinky finger, chirping. May brought it closer, and saw a hummingbird.

Somehow, some way, the bird made her forget her situation and smile.

"Zif," it said.

"May!" Raul roughly whispered. "We gotta get going, vamanos!"

The little bird zipped in front of Raul, twittering a long succession of clicks and chirps, then zipped down the trail, halting in midair a dozen yards away, looking back from the tunnel of branches. Its throat glowed as it bobbed up and down.

"Whoa," said May, "What was that?"

Raul's brow was furrowed. He felt out each word. "Zif said, to follow it . . . down to the cave . . . of the Bear Mother . . . and that she will protect us."

"That little bird is Zif? And it just said that to you?" she asked.

"She. Yeah. It was more like emotions or something. Fuck, I don't know. What do you think?"

"Who's the Bear Mother?"

"No idea."

"Fuck it. Let's go." May nudged him. "Better than those dudes."

"Yeah," said Raul. "Maybe."

The tunnel of plants twisted and turned, ending at a stone stoop at the entrance of a tunnel covered in roots and vines. They followed the chittering hummingbird down into the blackness. A dusty breeze flowed from somewhere below the earth, carrying with it the smell of dried herbs and cold stone. May kept one hand on Raul's back, unable to see. Raul's foot slipped, and they nearly collapsed before May caught him and held him up.

She squeezed him a little. He knew. They were glad to have each other.

Green glowing lights pulsed up ahead. They rounded a final curve, saw the light coming from the tunnel's end, and entered a massive cave. Its stone ceiling arched high, and the openings of several other tunnels lined the walls.

Squinting, they observed ribbons of green light running like fluid along veins in the stone. May was breathless, looking up to the cave ceiling. The hummingbird hovered high in the middle, and May focused on it as she spun in a circle. It was warm. Dry. Smelled like a bed of sage.

Raul cleared his throat, and the hummingbird chittered. Still spinning, May slowed down and lowered her gaze. When she had stopped, she jerked at the sight of an old woman staring back, flanked by a thin and very serious looking teenaged girl and a huge, muscular man. Behind them, a massive and ghostly bear shook dust from its fur. The red specks hovered in the light of the cave, like stars in the air.

"Uh, hi," said May, backing up. "How's it going?"

"Come," said the old woman. She turned and entered a smaller cave to the back. The girl and man stayed put as the bear let out a growl. The hummingbird flew to Raul and May, chittering.

"You still understand that thing?" asked May.

"Yeah," answered Raul, his eyes glued to the bear. "She says we should follow."

May sighed. "Well, should we?"

"Guess so." Raul looked at her. "Whatever happens, you are an incredible girl, uh, woman. And, uh, I think, well . . . "

As his voice drifted off, waiting for the words to come, May pulled him closer, wrapping her arms around his neck.

"Shh," she said, kissing him. "I know." Her breath hitched as they followed the group into the cave.

"Play the instruments, please," said the woman. She sat across from them with her back against the huge bear's belly. Beside her sat the girl with the intense eyes.

Raul found it difficult to meet the girl's gaze, but May was taken with her, so much so that she almost didn't hear the woman's request. Raul cleared his throat.

"Wait. Why? What's going to happen when we do?" asked May.

The old woman had eyes of stone. "It is good to question. Things will be set in motion. Your music will call those tainted with the silver."

"Tainted with silver? Called to us? What is that?"

"The blood silver is a means of control."

"Control of what?"

"A great deal," the woman said. "That is what we are doing. Taking a count, and perhaps a harvest. It will be . . . monumental."

May sighed, turning to Raul. "Alright, dude." She shook the chime side to side.

Raul nodded, put the flute to his lips. As his breath entered it, a great wind howled from the other end into the larger cave, shaking the air in tight waves. From the center of the tone came a ring. Its pitch rose higher, blending into the warm air.

Raul and May looked out. Tendrils of silvery dust vibrated, a cloud in the eye of the swirling wind, then whooshed out of the tunnels along the great cave's base. Stretching trails shone in their stead, then faded until the green lights pulsing on the cave walls were the only illumination.

25.

"It isn't fair," said Buddy between bites of his sandwich.

Myron shook his head. "That word, and that attitude, are for the weak."

Buddy, since the time of his captivity, had been wild and free out in the canyons. After being reunited with his mother things had gone pretty well. He loved her, and they had bonded. In that time, Buddy hadn't heard many bold statements directed at him such as the one by Mr. Fox.

"I'm not weak," he said.

"Then don't act like it. If you think you're a man, then be one." He walked to his own son, resting on the couch.

"How?" asked Buddy.

"Well, first of all, listen to your mom," he said. "If she says you have to stay, that's what you do, and without complaint. You may think you're smart, but your mom is smarter. So's Helen, and me."

Luna and Grifter followed Myron's gesturing hand around in the air, like he had a bone for them. Myron noticed them, adding, "And possibly the dogs."

"What's with this guy?" Buddy asked Helen.

Helen shrugged. Finally someone besides her and Buddy's mother thought the kid was a little too cavalier, and a man was saying it to boot. "Listen up to the fox man, Sugar," she said.

Luna barked.

"Shit," he said. "Okay, then."

"That's another thing," Myron continued. "The language. I agree with Miss Helen that it's a fine tool when used in an emergency. But here, among friends, it is not what we want to hear. Plus, if you use them too often, like any thing of power, it lessens the venom considerably."

Buddy let this thought roil around in his mind.

A crack, then a clatter came from behind the house. They looked up to see the monster, Crazy Garth, smashing through the back fence. The creature immediately rammed its face into a low-lying branch of the almond tree, which broke off and flew across the patio into the furniture set. The monster fell backward, and its body shook the the house when it fell. It groaned, trying to stand on its bullet-riddled legs, but they slipped from underneath it.

The long, solid note of a whistle filled the air with a silver ring, reverberating upon itself like a never-ending echo. Buddy felt a call, a stirring inside his spirit. He had no choice but to follow. But then the voice spoke within him, repeating Myron's words.

Lessens its venom considerably.

He concentrated on the black metal cones that drank of his spirit, thinking of how often they had done so. Each time, the cones seemed to have a diluted effect, until at the very end he'd gained a level of tolerance, and they affected him so little that he'd been able to conspire with Ysenia and escape the warehouse.

The combination of the tone and the warehouse memories made him feel murky, lost. There was something he was supposed to do, right? He looked at the large woman standing next to the man on the couch, watched her pick him up and hold him in her arms. Buddy knew her. Who was she?

The glass door to the back patio erupted into shards as the monster smashed through, roaring. It searched, darting glances from Helen to the coat rack.

Luna and Grifter ran between the beast and the boy, erupting in a stream of barks and growls. Hearing Luna's voice, Buddy's mind cleared the mist away that enshrouded it. He felt clear as he watched the crippled monster scan the room with its one working eye, a cold black orb. It faced the hook with the leash and ball hanging off, limping toward it, head cocked to the side.

"Get back, child!"

Over Myron's protest, Buddy sped to the leash. The monster's fist swung, whizzing inches from his head. He pulled it from the hook, but was stuck in the corner. Grifter saw this, and charged, biting into Garth's calf. The monster shook its leg and Grifter spun across the floor and into the wall, but it worked. Grifter hopped up, unhurt, as Buddy used the diversion to get around the monster and retreat near Myron, who swept the boy behind him.

"Come, Xorro," Myron said. Dark grey smoke curled from his sleeves, spilling beneath his crisp suit and forming itself into the fox.

Xorro, trailing smoke, launched into the air and landed on the monster's chest and shoulders, clamping her jaws down on its neck, then reverting to a column of smoke that hovered around its head.

The monster's attempt to punch the fox with an uppercut instead whiffed through the smoke and blasted its own face. Its head snapped back, and when it got its bearings again it was furious. It ran toward Buddy, sending the dining room table and chairs clattering to the side with one sweep of its arm. It reached out its hand and grasped the leash, hanging around Buddy's shoulder like a sash.

Buddy was jerked off his feet, flying toward the monster's gaping mouth, twisting and turning. Just before the creature swallowed him up, he managed to untangle himself and squirm enough to fly past its face, landing on his hands and knees.

The monster charged Buddy, and the dogs attacked. Luna zipped to the beast's injured foot, the one loaded with shrapnel from Clementine's gun, and sunk her teeth into the flap of skin trailing around its ankle. When Garth was alive Luna had bitten his face, and the acrid taste had made her almost lose her grip. Now was far worse. The taste of the man remained, but accompanying it was the flavor of corrupt flesh, made more pungent with the black mucous that gurgled into her mouth.

The creature didn't feel the teeth, but the flesh stopped ripping near the Achilles Tendon. As it caught, the creature tripped and crashed at Myron Fox's feet. It felt like the house had left its foundation.

"Stay behind me!" Myron yelled, corralling Buddy.

The creature was working to right itself, not an easy task for a four-hundred-pound dead thing. Buddy peeked around Myron.

Xorro, coming back to form, lessened Myron's solidity, one they shared. Buddy stared through the smoky haze of Myron's torso at the monster, realizing Mr. Fox would provide scant cover now.

"No, Xorro!" shouted Myron.

The fox, torn between protecting her master and listening to his voice, hesitated, and in that moment the monster managed to stand up, gurgling black pudding from its mouth. It hobbled toward Buddy.

Luna and Grifter charged in unison from behind, but the beast turned and swept its arm, hitting both animals and sending them sliding across the floor. Nothing stood between Buddy and the creature now except the ghostlike figure of Myron, still waiting for his smoky fox to join him.

Xorro finally saw, dissipating on the spot. Her smoke shot back into Myron, who solidified just in time to take the full brunt of the monster's fist. He crumpled to the ground.

The monster stepped over him, lumbering toward Buddy.

Buddy laughed. "There's no way you can catch me, you shithead."

It lunged, swinging the leash, but Buddy was too quick. Spinning to keep sight of him, it tripped on its own legs and smashed its temple into the corner of the butcher's block that separated the kitchen and living room. Black blood splattered on the wood, and it slipped to its knees. It raised its head, opened its mouth, and coughed. Black mist sprayed at Buddy. He dodged it, and when it hit the floor it smoked.

"Get away from it!" said Myron. "It'll burn you."

Buddy backed up and saw Helen and Gray walk out the back door. The monster inhaled, ready to spray more acidic spittle.

"What about them?" Buddy pointed at Helen.

"Hide, I said!" He shoved Buddy and faced the monster, arms in front of his face.

Luna and Grifter shot to the boy's side.

He pushed them behind the couch. "Stay."

Buddy knew he should listen, but Myron was moving slowly. He was hurt. The monster was going to kill him, and Buddy didn't want that. "No," he said. "We can take this guy. I did before."

He dodged to the left and the monster spit. It was far too slow to hit Buddy, but it melted into the couch, smoke rising. A flame trickled before Buddy picked up Myron's glass and poured it on the hot spot.

As the monster watched the steam, it tried to stand, but the damage to its bones made it no longer able to hold up 400 pounds. Its ankle snapped. The foot stayed planted as the leg popped off its base, sliding along the floor with a dark smear while the creature did the splits in a puddle of its own muck, holding Buddy's leash.

"See?" said Buddy. "Told you."

Facing Myron, the monster spat a great gout, lighting-quick. Myron twisted his body, but not enough to completely dodge it. White smoke poured off his shoulder from the acid burns.

Myron yelled at Buddy. "Arrogant child! Do as I say before you get us all killed!"

Buddy listened, retreating into his Mom's room with the dogs, shutting the door and pulling the chest of drawers down in front of it. Luna stood below the window, barking.

Following the dogs, he leaped out the window and ran down the paving stones on the side of the house, heading toward the path he had seen Helen carrying Gray, and saw a glimpse of their forms disappear over the cusp of the hill.

Just as he was about to run after, Luna whined. It was beyond their control right now. Escape was the priority.

Mind your mother.

He nodded, understanding. There was a time to follow, and a time to fight. And, like now, there was also a time to run. Flanked by the dogs, he sprinted toward the street. They hopped the fence in the far corner, avoiding any line of sight from the front door.

"Mom," he said aloud, running down the dark street, "get back home."

25.

Sitting in a puddle of its own filth, the monster had quieted. Outside, Myron heard the sound of a stone dropping into a pool.

Behind the monster stood a pillar of smoke, metallic and black. The air sizzled with charged molecules, swirling, then slowed, revealing the rag-clad body of Abraham Blackwing. He fanned his hand through the air, blowing the smoke away, and clocked his tongue as he walked toward the monster. Flicking a thick finger on top of its skull, he blew a smoky ring. It elongated into an oval and whisked up the great beast's nostrils. The monster ceased moaning, ceased moving, and awaited its next instruction. Dead eyes stared blankly at Abe.

"Myron, brother," said Abe.

"Hello, Abe." Myron gestured to the table. "Please."

As they sat, Abe chuckled. "So, are we all set? Damn that smells awful."

"Indeed. Not long now. I trust everything went well?"

"Well enough." Abe pulled two stone knives from his poncho. The monster swayed toward them, magnetized. Abe shook his head and it looked back at the floor.

Myron eyed them. "And it's going to work?" The blades pulsed, opaque light beating like excited hearts inside them.

"I believe so."

Myron looked serious. "Better than your grandson's theft, I hope."

"Ah, the unpredictability of youth. It all worked out, though,"said Abe, smiling as usual. He held the knives aloft. "Now, the words."

• • •

Gray blinked his eyes, trying to clear the murk clouding them. A big and beautiful woman set him down and walked alongside him, her face expressionless. Within his core a spark began. He knew this woman, but who was he? If he had no identity, how could he be sure of this connection? Behind the clouds, the rays of the moon broke through and fell upon them. As they hit his face, something triggered.

Wait.

He remembered a baby fox cub, running through the pines. A larger fox, identical in its markings, came up and touched his nose. Wake up,

Gray, it said. There is work to do.

Gray, he said to himself, that is who I am. The gray fox, silent scheming, loyal love, roots below, cloud above.

The scene shifted again. The larger fox sat beside a huge black bird inside a cage while a rabbit ran with dogs and birds around the outside. Behind them, bruised clouds circled, an approaching storm. The fox and raven, upon Gray's closer examination, were sitting on the struggling body of a toad-like creature. The toad would eat the world, and everyone in it.

Two glowing spires, small yet brilliant, shone near the toad.

Gray cleared his throat. It was hard to get any sound to come forth, but eventually he succeeded with a deep crackle. The vision dissipated.

His mind was far away, an echo of itself. The moon shone through the trees as he stood in front of the large woman, rubbing his hands together, then touching her behind both ears simultaneously. "Relax, Helen, and listen."

That was her name. The words came easier now.

She obeyed. The sounds of the world spoke to her as his touch melted into her skin, seeping through muscle and ligament, organ and bone. The silver ring bled into the ethers, and the milkiness began to drain from her eyes. As it swirled and diluted, she looked at Gray, slowed, then stopped.

He smiled at her. "Thanks," she said.

He felt alive. Invigorated. "Of course."

The leaves above them rustled, and the shadows twisted into a black, feathery smoke. Dropping to the ground, they gathered into a stout human shape.

Abe smiled and blew the remaining smoke from in front of his face. "Hello, friends," he said. "How's things?"

"Hello, Abraham," said Gray. Helen nodded.

"Helen, my dear. What is it about you? You smell so delicious, like secrets buried in sage. What's the big secret?" He stuck his nose close to her face, grinning, then backed away.

"Honey, I'm just tryin' to do my thing. Ease back."

"Yeah." He nodded. "That's it. Ease back. Not too far back, though."

Abe turned to Gray. "It is time, my boy, for the next step." He reached into his poncho and brought out the stone blades, offering them. "To slay the toad." The knives glowed, feeding off each other's energy.

"Yes . . . the toad." As he grasped the handles, his hair stood on end.

Abe laughed. "It must be done."

"Yes," said Gray. "It must."

"Wait." Helen grabbed for Abe's wrist, but her hand whiffed through, trailing smoke.

Abe laughed, fading from view. "No waiting! This is only the beginning, my dear. But time is running out. Gray's time is now. Haha! See you, secret-keeper lady." He unravelled into a smoky column, streaming back through the shadows to Clem's house.

"What the hell?" said Helen.

Gray touched her shoulder. "This is my duty. Thanks for looking out for me."

"But what is it?"

"I am to transform. Like he said, 'the next step.' I slay the toad, then protect the boy. It's the way."

"I'm going with you."

"No. It must be done by me alone. You have another mission. Listen and wait. You'll know when you hear it. If I don't make it, please tell Amy what's happened." His eyes brimmed.

Resolved, Helen stood back. "Okay," she said, sniffling. She watched him disappear, surprised at his agility so soon after being near death. He had been so weak. A sigh escaped her lips as she leaned back to look up at the moon.

Everyone has secrets, but not so big as mine.

She touched her hands to the course earth behind her, and could hear the grains rub along one another. She felt her consciousness pull along the surface, drifting in a circle among the hardy brush. Roots pulled her spirit down, gripping cracks in the eroding stone. She was the roots, the stone. The dust and the spiny branches were as much a part of her being as the body that lay above. Perhaps more so. This was a new level.

Expanding, she also felt herself drift up into the night air, parts of her gliding on gentle, eddying currents of wind that swept through the canyon. Up into the surrounding trees, tall eucalyptus from a world away. From a branch hung a sac made of grass and small branches. Patterns. As Helen's spirit snaked through the tree, the eyes of a hummingbird opened. It clicked its tongue and flew from the empty nest, the mother's young having grown up and flown away. From within the mist of her growing being, Helen observed the subtle intricacies of the nest, perfectly placed bits hanging down, strong enough to support a mother and her young. Strong enough to trust.

From there, she turned her focus from on high into an umbrella-like array. She thought of Max, her secret sharer, naturally. But also of Cora, and the emotions she birthed. Helen honed in on the female vibrations, separating them from the others. After a brief period, a frequency, came to her, as individual as Cora herself, and Helen smiled with satisfaction. Lines formed on the map of her understanding. She recognized their tint.

Cora was headed here. With Stewart, and Max.

• • •

When he had been pierced with the silver and maple tantō, Gray's spirit was sucked into the blade, where his existence was an illusion. He couldn't remember his captivity, nor did he ever want to. Only a cold feeling, a taste of metal on the back of the tongue, remained of that time. His body, having been violated by the blood silver, would never fully recover. He would never overcome its call. He knew that may not be true for all the metal's victims, but in his core he knew it was for himself. The blade was special, and Garth was no more a monster than he was.

He saw other parallels with Garth's monster as well, clear as day. Another path, then. His father's manipulations. Amy, Buddy, Clem, everyone had been touched by his father's wiles, making his ideas seem their own. Gray felt trapped by the genetic maze.

But right now, this feeling was the opposite. This was freedom. His life-force riding along the pulses of growth, of the very air currents sweeping through the canyons, mesas, mountains. Their powers swirled and embraced him, gathering. Electric energies sent rippling arrays off his body in preparation for a battle with another undead monster. Traces of the half-death, the tantō's ethereal ribbons, wound through his being.

It all leads to this moment.

26.

"Hey Pearl."

She jumped at the sound of her name. It was Eddie. "Hey yourself," she said.

"I heard you might know who did that prank on me a couple months ago."

He didn't need to clarify, everyone had been talking about it since it happened, and they both knew it.

"Mm-hm." Pearl said.

He was speechless, not expecting that.

She pulled a pack of gum from her jacket and popped a couple pieces in her mouth. Pearl was twelve, but she looked about nine, and acted about twenty. She chewed her gum and unlocked her bike, then sat on the seat and looked at some birds on a telephone wire, twirling one of her black braids around her finger.

"Well, you gonna tell me?" he asked.

"I guess so . . . " She paused, pushing his buttons. "I heard Lalo Alcaraz's little brother had his car messed up the night after your deal."

"So?"

"So you guys were hanging out in the canyon with the big oak right? Left a bunch of trash there probably, even though it's gross, right?"

"Whatever, yeah," said Eddie. Little butthole younger than he was, trying to tell him what to do.

"And somebody followed you and left all your trash at your house. Not too hard to figure out, Eddie. Some people care about shit." She wondered why anyone listened to this idiot. "Anyway, Lalo's brother Julio, the car guy, was spray-painting trees about a hundred yards from your trash pit, drinking forties. Not only was his car sprayed with his own tags, but the broken glass from the beers was poured in his sunroof."

"So probably the same guy," said Eddie.

"Probably. Or some other person who thinks people shouldn't be leaving their garbage and stupid gang tags in the canyons."

"Whatever," said Eddie. "You know who it is?"

"Yup. Julio saw him. It's that little kid with the dog. The cop's kid."

"How do you know that?" Eddie asked.

Pearl's face wrinkled. "He was around for a few days with that skinny black dude and the big white lady who hang out over there," she said, pointing down 25th Street to Golden Hill Park. "Before the big case broke."

Eddie's mind flashed to the canyon. The blonde woman. Connections. Control. He knew exactly who she was talking about. The blonde lady wanted him to snatch the kid. The same kid. He got a sick feeling thinking about the spider's web of coincidence.

"No reaction? You really don't pay any attention to the world outside of your little group of tough-guy friends, do you?" Pearl shook her head, disappointed. "The cop's kid. Huge case. On the news?"

Eddie snapped out of it. "I know about the cop's kid. The fuck you think you are, talking like that to me, Little Crow?" He cracked his knuckles, glaring.

Pearl walked the bike backwards until she was in full view of the clerk inside the store. "You're over eighteen, dude. I'm twelve. You freaking touch me and my brother will beat your ass, then you're going to jail. Plus I'm trying to help you, so mellow out."

He couldn't shake the blonde woman's face. He had to calm down before he compromised his mission. "Yeah, okay." Eddie breathed deep like the dipshit counselor at school had taught him. In. Out. Slowly. "So where's the kid?"

"I don't know. After everything went down a couple months ago he hasn't been around anymore. I did see the big lady once a few days ago, though. You should ask Julio. At least you two macho pricks could cry on each other's shoulders if you don't find him. Maybe a couple blow jobs."

She flipped her braids and pedaled away as she finished the sentence, just fast enough so he couldn't catch her.

"You keep talking shit and I might not go to jail, if they don't find your body." Eddie yelled after her. "Little Orphan Annie lookin' like motherfucker."

"It's Pippy Longstocking," Pearl shouted back, "And I'll tell my brother you said so!" She raced down the alley.

Stupid. He'd let her get him pissed. But his head was spinning.

Rick was the beefiest guy in their circle, and the closest thing to a best friend Eddie had. Though Rick and his sister traded barbs, he probably wouldn't take too kindly to Eddie threatening her life. Besides, their older brother Raul was some kind of local Robin Hood. Now he'd probably have to apologize to Little Crow. Ugh.

When Eddie reached Julio's, his brother Lalo was in the yard, looking inside of Julio's car. Most of the paint was gone, and patches of primer covered it.

"What's up, fool?" said Lalo, recognizing Eddie.

"Save it, dude. I know we're not friends, but I think we have a mutual enemy."

"Is it why my brother's not around?" said Lalo. "He was supposed to meet me three hours ago. Second time in a couple days."

"Maybe I can help," said Eddie.

"Oh yeah?" He took a swig of beer. "How's that?" He offered one to Eddie, who cracked it and told him about the kid.

• • •

Three blocks after leaving Lalo, Eddie rounded the corner of a house with a high fence and ran straight into a woman. His beer can dropped to the ground and rolled, spilling in a line until it stopped in the short grass next to the curb.

"God damn, lady," he said, his eyes following the can, then moving to her face. "Watch where you're go–" The words died on his tongue.

"Eddie," said Nuala, voice flowing like silk and velvet. "Did you find him?"

His hostility drained. Into its void poured lustful obedience, libido shrieking in anticipation. Here they were again, he and the woman who would guide him to an awakening. He knew this down to the cellular level. "I'm working on it."

"I know. I'm going to help you." She stroked his arm with her finger. "I've got something else to give you."

Where she touched him burned with sweet fire. It was as if every pore reached out for her. He'd been with a couple girls from his high school, but they'd never made him feel like this. He'd do anything for her, and she'd barely contacted his skin.

"Yeah. Okay," he said, his voice far away. His hand slipped into hers, and he lost himself inside the colors.

Minutes later, he came to. They were sitting on a log at the bottom of a small canyon. The woman had a sly smile on her face as she put the blade back in her bag. It was amazing.

Eddie grabbed the bottle and took a swig, doe-eyed. He reached out for her long neck, but as his fingers were about to caress her, she looked at him and made a low humming sound. His muscles froze, locking tight, heart constricting in his chest.

"What—"

"Hold on lover boy." Her soft voice spoke.

A glint of panic. He tried to move, to no avail.

"Not until you find him. But you're in luck. I know where he's going."

He swallowed, forcing it down, then was able to speak. "Why can't you get him, then?" His defiance crept through.

"Oh, I can't go there, honey. I need help," she purred, leaning forward and cradling his face in her hands. "And you can give it to me."

Sweat beaded on his skin, and his pulse quickened as Nuala leaned forward and planted her silken lips upon his, kissing him softly. His heart began to thud, a jackhammer he was sure the entire world could hear, and his pants tightened. Nuala's hand drifted down and lifted his shirt, touched the scar below his ribs, then brushed up to his chest, just over his hammering heart. He could feel their pulses match. His frozen body melted in her heat.

Eddie would kill or die. All for her. Today. Now.

"Not yet," she said, taking her hand away. "When we have him, then I will show you pleasure you've never dreamed of."

Eddie, groaning, couldn't wait to get started. He would get the kid, then he'd have her. Two of the things he most greatly desired, like it had always been so.

• • •

"Help you what?" said Rick, cranking a bolt on his sister's bike. "I'm not gonna kidnap a fucking kid, man." His deep voice boomed in the garage of the house he lived in with his sister and mother. "And you shouldn't either."

"Keep it down, dude!" Eddie bugged his eyes out, emphatic. "I need some help, here." He looked around for anyone listening.

"Man, first of all, Pearl told me what you said to her. That's not fucking cool, at all. That's my goddamn sister, shithead."

"I know, I know. I'm sorry. But she was pushing my buttons. I swear. Called me a fag."

"She use that word?"

"Not exactly. Hinted at it. She pissed me off."

"Yeah, she can do that," Rick said. "But you're still gonna have to apologize to her before I even talk to you about your shitty plan I'm probably gonna say no to."

Eddie sighed. "Okay," he said. "Where is she?"

"Right here," Pearl said from behind him, making him jump. She tried to appear nonchalant, looking at her nails,.

"Jesus," said Eddie. "What the fuck, Little Crow?" From the corner of his eye, he could see Rick stand up, and shifted tactics.

"I mean, Pearl. Pearl. You scared me," he admitted. "Anyway, Pearl, I'm sorry I threatened you. I won't do it again, I promise."

She stared, weighing her options. Something was different about Eddie, but in order to see what was really going on, she'd have to play along.

"Okay," she said. "I forgive you, I guess."

"Thank you," he said, then waited for her to leave.

And waited.

Finally, Rick said, "Pearl, could you leave us alone, please?"

She grunted, flipping her braids and walking out of the garage. As she rounded the corner she scampered to a vent on the wall near the ground and listened.

"So what the fuck? It's the kid who dumped shit on your porch, why don't you just beat his ass? Why do you need to kidnap him?" said Rick. "Dude was on the news. He's a fucking Detective's kid, for chris-sakes."

"We'll get a reward," said Eddie.

"How much?"

"Uh, five grand."

"For real? From who?" he asked.

"An anonymous benefactor. Who cares? it's five grand."

"Sounds like a terrible idea all around. Like a really bad idea. I'm out."

"Please? The lady said he'd be hard to catch without help."

"Lady, eh? So that's who. What lady?" Rick looked at him sideways.

"The lady with the money."

"You realize if we get caught, we not only don't get that cash, but we go to jail for a really long time, right?"

"I've got a plan," said Eddie, eyes on the ground.

"It better be good."

"It's foolproof."

"Fuck," said Rick. "If I help you, we'll be splitting that reward money." Rick finished the tune-up and stood Pearl's BMX up against the wall. "Fifty-fifty."

"Of course."

"Of course," Rick repeated, eyeing him. "So what's the plan?

Where? How?"

"He lives off Gregory Street. Canyon house. And he's there right now."

"How the fuck you know that?" Rick looked perplexed.

"Same way I know anything else; the lady," he answered. "So let's go."

Pearl hid in the bushes, waiting until the rumble of Eddie's engine faded down the street before running into the garage and hopping on her bike, all tuned up and ready to go.

The area Eddie had described was in a dense knot of streets, many dead-ending against large canyons. Getting there by car took a good knowledge of the area, or a map. Her brother and Eddie knew them well. This was close to their neighborhood, and they'd lived here forever. Still, you couldn't drive straight there, the route was circuitous.

Getting there was easy on a bike, though. The canyons had pathways perfect for Pearl's little BMX, and she'd know them with her eyes closed. She pedaled up and down the craggy hillsides, dodging the cacti and other thorny plants whose locations she had memorized, desperate to reach the boy before they could. Her brother did a good job. Her bike was tuned up and hauling ass.

She'd gotten a bad feeling from Eddie's conversation with her brother, like something terrible was going to happen. She liked the boy, or would if they got to know each other. She could tell. Pearl didn't like many people. Plus, what kind of future detective would she be if they beat her to the kid?

• • •

Eddie and Rick crouched on the sidewalk and peered through the thick plants between the fence and the house.

"Can you see anything?" Eddie asked. "I got nothing."

"Nah," said Rick. "This is shitty, dude." At first the money and excitement were alluring, but the closer it came to being real, the worse Rick felt about it. His grandfather wouldn't want it going this far, would he? "Let's get out of here while we still can."

"Man, this is like, a doorway. An opportunity to be involved in something. I thought you'd want something like this."

"Something like kidnapping a kid because some random old lady said so? I don't think I want anything like that. I'm out of here. Peace."

He turned to walk away, but Eddie grabbed his arm and spun him back around. The look in Eddie's face was manic, possessed. "She's not a fucking old lady, you crying pussy," spat Eddie. "And that little fucking dick of a kid is going to get what's coming to him. Just like you, bitch."

"Get your fucking hand off of me," said Rick, jerking his arm away. "And fuck-o, the next time you touch me you better be ready to eat your fucking teeth, then we'll see who's the bitch."

Rick outweighed Eddie, but Eddie had a boxer dad who wasn't afraid to use his skills on his boy. Several had translated into Eddie's acumen. Rick backed away.

"Don't fucking snitch," said Eddie, smiling sideways. "We wouldn't want anything to happen to Pearl."

Without a word, Rick ran at Eddie, ready to rock, but before he got there Eddie hopped over the waist-high gate and disappeared around the corner of Clementine's house, headed toward the back yard.

He knew Eddie was trying to lure him in through anger, which by itself wouldn't work. However, Eddie was getting dangerously out of control, and the threat to his little sister had Rick worried. Plus, if he knew Pearl she was going to show up here anyway. Shaking his head, he slipped around the opposite side of the house. If Eddie didn't blow it on his own, he might have to stop this crap. There was no time to get Grandfather.

At the side window, Rick looked into the living room. He could see Eddie, face transfixed, through the rear window. Craning his head around the curtains, Rick followed Eddie's line of sight to the obese man with tattered clothes sitting on the floor. He was wounded in several places, and oozing a blackish pudding onto the tiles, propped against a butcher block cabinet in the middle of the floor.

Its black eyes blinked once, or else you wouldn't know it was alive.

"Shit," Eddie whispered. It was only a faint sound, almost lost on the breeze, but when Eddie made it the monster swung its head around and roared, seeing Eddie through the doorway. Its voice was a gravelly thing from between the worlds of the living and the dead.

Another sound behind him, and Eddie turned his head. Through a hole in the back fence came a man holding two stone knives which glowed in the moonlight. Glints ran along their edges. He moved like a ghost on the wind, effortless and swift. The man's skin was pulsating, like it was lit from within by some sort of rippling electricity trying to get out.

27.

Gray ran through the doorway, leaping in the air, a knife in each hand. The monster was quick. It ducked under the blades and swung its fist. Gray contorted, but the blow nicked his foot, sending him spiraling through the room. He crashed awkwardly onto the kitchen floor. As he stood, it bashed its shoulder into his kidneys, driving his face into the wall. Pictures fell from their mounts, and the green blade fell from Gray's grip, clattering to the floor. Gray couldn't turn around; the monster had him pinned with its belly in his back, raising both fists into the air.

Gray swung an elbow into its ribs. It stumbled sideways, and Gray jumped out of its grasp. Clutching the gray knife, he faked to the left, in line with the monster's working eye. It bit on the feint, and he spun around to the blind side, burying the knife to the hilt between its ribs.

Its screams were sonic as it tugged on the blade's handle. It wouldn't budge.

Gray stayed in the monster's blind spot as it turned, creeping along until he located the green blade. Picking it up made the light in its core shine brightly, and the monster snapped its neck around, focusing on it. From its mouth, black sludge and bile dropped onto the floor, chemical smoke drifting off their sizzle.

With its eye on Gray, again it pulled at the knife handle, but the blade had fused to its flesh. Its severed foot flopped around, attached by a small strip of connective tissue. It spat at Gray, who put his hands up. Blue steam whistled off his skin, but when it cleared, there were no signs of burning. As he inspected his hands, the monster charged him.

Gray braced himself, knife held rigid, but the monster moved like a blur, hitting Gray's hand and sending the blade flying into the corner. As it smashed into him, Gray rolled backwards along the floor until his head slammed into the wall. The monster took two steps and jumped on Gray, landing with its ass on his ribcage and slamming its fists down. Gray blocked them, with his forearms, and a stabbing pain shot up to his shoulders.

The monster gurgled, and a gout of chemical spittle poured onto Gray's face. "Aargh!" he screamed, pawing at it.

Myron rose from his chair, but Abe clocked his tongue. "Mustn't help him, friend. It won't work that way. We've worked so hard. Let it happen."

Myron sat down, growling.

The creature gurgled again, readying.

Gray's skin was pink, but the acidic spittle hadn't broken through. He didn't know how many more burns he could take. As the monster opened its mouth, he pushed his feet against the wall and the monster slipped, ramming its head on the ground. The force sent Gray sliding along the hardwood floor toward the green blade. As he stretched for it, the monster, halfway standing now, lost its footing and flipped forward, above Gray.

Gray rolled out of the way as the monster's body hit the floor, its heavy impact sending him airborne. He landed on his feet, then, knife in hand, lunged at its eye.

With surprising speed, the monster cricked its neck, and the blade swished inches from its face. Then it snapped forward and bit down on Gray's bicep. He could feel the undead bacteria burst into his bloodstream. It was all he could do to hold on to the knife as he tried to shake out of the beast's grip. Its teeth cut deeper into his arm, scraping the bone.

In desperation, Gray pressed his arm close to the creature's face, then wrenched back. A large chunk of his flesh and muscle stayed in the beast's mouth, and his body began to tingle with a necrotic frequency. His electric glow dimmed.

He backed away as the monster spit the mouthful of bloody muscle to the ground. Gray pointed the knife in its blind spot.

It punched perfectly on the knife's tip, between the third and fourth knuckles. Pulling back, it looked at the knife fusing to its flesh, bubbling and hardening into a bulbous mass.

Its scream was cut off midway as its throat collapsed upon itself. Ribbons of flesh peeled off and fell to the floor. Black muck bubbled from the wounds, which started as slits, then burst open in long lines from its head to its feet.

The creature clung to its half-life, panicking as its body split into long strands and turned to an ooze on contact with the wooden slats and stone tile. The black puddle bubbled and boiled, foul vapors drifting on the air.

From the muck rolled two silver streams, magnetized to Gray. One touched each foot, instantly absorbing into his skin. The silver light brightened, pulsing beneath his skin as it coursed up his legs, through his manhood, and into his torso, neck, and head. He became so bright his features blurred. The toxins released into him by the monster were sought by the silver in his blood. He could feel them altering his genetic makeup. His whole being tingled with a metallic fire.

He blinked, and when he opened his eyes they were filled with complex and intertwining visions. Patterns. Gray watched webbed ribbons scrape the sky as his mind slipped into a different place. The puddle of the monster quivered on the floor. Gray could see the bones inside turning to jelly. He looked to his father and Abraham, who both appeared as shapeless blobs of energy. One greyish-red, the other black and metallic. The world around him moved in radiant waves, like fields of wispy crops rolling on a sentient wind. Burnt ozone permeated his nostrils, his lungs. His skin vibrated at a new frequency, pore by pore changing into something even denser and harder than before, armored like the shell of a beetle, yet supple and malleable.

Tar seeped into his organs, his muscles, veins. The dead energies of the monster trickled upward into his grey matter. Gray Matter. Between the light and the dark, the day and the night. His stomach turned in wet knots, and he vomited, cramps forcing him to his knees. He coughed and dry-heaved, unable to catch his breath, until he finally hacked up a glob of liquid metal. It shimmered on the ground.

The monster is me.

Like veins, another map grew in his mind's eye. Multi-colored lights twinkled along lines through the darkened canyons around them. Colors of web connected the neighborhoods and streets. So many webs, their number was overwhelming. He tuned his mind to the frequency of one that connected to all the others.

The child was walking into danger. The dogs might not be able to help him.

Leaving his father, he walked out the window and through the yard. The web was evolving, bringing a new wave. With that evolution would come games for control. The old guard would not like fresh blood pursuing the power that had been theirs for so long. And now people were making monsters.

Like him.

Gray walked into the canyon. The breeze blew through him as ancient harmonies played in his mind. The plants stretched out to touch his skin, sending him messages as he headed for the caves.

He was the walker between the worlds.

• • •

Inside the house, Abe smiled. "I told you."

"Yes. It seems to have worked." Myron wiped his brow. "So far, anyway." He stood, nodded to Abe, and walked after his son.

Abe watched him, an amused grin on his face, then rose from his chair and followed Myron as far as the back fence, where he turned to smoke and billowed up the tall trunk of a Torrey Pine.

• • •

Having seen things he could never explain, Eddie ran low to the ground through the front yard, jumping over some bushes to the neighbor's yard rather than hit the sidewalk. He crouched down as the sound of a motor purring along the street. Ducking beneath a parked car, he tried to hide, but the car in the street braked and idled alongside him. A door opened. He heard the clip clop of heels on the street. Heels that rounded the car and stopped.

"Get up," said Nuala. "Time's a-wasting."

Two blocks later she located Rick, who, after some persuading, got in the back seat.

28.

The dogs inches behind him, Buddy made it over the fence and cut left. Halfway down the block, Luna growled. He swung his head around saw blue headlights piercing the darkness, and ducked beneath a bough of overhanging bougainvillea, cloaked in shadow.

"Luna," he whispered, "come here!"

Grifter whined. Buddy turned around and saw someone ripping down the dark sidewalk on a bicycle, their body behind the parked cars and out of the headlights. His synapses fired. Luna growls at car, Grifter whines at bike, bike avoids car. Just as they had popped off, the bike came to a stop right in front of him.

"Hop on," said the girl with the black pigtails. "You gotta get out of here."

Buddy looked at the bike, then the girl, then took off running so fast it seemed to her that he'd completely disappeared. It was only from the dogs tailing him that she knew which way he'd gone.

"Shit," Pearl whispered, the headlights just missing her as a beat-up blue sedan came to a stop in front of Clem's house. She whipped her bike around, staying low and pedaling hard, hoping she could catch someone that fast. Two blocks later she heard a song. A woman's voice sang a simple and sad tune that rode upon the wind. Pearl followed it up the sidewalk until she saw the boy standing next to a trailhead above a canyon. The dogs were far behind him, sprinting to catch up.

The song grew louder. It felt like it was inside her brain. Pearl had to stop riding and put her fingers in her ears, the pressure building until it seemed she'd explode. The boy stood straight, lowered his hands to his sides, and waited. His posture looked different. Submissive, maybe.

A black convertible sports car pulled up, and a woman in black clothes and dark hair got out. Her eyes shone like blue lights as she guided Buddy, singing the hypnotic song, never letting the notes slacken.

With the dogs getting closer, she shuffled Buddy into the car, then hopped in and sped off. The dogs chased the car until they went over the ridge of the next hill, and the song faded.

Pearl was hot on their heels, pedaling like wildfire. "Wait for me!" she yelled, knowing they wouldn't listen. She was out of breath already, and needed to think. But there was no time.

She cut into a canyon, using her best guess as to where the car was going. As she rounded a group of bushes, she could see two trails up the hill with the car zipping down the street at the summit. On one of the trails ran the two dogs, dark streaking shadows.

Coming the opposite direction of the singing lady's convertible was a speeding vehicle that looked like an unmarked police car. As it flashed beneath a streetlight Pearl saw a woman's face inside. The police lady from the news; the kid's mom.

• • •

Inside the car, Marie whistled while breathing in and out through her nose. She looked at the boy beside her, his muscles frozen stiff. Nuala had taught her the song, said she knew it would work. Her father would be proud of her again when she brought the kid back. She wondered why he had Nuala tell her, rather than doing it himself, but as long as there was a plan to get on his good side, she was all for it.

Since Julio's death, she found her mastery of the web was growing rapidly. Beyond even when she was transformed through the machine. It was as if Julio's spirit was blossoming within her. It felt right. Her breath hitched. She chuckled, satisfied for the moment. The sky was the limit.

Buddy's consciousness swirled, as if playing an obscure dream on a loop. Nothing was clear. He was a rabbit held captive by a vibration. The sound of blackened silver scraping across a chalky plate caressed him with its chaos.

But then the sound stopped for an instant. He opened his eyes. Smelled the desert air. And he knew.

In the brief silence, he slapped Marie in the face and pushed the steering wheel hard to the side, aiming for a tree. As they sped toward impact, Buddy crouched down on the seat. Then, just before it hit, he leapt straight up in the air, flying past the tree as the car slammed into it. Marie's head rocketed into the steering wheel, splattering blood on the dashboard.

Buddy, mind moving at a full clip, rolled expertly along the grass. When he stood, he hightailed it down the street, so fast he was like a streak.

Marie picked her head up, wiped the blood out of her eyes, and found herself looking at the owner of the tree her car was smashed into. She started the car again while the man in his bathrobe looked at her in shock. His startled eyes met her glowing blue ones, and he forgot why he had come outside. Lights on the surrounding houses began to come on as she peeled off of the man's lawn and sped after Buddy, singing the Song of Control.

Pearl rode on the street with no sidewalk, and saw the kid running toward her, then suddenly move slower. She heard the woman's voice and the kid came to a complete stop. Over the hill's cusp, she saw the convertible streaming back. Without a second thought, Pearl pedaled hard toward the boy and skidded in front of him. She pulled and pushed him until he was riding her crossbar side-saddle, his stiff body propped against hers, then hauled ass down the street.

The car was gaining on her, she could hear it but didn't dare look back. The street cut to an "L" ahead, with a small trail into the wide canyon between the guardrail and a mailbox. The pathway zagged to the right and wound along a cliff that dropped nearly straight down. When Pearl reached the curb, she pulled as hard as she could on the handlebars, lifting up the front of her bike, then thrust her weight backwards as the rear wheel hit. It worked; her bike stayed low to the ground and she dropped down the trail just as she heard the car hit the curb.

Hugging the bike to the cliffside, she braked hard, looking up at the underside of the convertible flying high above the canyon. It came down hard on its nose, then flipped forward, coming to a rest right-side up with a snapped axle.

Buddy woke up on her handlebars, and before Pearl could respond he wriggled out of her arms and tore up the path toward his house. Pearl followed, falling behind. She knew where the kid lived now, though.

• • •

Marie hurt everywhere as she unbuckled herself and ran into the cover of the bushes. She'd screwed up again. Her father would be pissed.

She thought of Julio, and longed for him in a way that surpassed everyone, even her husband when she had first met him, before his transgressions and demise. A sadness overtook her. All this failure. But then she heard something. Julio's lost voice, stretching from the beyond.

I will guide you, Marie, it said. I am with you. We will prevail.

Deep inside, she knew their bond would stretch past the grave. It wasn't old, but it was deep. She let go of her concerns, and let her his presence guide her. She would prevail.

• • •

Clementine almost hit the black convertible speeding in the opposite direction.

"Fucking animal!" she yelled, middle finger out the window.

At the house, she ran inside. The place was torn apart with a puddle of sludge between the kitchen and living rooms. "Rupert!" No answer. Walking around the side, she spotted Rupert's shoe prints next to the dogs' claw marks in the dirt.

Panicked, she sprinted to her car and peeled out. One block later she had to slam on the brakes to avoid hitting the young girl waving her arms and sitting on her bike with Luna and Grifter behind her. The car skidded to a halt, missing her by inches.

Clementine threw her door open and ran to the girl, grabbing the handlebars."What's going on? Where the hell is Rupert?" she asked.

"Rupert's your kid, right?" asked Pearl. "A weird lady in a black convertible car just stole him. I got him back but he disappeared again."

"Shit! No!" Clementine said. "Get in the car."

She opened the rear door, but the dogs began to bark and wag their tails, running down the sidewalk. Pearl watched the streak coming toward them.

Clementine saw it too. "Rupert!" she cried. His name had scarcely escaped her lips when Buddy stopped beside the car.

"Mom!" he said. "They're at the house."

"Who are?"

"Abraham, and Garth. Myron saved me but Marie Stillwater kidnapped me and a girl . . . this girl, got me away from her. Thanks," he said to Pearl.

"You're welcome." Pearl smiled, batting her lashes.

Clementine's eyes seemed like they might pop out of her skull. She grabbed Buddy, hugged him, and shoved him next to her in the front seat. "You too," Clementine said to Pearl.

"No way," said the small girl. "I can't leave my bike." She picked it up and started pedaling back toward Clementine and Buddy's.

Clementine floored it past her. "What just happened? With Marie?" she asked Buddy.

"She trapped me with a weird song. When I had to run from the monster."

Clem was ashen. "Were they together," she asked. "Marie and the monster?"

"I don't know. Who can tell anymore?"

• • •

In the house, Clem surveyed the puddle of filth. Using a wooden spoon, she sifted through it, sliding an object out. On closer inspection, it appeared to be a bloated, purple foot with two bullet holes through it.

"Where's Gray?" asked Buddy. The house was empty.

"Gray has awakened." From the shadows off the back patio, a stout woman's figure walked toward them. "He walks between the worlds, toward a danger he has been made for."

They recognized the voice. Luna scampered to Helen and put her forepaws on her leg. Helen scratched her ears, then hugged Clem and Buddy.

"What are you talking about? What happened?" asked Clem.

"Many things. The monster's gone, but now there are others. We need to go."

"Where?"

"To the cave of the Bear Mother. Time is short. We aren't safe here."

"And we're gonna be safer walking through the canyons to a bunch of caves?" Clem was incredulous.

"I know it doesn't seem that way, but, yes. We are."

Clem sighed, then shooed the kids in front of her.

As they neared the back door, Buddy felt a small hand wind like silk into his own. He smiled at Pearl. "I'll take care of you," he said.

"I know." She kissed him on the cheek.

Clem looked the little girl up and down. Everywhere was suspicion.

"Now," said Helen, entering the canyon, "I'm going to give myself over to the call of the blood silver, and won't be able to speak for a while. Don't disturb me, just follow. It's the only way to find Ursula's cave."

The wind picked up, and with it came a distinct ring, high and light. Helen's eyes grew cloudy and her joints stiffened. She walked through the patio area into the canyon. Clem, hands on the shoulders of Buddy and Pearl, followed on high alert.

29.

Berserker fire had overtaken Stewart's mind. The taste of Garth's mutated blood let him see beyond the veil that separates the living and the dead. He hadn't been ready for this. A chill crept up his hand that held Garth's finger.

As he sprinted down the overgrown trail he could see a pink sheen over the living plants, mixed with blueish images where others had grown in the past, and for whatever reason had died or been chopped down. It was like a forest of phantoms drawing his attention. Seeing an oak right in front of him, he threw his hands up, and was shocked when he passed through the sturdy-looking thing. Plunk, tweet, chshhh. The rhythms continued, speaking to him, guiding him with their patterns.

He looked closer into the bushes and slowed to a jog. Hundreds of ghostly blue birds and animals sat deep in the foliage, following his movements with spectral eyes. They sang a droning song to the rhythms of the canyon.

The call of a Great Horned Owl startled him. He could see ruby trails of blood pulsing through it. The spirit creatures avoided the owl, as scared of it after death as they had been in life. Klia hopped low to the ground, skirting the tree trunks, wary eyes on it.

Stewart thrust headlong into the brush, racing along the faintly visible scent-thread left by Garth. Like a hound, he tracked the acrid stench, glowing blackish-brown among the trees. He could hear it. He could smell and feel it.

The path rose and fell along slippery sandstone, crossed a couple streets, then wound into an overgrown game trail. Squinting his eyes, he recognized Clementine's back fence, splintered apart on the ground. This wasn't good. He leapt over it. The line he had been following terminated amidst a puddle of black sludge.

Klia, still shadowing him, flitted from tree to tree and made a few clicks, perched well away from the house, eying the stinking goo. Stewart stood, mouth agape, drooling. After a long second she swooped down, landed on his shoulder, and rubbed her head on his cheek, cooing. The bird's trick worked. The dead blood's effect drained from him and he dropped the finger on the ground.

"Damn," he said. "Thanks, Klia."

"K-l-tttt-kk." She clicked her tongue and buried her head into the base of his neck.

Stewart felt heavy. The experience had been draining. Disgusting. He could still hear the faint beat of the plants and animals course through him. "I've gotta stay here. Can you go get Cora and Max?" he asked.

She gave two decisive click-chirps, then jumped off his shoulder, rocketing out the back door and down the trail.

Stewart walked into the house, carefully rounding the puddle of muck. When he stopped inside the living room, he squinted at a chair, approaching it slowly. The indentation in it was much bigger than any of the people's asses that had been in the house. He saw, trapped on the nappy upholstery, a solitary black feather, stuck between smoke and solid. He reached to pluck it off, but it dissipated and floated on the breeze that wafted through the house.

"Where the fuck are you, Abe?" he asked, focusing on the whiff trailing out the window, thin as a spider's web. Walking beneath it, he unfocused his eyes, peering deep and shallow at once, and could see it fade off into the trees. Stewart followed it, squinting so he wouldn't lose it to the night.

He tripped on a root. When he had corrected himself, he frantically tried to locate the smoke. It had thickened, and was circling upon itself, waiting for him, then it billowed up the branches of a tall Torrey pine. Looking through the tree limbs, Stewart could detect the shape of a burly man.

"I can see you, you know," he said.

The thing, more of a shadow, unraveled off its perch and spilled to the ground through the branches with a flowing grace, gaining substance as it landed on the bed of leaves. They crinkled, and soon the grinning visage of Abraham Blackwing looked back at him.

"Congratulations. What a treat." He propped against the tree, as relaxed as you please.

"Jesus, you're such a fucking prick," Stewart said. "What's your game?"

"Game? If you would have done what you were supposed to do, you wouldn't have to ask that question." He chuckled.

"What, kill Frank? No thanks. Even after whatever you did to me, I'm not about killing people." Stewart remembered the contradictory feelings that raced through him as he had stood over Frank Rawls defeated body at the battle of the warehouses. He'd barely fought off the urge to end Frank's life, a life that was taken by Amy shortly thereafter.

"He died anyway. Would you tell a hawk not to eat a pigeon? It's simply the laws of nature, Stewart Zanderson. Transformations sometimes cannot wait. You blew it, again. Gluck."

Stewart felt a shift, but Cora had prepared him for this. In his mind, he changed the frequency of the old man's voice. With the change in pitch the spell, born of Abraham's intention, lessened, then dissipated entirely, fog in a headwind.

"You're actually learning." Abe could see the effects, could feel them in his belly button. "Very good," he said. "Quick, too. Only took you an entire season."

"Huh. I'm still just an experiment to you after you ruined my life."

"You poor victim." He gave fake puppy dog eyes. "Please explain to me how I did that. Because, my simpering friend, if you look back you will see nothing but opportunity knocking on your thick skull. Haha!"

"Yeah, right." With the suggestion, his mind began to trace their relationship to its roots, despite Stewart's wishes. A flickering movie of memories. Fuck. Was he right?

Even at the beginning, twenty years past, Abraham had waited for him. But Stewart didn't show up, forcing the Raven to give his gifts to Nuala and Frank. They'd tricked him, sure, but that proved them to be more worthy of the Raven's gift. Stewart, try as he might, couldn't take umbrage with that. Abraham's pattern wasn't one of betrayal, it seemed. But it didn't matter how things seemed, only how they were.

"Is this another trick?" Stewart shook his head, trying to clear it. Was Abe trying to teach him something?

"Poor guy," said Abraham. "Poor, poor, poor man. Always so suspicious and paranoid everyone's gonna stab your back. Maybe I just like the shiny knives, or maybe I'm keeping them away from someone. Or perhaps they've served a beneficial purpose. You ever think of that? No. Because it's all about you."

"Fuck that. What about the monster?"

Abraham erupted in laughter. Stewart briefly entertained the idea of braining the old bastard with a rock before Abe caught his breath.

"The monster. Heh." He chuckled, wiping his eye. "I didn't kill him, I just got him away from my house. He might as well have a job.

"There's a game happening here, a struggle for control. Don't you want to play, Stewart?"

"Who are the teams? The Coyotes?"

"You know of the agents of chaos?" Abe smiled broadly. "Well, you seem to have everything figured out, smartie."

"Cora figured it out."

"Cora's a pawn, assigned by the Council to make sure I don't stir up any trouble."

"Maybe she is, and maybe she's not," said Stewart.

"You think you know her. That's so cute." He smiled, but wistful. "My world is coming to an end. The old way. It will be up to her, and to you, to see how the new one begins. More than either of you, though, it will be up to the children of Miguel Dos Santos. There are those who do not want the old ways to die."

"The Council?" Stewart asked.

"Certainly some of them, but the Council is never truly of one mind, despite how those at the top view it. Technically, I am on the Council, much to Golden John's chagrin."

"Golden John?"

"It shouldn't be too hard to figure out who he is, right Stewart?"

"The head honcho, then. And fuck you, you condescending prick."

"Think of the children," said Abe. "Glunk."

His mind drifted. Stewart knew how important Buddy and Ysenia were. Kids on the cusp of adulthood with talents that rivaled the ancients. Ancients who may want to end any threat to their reign. Still, hearing Abraham hint at his own demise was jarring. Stewart had come to accept an immortality to the old Raven Master, but what if it were something else? Maybe they just grow old very slowly, over centuries. Or maybe this older world really was morphing into a new era, like they'd all been saying.

"So what do we do now?" asked Stewart.

Abe started to fade into a smoky pillar. As huge black wings rose above his head, he croaked, "You're so smart, you figure it out, shitwad!"

Stewart raised his middle finger at the cloud as it drifted into the sky, listening to the throaty chuckle disappear among the branches. Naturally Abe had made him feel like an asshole. Of all the old man's skills, that was the most honed.

• • •

"Where's he going?" asked Max, racing to keep up with Cora, who sprinted through the bushes. Damn she's fast.

"I'm not sure, but I bet we find the monster there as well." She slowed, looking at a bush. Its leaves were stripped along one side, drops of wet sap ran from the wounds. "Clementine's house is this way."

Max walked around her, then stopped short.

Cora pushed him from behind. "C'mon, Max."

He didn't budge, taking up the gap between the trees. Cora couldn't see what was happening to him, but she could hear a light ring on the breeze. A bell, or a whistle. Maybe a combination. He turned and stumbled through the willow brush, sprawling on the ground, then righted himself with stiff movements Cora recognized.

She spun Max around and could see the milkiness covering his eyes. For an instant she listened to the pitch of the silver tone, then matched it with her voice. From there, she began to lower her pitch, creating clashing frequencies. The lower she went, the longer and more pronounced the soundwaves became, until her throat hit in the baritone range, and she could feel it in her bowels. She stared into Max's eyes, never blinking, never moving. She saw something there.

Max, from deep within a dream of silver water, felt the world rumble like the belly of a magnificent whale. The silver became white milk, which bled from his pores and turned to a vaporous cloud surrounding him. The rumbling wind pushed it away. It thinned like smoke, fading. The face that looked back at him was shrouded in darkness and making a tone that had him on the verge of crapping his pants. He was a sponge, and the voice wrung him of the silver's call.

"Cora," he said. "Stop. Please. It's over." He felt his knees buckle and sway, and the ground rushed up to meet him.

Cora caught him, her arm cradling his head. His ear landed on her wrist and he could hear blood pulsing through. She smelled of a million herbs.

"Got you," she said. "Relax for a second."

Max felt fatigue overtake him. He gasped for breath. She said something he couldn't understand, then leaned down and exhaled with her mouth near his. A feeling like wings of light fluttered into his lungs, uncomfortable at first. When his stunted breath was able to draw in once again, he could feel his being inflate. With the air came energy, buoying his spirit. All that had been opaque was clear, and he noticed details on her face he'd never seen before. He slowly rose from her lap.

Behind her, disappearing into the trees, a white canine figure trotted. Max stared, unsure if it had seen him. Though it was dark, he could see colors, shades he never could have picked up on before. He looked past her at a blue glowing trail of smoke, or dust, winding through the trees. "What's happening to me?"

Max, cool as ice. It was the first Cora had seen any worry on his face. Not that she blamed him. She had skills, taught to her by ancients in the craft, and that was still worth something.

"You are healing. Relax for a second. I've freed your blood of the silver."

"Thanks. I guess we should get going?" He started to rise.

"In a second," she said, placing her hand on his chest and holding him down. "There's something else, isn't there? Something you haven't told me."

"No." Max looked straight, his eyes fixed. "It's time to go."

"How long have you been with them?"

"Who?" Max stayed solid. "I'm not following you."

Cora shook her head. "No. You're leading me, in fact. You know exactly what I mean." Her face drew closer. "How long have you been with the Coyotes?"

"Now what would you say that for?"

"When I pulled the silver from you, I could see the connections to members of the Pack known to the Council, clear as day. A side effect, apparently. But there's no denying it. What are you doing with them, and why have you kept it secret?"

Max sighed. She was right. There was no denying it. He thought of Helen, and his cousin, Auntie Frieda, hoping he wouldn't get anyone in trouble. "That's how the three of us entered this world. The Coyotes helped us with a problem, then we were just in, you know? They taught us things, and we assisted them with their missions, which became our missions."

"What kind of missions? They're criminals."

"To you they're criminals, but you work for the Council, specifically for Golden John. He's trying to stop Buddy, stop the future. Stay mired in the past while the web passes him by. We are the agents of chaos, of change. That's why we couldn't tell you."

"And now?"

"No coincidences. Now it's time for you to join us. Help transition the world."

"No coincidences? I thought you were agents of chaos."

"Chaos is merely patterns that are not so easy to recognize." He smiled.

Cora was suspicious, but the longer she thought about it, pieces began to fall into place. "Who are the other Coyotes?" she asked.

"I don't know all of them. It's strictly splinter cells. Five at a time, more or less. Besides Helen and Frieda, I only know a couple people."

"Who?" she insisted.

"I can't say. You gonna turn me in?"

"Not yet."

"Then it's my turn. What is it with you and Stewart?"

"Hmm." She sized him up, reluctant to let the conversation turn. "I've been watching him since he was eighteen years old."

"The bet?" asked Max, referencing the wager Abraham Blackwing had made with Peik Stillwater decades ago.

She nodded. "A by-product. His life and my own were wrapped together before he was born, perhaps before I was. It was a job from the Council at first, monitoring the ridiculous wager, but then I had empathy. He has a good heart. Plus he's pretty funny."

"Yeah," said Max. "But not funny ha-ha."

They sat, looking off into the trees, smelling the warm night wind through the canyon. Cora broke the silence. "Let's get going, see how this all shakes out. How's your vision?"

To Max, the canyon, cloaked in the shadow of night, looked like daytime. "Fucking amazing."

They walked. She sped up then checked his progress. He nodded when she did, and they tore off down the trail. From up ahead, they saw a small shape flying in their direction. Klia called as they raced past her, then she swooped around and flew after them.

Max's breath came in deep and strong, filling his lungs, letting him run farther than he would have been able to go ordinarily. Damn, he felt good. His new breath was something else. They followed the tendrils of light, winding their way through the canyon and the patio to Clementine's house. A familiar figure stood outside the door.

"Stewart!" called Cora. "What's happening? Are you okay?"

He smiled warmly. "Hey, babe."

She ran to him. "Oh, thank goodness." She planted a kiss on his lips.

He hugged her back, tightly, letting her scents rush over him.

"Man, what the fuck happened to you?" Max was looking behind Stewart at the blackish muck that was sinking into the floor of Clementine's house. "And what is that shit?" he said, covering his nose. His heightened senses were on overload with the stench of death.

"That shit's Garth," said Stewart. "I didn't kill him, though. I just found him."

"Jesus. Where's everyone else?"

"That way. C'mon."

"But what happened?" asked Max.

"Not sure." Stewart shrugged. "It's just starting to happen, I think," he said, following Cora beneath the busted tree limbs. She knew where they were going.

Max could faintly see different colored threads trailing into the canyon. Rainbows of web connected everything. Shimmers ran down them like impulses firing along nervous systems. The sight was breathtaking. From the limb of a paloverde tree, Klia chirped, hurrying Max along from his stupor.

30.

In the lab, Amy stared into the vial. The silver swirled inside the blood, swimming in fluid knotwork patterns. The gel apparatus alarm went off, a high beep signaling results of the DNA test were done. As it rang, the silver stopped its dance and separated from the blood, hitting the top of the vial while the blood remained at the bottom. The beep ended, and the two parts mixed again. The silver stayed still for a moment, then resumed swimming like elongated tadpoles. Another beep, and they repelled one another. Something occurred to her.

On her phone, she downloaded a free keyboard application. While she waited, she looked at the vial. The silver had stopped swimming. It was pressed against the near side of the glass. Amy couldn't shake the notion it was looking back at her. Waiting.

On the keyboard app, she hit a note, much lower than the one from the machine. The silver separated. A pattern. A knot. Three corners. Simple and even. She hit two notes, and the pattern shifted. Eight sides. Complexities. She hit three notes, making a chord. Rings within rings, rippling. She stopped, looking into the vial.

Again the silver pressed against the closest side. Her backbone felt like ice.

She called Clem's house. No answer. Tried her cell. Voicemail. Not good. She leaned over to grab her car keys when, from nowhere, her eyelids grew heavy. She had been going for so long. She couldn't sleep, but maybe if she just put her head down for a second . . .

With lids barely slit, she saw the vial. The silver moved through the blood like waves. Amy loved the beach. Always would. She drifted away to the sounds of the surf, and the silver's mesmerizing movements.

• • •

The trees pulsed lights. Bark exoskeletons shone dull and transparent. Amy drifted among the live oaks and willow scrub, flying low. She recognized the dreamtime, and tried to look at her palms, the key to dream control, but found she couldn't rotate her wrists. She was conscious, but far from lucent. Small black feathers swirled on an ethereal breeze.

The trees rustled. A large hawk followed her with its eyes as she drifted along the dry, rocky wash. Around a copse of laurel sumac, three falcons sat on a dead branch. She noticed more birds of prey; on wires, cars, trees. Far too many. They didn't appear friendly. If they chose to, she was sure they could harm her. Kill, even.

The canyon ended in a fence, and Amy saw Clem's house beyond the thrashed patio. Two owls spoke to each other as she drifted up to the back door, shattered off its hinges. They sat just beyond the fence, as if unable to enter the yard. There was only one bird inside Clem's patio area; a ruby-throated hummingbird. It was perched on a feeder, still and calm. Amy put her face close to it.

Chick-wheet! It hovered, rising in the air until it was lost in the night sky. The birds of prey held their positions.

Something else rustled in the bushes. A fox cub, smoky and silver like luminous ink in the shadows of the bush. Something told her to not be afraid, and she reached her hand out to it. The small animal made of silver smoke stretched out its neck, sniffing at her hand. Amy touched it, and it dissipated into vapor and flowed onto her skin.

Part of Amy's being was pulled down along the roots and up through the limbs of the manzanita bush and live oak tree the fox stood beneath. It spoke, deep inside her dreaming mind.

I am the gray fox, it said. I will run with you through the fields.

Gray? thought Amy. Where are you?

I am with you. And also elsewhere. I am the Walker.

Amy began to cry. When she wiped the tears away, she walked toward the house, feet floating off the ground, wisping through the door. On the threshold lay a bloated finger, roughly hewn at the end. She reached down to pick it up.

This is what I would do if I were awake, she thought

She held it in her hand and observed it, then walked into the kitchen and pulled on a drawer, feeling its solidity against her fingers. It opened. Halfway disbelieving, she got a plastic zipper lock bag out and dropped the finger into it. She could smell things now.

Marveling at the feeling of actually being in the house, and not just dreaming, she continued. In the bathroom, she grabbed some swabs, then took samples of the spots of blood, the weird fibers from the couch, and the reeking puddle of black sludge between the kitchen and living room. cradling the evidence, she walked out the back.

Myron sat at the patio table. Klia chirped at him and jumped into a bush.

"You're getting pretty good at that," he said.

"Thanks, I guess. I don't know why, though."

"The raven's gift is becoming manifest."

"I never got a gift," she said, feeling the words stumble off her tongue.

"But you did, when you killed Frank."

"Why did it take–" she stopped. "Solstices and Equinoxes."

"Exactly."

"Shit. Just what I need. Where's Gray?"

"It has happened. My boy has walked between the worlds."

"What does that mean?"

"It means that he has gone into the next world, while remaining in this one."

"What? How?"

"By following a very complicated recipe which included defeating the monster," said Myron, pointing to the black puddle. "I wasn't sure it would work. It's almost finished."

"That's Garth?" She was mystified. "Wait. What would work?"

He stared at her. "You have to get back to the lab."

"I have to get back to the lab."

"Do tell." He snapped his fingers.

She picked her head up off her desk, and the plastic bag crinkled. It took a second to realize she was looking at several pieces of new evidence in her hand.

31.

Dazed and lost, Marie let the voice guide her. Behind some one-story stucco houses and down an eroding hill was a copse of trees. She saw movement in the shadows. A silver peal, smooth as silk, rang on the breeze. It piqued her curiosity. Surely this was from the flute, but where was it?

Turn here, said Julio's voice.

The pathway between the houses wound down a seldom-used trail separating two wooden fences with a strand of prickly pear cactus between them. At the end of the trail, near the bottom, she saw branches sway. Darkened figures walked through a small section of the trail in the center of the uncovered path, moving quickly. Stewart, Cora, and Max stepped beneath a moonbeam piercing the trees. Max eyeballed the bushes near her hiding place.

She crouched down beneath the fleshy ovals of the prickly pears, looking through a keyhole-sized gap as they disappeared into the trees.

Now, said the voice.

She obeyed, staying low down the dusty hill.

This way. It came from the right.

Turning her head, she saw a smaller side canyon, its entrance completely covered over with dense brush. Beyond it, she could see the tops of tall eucalyptus trees, silhouetted against the night sky.

As she rounded some brush a thin trail came into view. Doubt jabbed her mind as she entered a gap in the branches. How was she going to get the boy back and save face if she was headed in the opposite direction? But Julio, with a will so strong he instructed her from beyond the grave, must know best. Perhaps a shortcut.

Pushing the doubt away, she entered the eucalyptus canyon. The light was gone in this gully, plants much taller and the sides steeper. Marie struggled to see even a few feet in front of her face.

Closer. He sounded excited.

She pushed into the heart of a scrub willow, limbs growing together like a wall. She bent the branches back, listening. When she let go, they snapped into place, sticking tight, trapping her in a small clearing next to the thick trunk of a eucalyptus.

A thump sounded from the other side of the tree.

Deep in her mind, she tried to get the message out; Julio? Is that you? What should I do?

Her temperature was rising. Sweat started to bead on her skin.

Julio? Where are you?

A twig broke as the figure emerged around the tree's trunk. Marie found herself looking through the darkness into black orbs on a face that grinned with cracked, yellow teeth. The spidery teenage boy's mouth did not move as he spoke back to Marie, using the voice of Julio.

"Julio's dead, you stupid idiot," said Oliver, voice echoing inside her head. "Just like you."

• • •

"I wonder where Marie is," said Nuala, twirling her hair on her finger. "She wanted to be here for this."

"It is curious." Peik scowled. "Regardless, we need to get started." He shut the safe in Marie's room, handing Nuala a canvas bag that clanked.

Nuala followed him into the living room, where several young males stood in a circle. As she entered, someone palmed her ass. She twirled around and smacked the young man's face. "Fucking slime," she said. "Who are you? Why are you here?"

"Lalo Alcaraz, bitch. This dude invited me." He nodded to Eddie.

Nuala shook her head slowly, vision sliding between Lalo and Eddie.

Lalo looked at her, leering. "What?" he said, turning to Peik. "I grabbed a bitch's ass? You wanted some heavy hitters, and you're parading some fine old whore around here? I thought it was all good, like refreshments. Anyway, you got a problem, let's go. I'll fuck you up, old man."

Peik's tone was mocking. "Your terms are agreeable. I'll even give you the first strike for free."

"Well, get ready then bitch, 'cause here it comes." He cocked back and rocked a solid right cross to Peik's cheekbone. Peik's head didn't move. Lalo howled in pain as his middle knuckle compacted against Peik's skull. It jammed into his palm, all the way through his hand, puncturing the skin.

"I'll handle this." Nuala held a black cone in her palm. "Aash Kazhoul."

As she said the words, the cone glowed, only slightly, and Eddie Calhoun's eyes frosted over. On stiff legs he walked over and took it from her open hand.

Lalo cradled his broken hand, blubbering. "Hey, hold up," he said when Eddie got close. "What the fuck, man?" He began to struggle in earnest, but Peik grabbed his right elbow with one hand and forearm with the other, then jerked them both the wrong way. A muscle ripped in his arm as his shoulder dislocated. Peik put him in a sleeper hold with Eddie standing in front of him.

"Fucking Eddie! Fuck this shit! You fugugu–" His voice gurgled with blood.

Eddie slowly pulled the black cone from between Lalo's ribs. He'd buried it there so quickly the others only saw a blur.

Lalo folded to the ground, holding his guts as the blade clattered to the floor. Eddie vacantly walked to the window, staring into the canyon. Lalo breathed shallow sips of air on the ground, then coughed up a glob of blood.

"What have we learned?" asked Nuala, picking up the cone.

Uncomfortable murmurs floated around as Nuala held another black cone above her head. The jagged letters inscribed on its surface glowed hot silver, contrasting against the black.

The youths were wide-eyed with shock. Nuala sang a slow, hypnotic song, and held her palms in front of her. Clusters of tendrils grew from her hands, swaying upright like entranced cobras in front of the boys. They slithered and swirled around their legs and arms, and a hum caressed their bones.

They reached out, lightly caressing the filaments as they passed. Nuala walked to the rear of the group, holding the conical blade below the last boy's ribs on the right side, then slowly pushed the point beneath his skin. He made no sound, no response, and no one could see the milkiness seep into his eyes. Stepping forward, she did the same thing to the three boys just in front of him one by one.

Rick Oca noticed before they touched him, but when he tried to move he felt a burning pinprick near his kidney, and his mind was filled with a rich, milky feeling.

A ripple of fear passed through the remaining youths, and they realized that something very bad was happening. They tried to turn their heads, now flooded with terror. Before they could, she stabbed them, and they were overcome with a mental void, sending their spirits into limbo.

When all their eyes were filled with milk, the filaments of web retreated, slithering back to Nuala, then up her legs and body, down the arms and back into her palms. She walked up to the prone body of the youth who had groped her.

"Heavy price to cop a feel, eh?" she said, chuckling. "Now, hold this."

Lalo did as he was told, taking a short, curved knife made of silver from her hand. She leaned forward, whispered in his ear, and leaned back as he gripped it firmly, then jammed it into his own neck just below the ear. He strained as he drew the blade across his tendon, muscle, and windpipe. Blood welled up and spilled over the tattooed spider on his neck and down his shirt, soaking into his pants. He collapsed to the ground, a puddle of blood flooding the floor.

Nuala turned to the others. "Clean this up so we can get started."

Peik watched the boys busy themselves, concern on his face. "That was . . . unexpected."

"They need to learn a little respect," she countered. "Whether or not they're under the influence."

"Well, I'm sure they have it now," said Peik, walking back to the trapdoor on the far side of the room, and the massive silver tube with the jagged markings etched upon it. Small curved horns perked toward the floorboards like steel stalagmites, ending in sharp openings just beneath the planks. Without the instruments, a useless pile of scrap. With them, a machine to turn the tides of life itself.

"Those fine minds of yesteryear at HOME didn't account for someone stealing their precious musical keys," he said, referring to the architectural movement using web-bending and sound-bending machinations they had built into so many structures in the early 1900's, almost all of which Peik owned. And one of them was built here, into Marie Stillwater's house. They looked at the machine, as shiny as if it were polished every day.

From somewhere, a slight ringing echoed.

"Curious," said Peik, cocking his head to listen. The machine buckled, but didn't start. The signal was too weak.

"It's not from that," said Nuala, motioning with her head to the machine. The group of boys had started to shuffle their feet. She pushed her way through them like they were sheep in a corral, heading for the front door. When the slow hydraulic pump opened it, the sound increased, and the young men filed out.

"There," she said, pointing to the canyon. "The flute and chime, and presumably those two who stole them."

"Well, this is going to be easier than I thought," said Peik, watching the boys enter the shadows through a hole in the trees. He chuckled and pushed his hands on the small of her back, gently picking up the pace.

Up Switzer Canyon, they entered the tunnel beneath 30th Street. At the center a cool wind blew, and Peik sang a song into it. The old bricks moved, revealing a cobblestone tube into blackness. When they came out, a mile later, a long trail wound through the chaparral. They stopped in front of chiseled steps, and another tunnel..

They were heading down to the home of one of the few people who was more than a match for Peik; Ursula, the Bear Mother. This sort of action, turning a whole group of young thugs into shell-people, wouldn't go unnoticed by her or the Council. He knew that, was counting on it. It was time to make his move. Nuala's idea was actually panning out for once.

• • •

Her eyes shone electric blue. Marie, face-to-face with the adolescent assassin, overcame the shock of the deception, as her life depended on her mental clarity. She had an idea. All his life, Oliver had been cowed by fear and control.

"Poor man," she said. "No one gives you the respect you deserve."

Man. Respect.

Oliver was confused enough to pause, his teenaged brain reeling. Was she speaking to him like an adult? No one did that. His shoulders relaxed, poise softened. Why, he couldn't tell you.

"That's it," came the soothing voice of Marie, trying not to betray herself with the excitement she felt at how easy and, well, natural, this all was. Like this is what she was meant to do. Manipulate. Evolve.

"No one really pays attention to you, do they?"

Oliver's face drifted into a relaxed grin, something the muscles at first rebelled against as they hadn't ever turned that particular way before. His head was cocked to the side, enough to tell Marie that this was the one chance she'd get.

"They don't really understand you." Her voice was relaxation, harmony, like honey. Not daring to take her eyes off him, she crouched down and searched with her hands, sifting through the eucalyptus leaves and branches until she gripped a good-sized rock.

"I would listen. I would really hear you."

He drooled a little, eyes like a lovestruck pup.

Crack!

She smashed it into his temple and he folded. She stood over his head, about to bring it down straight into his open mouth, but stopped. Killing the young psychopath would certainly eliminate a danger from her life, especially after this little episode. However, he was also a danger to everyone else. If she could control him, she had a surefire weapon. Besides possibly her father, her best ally at this point was Julio's murderer, lying rapt in front of her. Maybe with him she could appease her dad and recapture Buddy. But wait. Now that didn't make sense to her. The realization hit. Nuala had sent her on a fool's errand.

From a small pocket on her pant leg she pulled some sturdy zip-ties, putting them on Oliver's wrists and ankles, and waited. A few minutes passed, then his eyes regained awareness. He began to struggle with the restraints.

"You shithead. You should have killed me," said Oliver, his yellow teeth snapping. "What are you, stupid?" His words sounded harsh to his ears, as if he no longer felt the hatred towards this woman that he felt for everyone else.

"What the hell have you done to me?" he asked, trying to suppress his desire.

"Nothing," said Marie. "I don't even know what you're talking about."

"Whatever you're doing," he said, "don't stop." He'd meant to say "stop." What was wrong with him? His pulse was racing, and he felt feverish.

"I'm not doing anything," she said.

What was it with this lady? Oliver wasn't used to good feelings, unless they accompanied an equal level of brutality. This was different. He was at rigid attention.

A light went on in Marie's mind. Levels of intention. She dialed it up, hoping for a soldier. "It's a shame we never talked much," she said. "You just need a friend."

"Yeah." What? Oliver stopped struggling with the zip-ties, sitting up with his bound hands behind him and his knees to his chin, eyes glossing.

Marie felt a ripple within her spirit, and in that moment realized that another thing had been awakened within her. She didn't know if it was the machine, Julio's death, or a combination of those, but this new talent was thrilling. He yearned for her.

"So, before I untie you, Oliver." She had it dialed now. "We need to talk about our particular futures. But my plan is only going to work if we do this together."

"Yes. I swear I won't hurt you, and I'll kill anyone who tries. I know something." It poured out.

"Hmm? What's that?" The fish was hooked.

"Nuala's moving on," he said. "Moving up."

"What does that mean?"

"She's gonna make a play. Try to get on the Council."

"Where? When?"

"Where they're headed now." His black eyes glinted. "At the Bear Mother's cave."

"Shit. I've got to get down there, then," she said.

"Wait! What are you doi–"

Crack! The rock. His skull.

She left him bleeding from both temples beneath the tree and tore through the brush to warn her father.

32.

Fully awake, Amy turned on the lights and put her kit bag full of evidence on the counter, keeping it closed, then turned on the machines. Various hums and whirring sounds filled the lab, so much so that she was caught by surprise when Jim Garrett's baritone voice came from right behind her.

"Hey Munoz," he said in his smoothest voice, one always full of innuendo towards any female but Clementine. "Fancy meeting you here."

Why didn't cavemen know how ridiculously stupid they sounded? "Yeah, crazy how I'm at the place where we work." she answered, staring at his forehead. "Fuck, what's up with the lump?"

"Nothing," he answered. "It is kind of crazy to be in here right now, though. What is it, 3:00 in the morning?"

"3:36. And I do the work when the work needs doing, Jimbo."

"That a fact?" He shrugged off the nickname.

"It is."

"Well then, what's the nature of the work you're doing?" He leaned in, reaching for her kit.

With his hand about to close on the handle, Amy slid it out of the way. "It's something for Clem," she said.

"Clem's my partner, Munoz. What's the evidence?"

"Not on this she's not. What I have in here," she patted the box for emphasis, "is something special she was running for the Loo. So, unless you feel like calling him at almost four AM to ask if you can check this out, you can hit the road, dude."

"Maybe I will. We're on pretty good terms lately." He pulled his phone out.

Amy didn't budge, didn't waiver, looking in his eyes as his finger levitated over the screen. "You lose his contact or something? Make the call."

"Fuck it, I don't care," he said, pocketing it.

"Thought so," she said. "Anyway, what are you doing in here at this hour?"

"A detective's work is never done."

"Well, go detect something else. I've got work to do." She pointed to the door.

Jim liked to get the last word. This time, however, he had to content himself with a grunt as he walked out of the lab. Amy had already gone back to ignoring him, something she had honed over the years. When he was gone, she brought out the evidence from her kit and got to work.

The finger was bloated and grey, smelling somewhere between old fish and dead rat. Amy pulled it out of the plastic bag with long tweezers, then set it on a the stainless steel rolling tray. She held her breath until she could put vapo-rub and a dust mask over her mouth and nose.

When she placed the vial containing the blood next to the finger, the metallic filaments were repulsed by it, swimming against the far side of the container.

"I don't blame you," she said, then looked around self-consciously. Seeing no one in the lab, she relaxed, telling herself to keep the inner voice inner as she busied herself for the couple hours it would take to get the results.

• • •

When the machine signaled its cycle was over, Amy checked the data, and was surprised to find the finger had four separate DNA signatures on it.

The first was no surprise, they'd guessed it belonged to the bloated creep Garth, the drunk from the park. Having been locked up dozens of times for alcohol-related incidents, the big perv's prints and DNA were readily accessible to the SDPD.

The second, a minute piece of skin from beneath the nail on the finger, was strange. It contained human as well as avian DNA. Before she had been thrust into this world, she would have agonized over this illogical information. Now, however, since the crime scene had been at Abraham Blackwing's house, she figured the signature would be his, and it probably was. He had no sample in the system, though, so that bit of information would remain elusive.

The third was saliva that matched Stewart's DNA, who was in the system from a previous arrest for a "drunk in public" years ago. He had apparently put it in his mouth, which is how he brought it to Clem's. What a freak.

For the last sample, the screen flashed red. Another match.

Amy nodded knowingly as Jim Garrett's saliva was matched to the finger, cementing what they'd suspected; Jim didn't just happen to bleed at the crime scene, Jim bled and threw up during or after killing Garth.

She collected the finger and the printouts from the DNA samples, putting them into her kit, away from prying eyes, and moved the information in the computer to a file folder which she gave a nonsensical name to, hopeful that that would cover her tracks for the time being. Now she had to figure out what she was going to do about the silver inside of the vial of blood, and the bottle with the silt.

She held the vial up to the light. With Garth's finger safely away from the metallic strands, they floated calmly in the ruby fluid. Amy walked over to the part of the lab which housed the gas chromatograph mass spectrometer, and after a thoughtful pause began to unscrew the lid of the vial. The hydraulic whoosh of the outer doors stopped her from opening it all the way. Someone was coming. She pulled her mask off, palmed the vial and the finger, then turned to face Rory.

"Hello, Amy," he said, "What's that smell?"

"I haven't figured it out yet," she answered. "What's up with you?"

"Following up on that presumed homicide from 21st and B Streets," he said, plugging his nose and walking toward the machine Amy had just used. He clicked the screen back on and looked at it with his head askew. "Is this new folder yours?"

"Yes, it's like we thought with Garrett," she said. "So what's going on with that evidence? What went down at that house?"

"Some poor schmuck got most of his blood drained out, although we don't know where," said Rory. "The only blood we found near the body seemed to be mixed with someone's stomach contents." He brought up his information on the screen, then began to check the data. "But he didn't have a whole lot left in his body."

"Do you mind?" asked Amy, looking over his shoulder.

"Not at all," Rory replied.

She scooted nearer, and could see. There was a hit on the stomach contents, matching the sample of the boy who had attacked Clementine at Nickel's house three months ago, and shed some blood on the way out. Now he was the murderer of some man in Golden Hill. Amy looked at display, remembering the spidery and dead eyed youth she remembered from the ballroom.

Oliver, Buddy's nemesis. Why would he kill some slacker musician?

"This signature ties into you and Detective Figgins' case with that guy who ended up decapitated at those warehouses," said Rory. "Shit, it's kind of looking like we might have a serial."

"Hm," Amy said, "or an assassin."

"Somebody putting out hits on slackers?" Rory's eyes narrowed.

"That's quite a conclusion. I'm reaching a conclusion, as well. Jim Garrett could be either one of those things, too. This is getting sketchy."

"Yeah. Jim's bent." Amy viewed Jim as much more of a bungling fool than someone with a concrete plan for corruption, even with the finger situation. More like someone trying to get his, and stepping on a few people along the way. But if Jim just played at being dumb to run a quasi enterprise, murdering whoever got in his way, he wouldn't be the first. She opened her palm to reveal the finger.

"What the fuck is that?"

"Garth's finger."

"Ew. Where did you get it?"

"Found it. With Jim's saliva. Like he bit it off in the course of a murder. Who's Jim working for, I wonder? This is outside of his pay grade."

"I think maybe a trafficker, or a bent border patrol agent, or both."

"Why do you say that?"

Rory looked around. "Well, I saw him in the parking lot, and he was at his car, facing the street. When I got close behind him, I saw he was on the phone. I kind of hid, and I distinctly heard him say 'They'll have to ask the coyotes,' into his phone. Then he saw me and hung up pretty abruptly. Gave me a look, too. Not a good look, either. I mean, who's called 'coyote' except human traffickers?"

"Nobody." Amy's mind was racing fire. The room swayed. She clutched the vial, but the silver fanned out into an array, and her view of the lab rippled. Numbness raced along her arms and legs, goose pimples shooting up her skin. Her grip slackened. Rory saw the blood evidence in the vial fall from her fingertips and tumble end-over-end toward the floor. Diving, he shot his hand beneath it before it could smash on the ground.

He breathed a sigh of relief, cradling it.

"Did you—" Amy swooned.

"I did," he said, opening his hand.

The vial was nestled in his palm, but Amy could see the cap was cracked slightly. Through the threads of the cap spilled the blood silver.

"What the hell?" said Rory. He tried to scoop the contents back into the vial, but the silver, with a mind of its own, separated from the ruby liquid and disappeared up his sleeve.

Amy wasted no time. She ripped open his shirt, buttons scattering across the floor. Rory followed her lead and peeled the shirt off. The metallic glob ran like a living thing, rolling up his arm toward his head.

With nimble fingers, Amy grabbed a plastic hazardous waste cup, slightly larger than her fist, and with its edge scraped down Rory's neck toward his shoulder, corralling the silver into it. It righted itself and exploded toward the open top. A stream of silver the size of a knitting needle shot into the air and flew across the lab, Amy running beneath it. It landed on the concrete floor near the drain, then slithered away as she watched helplessly.

As they caught their breath, Amy looked in Rory's eyes, and couldn't blame him for the anger she saw there.

"You have got some explaining to do."

Amy couldn't argue. "You're not gonna like it."

Rory scoffed, twisting his head around, making sure no silver remained on his skin. "Oh, I already don't like it."

33.

"Pearl?" Raul watched his little sister enter the cave with a big lady leading, then the lady cop and kid from the news. "What are you doing here?"

"Me?" she said, looking up the high arcing walls. "What about you? You probably started this thing."

"Kind of." He smiled. Pearl ran over and hugged him, smelling her older brother's earthy scent. He'd always protected her. She felt safe now.

Ursula's voice echoed through the cave. "Hurry. There is little time. We must begin the ceremony." No introduction, no chit chat.

"Ceremony?" asked Clem, confused. Her eyes flitted between the cast of strange characters.

"This will ensure their protection." The Bear Mother's eyes were steel fire as she walked to the center of the great cave, beckoned to them, and sat down. When they had formed a semi-circle around her, the bear completing the round, she lifted her voice, filling the cave with an ancient flowing melody.

Filaments of deep silver cascaded from the high, arching roof. Ursula let loose her braided hair, and the strands unraveled themselves, magnetizing toward the tendrils of dark light. The filaments met with her hair and weaved together. Slowly her eyes lost their focus, and became electric silver. "Now, Buddy and Ysenia, come to me." Even her voice was metallic.

Clementine's face twisted with shock. "What? Wait, please tell me what's happening."

"We must hurry. There are people coming for him. If this isn't done he is very vulnerable to attack," said Ursula's voice.

"He won't be afterward?"

"Not nearly as much."

"I thought he was already transformed." Clem held his shoulders, prohibiting him from joining Ursula and Ysenia in the circle's center. "Why does he need this?"

Ursula softened. "There is much danger surrounding him. This will temper his spirit."

Buddy turned around. "Mom, I love you, and I'm staying with you. But I have a place, and a role in this whole thing, just like you."

She wanted to be the protector of her son, but she also realized that she would never be his equal in the ways of the web. He was the new breed, and she was a cop. Tears rolled down her face as she let him go, but not before leaning down and kissing his cheeks. "I just don't want anything happening to you again."

"I know." He held her tight, then turned to join Ysenia on the ground in front of Ursula. "This will help."

When he sat down, a chanting voice rained down from the domed ceiling, transmitted through the filaments. Wordless and beautiful, it rang as dark webs ran through Ursula's hair. They filled her, making her skin glow with a neon-green fire, pulsating with wild energy.

The old woman held out her hands, and the giant bear stood up from its slumber, shaking its fur vigorously. The ensuing cloud of dust drifted over Ursula, electrified like a storm cloud. Dry lightning coursed through, whirling around her hands. A crackling energy built.

Her voice rose by octaves as her fingers flexed, then relaxed. On the exhale, two stout braids of light emitted from her palms and twisted out toward the two children, enveloping them in a bright silver haze. Buddy could feel his very being, his cells, filling up with a coded knowledge. Systems. Patterns. How. What. Why. He thought to look at Ysenia, his mother, Pearl, anyone, but the welling information overtook his intentions.

Pearl's jaw dropped. She walked toward the magical scene, stretching her arms out to touch the filaments. Looking back to her brother, she gave him a a questioning glance. He nodded. Maybe he wouldn't have if he knew.

Clem looked curiously at the little girl, Buddy's age but so much smaller. She left her place in the circle to try and halt her, but a filament broke out and zapped her skin. It wasn't the force of the shock–which wasn't much–but the surprise that put Clementine back in her place. Pearl continued walking, then sank to a cross-legged position directly between Buddy and Ysenia and looked into the eyes of the Bear Mother.

The great bear gave a roar that rumbled the cave, standing on its hind legs behind Ursula. It put its paws into the air, mimicking the old and beautiful woman, winding its deep voice around her higher one and creating an ancient harmony in the bowels of the Earth.

A third filament, split from between the two others, broke and touched Pearl between the eyes.

Pearl spun around inside the marvelous visions racing through her mind. She'd never dreamed of anything like this. Fields of web blew on a breeze far beneath her as she sped along a rainbow bridge of tendrils. Colors whizzed by so fast that everything took on a metallic hue. In the distance, massive braids rose like towers to the sky. She could see far off hills and mountains, hazy in the distance. Peering deeper, she noticed the haze was actually static in front of her eyes, which made it impossible to judge how far away the geologic formations were. Smells battered her, from burnt atmosphere to dirt and herbs to wet fur and boiled food. Exhaust, asphalt, a wind through the shimmering trees.

It was too much. Just as she began to feel overwhelmed, and scared, her body came to a halt, suspended snugly in midair above the sweeping fields of web, woven plants swaying and sparkling. Opening her eyes, she looked at her hands, and could see the systems–blood, nerves, muscle–at work, coursing through her translucent skin, each a different color. It was fantastic.

Smaller threads appeared as she focused. They spilled off the ghostly shapes of Buddy's mom and her friends, down on the ground, frozen in time. Pearl looked again at her hands, then through them, noticing the same effect at work. The systems pulsated with colors, weaving into a bridge of rainbow, gleaming beneath her suspended feet. The hues continued into and through her, and ran along tendrils to Ursula, Ysenia, and Buddy. The sky was static, gold and silver blending and separating, mixed with black spots like confetti from a void.

The webs shimmered and shifted, and Pearl's body glided forward until she was in the center of a triangle formed by the others. Feeling uneasy, She glanced at Buddy. He was as confused as she, and didn't really fool her when he grinned and shrugged.

Pearl could see Ysenia's body hanging limp with her eyes shut. She whipped her head forward and met Ursula's gaze, and the Bear Mother's voice spoke within Pearl's being.

"Calm yourself, Little Crow. Be at peace."

In the past, the name had been used to mock her, mostly by Eddie. However, this was different, and Ursula, translated by the webs, communicated so much more than simple words.

It was her true name.

Smiling, she looked at Buddy, but his eyes were closed. Feeling more at ease, she shut hers. As the lashes and lids came together, Pearl was lost inside the growl of the bear and the slow moving grind of tectonic plates. Their voices spoke to her. A shift, and she snapped her eyes open.

From high in the cave, a golden light shone. Small at first, it gained in size and momentum. Soon there was a flock of razor-sharp discs of spinning lights, flying and shifting into patterns, blinding in their array. Their bodies hung like a great mobile, pulled and pushed like kelp in a riptide. Ursula growled, trying to bring the children closer to her, but the tendrils didn't respond to her commands.

All eyes were fixed on the phenomenon, but no one could move to do anything about it. The golden lights concentrated on the three children, then a great explosion rocked the cave. When the ensuing dust cloud settled, the children were gone.

34.

It was dark, but Buddy could make out Ysenia and Pearl behind him, and a tall standing stone in the center of a room with old and rough walls. A small fire flared up in a clay bowl beside of the stone, and two figures rounded it. One was a muscular woman with short bobbed hair, black salted with generous grey. Dark robes hung off her shoulders. She had large, round eyes that drank in the scant light and widened upon seeing her guests. The other was a tall man with long, thick arms. The fire lit his skin, which seemed not a pigment of brown but of gold, deep and metallic.

"Hello, Rupert," said the man.

"Hello yourself. Who the fuck are you?"

"My name is Golden John." His gaze was piercing. Buddy shivered, fearful. "And this is Weela."

The woman stared at him in silence, unmoving.

From the standing stone came a rumble, and it began to glow, changing from a deep grey to red, then lightening through orange and yellow until it was rippling with white heat. The small fire was a few feet from it, but wouldn't explain the rock heating up so rapidly. Beads of sweat bubbled up on Buddy's forehead from the radiating waves. The rock rang in a high-pitched tone and became transparent, its shape and texture warping. Slowly, it separated into three thick and opaque tendrils. When they were long enough, their weight pulled them down to the floor, where they furrowed up clouds of dust, slithering toward the children. They were bulky and cumbersome compared to the other filaments Buddy had seen, and larger. Like colorless tongues oozing along the ground.

Buddy gulped as the one in front of him raised up its head. "What are you doing?" He forced his lips to move.

Golden John was surprised Buddy could speak. "I'll tell you, but before we get started, there are a few things I'd like to know."

Buddy felt his throat relax, muscles sliding back into place. "Like what?" Golden John's face grew strands of web changing his appearance. The beak of a bird of prey curved over his nose and mouth. Golden John was the Eagle. Of course he was. And Buddy was a rabbit.

"I wonder if you feel different from before. Specifically before you met Myron Fox in the warehouses a few days ago." His gaze was hypnotic. Buddy felt like a hunted animal.

Weela looked at Buddy like he was meat. "Why do you bother talking to him? You know what needs to be done."

"Still, we must seek knowledge." Golden John sighed. "It's not the boy's fault he's an abomination. At least we can let his final moments be ones where he is respected."

"Wait, what?" said Buddy as Weela bored her eyes into his. He was horrified when he looked behind her and saw the clear tendrils, like thick and hungry anacondas, inching toward the girls, almost upon them.

Golden John smiled, not pleasant. He pursed his lips, and a robust tenor note filled the room, halting the breeze that lilted through. The girls were deathly still, crystalline worms enveloping the tops of their heads, inching over the hairline. Buddy could see electrical impulses trapped in stasis, locked by the golden tone.

"I know what's going on here," Buddy said.

Golden John's eyebrows raised. "Really? Do tell."

"You're a fucking Eagle and I'm a rabbit. I'm not so hot at math but I'm a quick study. You're going to fuck me up when we get in there."

"Why would I do that, little foul-mouthed boy?" He looked down his nose. "When I could do it now?"

His voice was gentle, a perfect accompaniment for his easy charm. Buddy could feel himself calming, his suspicions drift away, as the man spoke. He recognized another trigger.

"Because there's something in there that needs to happen. Because I'm a threat to you," he said.

"A threat?" Golden John laughed, maybe nervous? "But as you said; you are a young rabbit, while I am a very old and experienced Lord of the Air, chief of this region for a very, very, long time. Eagles are not easily beaten by rabbits, my friend, but maybe you are right. Maybe you are that one special rabbit. Tell me, Buddy; what is it you think that we do?"

"I don't know, weave webs?"

"But why?"

Buddy thought about it for a while. "To protect them."

"From whom would the Web of Life need protecting?" Golden John asked. His gaze passed from one of Buddy's eyes to the next as if monitoring changes in the cornea.

Buddy thought of his past. "From people. Bad people?"

"Certainly. That would be one among many other things. I will tell you something about myself, young rabbit. In my long life I am, and have been, the meter of justice. If I have to leave my aerie here at the Council, someone has disrupted or perverted the web to their own ends, and I am sworn though blood and fealty to protect her, and to lay waste to her enemies. I am the swift judgement."

"You mean kill people?"

"If need be."

"So how do you do it?"

"Which way the Web weaves is up to Her."

It all made sense to Buddy now. Why they were apart from the others. He needs to sacrifice me to the Web, inside it. The location is important, somehow. And the action. The chase. That was it. They need to hunt him. The great ceremony and ritual of The Hunt.

Tendrils had grown from below him, binding his limbs before he could react. As he stood helpless, the last crystalline worm opened its mouth and crept down his face. It came to rest with its crystal lips around his torso, electrical nodes on either side of his heart.

Control trickled back into his muscles, and he kicked and struggled, to no avail. At first he thought he couldn't breathe, but then discovered it was simply a heavier type of air, piped up through the tube. Air from beneath the Earth. He felt heavy. Slow. He was going to die if he didn't figure out how to turn this situation around.

As he looked down the strand, it caught reflections that quivered and spun. The kaleidoscopic effect mesmerized him. Visions danced and twirled. Static sky. Rainbow wires. Clouds that were invisible until you changed perspective, like water on a tabletop. Everything spun faster, blending together until nothing was recognizable. Direction ceased. No up, sideways, down. Only is. Far in the distance, he beheld something else he recognized. A moving shape.

Glancing through the tube's skin at Golden John, Buddy saw his attention diverted. He looked back, and the shape was closer, then it disappeared behind a rolling strand of woven webs. On the other side, it poked its head around, and Buddy saw it; the rabbit made of webs that had spoken to him near Helen's camp in Golden Hill Park.

Run, it said.

A metallic, sliding sound came from behind him, pulling his attention. Next to him a green flash sparked, and without thinking Buddy kicked his legs, propelling himself down into the tube, giving his spirit up into the embrace of the web. He lost form, slipping down its crystal throat like liquid, and falling into a state between dream and reality. Between the worlds of the known and unknown.

His other trips into the web were never like this. The static sky above loomed over the spinning landscape. Tall trees filled with a black light hung over him, bare branches scratching against the air. He fell sideways through the trunks, impossibly fast, adrift and alone. His terror folded upon itself and became silence, though Buddy felt his mouth still releasing a bloodcurdling scream. Then beside him the rabbit appeared, churning its powerful legs to keep up, its huge green eye as big as Buddy's whole body.

Run, it said. Tricks.

He noticed a shift in the wind whipping his face, and turned his head in time to see a great talon sweeping down upon him. Without forethought, he curled into a ball, and was surprised when the talon swished to the left. He chanced a peek, and saw the rabbit, streaking away from him like a blur, the Golden Eagle right behind. It was difficult to focus on anything in the web, and soon their bodies disappeared among the wires, stretching as far as the eye could see. The sky above was a multi-colored static of constant shift and change. Swirling, and either growing or shrinking, hard to tell which. He suppressed the bubble of excitement rising in his throat as he watched the Rabbit lead the Eagle away from him. Then from behind a braided column stretching straight up and losing itself in the sky like the beanstalks in fairytales came the huge black mass of the owl. Brilliant yellow eyes like twin suns. A shiver of terror shook Buddy. He was meant to be this creature's meal. Destiny. The Hunt.

As the huge owl tucked its wings, plummeting towards him, his mind rid itself of the terror she transmitted, but he waited, giving no signal. At the last moment, he leapt to the side, and her thick talons sliced the air beside him, missing by the width of a rabbit's hair. Buddy exploded in the direction she had come from before she could turn around.

He raced down the bridges of web, lost in its bizarre landscape. I make my destiny, he thought.

How to get out? Something twinkled on the horizon, closing in. As he neared it, he saw it was a rippling hole in the air. Through it, he could see the room with the standing stone and the girls. He ran straight for it. As he entered, a wet sound filled his ears, then he popped out into the room, his head and shoulders trapped inside the crystalline tube. He wriggled around, trying fruitlessly to escape. After he'd exhausted his energy, he forced himself to calm down. What would help here? How would Helen or Max get out of this? Sensing time was short, he sang a low note. Nothing. He raised his pitch until he felt a tremor along the tube. Closing on that note, he sang it with more force, and fissure ran down its side, then it fell limp. It felt like he was holding a puddle as he wrestled it off his head.

To Buddy's relief, Ysenia and Pearl were moving, although the worms still held them.

From out of nowhere, Weela stood over him. "Where is the Eagle, child?"

"I don't know. Fuck that guy." Meeting her eyes, he recognized them. "And fuck you, too, Owl lady."

Weela clicked her tongue and tilted her head, saucer eyes freezing him in place. She began to sing an old, croaking song with jagged notes. As her voice filled the air, the cave transformed into the rainbow terrain. Beneath their feet, the floor swirled and bubbled into a round chasm, like a bowl into nowhere. She reached down and brought forth a translucent egg. Tendrils beaming with energy licked from the inside, lapping at the shell. She held it in front of his sweating face, burning so brightly it was difficult to tell exactly what it was. As it cooled, something insectoid skittered inside, a shadow crawling.

The light shifted, and from the distance soared the Eagle, filling the static sky. Buddy's stomach did flips as he watched it fan its wings down, bringing its great chest forward. Then it was Golden John, walking toward him and smiling. A scratch on his cheek dripped blood.

"Where were you?" Weela asked Golden John.

"Taking care of an unexpected problem," he replied, grinning in his smooth way. "Let us begin."

Golden John clapped his hands, and suddenly Buddy's body was not his own. His thoughts were snapped apart as the whole scene shifted and spun. Slowly at first, the sensation increased until everything was a blur. Everything, that is, but the face of the Eagle, laid over the now-human visage of Golden John, his chiseled face expressionless. His hands enveloped Buddy's, clasping the eggshell between Buddy's palms, then he and Weela sang a different song.

Between his fingers, Buddy felt the delicate egg lose its substance. His hands tingled with the prodding of sticklike feet, traveling up his wrists and forearms. A stream was running through his body, filling his brain, body, his very cells with knowledge and information. He came to an understanding of the fine balance that was the relations of the web, the council, power, the Earth and its inhabitants, from the planet itself, to the huge blue whales, down to microscopic insects that rode on the back of grains of dust, wings humming as they tickled the air. A web of every imaginable color ran through it all.

Then he saw himself. Webs shriveled and died around him, his black touch choking them of life. He was a threat. Sadness overcame him. He was the poison to the Web.

This is a lie, said the rabbit's voice. You are the now. They are the past. They are the poison.

He opened his eye. The egg in Weela's hands was right in front of his face. A shadow play of skittering chaos happened inside.

Do not let it hatch.

Buddy clapped his hands hard over Weela's. The shell cracked. Yellow and brown ooze, joined by a sticklike leg, fell to the ground. He twisted, ducking down and popping out of Golden John's grip as the discolored guts from inside the egg dripped. Smoke poured off Weela's burned hands as she screamed.

The sound of her voice was brutal, so much so that Ysenia awakened. Immediately she was able to muster a scream of her own, shrill as steel scraping porcelain, that created jarring waves against Weela's voice. The clashing tones shattered the crystalline worm draped over her head. Even Golden John had to cover his ears to block the noise.

"Leaakk Kulauw!" he shouted, and Ysenia's body was pulled against her will toward the rounded doorway. She tried in vain to claw her way back through the air, grabbing onto the doorjamb and bracing herself against the repelling tide of his will.

A smile curled on Golden John's lips, and in a cold voice he said, "Begone," waving his hand.

Buddy looked on in horror as Ysenia disappeared through the door.

He felt hopeless, seeing the ease and agility with which Golden John had drifted from the waking world to one of webs and dreams. He had power. Real power. It seemed he could do anything. It was mesmerizing. Golden John's fingers stretched out toward him, talons reaching for Buddy's neck, but he didn't care. There was nothing he could do against these people. If they wanted him dead, then he was going to die. Same as Ysenia. And Pearl.

In his mind. Pearl. Ysenia. A shift, then.

His eyes narrowed, and from deep within his core he began to shake. As the talons closed on him, he envisioned strands of web snaking from his center and flowing over to Pearl's side. He knew how to do this. In an instant, He was sucked into the swiftly moving tide of webs, shooting down their length for a nauseating instant, then came out standing very nearly on top of Pearl. He looked back with equal parts surprise and arrogance at Golden John.

Confusion spread on Golden John's face. "It cannot be," he said.

Buddy reached out, and just as Pearl put her hand in his, Weela attacked, turning to a huge shadow of blackest ink as she shot for them.. Almost invisible, save for petrifying yellow eyes. Before she hit them, Buddy envisioned himself inside the web again, this time with Pearl. This jump took them over to the doorway. Pearl swooned, sickened. Buddy lifted her up. Her legs were wobbly.

Screeches ripped the air as the Owl and Eagle flew apart and streaked at them from either side. Pearl's eyes looked drugged as she saw the advancing birds of prey, one darker than night, the other shining golden. She wasn't scared. They were so beautiful . . .

"Pearl! Come on!" shouted Buddy.

She pulled herself from the dazzling display and obeyed. As she embraced him, they whipped down crackling landscapes of living light, deep into the embrace of the Mother Web. For an instant Pearl thought she saw a gathering of caves along the base of the shimmering hills, but they were moving so quickly she couldn't be sure.

Ahead of them waited the Rabbit, tapping its foot on the rainbow wires. Buddy clutched her hand tightly and hoped he knew what he was doing.

Pearl looked behind. Far away were two flashes; one of light, the other a deep metallic black. They looked so beautiful. We should just stop. She was going to tell Buddy, but he took off after the rabbit made of lights before her mouth formed the words.

Over endless wires they followed the Rabbit-on-the-web, who spoke warm words into Buddy's spirit. Buddy followed, speeding and jagging, losing the predators. They had experience though, and in a forest of green and blue waving tendrils they surprised them. Buddy reared up as he rounded a trunk and came face-to-face with the open beaks and terrible song of the Eagle and Owl.

Pearl screamed, her voice directed fully at the birds of prey. Waves of sonic pressure crashed against them. They flapped their wings against it, but her voice sent them careening away into the static void. Feathers hung in the air, circling to the ground. Pearl kept screaming, as if she couldn't stop. The pressure began to pull Buddy away from her. Their hands slipped as the two massive birds of prey got their bearings, then flew back toward them.

Buddy strained every muscle, trying to pull her in close, but it was no use. Golden John, speeding at them, repeated the phrase that he'd used on Ysenia, waving his hand. Pearl tried to scream but her throat was frozen.

Buddy watched as she was sucked away, her tiny body disappearing into the electric forest. He didn't know what the words would do, but he looked Golden John dead in the eye and said, "Leakk Kulauw!" His intestines became a squished-up knot.

A bright flash filled the air, as if all the wires suddenly were sparked with a massive jolt of electricity. When it cleared, Weela and Golden John were gone. It was dark and silent as a grave. He was in a very strange place. Blackness surrounded him, interrupted by shimmering blips along strands he couldn't see.

A loud thump cut through the suffocating silence.

35.

When Ysenia returned alone into the cave, Clementine was frantic. "Where the hell is Rupert?"

"I don't know," Ysenia said. "We have been betrayed. Attacked."

"By whom?" Her words were cut off as the air pressure in the cave shifted dramatically, and hushed voices could be heard echoing from one of the farthest tunnels. Out of the dark opening stepped Eddie Calhoun, fists at his sides. He focused on Raul and May through hazy eyes as he took four steps and stopped, his vacant gaze coming to rest on the green bag around Raul's shoulder. Behind him, single file, came the other youths from the neighborhood, milky-eyed and stiff.

Clem recognized a couple from the drunk tank or lockup. Eddie, the boxer's kid, most of all. Raul watched his brother join the other boys, taking their places in a 'V' formation around the entrance.

Next came Nuala. Her expression was uncaring and cold.

No one spoke. The air rippled with anticipation.

A pop sounded, and the dust in front of Eddie shot up in a cloud. Then Peik was there, smirking as he looked around.

"Ursula!" he said. "Always such a pleasure to see you! My respects to you and yours. Markuz, old friend! I've missed you." He smiled, walking forward. Markuz didn't smile, but nodded slightly, deferential.

"You are not welcome," the Bear Mother growled as she reached into her skirts and pulled out an old, ragged glove covered in patchy fur. Four spikes protruded from the knuckles and curved at the end. She put it on her hand, pulled a strap taut and tied it off. "You may as well turn around now."

"Don't be ridiculous," he said, snapping his fingers and reciting a word few of them had ever heard. "Zhivaat." The boys advanced stiffly. "Things change so quickly these days," he said.

Clem leveled the pistol at Peik. "Stop whatever it is you're doing to these kids and get my goddamn son back."

"Me?" He stopped, hands in the air. "Back from where?" he said, looking around. He craned his neck, leaning here and there comically. "You lost him again? I don't have him. I don't even want him. Reminds me of that idiot Frank and his worthless ideas. I want what they have." he pointed to Raul and May, then made a swiping gesture with his other hand. "So excuse me Officer . . . "

"It's Detective. Detective Figgins."

"I know who you are, my dear."

"Then address me properly," she said as one boy tried to rush around her. Clem didn't miss a beat as she slammed the butt of the gun into his nose. He crumpled to the ground, stopping the other boys short. "Nobody fucking move!" she shouted, keeping her body between the attackers and Raul, aiming at the kids one by one. "You're not taking anything."

A massive roar, then great thuds shook the cave. Peik turned around to see the bear charging him. Just as it was upon him, the air around him popped, and he vanished.

"No!" Clem ordered the bear, barreling for her.

The youths saw the bear speeding at them, jaws wide and frothing. Fear momentarily shook them from their stupor, and they scattered out of its path. One boy got turned around, and the bear rammed its head into him, sending him flying through the air until he hit his face into the wall, then fell limply to the ground.

The bear turned, keying in on Nuala, running through the cloud of dust it had created. Using the poor visibility to her advantage, she leapt up in front of it, twisted around, and grabbed onto the wide scruff of its neck, whipping her legs around until she was riding between its shoulder blades. The bear stood on its hind legs and shook, but Nuala's grip was sure. Her voice bounced off the cave, a high shriek that sent the pressure soaring. The youths swooned.

Clementine crouched down as the ground next to her exploded with dust. The bear raced past, missing her by inches. She chanced a peek and saw Nuala growing a sharp, jagged filament from her hand, black as ink.

Nuala placed her palm on the base of the bear's neck, and black lightning exploded beneath its skin. Its backlit ribcage shone in great sweeping shadows across the cave. Its wailing voice made the ground rumble long and low.

Ursula winced, legs unable to stay upright. Markuz ran at Nuala, fists the size of cinderblocks clenched tight.

The bear was zapping like a lantern, its body losing definition, reverting to a thick, heavy smoke, then reappearing as Nuala kept her energy streaming through it.

Smoke. It happened again, lasting longer. When the bear solidified, its eyes were manic and crazed. Nuala kept up the intensity, throwing all her power into the great beast. Balls of dry lightning coursed from nose to tail before it changed fully into a floating mist. She dropped down to the ground as the bear's black cloud twisted well above the floor of the cave.

Markuz was closing in on her when his body slowed as if he was traveling through molasses. Confusion spread on his face. Nuala turned and raised her palm, blasting him with a black filament, thick as a ship's rope. It hit him square in the face, snapping his neck back. His body cartwheeled through the air and he landed in a heap, unmoving.

Nuala's knees buckled. She tried to hide it, but she had used an appalling amount of energy to trap the bear, then further weakened herself on Markuz. It's about time, she thought, looking up at the gold stardust floating at the apex of the domed cave. She lay limply on the ground while Eddie and two others ran to her side and dragged her over to the tunnel they had entered through. She sat against the wall and caught her breath.

• • •

A breeze floated from nowhere, carrying a deep bass note, then ribbons of gold light grew from the specks of hanging dust, whipping around the walls. They gained in speed and brilliance until the cave was lit like noonday sun. The ribbons slashed, thickening and collecting lower and lower before they gathered into a humanoid shape. Tall, fit, muscular.

"Hello, friends," said Golden John, smiling. He spread his arms wide, assaying the groups. Golden tendrils hung from his skin, dangling in unison like shimmering feathers. "Impressive gathering." He cleared his throat, looked at Nuala. "But so far your new recruits have been useless. Has the boy not returned?"

Peik's eyes darted between the two of them. "Excuse me? What are you—"

"Silence little man," said Golden John. "The only reason you walk this Earth is from a trick of the Raven. But I believe I've solved that problem"

Ursula whispered to Ysenia, then walked toward Golden John, claw-glove raised. Ysenia hid behind Markuz's body, using it as a shield, and peered over.

"Where the fuck is my son?!" Clem shouted, but no one chose to hear her.

"You are an abomination to the Council," Ursula said to Golden

John. "A twisted narcissist." Her long braid unraveled and her locks cascaded down. They stood on end, shining like flame. The bear-claw glove glowed hot, the luminosity of a blinding white star. Everyone but Golden John backed toward the walls, keeping their distance from the two, as well as from one another. Peik moved more slowly than the others, watching the ancients. He wondered how far it would go.

"And you are a simpering fool with too much love for these people to see they are a menace, a plague upon the web," said Golden John. His brow creased, and feathers, metallic and hard like armor, began to grow over his skin. From the tip of his finger grew a long, lean feather, which flew like a beam of light when he flicked his wrist, shooting at Ursula.

Without moving her body, Ursula used her strands to bat it away. She now appeared to be almost entirely made of silver light. Only her eyes broke through the shielding glow surrounding her. Filaments from her hand braided together into a thick rope which she whipped at Golden John, who ducked and dodged as the ground next to him exploded in a cloud of dust. The rope skipped on the ground, swinging hard at Peik.

Peik couldn't get out of the way fast enough, and it hammered into his leg with a crunch, spinning him around. He fell, holding it and wincing.

Golden John advanced on Ursula before she could gather the weight of the rope together. The heft worked to her disadvantage as he ran in its wake and slammed into her. Her shield held, if barely, but she rolled along the ground like a tumbleweed. He was gaining the upper hand, which she couldn't allow.

Getting up, he was upon her again. She braced her feet and pushed hard with the shield in front of her, and he lost his balance, skittering backward and landing in a crabwalk. Her braid smashed into the ground. He rolled out of the way as it smashed over and over, missing him by inches each time. Clouds of dust plumed.

Finally on his feet, Golden John let loose with two flying feathers at the same time. They separated, then intersected each other's trajectory like a helix. Jagged trails of light shone in their wake. Ursula tried to gauge their flight, and curled out of the way, but a slight misjudgment sent one of them slicing through her shoulder. The feather dissolved into a spraying mist. The other flew past her.

She jumped up and countered with a blast of filaments. Golden John waited until they were about to hit him before grabbing hold of them. As they touched his hands, he moaned a baritone note, rumbling.

Veins of gold crept into Ursula's silver, spreading and forming jagged arteries, like an infection. To avoid the corrosion from reaching her, Ursula dissipated both her braid and shield of filaments. When they vanished, Golden John raised one hand and flicked a feather at her. The golden blade sped, unencumbered by resistance.

She bent to the side, and as it whizzed past her ear she reached out and sliced through it with the blazing claw. Something tweaked in Golden John's center. Extreme discomfort. She punched the air as his attention was diverted, and it rippled off her fist, ramming him in the chest like a tsunami of wind.

Falling back, he felt actual pain. It had been a while. His mind couldn't focus. Muddled thoughts ran into one another as he looked up at the woman with the bear claw standing above him. By the time he had figured out which way was up, she attacked. In a panic, he shot a bundle of sharp quills, but they all somehow missed, curving around her body as if she were frictionless. Most of them hit the cave wall with hollow thuds. One of them, however, swirled like a boomerang, flying high up in the cave until it was lost in the cloud of dust and smoke.

A smaller tunnel lit up like blue fire, far on the other side of the cave, and Marie Stillwater dashed in. She located her injured father on the ground and ran toward him. "Dad!" she shouted, "It's a trap!" Once she'd reached him, she grabbed under his armpits and pulled.

"It would seem," he said, pushing along with his good foot. "Where were you?"

"Nuala sent me after the child, telling me it was your wish. I was nearly killed by Oliver. She's in bed with the Council." She kept her eyes on Golden John and Ursula. Golden John's hatred of her father was well known since the theft of the spirit of the still water by her father and Abraham Blackwing.

"It seems we are alone, my dear," he said, watching the dome of the cave with a furrowed brow. High above Marie's head, something sparked. Peik saw the golden blade curving back down, cutting a path through the air. If his guess was correct, it was coming straight at him. Nothing was ever an accident.

"Marie, look out!"

"Shut up, Dad. I've got you." She kept shuffling backwards, everyone in her field of vision. With Ursula and Golden John's pyrotechnics, no one was paying much attention to them. They were almost to the wall, but Peik could see they weren't going to make it. He tried to pull Marie into the Web and jump across the cave, but something was stopping him. He caught Nuala looking back, lips moving rapidly.

"Duck!" he screamed, trying to buckle his body so she would fall over. It swished past his ear, and a sickening thunk sounded from right behind his head. When he turned, the blade was sticking out of Marie's cheek. Her eyes were wide and full of tears, barely containing the blue glow. Through her cheek, her teeth were visible. Peik watched in horror as his daughter crumpled, blood spilling from her face. He cradled her head in his lap.

From the center, Golden John turned to see, and Ursula's swinging braid hit him full in the temple. He wobbled to one knee. The braid rose high, waving above him. Behind Ursula, he could see Nuala rising, as if energized from the bloodshed. A deep rumble came from Nuala's throat, rising to a shriek as she ran, focusing her voice until the brunt of its impact was centered upon Ursula's spine. The shriek hit Ursula like a kicking mule, and she stumbled. She swung with the glove, but her strike fanned wide and Nuala punched her in the kidney. Ursula doubled over, her braid falling limp. When she straightened out, Nuala swung again, cone-handed. She shot a small, black metallic filament from her fingertips that punctured the Bear Mother's skin near the top of her stomach, then she plunged her fingertips beneath Ursula's flesh. Fanning them out, she pushed through innards and around the lungs, staring into Ursula's wide eyes, then wrapped her hand around her beating heart. Ursula gasped, blood flooding her mouth and running down her chin.

Nuala calmly met her gaze, to let her know, then in one motion ripped Ursula's heart from beneath her ribcage.

Blood spilled in waves as Ursula watched her own heart beat one last time. Then her body collapsed into a lifeless heap.

Nuala held the heart above her head and laughed. Her eyes were on fire as the blood dripped down her face. She tilted her head back and stuck her tongue out. It tasted sweet, like destiny. She was so taken with the bloodlust that she didn't notice a silver wisp depart Ursula's mouth and slither across the floor of the cave.

The silver snakes came to rest in front of Ysenia. She was shaking and crying on the ground, having ducked down after seeing Nuala defile Ursula's heart. The strands stood on end, swaying like snakes. Like the braid. She stopped crying as they whooshed up her nostrils. No longer was she shaking, or crying. Or scared.

"Now," said Nuala, holding the heart in her hand. The neighborhood boys magnetically turned their heads. She signaled, and the youths turned and crept toward Raul. The dogs growled, tightening ranks.

Clem shooed them behind her and shot her pistol into the dust. One boy jumped back as a massive cloud exploded.

Having snuck around the group, Eddie grabbed Raul's bag, yanking him off his feet. Luna attacked at once, and yelped in pain when Eddie kicked her in the ribs. As she skidded across the ground, Raul landed a glancing blow off Eddie's cheek. Eddie didn't feel it.

As Helen turned to help, Eddie caught hold of her. He held her tight, but his face wrinkled in confusion as he smelled his mother's tortillas, from a time she was still alive. He looked at the large lady in his arms.

"Go home," she said. "Have tortillas."

He let her go, nodding in agreement, then walked toward one of the tunnels.

Peik saw it. "Aash Khozhoul!" he shouted at Eddie, to no effect. Nuala said something Peik couldn't hear, and the kid stopped. Peik glared at her.

Raul was in a panic. They had him, and the bag. He kicked, trying to get up, but hands kept grabbing at him. He felt a body thrown off him, and looked up to see Helen tossing another kid off like he was a feather pillow.

Golden John ignored the skirmish, and Ursula's body, instead walking toward Peik. "Let me help you, Stillwater." It was hard to tell if he said it mockingly. Such was his way.

Peik's situation was dire. "I think I've got it, thank you." He picked up his daughter, blood trickling from her face. Golden John walked faster, then jogged. Just as he got up to full speed, Peik and Marie vanished with a pop. At the same instant, they appeared right next to Helen, who stood guarding Raul and May. Before the large lady could react, Peik wrapped his hand around her neck. As his skin touched hers, she heard a great suction, and the next thing she knew they were on the far side of the cave, far behind May and Raul.

Helen looked back, and beyond all the dust clouds and commotion saw Max running from the tunnel where she had just been standing.

He saw her too. "Helen!" His eyes were wide.

"Max!" Helen called, but the pop sounded again, and she was inside the tunnel, far away from her man. The hand was still on her neck. One more pop and they were in the dark reaches of a desert canyon, warm night air running through the brush. She turned her head and looked Peik in the eye, then saw his daughter's bloody face. Another pop, and they were gone.

• • •

"Sit," said Myron.

"There's no time." Gray kept walking.

"If you go before we are finished, all we've done is useless."

Gray slowed, turning. "You're sure?"

"Sit."

Gray obeyed.

Myron spread dirt on Gray's lap, walking around him in a circle, then laid a bough of sage on top of his head. "I'm as sure as I've ever been," he said, then started an ancient chant to wake the stones.

36.

Max sprinted into the cave, but Helen was gone. He stopped, staring as she vanished with Peik and Marie Stillwater, then followed another pop toward one of the tunnels. How could he tell which one? To the left, he saw Nuala, a bloody heart in her hand. She stood next to a tall, muscular man with golden skin who nodded to her.

When Nuala ran toward the closest tunnel, Max ran to cut her off. "What the fuck did you do? Where are they?"

Nuala realized she wasn't going to beat him there. Running low on options, she tried the web-riding trick, like Peik could do. Her body faded to translucence.

Max ran faster when he saw her flicker. She was there, then she wasn't. Or was she? He could see the wall through her ghostly figure as he rammed his shoulder into her ribs, slamming her against the column of stone between two tunnels.

With the impact, she gained full substance, and the heart bounced from her fingers onto the ground, then rolled into a crack in the wall. They ricocheted off the lip of a tunnel, then tumbled inside, bouncing down an incline, headed somewhere deeper than the cave. As they struggled, Max was unable to keep his grip. Nuala tore free, and in the blackness he lost her.

"Shit!" he said, running back to where the cave should have been. Instead there was only dark tunnel. He turned around, running twice as far, but it was still just blackness. He stood still, breathing deep until his heart quieted, then he snapped his eyes open.

Bridges of woven light stretched into the distance. The entire landscape was composed of illuminated tendrils, writhing and sparking. On his skin, he could feel the difference in the air. It felt heavier. A map stretched in front of him, pulsing like an organic being. Max suppressed his fascination and began navigating the strange terrain. In front of him, he noticed a trail of light pink sinews. Sniffing, he picked up the scent of desert sage. Helen's trail. It shone bright, then faded into the distance.

Far behind, he heard Clem's voice calling him back, but he was already gone.

• • •

"Come now, boys," said Golden John, gathering the youths around him. The street kids, including Rick, followed his cue, surrounding Clem's group, who formed a defensive circle.

Clem leveled her pistol, aiming at Golden John between the bobbing heads of the young hoodlums. "What did you do to my son?" she asked.

He turned around. "Nothing, yet, my dear. Do you expect me to believe you'd—"

She fired. The bullet whizzed through Golden John's shoulder. A golden trail of smoke wafted in its wake.

He looked at her in astonishment. "That was unwise." The bullet seemed to have no effect.

She holstered her gun, then pulled up her pant leg and brought out Tommy Whiteoak's .22.

Golden John puffed his cheeks and made a bursting sound, and Clem felt her muscles freeze. She recognized the feeling and concentrated on her trigger finger. At first it was locked up, and the dread crept along her spine. One thought pulled her through; Rupert. The love, once lost, then regained. If she couldn't fight through this then he may be lost again, permanently. In the midst of her intention a lock was undone. Her finger squeezed, and the small blood silver bullet exploded out of the gun and hit Golden John's neck with a splat.

He coughed, placing his hand over the wound. Soon blood seeped between his fingers, then flowed.

"You will pay for that," he said, voice cracking. He waved his hand, and golden spirals swirled around him and the group of young toughs, bright as stars. They faded.

Clem shot again. Golden John's display of lights spun away from him and blood exploded off his shoulder. The young toughs came back into view.

"Enough!" His eyes were full of hate. Maybe fear. His hand glowed hot, and he threw a volley of golden balls at Clementine, hitting her with two of them. They felt like bean bags from a shotgun as they slammed into her and sent her flying backward into the mouth of a tunnel. A bang, then a flash, and the next thing she knew she got sucked head-over-heels into a vacuum. No matter how she twisted and turned, she couldn't fight the current shooting her away.

• • •

Near the surface, Stewart and Cora heard the air rip from down the tunnel.

"Shit!" said Cora, accelerating.

"What's going on?" Stewart was having trouble matching her speed. He ran behind her, relying more on the sound of her feet than his sight, stumbling over the uneven ground.

"Not sure." Her voice sounded far away.

From up ahead, a faint glow appeared, brightening until it seemed the light was in the tunnel with them. After a few steps it dimmed. When they ran into the cave they saw Golden John in the center holding his hand over his neck. Scarlet drops trickled from between his fingers. Off to the side were Ysenia and Markuz, and across the cave were the neighborhood boys, crowded around Alec and his bandmates. Then they saw Ursula's body on the ground.

"What in the fuck is going on?" said Stewart. Something happened to him upon sight of Ursula laying there. Rage bubbled, though he hadn't tasted blood. He looked at Golden John, eyes aflame. "I said, 'What in the fuck is going on, asshole?'"

Golden John turned. "Your little club is dying. I've come to clean things up, and you can be next piece of filth to be disposed of." He turned to Cora, dismissing Stewart entirely. "Cora, control your subject if you value your place on the council."

"I'm sorry, my lord," she said, "but I don't think I do."

"A pawn rises. Suit yourself." He looked through her, cocking his head.

Stewart stepped between them. "Come get some, bi–" his words fell from the air as a golden orb the size of a golf ball slammed into his stomach, sprawling him along the ground. He got up, short of breath, and Golden John threw another small golden cannonball. Stewart contorted wildly to avoid it, but it nicked the inside of his elbow. White-hot pain burned in a line up his arm, but wrapped in the cocoon of rage Stewart could give a fuck about pain. That was for later, if there was a later.

A third ball whizzed by his head and skipped along the floor. Cora dove to the side to avoid it. It hit a rock on the ground and careened into the spine of one of the youths behind her. The kid crumpled, then got up, looking around with fresh and clear eyes.

Golden John paused. "sleep," he said to the boy, waving his hand. The kid turned around, fell face-first to the ground, twitched once, and lay still. Then a rock smacked into the side of Golden John's face.

Stewart stood smiling. "C'mon, shitheel." He ran at Golden John, staying low to the ground, then leaped into the air before Golden John could respond. Stewart's vision of success slammed shut as Golden John landed an uppercut to his chin, and he flew into the air before falling down in a heap, unconscious.

Cora had to act. She was no match for Golden John, and she knew it, but that hadn't stopped Stewart. And he was injured.

She whistled to Klia and the dogs, who answered with high-pitched whines. Over all of it, Cora sang a piercing note, crags in her voice popping like an old record. She didn't notice a spidery figure run into the cave.

Golden John's head shook and pounded with the song. He tried to launch another ball, but in his confusion he shot it straight up into the roof of the cave, where it lodged. Shards of stone fell down upon him, sticking in his skin. He looked vulnerable.

Holding the note, Cora picked up a stone and cautiously walked toward Golden John. He didn't recognize her. She held the stone above her head, but from behind she heard a hollow clicking, then Grifter yelping in pain. She whipped around to see Grifter on the ground and Oliver with his foot raised from the follow-through of kicking the dog. In one hand he held a small black knife which curved at the end. Shit, she thought.

When she looked back at Golden John, he didn't look vulnerable anymore. He caught her throat in his viselike grip. Taloned fingers cut into her neck. Gasping for air, she reached out and pushed her thumb into his eye.

Luna ran to Grifter's side as Klia dive-bombed Oliver. He tried to smack her out of the air, narrowly missing. The dogs ran behind him, nipping on his pant legs to keep him occupied. He tried to kick them off, whipping around and staring them down as they kept him from helping Golden John. Klia flew down and pecked him in the temple. In an effort to slap her, he clubbed his face with his hand, and felt humiliated. He realized the birds were trying to enrage him into making a wrong decision, and he forced himself to calm down. Changing tack, he began to creep toward Ysenia, who lay behind Markuz's sleeping mass. His eyes shone black and he clicked his yellow teeth, smiling with grim delight at the girl.

Grifter followed, rushing to intercept Oliver, who heard and faced the dog, crawling like a spider. His legs released like springs, and he flew at Grifter. The dog reared back, biting into Oliver's leg. Oliver slashed his blade, cutting through Grifter's thigh near the tail. Blood spurted out of the wound at once.

Grifter yelped, limping over to Markuz's body and leaping into Ysenia's arms. She caressed the wound, and a dull light shone from where she touched him. When she pulled her hand away the bleeding had stopped, and she set him down. She stood, Grifter next to her growling, and with her hand dared Oliver to step closer. He obliged.

Luna and Klia had rushed to help Cora, who was starting to turn slightly blue as Golden John choked her. Klia swooped by his face, pecking his eyebrow, then flew straight away. He opened his hand and a golden ball shot at her from his palm. As it neared, she tucked one wing in, spinning around, then fanned both out when she was facing it, hovering in its path. She chirped, and the gold ball stopped in midair, spinning in place. She barked, and it fell to the ground, dust billowing.

Golden John was incensed. He felt a sharp pain in his ankle, and looked down to see Luna sinking her teeth into him. "Enough!" he shouted, grabbing the scruff of her neck, then hurling her up into the air. Before impact with the ceiling she barked. The rock rippled, and a smoky fissure opened up above her. It flashed as she entered it, then closed. Golden John stared at the space where her body had been, furious to be fooled by a dog. "I will kill you all!" he shouted, tightening his grip on Cora's neck.

A voice came from behind him. "Well, then. Start with me." From the shadows stepped the impeccably dressed figure of Myron Fox. He smiled as he let the smoke roll from his sleeves. Wisps spiraled to the ground and became Xorro. Once her body was complete, the smoky fox rushed at Oliver, snarling.

Oliver smiled, making a combined whistle and hum sound through his teeth. Xorro, racing toward him, yelped, then turned to smoke, swirling along the ground in wider and wider circles. Oliver drew a breath, then blew the cloud up a tunnel. Myron's knees buckled.

Golden John chuckled. "Some savior you are. Couldn't even get past the boy." He motioned to the crack that contained the heart, looking at Oliver. "Now's your big chance, young man. It's over there."

Oliver ran toward the tunnel, a ruby glow bleeding out. Myron moved to intercept, and Oliver cut toward him, swinging his fist. Metal flashed in the cavelight. Myron, ready for the feint, ducked under it and punched with the butts of both hands into Oliver's ribs. Oliver tumbled across the ground and ended up a pile of knees and elbows, unmoving.

Myron came up behind him, pulling rope from his jacket pocket to bind his limbs together, but Oliver swung round like a blur.

"Thought you knocked me out? Ha!" He spat.

The taste of cold metal flooded beneath Myron's tongue. Oliver was so fast that Myron had already started bleeding before he felt the steel enter below the ribs. He watched crimson drops fall from Oliver's knife. The floor went sideways, and Mr. Fox was left staring into the dirt, unable to turn his head. His joints were freezing up, vision clouding. In front of him, spidery legs came to a halt. As the dogs' barking neared, he felt his heart seize up, and looked into the cold black eyes of Oliver, who grinned with his filthy teeth as he stabbed Myron in the chest, twisted, then pulled the blade from his heart.

The dogs knocked Oliver off of Myron, biting and barking. He slashed, but they were too quick. Grifter caught Oliver's wrist in his mouth and twisted, making the knife plop in the dirt. Luna darted in and grabbed it, but Oliver caught Grifter in his wiry fingers and lifted him up, pulling the dog's head back to expose its neck. Sharp yellow teeth chomped in anticipation.

Before he could bite, however, a whirring filled the cave. He paused, raising his eyes to see a column of sparrows flying at him from the fissure Luna had disappeared into. They flew in a tight formation, streaming down and pummeling him in the face like a feathered maelstrom.

Sharp pains on his face and neck filled with blood. He let go of the dog, and the flurry of birds dodged around him, making a wall between him and Grifter. His face was swollen and his vision cloudy, but he could still make out a man coming from the hole behind Ysenia. Focusing, Oliver recognized the cop who had died. Silver burst off him in waves. He looked like a glowing god. Oliver had to turn his head from the lights.

Klia flew to Myron, sitting on his chest, chirping and clicking up his nose.

"No!" Gray screamed as he ran into the cave. He could see his father's body on the ground, unmoving. Ignoring everything, he ran to his side, cradling Myron's head in his hands. Tears began to break down his cheeks when Myron's eyes cracked open.

"Good-bye . . . my boy. This . . . is the last . . . phase. Only you . . . can . . . preserve . . . the future." A hollow rasp rattled from his throat, and his body went slack.

"Dad? No! Stay here! How can I do this?" Even as he spoke he could feel his cells undergoing yet another evolution. Answering him. They were bouyant, light. His breath expanded, and Gray saw timelines stretching like pathways through the air. Events. He raised his fist and the cloud that had been Xorro coiled downward. He breathed in, and the smoke wafted up his nostrils. From his core he could feel his father's wisdom, knowledge, memories fill his mind, embodied by the smoky spirit of Xorro, who nestled into a place within him, bonded. His father was gone from this plane. He was the Gray Fox. He opened his mouth wide and smoke billowed down like vapors of dry ice, weaving into four paws, then up into the torso, neck, and head of Xorro. She looked different. Her shade was lighter, and she looked younger, stronger.

• • •

Stewart woke to the sight of Gray lit up like a ball of dry lightning, holding his dead father's body with a fox the size of the bear next to him. A hacking sound made him tear his eyes from the scene and see Cora being strangled by Golden John.

Stewart wasted no time in rushing to her aid.

Gray listened to the patterns, and anticipated Golden John's next move. "Get down, Stewart!" he called just before Golden John slashed his talons at Stewart's face.

Stewart did. The talon missed, but his momentum carried him too close, and Golden John's knee rammed Stewart in the breastplate. Stewart flipped backward, tumbling down and slamming the back of his head into the packed earth. When he stood, his head was throbbing and his sternum felt shattered. He put his finger to his earlobe, and it came back blood-soaked. He chuckled, put it to his mouth, and entered the curtain of the red rage.

• • •

Gray held his father, who lay dead in his hands. He saw the spidery boy almost upon Ysenia, Markuz asleep in front of her, and Cora and Stewart about to be killed by Golden John.

Standing, he stomped his foot, and a ripple spread along the ground. When it reached Oliver, he was thrown into the air, churning his legs. Cuts had swelled up half his face, and it was hard for him to see how quickly the ground was rushing up. He landed at a bad angle, twisting his ankle and slamming onto his side. Looking back to Gray, he was blinded by his brilliance, Out of the glare came the fox, bigger than before, growling. Outnumbered and unable to see, he ran. The youths waited near the wall.

"Let's go," he said, shooing them along.

They looked at him, then all heads turned toward Eddie, waiting for his okay. Eddie, shaking his head, said, "No. We wait."

Oliver flew into a fury. "You want to replace me? That's what's going on? They did this to me and now I'm all used up? I don't think so." He rushed Eddie.

Eddie was a natural fighter, and landed a few good jabs to Oliver's face. Impervious to pain, Oliver didn't give two shits about technique, and continued to scrap past the blows. Eddie swung a left cross, but Oliver countered, grabbing Eddie's wrist and turning it the wrong way. He bit into his forearm and tore off a hunk of flesh, blood flowing out. Eddie screamed as he was forced to his knees, and Oliver swung his head forward in a blur, biting deep into the soft tissue of Eddie's neck.

As Oliver drank his blood, Eddie wailed him in the face, five times, but Oliver was clamped on. Eddie's blows got weaker and weaker until his hands twitched at his sides. Oliver let his spent body drop to the ground.

"Let's go," he repeated. The others had no one to turn to, and they made their way into the tunnel and away from the battle of the caves.

From the tunnel they heard raised voices, then Rick tumbled back into the cave.

• • •

Golden John watched Oliver and the boys depart, shaking his head in disgust. Gray was headed toward him. Stewart, also advancing, grinned like a madman.

Golden John was alone. No matter. He was the Lord High, and these were helpless peons. The real threats, the traitorous Fox and Bear Mother, lay dead in the dirt, and how was the Fox's simpering child going to succeed where he had failed? He curled Cora into a headlock and raised his palm. "Would you sacrifice her for your own gain?"

Gray didn't speak, walking straight. Without moving his arms, a bolt of light appeared from between his eyebrows, sparking off Golden John's face. His head snapped back and Cora curled out from his clutches. Another bolt zapped Golden John in his navel, traveling through his body and lighting him up. His back arched like a tortured puppet. Sparks shot from his eyes. The smell of burnt flesh hung heavy in the air.

Waving his arm, he threw a golden ball perfectly at Gray, who watched it approach, then caught it. Steam poured from between his fingers. When he opened them golden wisps drifted away. Nothing solid remained.

Gray punched his fists into the Earth, and the ground cracked. Deep rumblings traveled under the floor of the cave, then erupted from beneath Golden John. His upper thigh was clipped by a stalagmite shooting up from the ground. Thin and jagged, it sent a mist of blood into the air.

Gray sang a subsonic tone. Golden John now felt himself unable to move. Never in all his years had someone used the sonic arts against him in this way. For the first time in a thousand years, he felt honest fear.

Holding the note, Gray punched down again. The ground rippled, then stalagmites shot up onto Golden John's arms, enveloping his hands. They pulled at his spirit in a sickening way, churning his guts.

A thought. Rather than pull away, as Gray would expect, Golden John pushed his fists deep into the earthen spires and let loose with unbridled power. They flashed, lighting up like lanterns. Gray doubled over and gasped for breath,as the stalagmites crumbled.

Golden John brushed them off his hands, walking toward Ysenia. She rose, defiant, and he laughed out loud. "Look who's all growed u—!"

Crack!

Stewart hammered a stone the size of a grapefruit down on Golden John's cheekbone. Golden John swung, hitting Stewart's ear with his palm. Stewart's head felt like a melon in a vise grip. Golden John readied for a death strike, but the a sharp stalagmite thrust up and pierced his calf, narrowly missing his torso, then wrapped around his forearm, pulling down and constricting. Drops of amber liquid began to fall to the dust, splattering on Stewart's leg and burning like magma.

Gray had risen, staring dead into Golden John's eyes.

Golden John blasted him with a shower of needle-like golden quills, but they bounced off Gray's skin harmlessly, like it was steel. When he was near enough, Gray reached out and touched Golden John's neck.

Golden John's skin rippled, then burst into a tornado of feathers. They rose into the air then rained down on Gray. He held his arms up, all he could do amidst the flurry, before realizing they weren't affecting him. He lowered his arms, and the quills swarmed to the far side of the cave, spinning in the shape of an elongated ball.

A scent, wooden and earthy, permeated the cave, and Ysenia's voice rose above the chaotic sounds of battle. The ball of feathers gathered as far from her as it could, swirling like a flock of swallows, then stopped, shaping itself. Golden John appeared in front of Oliver's tunnel, breathing heavily. He looked defeated.

Raising his arms above his head, golden feathers whipped around him, faster and faster until they thinned to a golden thread of energy. It crackled, then zapped across the cave like lightning, forming into Golden John when next to Gray. Gray had no time to react. Talons wrapped around his throat so tightly no breath or sound could come out, then Golden John leaped upward, shooting like a rocket toward the high arching ceiling of the cave and throwing Gray into it. A loud crack filled the dome as Gray's body hit the rock, hard enough to lodge him there. Rocks fell, but Gray was stuck.

Golden John landed, then reverted to the tendril of energy, zapping up into Gray and continuing through the ceiling, dislodging stones as he went.

Electricity coursed through Gray. His eyes bugged and rolled as larger boulders cascaded down, followed by Gray's body. Stewart ran, trying to get beneath him, dodging boulders and clouds of dust. When he got there, he realized trying to break Gray's fall was going to get him killed.

A much larger body than his nudged him to the side, and Stewart glared with his customary hostility at Markuz, then softened and obliged. Markuz followed the falling body with his eyes, then at the last moment brought his arms up and caught Gray, tossing him over his shoulder.

"Everyone, this way," cried Ysenia, running for the smaller cave. The large cave floor was filling up from the falling rocks.

Markuz handed Gray's prone body to Stewart and nudged him toward the opening, turning and running back into the cave. Stewart made it about ten steps before he couldn't see. Dust clouds obscured his vision, and he couldn't make out the opening. Trying to see, a stone hit between his shoulders and spun him down, falling with Gray on top of him.

Markuz picked up Ursula and Myron's bodies, dragging them into the cave behind Alec. As Markuz ducked under, pulling the bodies behind him, A great roar filled the cave. Markuz pushed them in and tucked into a ball, filling the opening with his body. The cloud of dust and debris hit his back, nicking cuts through his clothing and skin.

"Where is Stewart?" Cora was wild-eyed. "And Gray?"

The mood switched as two more friends had fallen. There was little hope of defeating–or even surviving an attack from–Golden John without Gray around. It was only a matter of time, now. Hope was a fleeting emotion in the small cave. All was quiet.

Then, a shifting. Course pebbles of sand grinding against one another, and the clock clock of stones hitting. The sound rose until it sounded like a bulldozer was coming through the pile of rocks outside. Markuz stepped back, watching as the stones shifted, ignoring gravity as they spiraled apart. A pale silver light poked into the room, widening until it was flooded. Outside, they could see a being comprised of light holding another figure unconscious in its arms.

Through the hole stepped Gray, cradling Stewart.

Stewart saw Cora once they were inside. Red claw marks emblazoned her neck. "Are you . . . okay?" he managed to say.

"I'm alive," said Cora, touching his arm. "Thanks to you."

"Well, I'm alive thanks to him." He thumbed at Gray, patting his shoulder. Gray put him down and Stewart swooned. "Got clipped by a shitload of rocks and thought we were dead, but he put his body over mine like a tent until they stopped falling, then he made the rocks move–I don't know how–and walked right in here." He was short of breath, and had to stop talking. Cora kissed his forehead, then turned to Ysenia.

"Sister," said Cora, pulling her into an embrace.

As they touched, a story from shadows grew. The bear mother living on, commingling with the spirit of the little girl. Guidance. Consciousness. A path through the tricks of power. It made sense to Cora in this instance.

Ysenia was Buddy's sister. She was also the Bear Mother. Just as Markuz was both himself and the Great Bear, bodyguard of Ysenia.

Cora looked into the Bear Mother's eyes. "We are with you."

"Thank you, sister," replied Ysenia. She turned to the opening, a tunnel leading out that Gray had made, and sang a simple, eerie song. Silver tendrils, almost invisible, snaked out into the large cave, brushing aside silt and small rocks. After a time, they danced back in, holding Ursula's heart aloft on their thin tips. They bounced it through the air and deposited it into Ysenia's hands.

37.

As the rocks started falling, Raul had followed everyone into the small cave, guiding his brother, who walked on wobbly legs. "What the fuck are you doing, Rick?" Raul asked, safe for now in the smaller cave. "That wasn't the plan."

"Shit, that was weird," said Rick, rubbing his head. "It's like a dream that's already scripted, and you just watch your body get swept up in the tide. They appeal to what you individually want. She made me think that Pearl was in danger from you guys, and I believed it with all my heart. It's like a wall of cotton in your head."

"Who made you think?" asked Cora.

"Nuala, the lady, is the one we listened to. Made me forget my mission." He looked around at the group.

"And what is that?"

Rick's eyes rested on Markuz and Ysenia against the far wall. "Is it okay?"

"Yes. It is time," said Ysenia.

"Alright. My mission is from Abraham Blackwing, my grandfather. I was to infiltrate Nuala's group and make sure no one interfered with Gray's transformation."

"Excuse me? Transformation into what? What happened, Gray?"

"Into a weapon. One strong enough to take down Golden John and the Council." Rick answered for him.

"Oh, dear," said Cora.

"Yeah," said Rick. "Pearl and Raul had missions as well. Raul was to get the instruments, and Pearl was monitoring Buddy." His eyes got wide. "Where is Pearl?"

"With Buddy, but we don't know where. That's one thing we're trying to figure out," answered Raul.

"Where's the bag with the instruments?" May asked.

Ysenia answered. "They have been taken by the Stillwater's."

"What? They can't use them," said May. "Only Raul and I can."

"That is no longer the case." Ysenia said.

"How do you know?"

"It is good to question," she said. "I know because I speak the language of the moving stones and burrowing roots, the web's voice calls from within my spirit. But the Stillwater's aren't the focus, now." Ysenia's eyes were hypnotic."Later, perhaps."

"Who, then?" asked May

"Find Nuala and her followers. Rick must make them believe he's recruited you. Deceive them, turn them against one another."

"What if it doesn't work?" asked May.

"It must," said Ysenia. "That is the way. But not for you, May."

"Bullshit. I'm going, too." May's voice was firm, final.

"I don't suggest that, it's very dangerous."

"Well, dangerous or no, I'm not staying here. I'm with Raul."

"Then go," said Ysenia. "All of you. Now." She clasped her hands together and put her thumb knuckles against her pursed lips. A high pitch, strong and true, rang from her hands. It shifted the pressure in the cave, and trail through the air appeared, leading out the opening.

"That is your route," said Ysenia. "Quickly now, you must go." She shooed them along.

As they left, Ysenia closed her eyes, holding Ursula's heart close. She picked up the glove and fastened it to her hand as she had seen the Bear Mother do. When it was tight, she walked to the center of the small cave. Raking the earth with the claw, she made a gaping hole, then placed the heart inside. She wiped her finger across it, then smeared the blood and dust between her eyebrows.

The green strands along the cave's sides grew brighter, and the stripe of blood shone silver on her face. Using the glove, she raked the dirt over the heart. When she had finished, she raised both hands in the air and brought them down beside it. The dirt rose in the air, and silver-green light glowed brilliantly inside the hole. The glow concentrated itself, rays closing like a fan until one brilliant beam shot up from the heart, inches away from her. The beam turned into a writhing serpentine thing as it neared the ceiling of the cave.

The tendril's tip caressed the rock on the apex of the ceiling before shooting downward, whip-like end snapping around Ysenia's head in a tight crown, and her eyes changed to steel green. Markuz stepped toward her, but she raised her hand and stopped him in his tracks.

Her facial expression hardened. The rope lifted her up, connected only between her brows while she floated in the center of the cave. Vapors, lit like a silver cloud, snaked from her skin. Her eyes were deep, full of mystery.

The cloud floated, heading for Markuz. Nearing him, the vapors formed patterns. First an eye, then the face and neck, then eventually the whole body of the great bear. Markuz watched, unafraid, as the luminous creature sniffed at him, growling softly. Tilting its head, it whined. With the noise, the strands of light blurred, then flowed in wisps up his nose, starting with the bear's face and unraveling like a sweater made of steam.

When the cloud had entered his lungs, Markuz groaned, deep and hoarse. He could feel the vapors in his core. Hardening, changing and chilling him, but he was not cold. Far from it. He was stoked by an inner fire as he gazed beyond the lights at Ysenia, floating in the center of the cave.

Her eyes were those of the Bear Mother. Markuz did not scare easily, but this had put him closer to fear than he had been since he had been retrieved from the Arctic Ocean so long ago.

In their gaze passed centuries of understanding.

He was the Bear.

But he had always been the Bear, before and after he had been dumped in the freezing sea.

He remembered now.

• • •

Night had fallen when Rick, May and Raul made it through the piled stones and out of the tunnel system. They found themselves under a bridge in a wide gutter. After walking out from under the concrete expanse, they saw the naval hospital looming above them. To the southeast lay Golden Hill, and home. They continued in silence, keeping wary eyes on the bushes across Florida Canyon. Avoiding the traffic signal, they moved past it, where the freeway offramp stuck to the side. They crossed the street and ducked through a hole in the chain-link fence that led to the city mechanic's yard. They'd lost the signs of Oliver and his entourage. No footprints, no more glowing trail. It was as if they'd vanished.

"Stop," whispered Raul. Rick and May obliged. Raul squinted at the edge of the closest structure, a corrugated metal shed the size of a small house. Sure enough, shadows shifted at the base, then one of Oliver's boys walked from behind the wall.

"Hey, bitches," he said, smiling. Two of his friends joined him.

"Hey, dudes," said Rick. "I brought some new recruits."

"Nah," said the boy. Duane was his name. A lost kid trying to fill Eddie's void. "They already told us you'd say that bullshit." He cracked his knuckles. The sound bounced off the steel door of the garage.

"No, really. She's going to be interested in the girl. We should find her and ask her before you get in trouble for fucking up."

The kid smiled. "I'm a little sick of you thinking you're smarter than everybody all the time. You and your brother and this bitch are gonna die right here. Right now."

"Three on three?" said Rick. "You got it, asshole."

Rick gave Raul and May the heads up. Behind them he could make out two more figures underneath a tree near the northern entrance. He looked back the way they'd come; three more kids blocked the hole in the fence. There was only one way they could go; down the fence line to the ten-foot-round drainage tunnel that ran underneath San Diego until spilling into the harbor. Even if they were being herded, it provided a better chance of escape than facing off with the gang.

Then another shadow, quick and lean, like a human spider. Fuck.

Bolting, they ran along the fence until they saw a rip in the links, then weaved through, back into the wide drainage ditch. Trees and bushes grew in the cracks, hiding them. Shoving branches out of the way, they sprinted south until they got to the brightly spray-painted mouth of the tunnel. Unlike the jagged stone tunnels of the Bear Mother, this one was a smooth technological marvel. The bushes above the tunnel rustled, and faint light glinted off Oliver's cracked, yellow teeth. His face was bloated.

They paused, listening to the others closing from behind them. Inside the tube was pitch black, dark enough to swallow a beam from a flashlight before it hit the ground. Oliver dropped down.

They fled beneath him as he let go of the top, barely making it past his kicking legs. The crew reached the mouth at the same time Oliver hit the ground, keeping their distance from him as they pursued the Oca boys and May.

Rick was in the lead, and vanished immediately in the dark. Raul listened to his brother's footsteps and held May's hand, trying to match the rhythm, hearing the excited shouts of the pursuant mob making their way into the tube. Their catcalls and threats bounced off the wall.

"We're gonna fuck you up, Rick the dick!" The voices got closer. Oliver's panting animal breath wheezed, echoing.

The tube bent, and they lost track of Rick's feet. Raul tripped, slipping up the side of the tube before May stabilized him. The voices were incredibly close, and Raul felt something whistle past his head.

The tube exploded with hot light. Pupils dilated on half-blind eyes. The gang halted, looking in terror behind Rick. Only Oliver kept going until a great squawk erupted and knocked him backwards. He careened into the gang and scattered them like bowling pins.

Behind them, May saw a massive raven, legs crouched as its body filled the high, arching tube, emanating a dark light. It opened its beak wide to reveal a row of drooling human teeth.

Without pause, Rick and Raul ran past it, farther into the deep tunnel. Once May had weighed the two choices, she followed the brothers past the thing. The Raven's lights went out, and the tunnel was as dark as the grave.

Oliver's gang fled from the sickening bird, sprinting toward the tunnel's entrance, blind in the suffocating darkness. Oliver hissed, defiant, then ran through their ranks, faster by far, and was the first out.

Raul, May and Rick kept running until their lungs were fit to burst. As they slowed to a walk, a cold wind blew, and in the blackness they saw smoke wafting past them along the ceiling. It gathered into a mass, then sprouted arms. The thick shadow lit a match, lighting a tar-covered cone; a cigarette, or joint.

Abraham Blackwing blew smoke at them. It stank.

"Grandfather?" said Raul. "What are you doing down here?"

Abe smiled, handing Rick the smoke. "Meeting you," he said. "Now, let's get to work."

May tried to smile, but found herself frozen in place, shivering and scared.

38.

"Fix her," said Peik.

Marie gurgled blood. The deep wound on her face still bled.

Helen was in a fog, trying to shake off the effects of Peik's short-hop teleportation trick through the webs. It was impressive. Pop by pop, a hundred yards at a time, they had traveled up the tunnels, out of the caves, and through Switzer Canyon to Marie's house. Each time Helen felt her body stretch impossibly long, then shoot through the iridescent webs to the next location. Before she could breathe, it happened again. When it had finished, their bodies were in the living room, above the huge spirit generator beneath the floorboards. She could feel something trapping her there. If she could break its draw, she could get out, she was sure. This was more than illusion, it was an evolution.

"How?" she asked. "What do you think I am?"

"I know exactly what you are. My daughter and I, however, are not what you think. So, please, fix her and no one else gets hurt."

"You're threatening me?"

"I could always go snatch the boy you're all obsessed with."

"Hmm . . . if you could find him. And with the Eagle on his tail you wouldn't dare."

"Daring is my strong suit. I could find him. The Eagle wants to kill us all anyway, to preserve his dying way. But I don't want to hurt Buddy. I rather like him. Right now I just want Marie to live."

Helen could hear the desperation in his voice, and decided not to test him further. She didn't know if she could save Marie or not, but she knew she had to try.

"Okay," she said, "stand back."

She bent down and sang a wordless, lilting tune. A scent filled the air. Autumnal and spiced, the smell birthed memories. A strand snaked toward Marie's face.

Marie's nose twitched and a ripple crawled along her flesh. The scent filled her mind, serpentining among the lobes. Her head tingled, raw and sharp. Peik could see her scalp rise with gooseflesh.

Helen moved her fingers up over Marie's ears, cradling them. Then she made circles with her thumb and forefinger, just above the ear canal, and lowered her pitch. With the alteration, the strand changed from transparent to a milky pink, streaking into Marie's ears. Next, Helen reached in her pocket and pulled out a vial filled with red earth. She sprinkled some on her palm, spit into it, and rubbed it into a paste, then spread it on Marie's flesh below the wound. "There is something trapped in her from the quill," she explained. "I need a cup half filled with water." As Peik retrieved it, she bent her head down and sucked where the mud was spread on the nape of Marie's neck.

Marie's eye snapped open, and she met Helen's gaze. Helen spit into the cup Peik had handed her. A gnarled thing, like a small branch made of dark gold, floated in the water. A bubble of blood and mucus popped from Marie's mouth, and some of it flew into Helen's eye. When she had wiped it from her face she looked down at Marie, somewhat surprised to see the smaller lady calmly looking back at her. Marie tried to speak, but more blood spilled out, running down her cheek and dripping onto the floor. From the edges, Marie's skin started to repair itself, stretching and bonding over the open wounds.

"Shh." Helen cradled her head, so as not to disrupt the process. Marie's skin wove together like a tapestry, pores and fine hairs appearing on the skin after it was stretched taut.

"Amazing," whispered Peik, trying to see, but Helen glared, freezing him in his tracks.

"This is not finished," she said, "so please, sit down."

Peik begrudgingly did as he was told, but his suspicions remained at full alert. As he watched her work, he said, "If you ever want to consider working for me, you know . . . "

"Kidnap little kids and make them slaves and experiments?" Helen asked, halting her work. "I don't think so, Mr. Stillwater."

"That was Frank's thing," he replied. "I'm more concerned with science. And survival. Long, drama-free survival."

"Heh," she snorted, "so was Frank, if I remember correctly. That's where Jeb came in. Plus, who were those new kids? Volunteers?"

"Of course not, they're Nuala's little hoodlums from the neighborhood."

"Not scientists, anyway. Well, I'm on the other team."

"So are they, it seems."

"Yeah, I saw that. Your team's pretty small, now. Serves you right."

"Says the murderer who got away with it." Peik, a grin on his face, saw Helen's eyes grow wider. "Oh, yes. I know about your ex-husband. The police are about to open that back up."

"I was cleared of that," she replied, "long ago."

"Yes, cleared. But guilty nonetheless. You forget how unconcerned

I am with the nuances of law enforcement."

"Only because some of them are your employees as well," Helen said. "Or are they still with you? I heard you got taken off of favorite status with the cops."

"Oh, did you? Well, whether or not they're still with me." His eyes narrowed. "There are those who can open unsolved cold cases. I know how you and your two friends shifted the investigation, and they will, too."

"Of course. But why would they care? If you're not still with the cops, who's digging around?"

"It seems Golden John has infected the police force."

Helen stared mutely.

Was he guessing? Or did he know? Every word from the pale alchemist's lips was a web of deceit. His tongue weaved honeyed lies amidst truths until it was impossible to know the difference. She had to struggle against his hypnotic words in a way that he couldn't tell. Several things set her apart from the others who had discovered the webs in this new age, but the greatest of these was the controlling of olfactory senses, and therefore of memory. The Coyotes had taught her to use her personal talents wisely.

"I don't have any idea what you're talking about. Whatever's going on between you and Golden John, leave me out of it. Now, if you'll excuse me, I should get back to your daughter. She's far from out of the woods."

Peik continued. "He needs to kill the boy, in his mind. Your boy. The one your pack helped to escape." He eased back into the chair. "You need me more than you know."

She ignored him, singing the one note, then, somehow, another, and a third. A melody formed, simple and strong, the three notes intertwining, painting a picture as they poured from her throat, nose, and mouth. The pale man hadn't seen this from anyone, in all his travels. He breathed deeply, watching in wonder. The accompanying smells opened him.

With the haunting song washing over him, Peik found his focus drifting. His eyes wandered over the ceiling, and he picked up the scent of the old house, catching a fleeting memory of his architect friends so long ago.

From there, his memories stretched farther into his past; sea snakes with rippling wakes.

• • •

"Where are we going?" Peik asked Abraham Blackwing. Over the course of centuries, they had kindled a sort of friendship, a camaraderie born of arcane knowledge. After Peik had shown Abraham the method from which to make a berserker, Abe had seen fit to introduce him to one of the higher-ups of the Council, the first step in getting Peik on board.

"You will see, phantom," said Abe, goading Peik about his pale skin. In front of them was a massive live oak tree whose branches arched down and swept upon the ground. Abe held them out of the way with his burly arm, pushing Peik through. Inside their umbrella-like array it was nearly pitch-black. It smelled earthy and dark.

"Who is this?" came a woman's voice.

Peik strained his eyes, and saw the light of two eyes staring back. He could barely make out anything else, mesmerized by their glow. "I am Peik," he said. "The man from across the waters."

"Hmm." She walked toward him. Muscular, strong. "And what do you bring to offer?"

"I'm sorry?" He looked to Abe.

Abe chuckled. "He offers his blood." He then, quick as a wink, grabbed Peik's hand, and pricked his finger. Abe squeezed, then pulled it toward the woman. Peik could make out her features now, graceful but hard. She put the finger into her mouth. Peik could feel her sucking the blood out, too fast. He got woozy, and they laid him down beneath the tree, where he dropped into slumber.

Hours later, he awoke, naked and alone. Gathering up his clothes, he felt different, like something had been taken from him. He reached into his bag, relieved to find the snare still in the box. When he was getting dressed, the branches parted, but no light crept in due to night having fallen outside.

"How do you feel?" came the woman's voice.

"I'm not sure," he said, sitting on the ground. "Who are you?"

She touched his bare chest, and a flame of desire kindled itself. "My name is Weela," she said. "Also I am known as the Owl."

"What have you done to me?"

"I've taken your gift, and am using it for our future."

"The blood? How does one use that?" He was bewildered.

"Not the blood. Another life-fluid." She smiled at him, and her dark beauty unlocked the mystery. He could feel it down below. "Soon we will have a family."

"I don't understand," he said.

Slowly, she bent forward, and he could see she was naked. She kissed him on the mouth. "I think you do. You don't join the Council by just asking. There must be a gift. A real gift."

He knew what she was referencing, and in that moment slipped into a sense of pride. He reached up and embraced her, pulling her down on top of him. Her skin burned him, a deep yearning fire.

When they were finished, Peik had to catch his breath. He'd never remembered anything like that before, even after a thousand years on this Earth.

"You will be a fine Council member," she said, smiling at him. "Our daughter will make sure of it. What shall we name her?"

Peik was speechless, watching the limbs of the live oak render a shadow play with their dark patterns.

• • •

"Dad!"

Peik snapped out of his stupor, and looked upon the beautiful, if slightly altered, face of his daughter Marie. Her nose bent to the side, and a wide scar covered her cheek. The glow was gone from her eyes, but she was awake and alive, and for that he was thankful. He was lying on the ground, having fallen off the seat, with his head cradled in her lap.

"Oh Dad," she said through tears.

Peik pulled her into an embrace. His head swooned a bit, but he held her tight. "I'm so glad you're alright," he said. "Thanks to–"

He looked around the room, but she'd vanished. One and one became two, and he realized that he had been duped, happening more often lately than he felt comfortable with. He had his daughter back from the clutches of death, though, and couldn't think too far on anything else.

"Thanks to Helen," said Marie. "She's gone."

"It doesn't matter now, Marie." He breathed deeply, halfway slipping back into the mysterious dream of her mother and his past. "You've lost the glow. Now what do we do? Helen was right. We're alone, the Council wants us dead, and we can't use the machine. Even if we could I don't think it's a good idea. We might be killed."

Marie met his gaze sternly. "If we don't do something about

Golden John, We'll definitely be killed." She brought the olive drab bag from behind her back, reached in, and pulled out the flute and chime. Light exploded off of them, then cooled. "So I say we go for it."

"How did you get those?" Peik's eyes bugged.

"When you grabbed Helen, I grabbed them."

"Well, well."

She offered up the flute, swaying the chime back and forth. The ring, light and high, changed the atmosphere. Peik brought the silver whistle to his lips and blew a succession of notes, eerie and cold. The instruments began to glow like hot embers as a knot of silver tendrils poked out, slithering between the floorboards and awakening the machine. More tendrils grew from the floor, and the trapdoor creaked open from their bulk. The tendrils writhed, showing visions.

Peik pulled the flute away from his lips. "It seems they're not bound to the musicians any longer." he said, voice cracking with delight.

"No." Marie smiled. "It would seem not."

39.

Pearl had lost Buddy. Alone in the dazzling world of the webs, she stood still, bracing her legs for support, and waited for the two red-tailed hawks in the static sky to get closer. She was sure they weren't friendly.

It didn't take long. Wings tucked to their sides, they rocketed over the shimmering landscape of iridescent wires, past hills and trees made of woven tendrils, zipping straight toward her as if on a rope. She breathed deep, filling her lungs, then screamed at the closest one. Feathers burst off, scattering in the tailwind, but still they flew, now almost upon her. She barely had time to react, ducking down at the last second and feeling the swoosh of tail feathers on her face.

The hawks split up, soaring opposite each other in wide horizontal loops, shifting strategy and coming at her from either side. Pearl readied herself, but for what? How far off would they be from colliding? Which one's job was it to snatch her, and who was the decoy? She had to choose.

When she had drawn a bead on one of them she saw one eye shift, and she knew where the attack would be coming from. Movement in the corner of her eye drew her attention, and a cloud of hawks appeared on the horizon, moving fast.

Beneath her feet, black smoke trickled from the path of tendrils. Just wisps at first, they quickly thickened into a blanketing mist, covering Pearl in their folds.

The hawks barreled into the smoke, raking their claws, searching for purchase. Their talons were empty when they came out the other side. Both had passed without a ripple of resistance. They slowed and circled back as the black smoke dissipated, landing close.

The other birds began to land; hawks, falcons, owls, eagles, osprey, crowding around the two red-tails as they alit.

The two hawks' feathers rippled, churning. When they'd finished, two very muscular men with deep red skin stood over the place where the smoke had been. One crouched down and felt the ground. Silently, he shook his head. Both men raised their arms, growing feathers. They flapped their wings as they reverted to hawk-form, then flew to tell Golden John what had happened, a massive tail of flying predators behind them.

Pearl sat on the back of the large Raven as it swooped through a smoky portal and flew below the live oak canopy. "What did you do that for, Grampa? I had them right where I wanted them," she said.

"Gluck," said the bird, and a funnel of smoke shot from its beak, trailing across her face and tickling her nose.

• • •

Webs. Everywhere the webs. Max scanned the distance, searching for anything that could signal danger. How would he know? He looked at his hands, then right through them. The neurons firing down his electrified system created a pattern on the braided tendrils. The feeling was new, and terrifying.

Watching the strings, he saw them vibrate at different rates. He sang a deep note, like wet soil rolling. The braided webs shook faster, and he focused on two strands, one of electric blue, the other soft pink. Their color and frequencies set them apart from the others. He recognized their particular shades. He could breathe now, assimilating to this harsh world.

As he followed, the strands would stretch long and fade into nothing, then reappear farther away. Around where they vanished were ripples in the air. Bubbling holes. Inside the webs, pulsating tendrils cast blinding light.

As he got closer to the holes, a great suction pulled him along. He tried to stop, but his heels slipped on the frictionless webs, gaining no purchase. Looking into the hole, he could see desert shrubs on the other side. Winds whipped through the branches. Another gust blew from behind him, sending him head-over-heels into the magnetic embrace of the hole in the air. He tumbled out into a dark canyon, coming to rest inside the limbs of a shrub. Thorny leaves and acorns poked his neck.

Something wet surprised him. When he turned his head Luna licked his face.

"Heh, easy girl. How'd you find me?" He petted her head. Behind her, he saw the white wolf dog sitting and watching. The pink and blue strands hung in the air, weaving into the trees. Sparrows flitted in the bushes around Luna.

"I thought you guys would know each other," said Max, smiling at the dogs.

Luna barked and chased the colored strands, followed by the wolf dog and Max. The small flock of sparrows flew overhead, low enough to hide from predators.

The webs glistened, one rosy essence braided together with two webs of blue; the Stillwater's and Helen. Along the route, they appeared in bunches, knotting up, then streaming off and tapering until they were all but invisible. Max had to peer into the distance to see where they took up again, which wasn't easy while running.

When he breathed in, rosy wafts drifted up his nostrils, and the essence of Helen told him the dogs were on the right track. Luna had made it out, finding the wolf dog, and they'd located him in the webbed world.

With the olfactory stimulation came an accompanying thought, or rather a suggestion.

Follow in the strand.

He'd learned a great many things in the years since Auntie Frieda, Helen, and he had met the Coyotes, and had a good grip on the webbed world. However, since Cora had shifted him, there was something newer, greater, within himself. Until this moment, he hadn't been able to put his finger on it. But now he knew.

He could travel along the strands.

With that in mind,, he kept his legs churning, and redirected until he was running down their length, into the next burly knot. When he neared it, he willed himself inside, and heard a whistling from everywhere. It rose in volume until he was upon it, then, just as the sound became unbearable, it ceased. A curtain of silence fell as he closed upon the rose-and-blue tangle, shimmering like nerves. Pressure built. Bubble gum on a dam.

Then he wasn't there.

He felt his substance turn to sound, information. Data whipping along strands of web. What was this? From the corner of his eye, he recognized the systems streaming by. A pop, then a whistle sounded, and he was in front of the sprinting dogs.

Max found himself bound to the tendrils. He focused his will on moving forward to the next knot, and as soon as he could think it, it was so.

Each time he felt in more control of the chaotic shift, and soared through the rainbow webs with ease, then popped out in front of the dogs. They'd already grown accustomed, but he was getting too far ahead.

The dogs would be able to smell his trail. He popped out at the next knot, and said, "Catch up when you can," then let his will stretch along the strands with dizzying speed until he was flying through blurred surroundings, his body blipping at each knot, not even attaining corporeality before vanishing again. He got it now.

His triumph darkened when he sped past a knot of pink lights, then popped out into a tangle of blue tendrils. In an instant they wrapped around him like a thousand snakes. He was pulled inside them, not a whiff of Helen to stabilize him.

This was cold, and angry. Everything turned upside-down and folded upon itself. When he emerged he was covered in an ectoplasmic slime, lying on the floor of the house he had burglarized days ago. A hum pulsed through the floor. Standing above him was Marie Stillwater, face all wonky. No crazy blue eyes, though. Next to her, smiling in his blue track suit, was the pale alchemist himself; Marie's father, Peik Stillwater.

"Hello, Max," said Peik. "Nice of you to drop in."

Max tried to rise, but felt glued to the floor. Through the cracks in the hardwood he could see minute tendrils waving like cilia. Peik brought the flute to his lips and nodded to Marie. Together they played a song.

The effect was nauseating. Max doubled over, his innards on fire. Peik looked down at him with piercing eyes. The music thundered in his brain. Below the floor, the machine bucked and fired like an old car.

Max strained, forcing himself to move his jaws. They creaked and popped until he could form words. At first, struggling against the pressure of the music and tendrils, his frozen tongue lolled around, producing only gibberish. Peik was surprised at Max's resolve as Max came out of his locked state and finally formed a sentence.

"I can bring you Nuala," he said. "I know she screwed you guys."

Peik stopped playing and lowered the flute. "How would you propose to do that?"

"You'll have to wait and see."

"Ridiculous." Peik laughed. "I'll just play some more. You won't last long. I can do a great many things with this machine."

"Let's see."

"Brave man, or stupid. So hard to tell these days."

"Your call," said Max.

"Marie, let's play." Peik turned his back and pulled the door in the floor open. As Marie obliged, the hum grew louder.

Max's head felt like an overinflated innertube. He looked for an out, and noticed a rosy remnant of web drifting in a circle across the room.

It formed a portal, and something growled, moving inside it. Luna and the wolf dog barreled into the room, snarling and barking at the Still-water's. Several sparrows followed, chittering wildly.

Peik was startled. The white wolf charged him before he could move. It bit his hand, and the flute fell through the trap door and into the works of the machine. Clanks and rumbles drowned out their barking.

Max wasn't going to get another chance. He dashed for the circle of lights the dogs had entered through "Let's go!" he shouted as he launched himself into the web.

Something was wrong. He sped, out of control, popping between the sprawling landscape of the web and the known world. There was no pattern, only chaos. He appeared in a playground, then an alley, then in the bakery parking lot. Each time he would get sucked back into the web. Its embrace more of a crush at this point. He couldn't hear the dogs. They were gone.

Inside the chaos he smelled something homey and comforting. Bread that his neighbor Helen used to make. In the distance, more bub-bling holes drew him in like bait, the scent of bread pulling him along. It was dark when he emerged in the canyon of Golden Hill Park, un-derneath the massive live oak. Helen was lying next to him with her eyes closed.

"Helen! Baby, wake up!" He shook her, relieved when she groaned, then kissed her.

She opened her eyes, smiling, but had a faraway look in her eye.

"What's wrong?" asked Max.

Helen raised a finger to hush him. Then Max heard it too; the bark-ing of the dogs. Luna came tearing down the log staircase into the canyon, wagging her tail. At the top stood the white wolfen dog. Max looked behind them and saw more shadows at the top of the stairs. Human.

The dogs quieted as a group of people flowed down, joining Max, Helen and the dogs under the big live oak tree.

Auntie Frieda and Tommy Whiteoak stepped into the moonlight. "Let's go, you two." said Auntie Frieda.

• • •

At Auntie Frieda's, Tommy and Frieda guided them through the door then bolted it. May stood with Raul and Rick Oca beside her. Two women and a man, all with long, sandy hair, stood farther away.

Black smoke poured from a door on the back wall, drifting to the center of the room, and Abraham Blackwing materialized, little Pearl Oca riding him piggy-back. She hopped off, and was promptly mobbed by her brothers.

"Friends," Abraham said when they had calmed down, his voice a raspy cackle, "it is time."

40.

Inside the small cave, Gray crouched down, stroking Myron's hair before cradling and lifting him. As he did, a puff of smoke came from Myron's mouth, and Gray saw a vision. His father's face in the smoke, smiling and proud. It leaned in and lifted a smoky finger, touching Gray between the eyes.

Gray tried to speak, but a rush overcame him. Dark caves, full forests wet with morning dew. A council formed from ash and bone. Trust games and betrayal. Ancient ways wove together in his mind, guiding him through years and years. When at last his father's ghostly fingers dropped from his face, they vanished in a wisp of smoke. Gray understood, and lowered Myron into one of two graves. Ursula lay in the other.

A sorrowful whine came from behind him, and Xorro trotted up, sniffing Myron's body from head to toe, circling. She licked him, then sat down between the two graves. The smoky fox raised her head and cried a mournful song. Within it were memories so thick Gray could taste them. They rolled through Xorro and Myron's adventures: joyous, dangerous, and everything between. A map lay itself over his vision. In his mind Gray could see the other players' routes and connections: Mr. Stillwater, Abraham, Ursula, Golden John. He saw his mother, younger than he'd ever witnessed, standing in an orchard.

As Xorro sang, Myron's body began to glow. Ysenia and Cora's voices joined Xorro's, and thin tendrils streamed from the ground, swishing as they pulled the dirt over Myron's body, then did the same to Ursula.

Ysenia approached with Ursula's heart in her hand. She led Gray and Markuz to the head of each grave. Ysenia lowered the heart, placing it between the two fallen Makers at Xorro's feet.

Ysenia's voice rose, a single high note that made the cave ring like a bell. From cracks in the walls came a responsive buzzing. Streams of insects poured in, and flew in spirals along the ceiling. She changed her pitch, and they dipped down, flying around Gray's legs, swishing the coat of Xorro. Without pausing, they flew over the heart, and from the current of their beating wings the dust swirled like miniature tornados. They converged above the heart, sending up a plume of dust, until the final waft of lacy wings brushed the last grain of earth away. It lay slick with blood.

Ysenia cut the note off, and the insects flew back to the top of the cave, where they circled. She held the heart and glove, saying, "Zoph Khulil Ur."

A dazzling array lit the air. Ysenia's hands buzzed as the ruby light from the heart traveled beneath her skin and spread up her arm. Xorro yelped at her, but was shushed by Gray, who watched in fascination.

The light spread over her body, coursing over her shoulder and torso. Its glow filled her legs and neck, then covered her face and head.

She held the heart high and cried out a song of the Bear Mother, whose pack had lived in the cracks and crags of mountains and caves for millennia. The quivering notes deepened as the blood of the bear coursed through her heart. The knowledge of hundreds of women over thousands of years entered her mind. The healing arts, as well as the way of cold ruthlessness. The strength, the mystery, and the Web. Of all the Web. Behind her, Markuz growled deeply.

The insects swarmed, forming patterns as they descended. Spiraling together, they lifted the heart from Ysenia's hands and rose, the combined effort of thousands of lacy wings, until it hovered far off the ground in the center of the cave, a glowing lantern of blood. Red dots of light, like tiny lasers, slipped along the walls as the heart rotated in the air.

Ysenia's hands grew bright red. Heat waves emanating from her body distorted the cave. The flurry of moths took flight, shadows ripping along the ceiling. The heart glowed, bending, white hot. Rivulets of rubied silver spilled from her clenched fists, falling onto the dust. It began to show a form, a bowl, crackling in the earthen pit. The shape crystallized, sending metallic beads sizzling through the air. Klia chirped from behind Stewart's ear, peeking around to make sure she didn't get burned.

The trickle of silver turned to a gush, and a gout of steam shot up. When it cleared, inside the pit was a deep ruby crystal, round as a bowling ball. Dust and steam drifted, swirling around Ysenia's hands as she picked it up. Her skin's glow faded, cooling to her normal tone.

When she rotated the heart, one side was caved in. Her eyes sparkled as she placed the crystalline helmet upon her head. It covered her ears, and its thickness tapered over the eyes to form a sheer visor, curving around her face. Her lips curled into a smile.

Shadows zipped along the walls as the moths flew into a frenzy.

• • •

Buddy raced along threads in the dark place, his rabbit legs pistoning away. He could hear objects whiz by as he gained speed. Out of control. Something seemed off, like the darkness was following him, smothering. As he tried to get his bearings, he saw a figure far on the horizon. It blipped, then suddenly appeared right in front of him, too big and too close for him to see anything but a wall of shimmering fur.

A concussive blast filled his ears, spurring him to run, and the landscape shifted. He was racing along brilliant woven strands, but now they had taken on a deep sheen. Gold, specifically. He scanned the sky, or whatever the static was, for the dreaded birds of prey. Something changed in his periphery. Next to him, a giant eye winked, attached to the head of the massive rabbit made of incandescent wires, and the darkness returned, suffocating in its totality. When Buddy chanced a look, he saw nothing. No wires, no color. The air had grown cold. Metal-laced voices whispered in echoes, zinging along like cracks on a frozen lake. He stopped.

A shimmer of fur, and small animals scurried forward, curious. Chipmunks, squirrels, rabbits, raccoons, mice, rats. All wanted to see the new arrival to their hidden world.

A familiar shape rose, and the eye peeked in from the void, curious.

"How do you like it here?" spoke the voice, a robust baritone, yet silky. It came from everywhere, but mostly inside himself. Familiar. Comfortable. The animals darted away when it spoke, then crept cautiously back.

"I don't know," Buddy answered. "Where is here?" He looked around. Deepest hues of black, blue, purple, swirling slowly.

"Here is a hole. A maze in the maze. The lost web." As the voice spoke, more features became clear. Cleft nose. Whiskers. Long silky ears.

"Who are you?"

"I'm the Rabbit-on-the-web, my boy." His huge back foot raised up and scratched the base of his ear, sending big brown hairs drifting down.

"But do you have a name?"

"Hm." The rabbit appeared wistful, and looked off in the distance, only there was no discernible distance inside the hole in the web. "Long ago they called me Miguel," he said. "Miguel Dos Santos."

• • •

Back at Auntie Frieda's, Abe stood on the stage, spreading his arms. "Sisters and brothers. We come together and reveal ourselves so we may save the future. Times are changing, and one has been altered to end the Council's corrupt era, and Golden John with it! Through a very long and complicated ritual we have made a human weapon that has never been seen." He gestured toward the front door.

The group turned their heads as a key slid in the lock, and Stewart walked in, surprised to see so many people staring at him.

"Haha! Not him!" said Abe with a grin so wide it was comical.

Next came Cora, then Gray, who rippled with wild energy. His eyes were cold fire. Stewart heard relieved sighs make the rounds.

Ysenia followed, ruby helmet in hand, then Markuz bolted the door. Markuz growled suspiciously at the size of the group, establishing his commanding presence.

41.

Amy excused herself from the lab to use the restroom. Rory was processing the vodka bottle for prints and analyzing the results of the silt in the bottom.

She ran the water cold, splashing it upon her face. When she looked in the mirror, thin trails of smoke wafted from behind her head. She spun around, but nothing was there. She shook her head, feeling like she was losing it. When she looked in the mirror again, her face was covered in black feathers. The blip of a memory, not her own, showing two people receiving a gift near a river from Abraham Blackwing. A man and a woman. The next memory was hers; shooting Frank Rawls to death at the warehouses. She could feel the correlation.

Now, instead of Nuala and Frank sharing the Raven's gift, it was Nuala and Amy. Killing him transferred the talents from him to her, but they had taken some time to manifest. Now she could feel ripples, slight changes in the atmosphere, electromagnetic impulses floating through the air.

A voice availed itself to her, and a location.

Emiliano Flynn.

Keeping the location in her mind's eye, she stared into the mirror. Behind her reflection, the landscape began to waver and distort. The bathroom faded, and in its place there appeared a two-story triangular house, old cracked eggshell paint over long-ago boarded-up windows. Behind the house were two smaller cottages, a concrete walkway dividing the three. Old newspapers and spent gallon jugs and film canisters littered the corners, with a well-trod lane through the debris.

Amy pushed, and the back door groaned open, dim red lights glowing inside. She walked through two flaps of heavy black vinyl that squeaked as they rubbed together.

The place smelled of chemicals, and photographs hung from clothespins on laundry lines. In one photo was Klia, then Max, Helen, Clementine, Buddy, and, most unnervingly, a few of herself. On another line were more photos. She recognized the baker from Golden Hill.

On a table were slim black cones with little holes, like someone was trying to make flutes.

This case, never simple, now stretched out like a spider web, drawing in everyone who came in contact with it.

The door at the other end of the darkroom was unlocked, and she opened it. The next room was pitch black. As she felt around for a light she jerked back. Her hand had brushed against something that felt like a human nose. She held her breath, and heard a wheeze. Stepping back, her heel hit something small and conical, and she fell backward to the floor, landing with a thud. She stayed down, listening. Another wheeze.

A faint light from the darkroom bled beneath the door, and as her eyes grew accustomed she saw a tall lamp next to the couch. When she turned it on she gasped. Sitting down was the baker she had seen in the photographs, next to a wild haired woman in a muumuu.

She picked up the black cone that had tripped her, and stepped in front of them. Their eyes were hazy with milk, and when she poked the baker with her finger he didn't budge. "Shit."

The room began to glow with a golden light, and she heard voices. Amy edged closer to the darkroom, and was in the doorway when a flash lit the room. Silently, she backed into the darkroom and closed the door, all but a crack. On the other side of the room, a door opened, revealing a tall proud man with golden skin. Behind him stood the man with the camera she recognized from the time Buddy had been discovered in the park: the photographer Emiliano Flynn.

Amy got a feeling of warring butterfly armies in her intestines, which worsened when the third and final man entered the room.

"Let's get going," said her Lieutenant to the golden man and the photographer.

• • •

Clementine's body flew like a rag doll in a hurricane up the tunnel. She calmed herself, thinking as long as she didn't struggle, the danger of bashing into the stones lessened. A light shone from the distance, nearing very quickly. She thought of Rupert. How could she get to him? Where was he?

Then, suddenly, she was in midair, flipping head over heels above the thick shrubs on a hillside next to a freeway. She twisted and turned her body as hard as she could toward a thick lemonade-berry bush. Her flailing worked; the bush cradled her gently and deposited her right-side-up.

"Thanks," she said, touching the leaves. She needed to get her bearings, fast.

The distance she had flown up the tunnel was almost impossible to gauge, as dark as it was. Behind her, at the crest of the hill, stood an apartment building. After scraping up the loose dirt pathway, she looked back down, and saw she was at the crux of the 15 and 94 freeways. Looking beyond the overpass, she made out the warehouses that had held Rupert for so long, abandoned for the last three months while the investigations had been undergoing.

She noticed footprints on the ground. Athletic shoes. A woman or short man's feet. No coincidences. She followed them under the freeways' clover knot.

A chill overcame her as she thought how well planned the Stillwater people were. The obstacles she was facing right now were a big reason the disappearances hadn't been put together sooner. Four different police substations operated around there, one in each of the neighborhoods separated by the freeways.

She heard a whir, then a scrape, and gripped her weapons. Two small shadows approached. One the size of her dogs and one zipping through the air, about the size of a golf ball. She held her aim until she realized it was Grifter running behind a flying hummingbird.

Tears welled in Clem's eyes. "Oh, boy, thank you!" She nuzzled the dog and he licked her cheek.

The hummingbird clicked off a succession of trilling sounds, then sped back to the warehouses. Grifter trotted alongside Clem, looking at her. He barked and started running after the bird.

"I hope you know what you're doing," she said, quickening her pace.

Having changed the lock on the gate to one of her own months ago, she popped it, put her keys on her belt, then pulled out Tommy's small .22. Checking the chamber, she confirmed she had three bullets remaining, the ones dipped in the blood silver. She was getting a feeling like she might need more.

"Chk-wheet. Zif."

She looked into the eyes of the hummingbird, hovering in front of her face. It made the sound again, then flew up to the door handle and started clicking its tongue.

Clem knew about Klia and her friends, how they could open locks. She walked back to the door and tried the handle. Sure enough, it turned. Apparently the talents weren't confined to mockingbirds.

She pushed the door open and Grifter went first into the dark building. He barked softly. The coast was clear. After Clem took two steps, the hummingbird landed on her shoulder and clicked in her ear. Almost like words. She reached up and stroked the bird's head, continuing through a hallway and into a small room. There was a hole in the wall, but the hummingbird flew past it and hovered over the pile of ripped-out wood and plaster in the corner. Grifter started pawing at it, and Clem spotted a small wooden box. Pulling it out, she dusted it off and opened the flap. Three metal balls, no bigger than large marbles, were inside. Clem reached for one, but the hummingbird got between her hand and the objects. It zipped past the one her hand was going for and lit on the furthest one from her. She picked it up, and her hand felt light, like the thing was pulling against gravity. She held it steady until Grifter nudged her hand, and she let go. The thing rose, only a couple feet, then levitated in midair, turning slowly.

It clicked, and rays of light shone from its top, forming a tightening array that fanned down the walls, until one solid beam shone down on the ground. The beam bowed into a circle, and she could see something inside it. A machine clanked and hummed, the likes of which she had never seen.

Grifter and the hummingbird looked at Clem, then at the portal to the machine. And she knew. They wanted her to come with them. This would lead her to Rupert.

The hummingbird twitted again, and the portal's edges rippled like they were made of gas. It flew into the hole. Grifter nudged her and she followed.

Her head felt like it was ripping in two, and her heart hammered. She couldn't smell, couldn't hear except the roaring din of static pulling her mind apart. Then, as quickly as it had started, it stopped. She sat next to Grifter with the hummingbird perched on his ear, trying not to heave out whatever food she may have left inside her stomach.

A snap of a latch and a creak of a hinge, and the door above her opened wide. Light flooded the space, reflecting off metal tubes, barely missing her fingers. She scooted back as a pale hand reached down and picked up something from the innards of the clanking machine, then the simple music of a flute and a chime sounded above her. The hummingbird flew from Grifter and landed on her shoulder. Very quietly, beneath the drone of the instruments, it told her what she must do to find her son.

42.

As the haunting melody filled the air, blue tendrils snaked from the tips of the machine. A hum joined the flute and chime. In its center, the largest tube lit up, glowing. Following the hummingbird's instruction, Clem waited until the metal was bright, then aimed the .22 and shot through the tube.

A clank, like a giant transmission falling apart, rattled the floor. The hum stopped, and smoke billowed out of the machine as the tendrils withered. It sounded like a jalopy losing parts, getting ready to explode. Clem couldn't stay down here.

She squeezed through the clanking tubes, popping out of the hole in the floor and leveling the gun at Peik Stillwater's face. Next to him, his daughter looked at Clem with calm, cool eyes. The ceiling had filled with smoke, getting thicker as Grifter and the hummingbird followed Clem out, flanking her.

Peik was ice. "That was a very old and expensive machine."

"Fuck the machine. You have others, anyway."

"Not like that one." He raised his eyebrows. "What's the plan, Officer Figgins?"

"You're going to do that thing I've heard about, and take me into the Webworld to find my son." Her hand was steady. It had to be.

"That sounds like a terrible plan. How do you know he's there?"

"Zif." Clem nodded to the hummingbird, hovering beside her. "This bird."

Chk-wheet! it said.

"Of course," said Peik. "In case you didn't notice, I'm not really welcome to freely go in and out of the web. The Council, meaning Golden John and his cronies, will be coming for me as soon as I enter, with or without you."

"Well," said Clem, "I'm out of options, so you're plan Z. Let's go." She waved the gun.

Peik smiled. "If you are going to force me to do this, which it seems you are, we're going to need a lot more bullets."

"Not an option right now," Clem said.

"But of course it is. Who do you think made yours? Stillwater Enterprises does a great many things." He motioned to Marie, who walked down the hall.

"Not so fast." Clem pointed the gun at Marie. Her free hand went to the small of Marie's back, where two small handguns were stashed. "Nice try."

"We're not going to be any help with your beloved son if we're killed before we get to him." Peik's voice was a soothing wave.

"Let's establish a level of trust, first." Clem put the guns in her pockets. "Then we'll see about arming you. She held the gun on Peik until Marie returned with a small ammo box.

Clem snatched it. "Can't you guys just use the whole web thing anyway?"

"Once we enter this realm, we will be hopelessly outmatched in that regard. I wish you'd reconsider."

"I'm not a genie. I don't grant wishes." She picked up Grifter, and Zif landed on her shoulder. "Now let's go get Rupert back."

"Very well." He circled his arms around Clem and Marie. Zif clicked in Clem's ear. She nodded, then the rug of the world was pulled from beneath her feet as they entered the chaotic dimension of the webs.

ABOUT THE AUTHOR

Ben Johnson has been a drummer, a delivery driver, a fisherman in Alaska, a night porter for the haunted El Tovar Hotel in the Grand Canyon, a singer, a bartender, a rapper, a busboy, a cook, a percussionist, an actor, a director, a river rafter, an outdoor enthusiast, a teacher, a barback, a student at the infamous St. Anthony's Seminary in Santa Barbara, a beatsmith, and an artist. He is proud to add the title of author to that list.

Blood Silver is his 2nd novel.

He lives in San Diego, California with his wife and daughter, and their dog Rooners.

ALSO FROM GRAND MAL PRESS

DEAD THINGS

by Matt Darst

Nearly two decades have passed since the fall of the United States. And the rise of the church to fill the void. Nearly twenty years since Ian Sumner lost his father. And the dead took to the streets to dine on the living. Now Ian and a lost band of survivors are trapped in the wilderness, miles from safety. Pursued by madmen and monsters, they unravel the secrets of the plague...and walk the line of heresy. Ian and this troop need to do more than just survive. More than ever, they must learn to live.

Dead Things has been called "an amalgam of Clerks and everything Crichton and Zombieland."

ISBN: 978-1-937727-10-9

Available in paperback and all ebook formats.

"Dead Things a first-rate triumph. Darst is taking the zombie novel in a really cool new direction."
-Joe McKinney, author of *Dead City* and *Apocalypse of the Dead*

"A first-class zombie story which takes place in a beautifully realized post-apocalyptic world. Highly recommended!" - David Moody, author of *Autumn*

ALSO FROM GRAND MAL PRESS

HAFTMANN'S RULES
BY ROBERT WHITE

The first full-length novel to feature White's recurring private investigator, Thomas Haftmann! Out of jail and back on the streets, Haftmann is hired to find a missing young girl in Boston. But what he uncovers goes beyond just murder, into a world of secret societies, bloodshed, and betrayal beyond anything he has experienced before. HAFTMANN'S RULES is an exhilarating read into one man's maddening journey for truth, justice, and self destruction.

ISBN: 9780982945971

Available in paperback and all ebook formats.

"Haftmann's Rules grabs you by the soul and doesn't let go!" -Simon Wood, author of THE FALL GUY

"White's recurring private investigator, Tom Haftmann, would do Dashiell Hammett proud!" - Sex and Murder Magazine.

ALSO FROM GRAND MAL PRESS

DEAD DOG

BY NICKOLAS COOK

It's the late 70s and Max and Little Billy are back from Vietnam trying to mind their own business when they stumble onto the murder of a local boy. With organized crime and local thugs on their trail, it's up to these two heroes to solve the murder.

ISBN: 978-1937727246

WALKING SHADOW

by Clifford Royal Johns

Benny tries to ignore the payment-overdue messages he keeps getting from "Forget What?," a memory removal company. Benny's a slacker, after all, and couldn't pay them even if he wanted to. Then people start trying to kill him, and his life suddenly depends on finding out what memories he has forgotten. Benny relies on his wits, latent skills, and new friends as he investigates his own past; delving deeper and deeper into the underworld of criminals, bad cops, and shady news organizations, all with their own reasons for wanting him to remain ignorant or die.

ISBN: 9781937727253

GRAND MAL
PRESS